CHRISTMAS IS DEAD

A ZOMBIE ANTHOLOGY

EDITED BY
ANTHONY GIANGREGORIO

OTHER LIVING DEAD PRESS BOOKS

CHRISTMAS IS DEAD: A ZOMBIE ANTHOLOGY

Table of Contents

FOREWORD

Instead of a boring old foreword, how 'bout a Christmas
poem to get you in the right mood?

CHRISTMAS IS DEAD

ANTHONY GIANGREGORIO

Twas the night before Christmas, when all through the morgue,
Not a creature was stirring, not even a corpse.
Its internal organs, were weighed on a scale with depth,
In hopes the mortician, would find cause of death.

The rest of the bodies, were snug in their deathbeds,
While visions of Heaven and Hell, danced in their heads.
The cadavers were wrapped, nice and tight in their body bags,
As the mortician settled down, with the day's bloody rags.

When out back in the cemetery, there came a loud sound.
The mortician investigated, as there was no one around.
Away to the back door, he flew like a wraith,
And tore open the portal, there was no time to waste.

The moon reigned down, over the new-fallen snow,
As the mortician searched, both high and then low.
When what to his searching eyes did he find,
But a corpse in a Santa suit was walking, the first of its kind.

The ghoul was stumbling, not too fast or too quick,
He knew in a flash, it was a living dead man named St. Nick.
His face was pale, his cheeks far from red,
And when he exhaled, it was foul, the legend surely dead.

Zombie Santa turned, and waved his claw-like hand,
And eight zombie reindeer, stumbled across the land.
"Kill them, Dasher Dancer, Prancer and Vixen!
 Eat their brains, Comet, Cupid, Donner and Blitzen!"

He shambled to his sleigh, and moaned to his deer,
Who joined him then, and snarled with a leer.
As zombie Santa and deer, flew off into the night,
The apocalypse had begun, the world over by first light.

The mortician heard Santa, call out to the night,
"Christmas is dead! It's no use to fight!
For the dead will walk, and eat your brains,
The world has ended, with blood and with pain!"

So hug your kids, your pets and your mice,
Because the dead now live, their teeth like a vice.
And run for the hills, for your death is in sight,
Christmas is dead, you can't stop the night.

DECK THE MALLS WITH BOWELS OF HOLLY

SCOTT M. BAKER

No one expected to see Santa Claus leaning against the shopping mall's dumpster, puffing on a cheap cigar he held in one hand while taking a swig of whiskey from a 200 ml bottle of Jack Daniels clutched in the other.

A bleached-blonde soccer mom decked out in a fur-trimmed leather jacket drove past in her Mercedes SUV, covering her daughter's eyes so the little girl couldn't see while flashing him a look that was equal parts haughtiness and disillusionment.

Jack placed the cigar between his teeth and used his free hand to tip his Santa's hat to her. The soccer mom crinkled her face in disgust and sped away.

Jack placed the Santa hat back on his head and removed the cigar from between his teeth, but not before taking a deep puff. He blew the smoke in the direction the soccer mom drove off.

The hell with her, he thought. Jack had met a lot of people like that in his life, the pampered elite who were arrogant and judgmental. To them, hardship was when the local wine shop ran out of brie. Let them live his life, and then we'd see how well they made out.

Four years ago, he never would have guessed his life would have turned out like this. As a major in the Special Forces, he was a few years shy of putting in his twenty and cashing in on an early retirement when an IED outside of Baghdad went off next to his Humvee, shattering his right leg. A year of therapy left him with a limp and an addiction to pain meds, both of which earned him a discharge from the Army. He broke his addiction to the pills by climbing into a whiskey bottle, and spent the better part of the next two years bouncing in and out of rehab until he finally got his life into some semblance of order. By then, his resume and reputation left much to be desired. He was forced to take any odd job he could get, which was how he wound up as a mall Santa.

At least he made enough to pay the rent on his run-down studio apartment, even if it meant he had to take a few shots of whiskey every now and then to dull the pain in his leg from having whiny little brats sit on and kick it all day.

Jack took another swig of whiskey before replacing the cap and sliding the bottle into the fur-trimmed pocket of his Santa suit. He shifted the padding in his pants and jacket, grateful he needed padding. It would have sucked if the mall hired him just because he filled the suit. He might have a little more around the waist than he wanted, but other than that he was in good physical shape.

The door to the employee entrance opened. Jack grabbed his cigar and prepared to toss it into the dumpster, afraid it might be Bert, the megalomaniacal mall cop who ran the mall like a third-rate dictatorship. Thankfully, his friend Sammy stepped out. Sammy worked at the mall's Christmas Village, ushering kids to and from Santa. He had a way with kids. They related to him, mostly because Sammy was a midget. A little person, Jack corrected himself. Too bad mall management wasn't as sensitive. The Ice Princess dressed Sammy in an elf costume and paraded him around the display like he was one of the decorations. Though he never admitted it, Sammy felt humiliated by the treatment, and he probably would have quit if he could have found work elsewhere.

Sammy pointed to Jack's cigar. "Those'll stunt your growth."

"How many did you smoke as a kid?"

"Ha, ha," Sammy replied good naturedly. "I'm surprised you haven't taken over for Letterman yet."

Sammy leaned up against the dumpster, yanked off his elf cap, and wiped his palm across his forehead. It glistened with sweat.

"Are you okay?" Jack asked.

"I'm running a fever and feel like crap. I think I got an infection from one of the reindeer."

"When?"

"Earlier this morning. The big reindeer with the antlers is a mean bastard. It bit me and the other reindeer in the pen." To emphasize his point, Sammy shoved up his sleeve and pulled aside a large white bandage stained with blood. Underneath sat a nasty looking bite that cut deep into the skin. Yellow pus oozed from around the edges. Bluish-black skin surrounded the wound, which gave off the sickeningly-sweet odor of rot.

"That's a serious infection. You need to get to the emergency room."

"Not until after my shift." Sammy replaced the bandage and pulled down his sleeve. "If I leave now, the Ice Princess will can my ass for sure."

Jack wanted to argue, but he knew Sammy was right. The Ice Princess, their less than affectionate nickname for the mall manager, showed nothing but contempt for those under her, Sammy in particular. If he left early to go to the hospital, she probably would use it as an excuse to fire him.

"There's only a few hours left to the shift. Try to stick it out. But if you get any worse, you got to promise me you'll take off early and head to the hospital."

"If I get any worse you'll be picking me up off the floor," Sammy replied.

"Where the hell did they get vicious reindeer?"

Sammy leaned back against the dumpster for support. "I overheard the Ice Princess telling Bert she got a good deal on them from a farm up state. I know now why she got them so cheap."

The back door opened again. This time Meghan appeared, the Christmas Village photographer. She was a young woman in her mid-twenties with shoulder-length strawberry blonde hair. Jack couldn't help but notice how hot she looked in her green mini-skirt elf costume and red nylons. She refused to wear the pointy shoes with bells on the toes and opted instead for black heels, which the Ice Princess accepted once she discovered that the slightly fetish look brought more fathers to Christmas Village, and by consequence, more money.

Meghan greeted them with a smile warm enough to melt snow. "I hate to bother you, but Miss Landers is hanging around the village asking where you guys are."

"What a...." Jack checked himself, not wanting to swear around Meghan.

"Don't worry. I told her you just went on your break. She'll never be the wiser."

"Thanks. We'll be there in a minute."

Meghan flashed Jack a flirtatious smile and went back inside. He watched her behind as it jiggled beneath the elf skirt, wishing he was twenty years younger. Jack tapped his half-smoked cigar against the dumpster several time to make sure all the loose ash fell off, and then slid it into a carrying case he kept in his pants pocket.

He turned to Sammy. "Ready?"

"Barely." Sammy pushed himself off the dumpster and staggered to the door. "I feel like I'm gonna puke."

"If you do, just tell the kids it's from some bad eggnog."

As the two walked down the aisle toward Christmas Village, Jack admired the work that went into organizing the display. The village filled the first floor atrium across from the main entrance, nestled up against the glass-enclosed elevators leading to the second-level food court. His throne, an old preacher's chair, sat atop a raised platform covered with fake snow. To the left stood a fifteen-foot live Christmas tree strung up with colored lights and decorated with large red and green glass ornaments. To the right, a propane tank fed the flames behind faux logs in a fireplace. Curved metal poles painted to look like candy canes and linked together by a garland-wrapped chain prevented the kids from getting too close to the fireplace. Directly opposite the platform, on the other side of the atrium, sat a plastic igloo and half a dozen animatronic penguins, which had nothing to do with Christmas but did cash in on the latest craze in penguins. To the right of the village, a maze of velvet ropes herded nearly twenty kids and their parents who patiently waited for Santa. Off to the left stood the pen holding the five reindeer, a twenty-foot square area closed off by a heavy log fence. The buck with the large antlers stood near the front of the pen, swaying unsteadily. Behind him, four does walked around lethargically. Jack knew nothing about animals, but even he could tell they weren't feeling good.

What upset him more than the condition of the reindeer was the presence of the Ice Princess. She stood with Meghan by the camera, arms tightly folded across her chest, her frosty glare fixed on the two men. Dressed in a dark business suit and sporting a short, professional hair style, she would have been attractive if her face wasn't frozen in a perpetual frown. As Jack and Sammy approached, she gave them a smile as real as the fake penguins and stepped over to confront them.

"Where were you two?" she huffed through the clenched teeth of her forced smile.

"Taking our break." Jack tried to sound as disarming as possible.

"You're entitled to fifteen minutes. You were gone for nearly twenty." The Ice Princess leaned forward and sniffed. She grimaced even more severely than before. "What's that smell?"

"Cigar smoke."

"That suit's coming out of your paycheck if we can't get the stink out of it."

"Yes, ma'am."

At that moment, Bert raced up on his Segway. He skidded to a halt by the group, the sudden stop causing the beer belly straining against his uniform shirt to jiggle like a bowl full of Jell-O. "You wanted to see me, Holly?"

"That's Miss Landers, to you."

"Sorry, ma'am."

"I don't want to give the parents any reason to file a lawsuit against the mall, so guard those unruly beasts and make sure they don't bite anyone."

Bert grinned, revealing a mouth full of yellow teeth. "I assume you mean the reindeer, and not Santa and his elf."

"Ha. Ha." This time, Sammy didn't sound amused. "Did your mother tell you that joke was funny?"

The smile drained from Bert's face. "Blow me, munchkin."

"Funny. That's what I said to your mother last night."

"Enough," the Ice Princess hissed through clenched teeth. "Just get back to work. All of you."

Bert sneered at Sammy before whipping his Segway around and driving over to stand guard by the reindeer pen. Jack and Sammy headed for the platform. They were greeted by a round of cheers and applause by their young fans. Jack bellowed a hearty "Ho, ho, ho" and waved. A minute later, now seated in his chair, Sammy ushered over to him a six-year-old with auburn locks who beamed as she approached.

The next fifteen minutes passed without incident. The Ice Princess hung around the village, keeping a watchful and distrustful eye on Jack and Sammy when not telling Meghan how to take photos. Bert circled back and forth in front of the reindeer pen as if guarding a federal penitentiary. Jack had just finished talking to a boy who requested the latest edition of *Guitar Hero*, and Sammy was ushering him away, when all hell broke loose.

The buck let out an anguished mewl and toppled over in the pen, its head twisted on the floor at an obscene angle, black fluid leaking from its mouth. The does backed away, moving to the far corner to get as far away as possible. Bert jumped off his Segway and raced over to the gate, unlatched it, and entered the pen. He knelt down beside the carcass and placed a hand against its neck.

Sensing a growing uneasiness among the children and parents still waiting in line, Jack tried to take control and calm everyone down. He stood up, held his belly, and forced a hearty laugh.

"Ho, ho, ho. Nothing to worry about, kids. My reindeer is tired after pulling my sleigh. He's just taking a nap."

"Nope," Bert blurted out loud enough for everyone at the village to hear. "It's dead."

Parents gasped and children cried. One little girl looked up at her mother, her lips quivering as she asked if Rudolph was dead.

"No, no, no." Jack waved his hands dismissively. "He's just joking. My reindeer is getting a good rest, that's all."

"He's right," said the young mother to the little girl who asked if Rudolph was dead. She pointed to the pen. "See. The reindeer's moving."

Jack turned to look. Sure enough, the buck's legs spasmed, lightly at first, then more forcefully. It flopped around for a second before struggling to its feet, eventually righting itself on wobbly legs. Bert stepped back a few feet to give it room to maneuver, backing up against the pen.

The Ice Princess stepped up to the outer rim. "You idiot. I thought you said that thing was dead."

"It was. It didn't have a pulse and was stiff as a board."

The buck spun its head toward Bert, attracted by the sound of his voice. The once dark brown eyes were now light gray and lifeless. It bared its teeth and snarled, then lunged at Bert. Before

Bert could react, the buck latched its mouth over his face and bit deep, stopping only when its teeth ground into his skull. It tugged at his face. Blood spurted from around the reindeer's teeth and poured from its mouth. Bert howled, as much in terror as in pain, most of his cries muffled down the reindeer's throat.

Some of the parents had already scooped up their children and were dashing for the safety of one of the mall's exits. Most stood there in shock, too transfixed by the sight to move. Jack had no idea what the hell was going on, although he knew enough to realize they all were in danger.

"Sammy!" he yelled. "Get these people out of here!"

"S…s…ure th…thing." Sammy turned to the crowd gathered behind him in the rope maze and shuffled toward them. He took two steps, wobbled slightly, and fell forward. His face made a horrible crack when it hit the floor.

Before Jack could react, the sound of more bodies dropping to the floor caught his attention. He turned to the pen as the four does, all of which had been bitten by the buck, collapsed one at a time.

Meghan took control of the situation, racing up to the maze full of parents and children. She clapped her hands in the air to get their attention.

"All right. You have to get out of here now. Please move in an orderly manner toward…"

No one waited for Meghan to finish. Shock gave way to universal panic as everyone rushed for the exits at the same time. Children were knocked down. Parents tripped over the velvet ropes, collapsing the maze, which caused even more people to get entangled. Meghan tried to maintain order, but no one would listen.

Jack ripped off his beard and Santa's cap, and began stripping out of his padded jacket. Shit, he thought to himself. This can't get much worse.

He had no idea how wrong he was.

The Ice Princess leaned over the wooden railing of the pen and pulled the can of pepper spray from off Bert's belt just as the buck yanked its head back. Bert's skin slid off his skull like a rubber mask. He fell to the ground and placed his hands over his face, whimpering into the palms. Blood gushed between his fingers. As

Bert rolled around in agony, the buck chewed the skin and swallowed.

Bits of flesh and gore dangled from its jaw.

"Don't screw with me and my mall, fleabag." Leaning over the pen, the Ice Princess raised the can of pepper spray and squirted a stream directly into the buck's face. It mewled in pain and thrashed around, shaking its head wildly to get rid of the liquid. When it finally stopped, the buck fixed its gaze on the Ice Princess. It sneered.

"Oh, shit!" She took a step backward just as the buck lunged, slamming into the pen. The top log flew off, hitting the Ice Princess in the chest with a loud crack and knocking her backwards. She cried out and grasped her chest. Putting pressure on her broken ribs, she tried to get to her feet, wincing in agony with every move. The buck used its front hoofs to knock down the last remaining logs, clearing a path for it to escape.

"Holly, look out!" Jack screamed. However, before he could react, a moaning to his left caught his attention. He looked to the base of the platform as Sammy struggled to his feet, looking dazed and disoriented.

"Sammy, how ya doing?"

Sammy spun around to face Jack, focusing on him with dead, gray eyes and growling like an animal. He lunged forward and raced up the steps of the platform, snarling, his tiny arms reaching out for Jack. Teeth clacked in preparation of feasting on Jack's flesh.

He didn't know what was wrong with Sammy, but he knew it wasn't right, so Jack waited until Sammy got within a few feet before kicking out with his right leg. He caught the zombie elf in the middle of his chest.

Bolts of pain shot up Jack's leg, the damaged nerves from his war wound protesting the action. The force of the blow sent Sammy reeling backwards off the platform. He slammed into the floor and slid for several feet, coming to a rest only when he crashed into the overturned rope maze.

Jack looked around for a weapon, but Christmas Village was not what one would consider an armed compound. He finally spotted something he could use. Running over to the fireplace,

Jack disconnected the chain from one of the metal poles painted like a candy cane and tried to pull it out of the platform. The pole moved only an inch or two. He twisted, trying to loosen its mounting, when he heard snarling again.

Sammy staggered back to his feet and raced across the atrium toward him. Jack yanked hard on the pole. It gave a little, but remained stuck. He yanked again, this time with all his strength. The pole broke free. He stepped back and held the candy cane like a baseball bat.

When Sammy came within range, Jack swung the candy cane. It connected with the side of Sammy's head with a loud *crack*. His friend spun around and tumbled back down the stairs, rolling head over heels twice before flopping to the ground. The body barely slid to a stop before Sammy started to get back up.

Shit, Jack thought, this was going to be tougher than he had planned. Shifting the candy cane in his hands, he brandished it by his side as if it were a rifle with a bayonet. Sammy already was halfway up the stairs and gaining speed.

Jack pulled his arms back. "Sorry, Sammy."

As his friend closed to within a few feet, Jack swung his arms forward, aiming the end of the candy cane right at Sammy's forehead. The metal end easily punched its way through Sammy's skull, scrambling his brain. Sammy twitched around on the end of the candy cane for several seconds before going limp. His eyelids closed over lifeless eyes. His snarling features softened, finally at peace.

A female scream echoed throughout the atrium. Jack spun around; afraid the cry came from Meghan. Thankfully, he saw her standing at the far end of the village by the penguin display, ushering the last of the terrified parents toward the mall entrance.

The scream had come from the Ice Princess. After being knocked down by the buck, she had just gotten to her feet when he charged, bowing his head and plunging his antlers into her abdomen. The buck repeatedly twisted its head from side to side, goring the Ice Princess with all the dexterity of someone using a chain saw on a piñata. She pounded futilely on the head and antlers until her screams became a gurgle. With a strained cough, she spat blood from her mouth and went limp. The buck flipped its head to one side, throwing aside the disemboweled mall manager and leaving a five-foot length of intestine and a ruptured stomach dangling off its antlers. Holly's body hit the floor with a sickening squish. The buck stepped over to her, put its head inside the gouged-out cavity, and started to feed.

Only then did Jack notice that the four does also had risen and were exiting the pen looking for food. The clamor of panicking mall patrons bunched up near the closest exit caught their attention. As one, the four reindeer moved off in that direction.

What could have been a slaughter was averted when Meghan spotted the does heading for the mall patrons. She grabbed one of the animatronic penguins and flung it at the first reindeer, clipping it on the side of the head. It distracted all of them, but now their attention was focused on her. The four does snarled and lunged. Meghan ran for the penguin display, dove to the ground, and scampered on hands and knees into the igloo just as the does reached her. The animals kicked and head-butted the igloo, their snarls and mewls drowned out only by Meghan's cries for help.

Being made of thick plastic, the igloo afforded some protection, but only for a minute at best. Already chunks of plastic were being torn off by the onslaught.

Jack quickly assessed the situation. He stood exposed on top of the platform, but as of yet none of the zombie reindeer had noticed him. That was his sole advantage. There was no way he could take on five zombie reindeer with just a metal candy cane. And he couldn't waste time trying to find another weapon, because Meghan would be zombie reindeer chow long before he got back. So he could either fight a futile, hopeless battle or...

What was he thinking? There was no *or*. He couldn't leave Meghan and the remaining mall patrons to be devoured by these Christmas nightmares. Running wasn't an option.

Jack had only one chance, as ridiculously slim as it seemed. Running over to the fireplace, he placed the candy cane down on the ground and removed the rear panel to the fireplace, exposing the propane tank. The meter indicated it was more than half full. He wished it could have been more, but this would have to do. He closed the valve on the propane tank, disconnected it from the fireplace, and placed the tank at his feet. Reaching into his pants pocket, he rummaged around until he found his cigar case, pulled it out, withdrew the cigar, and placed it between his lips.

"Hey, walking wall mounts!" he yelled out.

Five sets of dead eyes turned toward Jack on top of the platform. Jack lit a match and placed it against the tip of the cigar, puffing until the end glowed red. He flicked out the match and tossed it aside.

"It's time to play some reindeer games."

The five zombie reindeer let out a collective howl and lunged at Jack, covering several feet in a matter of seconds.

Shit, Jack thought to himself. *Fast zombies suck.*

Grabbing the propane tank and the candy cane, Jack jumped off the rear of the platform and raced for the bank of glass-enclosed elevators. Behind him, he heard the zombie reindeer crashing their way up the front side of the platform. As he circled around to the front of the elevators and slammed his finger against the up button, he prayed at least one of the cars was on the first floor.

Thankfully, the doors on the far left slid open.

The buck topped the platform first and slid down the back slope. Jack ducked into the elevator, dropping everything onto the floor and turning to the control panel. He pressed one thumb each against the second floor and **CLOSE** buttons, jabbing repeatedly. Nothing happened. As Jack watched, the buck reached the floor and looked around, finally spying him standing in the open door of the elevator. It snarled and charged, with the does close on its hooves. Just then the doors began their interminably slow slide shut. Jack didn't know if he was going to make it. He shoved his thumbs even harder against the buttons and braced himself to be mauled.

The doors closed enough that the buck's antlers slammed against the outside surface, preventing it from getting at Jack. It growled and spat at Jack, filling the car with the stench of death. The doors finally closed completely and the elevator jerked, beginning its climb to the second floor.

Beneath him, Jack could hear the five reindeers scratching and clawing with their hoofs at the elevator door.

When the elevator came to a stop, Jack waited until the doors opened before pulling out the **EMERGENCY STOP** button. Working quickly, he used the end of the candy cane to knock aside the access panel in the elevator's ceiling, pushing it completely aside to clear the opening. He then placed the propane tank in the corner of the elevator and turned the valve into the **ON** position. Gas hissed into the interior of the elevator. Stepping to the control panel, Jack pushed in the **EMERGENCY STOP** button, pressed the button for the first floor, and stepped out onto the second floor. A few seconds later, the doors slid shut and the elevator began its descent.

As the car descended, Jack wedged the end of the candy cane between the joints of the doors and pried them apart, then reached in with his hands and pushed them all the way open. He leaned out to watch as the elevator came to a stop on the first floor, and listened as the doors slid open. It sounded like a stampede when the five zombie reindeer rushed into the elevator, snarling and thrashing around as they searched for their prey. The buck glanced up, catching sight of Jack through the open access panel, as Jack looked down from the second floor. The buck growled and raised itself on its hind legs as if wanting to climb into the elevator shaft to get at Jack.

"Ho. Ho. Ho," Jack grinned.

On the last "Ho," Jack puffed on the cigar until the tip glowed bright red, and then flicked it down the shaft. It arched through the air like a tiny comet before disappearing through the open access hatch of the elevator car.

A moment later, a fireball mushroomed through the opening and into the elevator shaft as the propane gas ignited, incinerating the zombie reindeer. Jack dropped to the ground and covered his head just as the propane tank exploded. The floor beneath him shook. The explosion took the path of least resistance, shattering the glass walls into a million shards and venting a fireball out across Christmas Village, ripping Santa's chair into kindling and blasting apart the giant Christmas tree.

Jack rolled and looked out over the scorched remains of the atrium. All that remained of the platform was the metal struts of its base. The rest lay scattered across the area, pieces of wood and particle board mixed in with charred chunks of zombie reindeer. Pine needles, pieces of wrapping paper, and shattered fragments of ornaments rained down like burnt snow. Except for the settling debris and the crackling of a few scattered fires, everything was pleasantly quiet.

Jack got to his feet and stepped over to the railing to survey the carnage below.

Not a creature was stirring, he thought. Then Jack suddenly remembered that Meghan was still down there. Running to the stairs opposite the elevators, he rushed down them two at a time, careful not to slip on the holiday flotsam. Below him he saw the igloo, shredded from the blast and partially melted. There was no way she could have survived that. Even so, he rushed over to the penguin display and dropped to his knees.

"God, Meghan. I'm so sorry."

Jack flipped over the igloo, surprised to find nothing underneath it.

"Sorry about what?" a sexy voice asked from behind him.

Jack looked over his shoulder to see Meghan standing three feet behind him.

"Aren't you dead?" he asked.

Meghan placed both hands on her hips and rested all her weight on her right leg, striking a pose that looked all the more erotic in her short elf skirt. "Normally this would sound like a stupid question, but do I look dead?"

"No." Jack stood up and took Meghan in his arms, hugging her tightly against him, or at least as tightly as the padding in his Santa suit would allow. "How'd you survive the blast?"

"When I saw you leading those things away with the propane tank, I knew nothing good could come of it, so I high-tailed it for cover."

"Thank God you did." Jack broke the hug, but kept one arm wrapped around her waist. He was happy to see she didn't protest as they headed for the mall exit.

"You know," she said. "Since you saved my life, you get to buy me dinner."

"It's a date. What would you like?"

"I could go for a nice steak."

"Great. I know a place that serves venison."

Meghan wrapped her arm around him. "On second thought, maybe we should go for pizza instead."

*   *   *

Clint stopped the ambulance a few yards from the shopping mall's main entrance, fighting back a sense of uncertainty about what they would find. The initial dispatch had been unusually vague, saying something about reindeer *beating* people at a Christmas display, although he swore the dispatcher had said *eating*. Not that neither one made any sense. In any case, it sounded more like a situation for animal control rather than EMTs, and Clint had said as much, only to be ordered to get to the mall pronto. Of course, arriving in time to see swarms of terrified shoppers shoving their way through the exit and scattering across the parking lot didn't help assuage his uneasiness. Panicked crowds were never a good sign.

In the back of the ambulance, Kevin, his partner, gasped at the sight as well.

Jumping out of the ambulance and grabbing their gear, Clint and Kevin rushed into the shopping mall. They had to push their way past a couple strolling out arm-in-arm. The man was wearing a padded Santa suit and the young strawberry blonde was dressed in very risqué elf costume. Clint thought it unusual that, amidst the panicked exodus by mall patrons, these two weren't concerned.

Kevin, on the other hand, noticed the blonde. "Hey, did you see the ass on that one that just walked by?"

"No." Clint pointed toward the atrium where the charred wreckage of the Christmas Village lay scattered around. "I'm more interested in that."

"Holy..." Kevin let his words trail off. He broke into a jog, rushing to the scene in case someone was still alive.

Clint followed, though judging by the extent of the destruction, he doubted if anyone had survived. He stopped by what looked like a pile of dead plastic penguins and scanned the atrium, shaking his head.

"Man, nothing could have survived this."

"Someone did," Kevin responded. "Over there."

Clint looked to where Kevin was pointing. Across the atrium, near the remains of what once was an animal pen, a single figure stumbled through the debris, his hands outstretched in front of him, fumbling around as if he was blind. His back was to them, so Clint couldn't tell how badly hurt he was.

Given the fact that the man wore a light blue shirt with the tattered remains of a patch on his sleeve, and a utility belt hanging at an awkward angle from his hip--half the contents missing--Clint figured he must be mall security.

"Poor guy," Kevin said. "Probably stayed behind to help get everyone out and then got caught up in all of this."

"You check out the rest of the mall. I'll go see to him," Clint said as he crossed over to the security guard. The guard's hands fell onto the handlebars of a scorched Segway and clutched it tightly. He attempted to climb on, but couldn't get his feet up high enough.

Probably shock, Clint thought.

When Clint got to within a few feet of the guard, he called out to him.

"Hang on, buddy. I'm a paramedic. I'm here to help...Holy shit!"

When the guard turned around at the sound of Clint's voice, Clint saw that the man's face was ripped off.

Clint stared into a skull covered in gore and blood with strands of severed nerve endings dangled out of the sockets. It couldn't see Clint, but it heard him. When Clint squeaked a muffled cry of revulsion, the thing lunged at him, its exposed teeth ripping into the paramedic's throat.

RANDOLPH THE RED-NOSED REINDEER

ROB ROSEN

Santa trudged inside his workshop, sweat trickling down his wrinkled brow, a sad frown plastered to his usually jolly face. "Prancer and Dancer have the swine flu," he groaned, talking to a group of elves that had gathered around him.

"But Christmas is only three days away," cried Sam, the toy-train maker, his face suddenly pale. "What if they're not well enough to fly by then? Can the others pick up the slack?"

Santa shook his head from side to side, his jowls jiggling like a bowl of Christmas pudding. "If we skip China, maybe. Last time we did that, though, they stopped our shipment of plastic doll-clothes."

One of the elves grimaced. "And Barbie looked awful in burlap. What's option number two?"

Santa played with the whiskers that sprouted down his double chin, nervously twisting them between his chubby, little fingers. "Temporary replacements, I suppose."

"How many flying reindeer live around here, anyway?" another of the elves asked.

"None," came Saint Nick's glum reply. "That I'm aware of."

"Then we're screwed," the same elf groaned.

"Language," cautioned Santa, a warning finger held up high.

"In bad shape," amended the elf. "Up shi...um, up the creek without a paddle. What if we stick with China and bypass the United States? Tell them it's the recession. Or the Republicans. You can blame anything on them and get away with it, I hear."

"Nope. No skipping anybody," Santa said. "We just need to find a couple more reindeer. Been ages since I looked. Must be some left around these parts. I couldn't have found the only eight." He paused and glanced around the room, shiny elfin faces looking up hopefully at him. "You, you, and you," Santa eventually said, pointing to the yo-yo brigade. "Go down south and look. It's a tad warmer down there. Reindeer are bound to have more of a spring to their step."

The three nodded, saluted, and skedaddled, running out of the workshop as fast as their little legs could carry them. Yo-yos were going the way of the dodos, so this, they figured, was their way of getting back on everyone's good side. Not that tying string to wood would be much help in locating flying reindeer, especially since reindeer were missing the skill-set needed to do a good walk-the-dog or rock-the-cradle, but beggars, they knew, couldn't be choosers.

"There," shouted Jester, a short while later. "In the snowy valley below. At least six of them." The elves bounded down in double-time, their pom-pommed hats bouncing all the way.

"Excuse me, sir," Fester said, bowing ever so slightly once they reached the herd. "My friends and I were wondering if any of you can, er, fly."

All six laughed, antlers shaking like tree limbs in a strong winter breeze. The biggest one responded for the others. "Look around you, elf, and tell me what you see."

Fester did as he was told. " Just snow, sir reindeer."

"And some twigs," added Lester.

"And a large boulder," finished Jester.

"Bravo," said the reindeer, head tilted down, his big, brown eyes directly in front of Fester's little nose. "Now, if we could fly, would we be grazing in a field with snow and twigs and a large boulder?"

"Um, if you liked those sorts of things, I suppose you would." Fester again looked around, inching backward just a tad. "Do you, um, like those sorts of things? A lot you can do with snow and twigs."

"And a large boulder," threw in Jester, yet again.

The reindeer scowled, yellow teeth bared. "That would be a no, little elf. On all accounts. Especially the flying. Any more questions?"

All three shook their tiny heads, east to west, and started to move away, lest these reindeer decided to start chomping on them instead. Still, Lester did think of one more thing to ask. "Um, do you know where we can find any flying reindeer?"

"Besides Santa's eight?" the large animal asked. The three elves nodded their response. "Then, yes, just one. Randolph is his name. Lives in a cave about ten miles due south. But I'd stay away from the likes of him if I was you. Nothing but trouble that one is. Or so we've always been told."

But Jester, Fester, and Lester had already started running after the word *south*, just after the *period* and before the word but. In other words, the warning fell on deaf pointy ears. Well, deaf and dumb, to be frank, but that's neither here nor there. Mostly there.

Ten miles south, just as promised, they found an ancient cave, deep and dark, etched into the side of a huge, snow-covered hill. Tentatively, they neared the mouth. "Um, hello?" Lester meekly called out, his voice echoing off the walls inside. "Any reindeer at home? We need your help."

They waited, five seconds, thirty, a minute. Three seconds after that, though it seemed like an eternity, they heard the telltale clip-clop. They backed away, the animal's eyes appearing in the gloomy darkness.

"What do you want?" barked the faceless voice, the sound terrifying, deep and menacing.

The three elves, with chills running down their collective backs, clung to each other. "Can you, um, can you by chance *fly*?" managed Jester.

The animal moved into the light, eyes black as coal, nose the same horrible hue. His ebony coat was like nothing the elves had ever seen, dark as pitch, dark as a moonless sky, small for a reindeer, though scarier looking than a pack of wolves. "Yes, I can indeed. Why do you ask?" A sinister grin spread from ear to turned-up ear, yellow fangs jutting out from his gaping maw, saliva dripping over and down.

The elves cowered at the sight of him. "Santa n...n...needs a replacement r...r...reindeer for Christmas," Lester stuttered.

"R...r...really?" Randolph mocked, moving in even closer, his breath as foul as a stagnant pool of swamp water.

"But if you're too busy," Jester managed, barely in a whisper.

"All the time in the world, little elf," came the reply. "Though there's one thing you should know."

"W...w...what's that?" the three asked as one.

"My nose, you see, is what powers my flight." He bent down for them to get a better look at said nasal appendage. "Only, right now, it is, quite sadly, running on empty."

Lester pulled out a gumdrop from his vest pocket. "Will this help?"

The reindeer's teeth were bared yet again, eyes mere slits now. "Guess again, little elf." And then he raised his head up high, nose pointed to the sky. A black glow began pulsing from its tip, growing, swirling, around and around, brushing the closest elf. Jester's pink skin instantly turned ashy gray, blue eyes casting over, skin desiccating, cheeks going gaunt. A moan like an avalanche burst forth from a dropped jaw as the nose's light grew in intensity, black upon black upon endless, cold black.

Lester was hit next, the life-force sucked out all at once, the shell remaining, alive though not alive, both elves suddenly moving in on the third. Fester, wide-eyed, ran for dear life, Randolph's wicked laughter following in the breeze.

The zombie elves gave chase, arms outstretched, dead eyes staring out into nothingness, the ever-present moan echoing throughout the valley. All the while, Fester ran, huffing and puffing, tripping over rocks, stuck in one snow bank after the next. Randolph was now flying high overhead, his black-lit nose lighting up the sky like an eclipse.

Sadly for Fester, slow as they were, the two zombie elves were tireless, and soon closed the gap. Randolph high above, stared down in rapt delight as his creations backed the little elf into a corner.

"Dinner is served," came the devilish voice from overhead. "Dig in, little ones."

Fester cowered and quivered and shook, hands over face, no desire to see his friends' apparent appetites quenched. Oh, but he heard them, though, those moans of death swirling around his head; the stench of them wafting up his nostrils, acidic tendrils spiraling up inside his head.

Then, suddenly, a new sound, hooves galloping up from his side, the earth trembling beneath him as he was suddenly lifted up and whisked away. "Told you to stay away," said the reindeer they'd encountered earlier, galloping at amazing speed. "See what you've unleashed?"

Fester looked up, Randolph barely a hundred yards behind, losing altitude, eyes fierce, angry, the zombies far in the distance now. But for how long? He shut his eyes, holding on tight to the animal's flanks. "Santa's gonna be pissed," he muttered.

The reindeer beneath him laughed. "Gee, ya think?"

Pissed, of course, was a gross understatement. "You did what?" Santa bellowed, his face as red as burning coals, fists clenched tight, just after the story was related.

Fester, quivering and quaking, replied, "Uhm, seems like we unleashed a demon reindeer whose nose-light turns the living into the, uh, dead."

"Walking dead," added the reindeer that had rescued him.

"Yeah, walking dead," agreed the elf. "*Murdering*, walking, dead. And they smell something fierce, too." He scratched at his head and squinted his eyes. "On the plus side, this reindeer, Randolph, can fly, just like you asked for. So, you see, the day wasn't a total loss."

Santa tapped his foot and counted to ten. "Really?" he grunted, clearly perplexed. "Christmas is still less than three days away, we're still down two reindeer, and now we've lost two elves and have a demon reindeer barreling down on us. I'd say we're deep, deep in the red, little elf. How, exactly, was the day not a total loss?"

Fester scratched his head, and replied, "We found a reindeer that can fly, and, by the looks of it, faster than the other reindeer you have on your team. If we can persuade him to fly for us, our problem is solved."

Santa sighed, his big belly bouncing. "Unless he turns us all into zombies first."

Which wasn't too far off the mark, all things considered.

Randolph took his time now. After all, he knew where he was headed; Santa's workshop not exactly hidden from the North Pole denizens, even ones that have been unseen for so many centuries. Plus, his batteries were once again fully charged, so to speak, and with each mile he flew, his nose-light pulsed brighter and brighter, hitting whatever animals were beneath him at the time. In other words, within a very short while, the two zombie elves were being followed by a whole horde of zombie creatures, hungry undead monsters that devoured anything and everything in their paths, leaving a trail of blood and guts and gristle in their wake. And an army of flesh devouring chipmunks, and squirrels, and tiny birds of a dozen species, and foxes, and bunnies is not as adorable as one might think.

Santa and the elves smelled them long before they saw them, the stench of death traveling along on the cold winter's air, sending a shiver up the backs of the living. "Oh shi...," started one of the elves.

"Language," cautioned Santa.

"Oh, uhm, now what do we do?" the same elf asked, trembling in place.

Santa twisted his chin hairs, pushing his brain to its limit. After all, he had a whole workforce to protect, not to mention Christmas itself, and quite probably the fate of the entire world. A lot of pressure for a man who generally thrived on it. "We reason with this reindeer," Santa eventually said. "After all, who can say no to Santa?"

"No," Randolph said, nonchalantly. "No way, no how, no chance." This in all about two minutes after their meeting, Santa's elves behind him, Randolph's minions in the opposite direction. It was just after Santa had asked Randolph to cover his nose for good, restore the dead back to the living, and help him save Christmas. All noble deeds, though, but of course, noble was not a word used to describe Randolph. Not by a long shot.

Santa stood, arms akimbo, eyes glaring, all the jolly sucked right out of him. "What *do* you want then?"

"Want?" Randolph asked, blinking his evil, doe-like eyes. "Why, not much. A little place to call my own, my nose forever powered," he started, legs suddenly going rigid, eyes smoldering, before he growled, "Total world domination, zombie spawn bowing to my every whim." And then he relaxed again, his eyes reverting back to normal. Or as normal as possible for a demon reindeer. "You know, the usual stuff."

All those on the opposite side of the demon reindeer flinched. Those behind merely licked their chops. "Um, how about a space heater for your cave and the occasional gopher to keep your nose lit," offered Santa.

Randolph scoffed. "You seem to forget that I'm the one with the zombie horde and you've merely got a bunch of dipsy elves. Meaning, I call the shots." Frighteningly, just as he said this, his nose once again burned bright, its dark beam swirling around like a cyclone. It stretched out until it came into contact with an elf, two, six, plus Comet and Vixen, all of them at once going gray, dry, mouths agape, eyes dead. And then, as the saying goes, all Hell broke loose, the dead sinking their yellowed teeth into the living, blood squirting out in all directions, a veritable river of it that soaked the ground in a vivid bath of crimson.

"Retreat!" shouted Santa. Those still able to followed him into the workshop, those who couldn't were devoured, piece by chewy piece, a feast of elf flesh. Tender, if not a bit gamey.

All the while Randolph grew bigger and stronger, drenched with power, laughing wickedly in the center of all the turmoil. "Yes, run, fat man, run. But know this, you I will save for last. You will watch all your elves and reindeer die, and then I will turn you into Zombie Claus, and we will fly around the world, devouring souls, one by one, country by country, continent by bloody continent."

With the door locked and barricaded behind them, Santa, his elves, and his remaining reindeer, all breathed heavily. Their hearts madly pounded away, sweat-soaked, nervous eyes roaming back and forth, looking to see who was still among them. And who, of course, was not.

The banging started almost immediately, zombie elfin fists pounding against wood, tiny animal teeth gnawing their way inside. Everyone turned to the boss-man for an answer. Though this, naturally, was even out of his realm of expertise. Christmas magic was one thing, but how does one combat something like this?

There was one clear solution, of course, but no obvious way to come by it.

"We have to extinguish his nose," Santa said with a moan. "But he's too powerful now to get close enough to even attempt such a thing, even if we knew how to do it." He sat on a stool, covering his ears before looking to Fester for help. "Don't you find it strange that we're only now just encountering this demon reindeer? Why all of a sudden?"

"Beats me," replied the elf, who suddenly looked around the room, knowing someone who might be able to help. "Ask the reindeer who rescued me. He was the one who told us about Randolph in the first place."

Santa pointed to said reindeer. "You there. What do you know about this, this *creature*?"

The reindeer blushed as he pushed his way through the nervous throng. "Very little, Santa," he replied. "We knew of this Randolph only from stories. A reindeer that could fly by the power of his nose. An evil power. One we should never seek out." The reindeer paused, staring into Santa's sparkling blue eyes. "But how is it you can fly? Perhaps the answer to your question can be found within your very own powers."

Santa nodded. "Yes, that makes sense." He looked again to the little elf by his side. "Fester, what did you first say to this demon reindeer?"

Fester strummed his chin and stared at the ceiling. "Well, um," he began. "I think I asked if anyone was home." A pause, eyes shut tight. "And then I said that we needed his help."

Santa's smile instantly bloomed. "Bingo." He put finger to nose, then continued. "My powers come from the children. They believe in me. They need me. If they ever stopped needing me, I would cease to exist, as would all of us in the workshop. This Randolph must operate similarly. When Fester said we needed him, it woke him up, gave him enough energy to light his nose up again. Now he obviously runs on the souls he's sucked inside of him. It explains, in any case, why none of us have ever seen him before now. He must be even older than I am. Still, it doesn't help us in figuring out how to stop him."

And now it was Fester's turn to smile. "The light from his nose is his power. When his nose glows, the light swirls out, and whoever gets touched by it becomes the walking, and, um, devouring, dead." The elf stopped, formulating his words, thinking of a plan. "But what if we can reflect the light, send it backwards, away from the living?"

Santa finished his train of thought. "You mean, if we reflect the light it might turn Randolph's power against him." Santa thought it over and nodded. "But how do we do that? What few mirrors we have are back at the main house. We have none in the workshop, and, even if we did, they wouldn't be enough to reflect that hideous glow. Randolph is stronger now, and so is the light from his nose."

Fester snapped his fingers and ran over to his workspace. He returned a second later, a large box in his hands, and dumped the contents on the floor.

"I give you the *Power Yo-Yo.*" His proud face was lit up like a Christmas tree.

The elves grimaced, Santa included. "Forgive me, little one, but a bunch of common yo-yos are no match for a powerful demon reindeer."

"Maybe," Fester said, a knowing grin spreading like wildfire across his face. "But these aren't *common* yo-yos. Watch." He lifted one of the toys off the ground and hit a button, the string miraculously rising and lowering on its own. A slight twist of the wrist and it did a loop, then a trick, then two, all with just barely any movement on the elf's part. "See, children today want everything easy. That's why you don't see them playing with our yo-yos anymore. Not enough flash. Not enough pizzazz. Too much work for too little payoff. But not anymore. These babies are made of shiny metal, not wood, the string a conductive piece of zinc wire, a minicomputer inside. Programmable. Safe for kids, unless..."

Santa chuckled, the other elves still looking on in confusion. "Unless," Santa continued, "we reprogram them. Make them unsafe. Especially for demon reindeer."

And now it was Fester's turn to touch finger to nose before handing out the yo-yos to his fellow elves and teaching them, quickly, how to reprogram them into the dangerous instruments they'd soon become.

They looked up to Santa when they were done, all of them covering their ears now, the din growing louder and louder outside. Insistent hands and claws were pounding and pawing and scratching, the wood obviously just barely holding. Thankfully, the elves and forest animals outside were too small to reach the windows, but not Santa.

He unlatched the nearest one and poked his head outside, a cacophony of moans and groans going up at once, the sound like a million fingernails scraping across a million chalkboards. "We surrender!" he hollered, above the clamor. "Please, just let us come out and say farewell to one another."

Randolph grinned and bowed his neck. "Stop," he commanded. And stop they did, the zombies at once filing in behind their lord and master. They froze in place, dead eyes staring blindly ahead, emaciated limbs dangling from sunken, gray torsos. Death in stasis. "Come out now. And make it quick. I want total world domination by dinner time."

Santa cringed but did as he was told, the surviving elves and animals exiting as one, single file, all of them lining up against the side of the building. "A last request," Santa pled, eyes cast downward, a frown plastered to his face.

Randolph sighed and tapped a cloven hoof. "What now?"

"Just a North Pole ritual. As a memorial for our fallen comrades, we give a final salute." He paused and looked up, locking eyes with the demon reindeer. "With our yo-yos."

The evil one laughed, a wicked chuckle that shook Santa's very bones. Still, he nodded once again. "This I'd like to see."

Santa looked to his team and smiled. "Just hide behind your shields everyone," he whispered, then soon added, "Let 'er rip."

All at once, the yo-yos were activated. A flick of the wrist and the strings were flung to their full length, another and the metal balls went swinging, clockwise, loop after loop, crazy fast, with a harmonious symphony of buzzes and whirrs.

"We're ready now!" shouted Fester to Randolph, who, despite himself, was duly impressed with the nifty show. Still, world domination loomed ahead, and he was never one to waste time.

And so, fully powered as he now was, he set his nose to glowing, a black ring of light that burst forth in unimaginable fury, pushing outward like a tidal wave, and reaching Santa's little helpers in an instant.

Randolph watched all this, first in complete joy, then in abject terror.

"No!" he quickly hollered as his glorious, deathly beams were repulsed back by the spinning yo-yos, the light in an instant traveling in reverse, smashing into him and his zombie mob, spiraling around them, obliterating them from sight in a cloud of black. Soon enough, however, the black blurred, turning gray, then blue, then green, then yellow, brighter yellow still, then brighter than that. Until a blinding flash of white enveloped all of the North Pole and all that resided there.

Santa and the elves dropped their toys and covered their faces for a moment, standing still as a burst of energy flowed around them. When they blinked their eyes open again, Randolph was gone, the woodland creatures dashing off, reverted back to their former selves, the once-zombie elves, all rosy cheeked and toothy grinned, hopping up and down and shouting with glee.

"Fuckin'-A," Santa whispered, rubbing his eyes.

"Language," cautioned Fester, quickly running out to hug Lester and Jester.

"I mean, uhm, welcome back, little ones. Welcome back," Santa grinned.

And welcomed back they were, hugged and kissed, and, of course, tested for any lasting zombie side-effects, of which there was, surprisingly, just the one. "Get a load of Comet and Vixen," Fester whispered in Santa's ear.

Santa turned and stared, mouth open at what he saw. For where both reindeer once had black noses, they now had shiny white ones, and the more they were hugged and kissed and pet, the more said noses glowed, shooting out amber beams that filled everyone with an overwhelming sense of happiness and love. Enough power to circle the globe in one evening, which is just what they did a mere two days later.

And that very next spring, when all the animals in the forest were having their babies, Comet and Vixen were strutting around with theirs. Oh, and this was a feisty one, small for a reindeer, but special, very special indeed.

"A red nose," Santa said, with a long whistle, bending down to greet his new charge. "Well I'll be damned."

"Language," Fester chuckled, waving a finger. "And a poor choice of language at that. No more *damned* anything around these parts, if you please."

"Amen to that, little one," Santa said with a jiggling, jolly belly-laugh. "Amen to that."

IT'S A WONDERFUL DEATH

RICK MOORE

It started with the fresh turkeys.

Cyril Whittaker and his wife Glenda saw a report about it on the news.

"It has now been confirmed," the newscaster solemnly intoned. "That the recently deceased bodies of freshly killed turkeys are returning to life and attacking the living."

Cyril looked at his wife, who sat beside him on the couch. The fear in his eyes matched hers. He took her hand, and they sat there together watching the report, their entwined fingers trembling.

"What follows," the newscaster, Mike Hollace, said. "May not be suitable for younger viewers and you may want to ask them to leave the room."

The scene cut from the studio to a shot of a rural farm. The camera was shaky, hand-held. A man came running out of a low, windowless brick building, the fire exit door slamming open ahead of him. The man, who wore a bloody butcher's apron, ran screaming toward the camera. His entire right hand, up to the wrist, was buried deep in the neck of a decapitated, plucked turkey.

"Get it off!" the man yelled. "It's eating me!"

Behind him, the slowly closing door was pushed open, and three dead feathered turkeys, looking alive but for the twisted angles of their broken necks, came waddling out. Their familiar calls—*gobble-gobble, gobble-gobble*—sounded clogged and distorted, clotted blood coating their primary vocalizations. A woman wearing a hairnet and rubber gloves ran into the frame, hurrying to the man with his hand inside the turkey neck.

"What is it, Ned?" she cried. "What's wrong?"

"Get it off!" the man sobbed.

The woman grabbed the turkey's back legs, yanked hard. The turkey came free with a sucking sound.

In unison, Cyril and Glenda grimaced. The man remained in frame but a few seconds before staggering off, clutching his damaged hand. He'd been visible just long enough for Cyril and his wife to see the flesh on his hand was gone, dissolved as though dipped in acid, stripped to the bone.

Off camera, someone yelled, "Shoot it, Pete. Shoot it in the head."

The camera zoomed in on the three broken necked turkeys. The shotgun blast blew the head of one clean off its neck, and the bird stood there tottering. Blackish red blood sputtered out of the open neck cavity, hissing as it hit the dirt, sending up narrow tendrils of smoke.

Then the turkey with its head blown off continued its advance, some unknowable sentience guiding it toward the cameraman.

"Fucker's still alive!" he yelled, though the network, in the interests of good taste and not wanting to offend their viewers, bleeped the latter half of the sentence.

The camera panned down, showing the plucked and headless turkey righting itself, one lazy step taking it closer to the cameraman. The camera lifted again. Over at the doorway, more broken necked turkeys pushed their way outside into the daylight.

Gobble-gobble, Gobble-gobble.

The screen cut back to Mike Hollace in the studio.

"We now go live to Yvette Ibsen for further developments on this breaking story."

The screen went dark. Cyril sat with the remote in his trembling hand.

Glenda looked at him. "Don't you think this is something we need to know about?"

"Poppycock," Cyril said. "It's a gag. A Christmas prank. Like that fella Colbert puts out. And I for one don't intend to be a party to it."

"But why would they do something like that?"

Cyril shrugged. He looked from the TV screen and took solace in the Christmas tree, a beautiful six foot pine they'd strung with lights and tinsel and hung with ornaments. Beneath the tree were a dozen or so wrapped packages, gifts for the grandchildren and the kids, a few items that Cyril and Glenda had each bought the other. Glenda's gifts to her husband were beautifully wrapped, his for her less so, with too much tape and paper folds in all the wrong places.

In the morning, when their daughter Sally and her husband Aaron arrived with little Jack and Lucy, the number of gifts would triple, carried into the house from the back of the SUV, as was tradition. The tykes, excited at the prospect of what treasures waited beneath the gaudy wrapping paper, were each allowed to open one of the smaller gifts, the rest saved for after dinner, as was also tradition. Just like Cyril and Glenda had done with Sally when she was little, making the magic last, drawing it out, teaching her the reward of patience.

Family. Tradition. That was what Christmas was all about for Cyril.

No way was he going to let those idiots with their special effects and their tomfoolery put a dampener on it. Why he had a good mind to call the network and give them what for, scaring folks like that, especially at a time that was supposed to be holy. Not that he went in for the holy part, believing in it about as much as he did Santa Claus.

Glenda moved from the couch to the glass cabinet containing the sherry decanter. She poured herself a glass of the dark amber liqueur, knocked it back in one shot, and then refilled the glass to the brim.

"Steady on there, old girl," Cyril said. "It's not Christmas yet, you know."

Glenda turned to him, some of the sherry sloshing onto her hand, which was shaking.

"Mike Hollace wouldn't lie to us, Cyril," she said. "You couldn't find anyone more honest. That's why he reads the news. He wouldn't lie. Especially not on Christmas Eve."

"You give those nincompoops enough money," Cyril grumbled. "They'll do whatever you tell them to do." He picked up the television guide that had come as a free supplement with the morning paper, flipped through the pages, studied the schedule for Christmas Day. The cover was paper, not glossy like the real TV Guide, and Cyril did his best to ignore the ink it left on his fingers.

Glenda finished her second glass. "I can't believe you're not even the slightest bit concerned by what we just saw."

"The only thing that concerns me," Cyril said, moving the television guide closer to his face. "Is which James Bond film I'm going to watch tomorrow afternoon. Usually it's a toss-up between Connery and Roger Moore. And Connery wins, no contest. But tomorrow, if you can believe it, they've got Diamonds Are Forever and Thunder…"

From the kitchen came an enormous crash.

"What the Dickens!" Cyril cried.

Glenda stared open mouthed into the kitchen, which was situated off the living room. There was an arch overhead and carpet transitioning to tile underfoot; all that separated one room from the other. Cyril jumped off the couch, no small feat for a man of his advanced years.

Together they crept toward the kitchen, Cyril clutching the rolled up television guide for protection, Glenda close behind.

A second crash.

It came from the refrigerator.

Almost to the point of being on tip-toes, Cyril and Glenda advanced toward the fridge.

More movement. Something heavy thudding against the interior wall. Jars and bottles tipping over, clattering against the bottom shelf. Then the buckling of the spare aluminum roasting pan, used in this instance for the purpose of defrosting.

"What is it?" Cyril asked. "What's in there?

In a trembling, hushed voice, Glenda told him. "It's the turkey."

Cyril tried to find the words to contradict her. To tell her she was wrong. Instead, he remained silent, reaching out for the door handle. His fingers appeared to have lost their ability to grip, the strength in his arthritis-weakened hands abandoning him entirely. He managed to hook two fingers around the handle, and with a forceful tug, freed the door from its seal.

It was the turkey, all right. Just like Glenda had said.

"It's alive!" Glenda screamed, dropping her sherry glass, the shattered fragments scattering across the floor tiles.

The TV had it wrong. It wasn't only fresh turkeys that were being reanimated. For days this one must have contained sentient life. Three days to be precise, since that was how long ago Glenda had taken it out of the freezer. Looking at it now, Glenda shuddered at the idea of it sitting there all this time, awaiting the moment when the ice crystals binding its reanimated flesh melted sufficiently for it to regain movement. Why, just a few hours ago, she'd used the kitchen scissors to remove its bag and pour off the pooling blood; her fingers touching its bumpy flesh, making a mental note to remember to wrap its meaty wings in foil so they wouldn't burn. She shuddered again, remembering how she'd explored the edges of its inner cavity with her fingers, testing to see if it would be defrosted in time to go in the oven the following morning.

What if she'd reached all the way inside to remove the bag of innards and its neck, like she'd almost done? Would the zombified turkey have seized its opportunity to attack, to use whatever mystifying power it contained to clamp down on her hand and strip her skin, like the one on the TV had done to that man?

The turkey had no head, and yet somehow it appeared to be imbued with sufficient cognizance to recognize their presence. Their intended Christmas dinner, which was on its side, was pressed up against the fridge's wall when Cyril opened the door. It dropped back to the glass shelf, flattening its overturned aluminum coffin and knocking over the last few condiment bottles.

Cyril and Glenda watched in transfixed horror as the turkey strained against the plastic tie holding both legs together, one crossed over the other. Its legs trembled and its wings wiggled, and beneath the fat pockets that created the bumps on the surface of its pale skin, Cyril saw tension in the leg muscles.

"What's it doing?" Glenda asked.

The plastic tie snapped in two, and as the legs parted, her question was answered. Out of the dark cavity came the bag of innards, shooting at incredible speed from the turkey's ass (or the widened hole where its ass used to be), the slippery, blood-drenched plastic bag smacking Cyril between the eyes, sending him staggering backward.

"Son of a bitch!" Cyril yelled, wiping blood out of his eyes with the sleeve of his Christmas sweater.

Glenda knitted him a sweater every year, and though he was due to receive a new one in the morning, she couldn't help thinking--somewhat absurdly, she realized, after the thought that popped into her head--the blood would never come out of the white wool she'd fashioned to resemble snowflakes, not on a cold water wash cycle, anyway.

"Son of a bitch!" Cyril yelled again, charging forward, the rolled up television guide with Jimmy Stewart on the cover clutched tightly in his hand; some long dormant, long assumed defunct aspect of the protector instinct waking within him, alerting the need to retaliate.

"Yaaaahh!" Cyril cried, cuffing the bird on either side with the television guide, then bringing his weapon down repeatedly in a club-like fashion on top of it.

The turkey, which hailed from the order of Galliformes and was of the genus Meleagris gallopavo, had, in its short lifetime, been through unheralded quantities of shit. Both literally and figuratively. Literally, since it had been caged in a space providing little opportunity but to crap where it ate and utilize said space to walk in circles all day. And figuratively, which is to say that the fowl presently receiving a pounding from the printed face of an inexplicably popular long dead actor had, during its spectacularly irrelevant existence, been force-fed and decapitated, plucked and disemboweled, injected with broth and frozen, defrosted and now, finally reanimated.

In life it had been blissfully unaware of its own unfortunate fate. But in death, possessing an entirely new, hitherto inexperienced form of supernaturally powered super-consciousness, turkey number 4431887163, was not only self-aware, but also aware that these creatures--who it saw as big red blobs despite having neither eyes, nor a head nor a brain--had intended to chew its skin and eat its flesh and suck on its bones. That they were, in short, the personification of evil incarnate.

Now, like its brethren all across the world, it was back to offer a taste of the torment its kind had endured for hundreds of years. And what better time than this? For wasn't this, after all, a time of giving?

"What's it doing now?" Glenda asked, seeing the turkey employ its wings to raise its body to an upward facing angle. The wings moved up and down, up and down, like the turkey was testing their strength. All through the Whittaker's house not a sound was heard.

Leaning over with his hands on his thighs, Cyril looked into the dark chasm of the turkey's butt end.

A split-second too late to get out of the way, Cyril realized 4431887163's intentions.

Into the air the turkey sprang, a squelchy slap breaking the silence as its butt end attached to Cyril's face, covering his eyes, nose and mouth. The legs spread wider, then clamped tight against his ears. Cyril made muffled cries, cries that intensified as ectoplasmic, black-red goo that crackled and popped, oozed from the edges of the orifice and trickled down his cheeks.

"Help!" Glenda cried to no one. "Help! Help!"

She heard bones cracking, saw the orifice opening wider, the cavity expanding to accommodate more of Cyril's head; sliding over his ears, his hairline, his bald spot, down to the nape in back, and in front past the chin to his wattle; which, coincidentally, bore more than a passing resemblance to the type found on most domestic turkeys.

The bird sat atop his neck, its legs dangling onto his shoulders, its wings moving up and down.

Cyril whacked the turkey covering his head with the rolled up television guide. Fizzing ectoplasmic goop oozed out of the orifice, running down his neck.

Flesh smoldered.

Cyril yelled a desperate, wordless plea for help. The television guide fell from his hand, unfurling as it dropped to the tiled floor, Jimmy Stewart's face now an unrecognizable smear of black ink.

Glenda smelled cooking pork. The realization that it was not pork, but her husband's burning flesh unlocked her fear-induced mental freeze frame and got her moving. She ran to him, grabbing the turkey by the wings and pulled with all her strength until it lifted from his head.

Only the turkey didn't lift from his head. It lifted from his neck. And his head, well, that lifted off with the turkey. The goop continued to eat its way through the top of his spinal cord, the vocal cords snapping free, dangling out of the turkey's butt end before being suddenly sucked inside.

Glenda stood there in frozen horror with the turkey containing her husband's decapitated head in her hands, the cavity of his neck gushing a fountain of blood that splashed down on top of her, coloring her crimson.

The bird flapped its wings and kicked its legs, almost like it was doing some sort of celebratory victory dance. The headless body of the man she'd spent the last thirty-two years married to dropped to its knees, decorating every surface in the kitchen with a torrent of blood. Then it collapsed to the floor and finished bleeding out across the tiles.

From the butt end cavity, dangling from dark, snot-like threads, came two pink shapes Glenda recognized but couldn't place. It only took a few seconds to realize what the pink things were, and why she hadn't initially identified them. She was used to seeing them attached to either side of Cyril's head. They were his ears. Each of the turkey's legs moved toward the ears, the knot of bone where its feet had been severed docking with the hole where the ears had been separated from Cyril's head, the two forms of flesh and bone uniting.

And then she felt it.

An unmistakable sensation of something moving inside the bird.

A moment later Glenda witnessed the unholiest of nativities.

Out of 4431887163's neck cavity pushed Cyril's head, strands of sticky, black-red ectoplasm clinging to his sodden hair and face like afterbirth. The first sounds out of Cyril's mouth, produced by the reborn vocal chords, belonged not to the man, but the bird.

"Gobble, gobble."

Glenda blinked in shock.

"Hello there, Glenda," Cyril said in a voice that sounded strained and high pitched. His eyes were brightly lit, never more pleased to see her. "I must say, you're looking very festive. Red-*gobble-gobble*-suits you. You ought to-*gobble*-wear it more often."

"Naaggghh!" Glenda cried, heaving the bird sporting her husband's head away from her, sending it skittering across the counter top and clattering into the sink.

The Cyril-thing righted itself, raised up over the edge of the sink to look at her.

"It's a Christmas miracle, Glenda," Cyril cried jovially. And then this thing, with a turkey's body and her husband's head attached to its neck, started to sing.

"Away in a manger, a sink for his bed, tomorrow's Christmas dinner, just got a new head."

Up from the sink and onto the rim, the Cyril-thing hopped.

"And that's not all, Glenda!" Cyril grinned at her. "The gifts just keep on coming. Baby needed a new set of feet, and papa provided. Check 'em out!"

When the creature that had taken possession of her husband's head started to tap-dance, using the soft bones of his ears to make the requisite clicking sounds against the stainless steel rim, Glenda threw her arms in the air and ran screaming.

Cyril's headless body, it transpired, had also been invited to this impromptu Christmas shindig. One of its hands shot out, grabbing Glenda's ankle. She screamed, looking down at the bloody fingers gripping her leg, at the hand she'd held countless times, at the gold band she'd slid onto the ring finger over three decades earlier. With her other foot, she stamped down on the back of the hand, dislodging the fingers.

Screaming, she ran through the house for the front door. A backward glance showed her a snapshot of Hell. Cyril's headless body pulled itself along the floor, sloshing through its own blood. At its side ran the Cyril-thing, a dead bird with her husband's head atop its neck and his ears for feet.

"Glenda, wait!" Cyril called. "You don't have to be left out in the cold. Not at Christmas. Come back. There's plenty of room in here for two!"

Glenda got the front door open and saw the pandemonium out in the street.

Through the snow stumbled people wearing turkeys over their heads, arms flailing wildly in front of them. She saw her neighbor living on her right, Joyce Green; or her head anyway. Joyce had been reconfigured just like Cyril, the darting turkey carcass her head was attached to leaving ear shaped footprints in the snow.

Across the street was a leg of lamb and shoulder of ham that moved of their own volition. They took turns beating to a bloody pulp the face of a man she thought might be Alan Daniels, her neighbor to the left, but could no longer tell for sure.

Overhead she heard bells. Her eyes lifted toward the sky.

But these were not sleigh bells. Only Hell alone could own a sound of such soul-searing cacophony.

Glenda saw a flash of red and white. Leathery red flesh instead of a suit. Gleaming white horns instead of a beard. It wasn't Santa, though the movement of one letter was all it took to provide the right name. It wasn't reindeer she saw, but eight hounds of Hell, dragging the death-sled through the sky. Within the carriage made of human bones, she saw the instigator himself, saw the one who'd unleashed Hell on Earth, who'd chosen this night to commence his dominion over mankind.

"Ho-ho-ho," Satan called, grinning down at her, the points of his countless teeth sharper than ice picks. "Happy Holidays, Glenda! A merry Anti-Christ-mas to you and yours. Ho-ho-ho."

Glenda sensed a presence behind her. She started forward, refusing to give-up, refusing to accept this was the end. Her foot went no further than the threshold. It was the Christmas lights that got her; the ones she and Cyril strung around the tree every year. The lights snaked around her neck, constricted, choking her. They were still on, still flashing their multitude of colors.

Then she was yanked back inside, into the waiting embrace of the pine tree. The strings of lights were used to lift her off the ground and turn her into the world's largest Christmas tree ornament. The pine tree trembled, shedding loose needles, its branches flexing and thrashing.

As Glenda hung there, arms and legs flopping uselessly, her tongue protruding from her mouth, the flashing string of lights crushed her windpipe, making both her eyes pop out and lay dangling on her cheeks. The last thing she saw was Cyril's headless body sitting cross-legged at the foot of the tree, unwrapping his presents, while the Cyril-thing watched with an excited glint in his eyes.

Looking up at her purpling face, Cyril smiled, the corners of his eyes crinkling.

He said, "Don't worry, Glenda. You'll be-*gobble*-back in just a jiffy. And then, side-by-side, we'll-*gobble*-welcome the rest of the family home. Family, Glenda. They're what Christmas is all about! The rest of it, that's just-*gobble*-just the trimmings. Don't you think, hon?"

Glenda's lifeless body slumped forward.

Cyril looked away, watching as his hands tore the wrapping from his gift and held it up for him to see.

"A new sweater!" Cyril cried, flapping his wings. "It's exactly what I wanted!"

THE WORST CHRISTMAS EVER

KEITH ADAM LUETHKE

Ben Gram was five years old and waiting for Santa Claus on Christmas Eve. His babysitter, Cheryl, made him go to bed an hour ago. Cheryl wasn't nice like his mother. She didn't read him a bedtime story and was always talking on the phone instead of paying attention to him. Ben had argued that he wanted to stay up late and wait for Santa, but Cheryl told him that the jolly fat man in red didn't exist. Ben knew differently. Instead of going to bed, he stared out the window. He could still hear Cheryl on the phone downstairs, laughing about how he still believed in Santa. Ben knew Santa was out there. He made a wish on a twinkling star and within minutes it came true.

Across the street, he witnessed a large, white bearded man in a red jumpsuit, black boots, and a Santa hat. He was moving really slow and carried a sack over his shoulder which must've been stuffed full with presents.

Ben couldn't believe his eyes.

"Santa Claus, you are real," Ben gasped.

The big jolly man stumbled to the Carpenter's house and beat on the door.

Ben frowned. Santa was supposed to go down the chimney, not through the front door.

Maybe the Carpenters' didn't have one, Ben reasoned.

Mr. Carpenter opened the door to greet Santa. Ben was over-joyed, until Santa grabbed Mr. Carpenter by the neck and sunk his teeth into his head.

Ben gasped. He wanted to scream, to call out to Cheryl for help, but he was motionless.

Mr. Carpenter's blood leaked onto the porch and painted the snow red. Santa dropped his gift sack, broke Mr. Carpenter's head open like a watermelon, and feasted on the brains inside.

Then, Jamie, Mr. Carpenter's mother, came outside and screamed. She ran back into the house and attempted to shut the door but Santa barged right on in.

Ben's heart turned into a jack-hammer. He didn't understand how Santa could do such horrible things. Unless...yes that was it. Mr. Carpenter and Jamie must've been bad this year, really bad. Ben racked his mind to make sure he hadn't done anything wrong, so Santa would give him presents instead of breaking his head open. He'd lied to his mother about breaking the cookie jar, but it wasn't his fault because she'd put it high on the shelf where he couldn't reach it. Santa would understand. Yes, Ben had been a good boy all year long, but he still felt bad about his neighbors. He pulled himself away from the window and peeked out of his bedroom and into the hallway. From upstairs he could still hear Cheryl's constant babbling.

"Cheryl," he called out to her. When she didn't answer he raised his voice. "Cheryl, I need you!"

"Go to bed, Ben!" she snapped.

He heard the springs creak on the couch as Cheryl got up.

"If I find you out of your room, I'm going to call your mother and she won't be happy."

Ben shut the door and ran to his bed. He ducked under the covers and feigned sleep. Cheryl checked on him. The light from her cell phone cast his room in a dim blue light.

"You'd better be asleep. If I find you awake again I'll make sure you don't get any presents tomorrow."

Ben couldn't pretend to be asleep anymore. He sat up quickly to address her.

"But, Cheryl, Santa's next door and he's..."

"Shut it. Go to sleep or no presents," Cheryl said, and slammed his door.

After Ben heard the couch springs again he went back to the window. Mr. Carpenter was on his feet now and standing in the street. Gore ran down his face from the opening in his head, but he was still alive. He didn't move from the spot on the street, but just stood there, letting brain matter run onto his face

It was like he was waiting for someone.

Ben's hands were shaking. He grabbed his flashlight from the dresser and held it tight. A moment later, Santa and Jamie lurched outside. Mr. Carpenter's mother looked different than before. She wobbled as she followed Santa, and when she got under the streetlight, Ben's mouth dropped. Jamie was missing her left arm, only a boney stump remained. But that wasn't all; her neck had a gaping hole in it and her nightgown was plastered with blood.

They're dead. They're all dead!

Ben had snuck out of his bedroom one night and spied on his mother. She was watching a movie with Dan, her boyfriend, and Ben was frightened by what he saw. The movie depicted a bunch of dead people making their way to a city. He had trouble sleeping that night, and when his mother asked him what was wrong, he told her he'd seen the bad people from the movie. Her mother laughed, called them zombies, and reassured him they didn't exist. But as Ben looked out his bedroom window, he could see the zombies clearly.

His mother had lied, they did exist.

Ben turned on his flashlight and shone it through the window at the zombies in hopes that they would go away.

Santa, Mr. Carpenter, and Jamie jerked around to look at where the light had come from. Then, to Ben's horror, they started to walk towards his house.

Ben flicked the light off and shut the curtains, thinking that if they didn't see him, maybe they would stop their pursuit.

He locked his bedroom door just in case, then hid under his bed. In the movie, the zombies would stop at nothing to get to the city and eat the people within. They even went underwater. Ben hoped these zombies were different. He moved his toy box out of the way and huddled behind it.

This was the worst Christmas Eve ever, he thought.

*   *   *

"I feel like the worst parent in the world," Kate said. She walked beside Dan and stared at the sidewalk. "What kind of mother leaves her son on Christmas Eve?"

Dan, middle-aged, handsome, and supportive, put his arm around her shoulder.

"It's not your fault. You didn't get your paycheck until today. How are you going to get him a gift without any money?"

Kate smiled at him.

"You're doing great. We'll get him a Christmas present and return before he knows you were out shopping for him," Dan said.

Kate laughed. "You don't know my son very well yet, do you? He's probably trying to get Cheryl to let him stay up so he can see Santa Claus."

Dan held her closer and squeezed her butt.

"Boys will be boys."

Kate playfully shoved him.

"You're so dirty sometimes."

"You love it," he grinned, and leaned in for a kiss. But before their lips met, someone ran down the street screaming.

"Get out of here! Run for your lives!"

They watched as a skinny man in a big coat ran past them and didn't stop. He disappeared behind a building, but they could still hear his shoes slapping the concrete.

"What was that about?" Dan asked.

"Maybe there's a sale we don't know about," Kate joked.

As they continued walking, the streets grew ominous. Cars sped by blaring horns, a few more people ran past them, and somewhere nearby an ambulance whined.

"What's going on tonight?" Dan said, shaking his head.

"I don't know. Let's get Ben's present and go home. I don't what to be out here any longer than we have to."

"I agree with that," Dan smirked.

They continued down the sidewalk until they came to a store open for twenty-four hours, the special hours just until Christmas. The parking lot was nearly empty, save for a group of teenagers milling about the entrance in a drunken stupor.

Kate and Dan quickened their pace.

The group of teenagers saw them coming. A few of them groaned, deep-throated sounds which sounded like they'd gargled with broken glass. Three of them: a boy in all black, another in a wool jacket, and a girl wearing a Prada jacket, stretched out their arms and reached for them.

"We don't have any money to give, I'm sorry," Dan explained.

"Just ignore them," Kate whispered.

As they slipped by the teenagers, Kate noticed the girl in the Prada jacket was missing part of her face. She tried not to stare at the deformity out of politeness and continued into the store.

The gang of teenagers followed them inside.

Upon entering, they heard Christmas music playing throughout the store.

Dan took Kate's arm and walked her to the electronic section.

"Crazy kids, what are they doing here on Christmas Eve anyway?"

Kate wasn't paying attention to Dan or the teenagers behind them anymore. She was looking around in panic. Most of the shelves were empty; whatever remained of the merchandise was on the floor. There were no customers at the checkout and the shoppers in the store were moving strangely, as though in a trance.

"Something's not right here," Kate muttered.

"Everything's fine. Don't worry about..."

Dan's sentence trailed off when they reached the electronic department. Three male employees wearing red Santa hats were bent over a lifeless body. Their hands plunged in and out of a wide opening in the stomach cavity, digging out ropey intestines and stuffing viscera into their mouths.

Kate screamed, loud and shrill.

The three employees took their attention away from the body they were mutilating and advanced toward her.

"Get back. Get away from us!" Dan ordered. He shoved the largest man in the group and knocked him onto the floor.

Kate yanked on his jacket sleeve. "Come on, let's get out of here."

Dan turned to go but a gnarled hand wrapped around his neck. He was pulled away from her in an instant.

"Dan!"

Hands curled around Dan's head as fingers probed his mouth and ears. Dan was dragged onto the linoleum floor. He thrashed like a baited shark, kicking his legs out and trying to tear away from his attackers. Blackened teeth clamped down on his hand, severing the skin and the tendons underneath.

Then, Kate bashed the employee who bit him with a flat screen television. There was a loud boom as the head of the Santa wearing worker smashed through the screen. Dan managed to shove the other one away. He gripped his wounded hand as he bled onto the floor.

"That son-of-a-bitch bit me."

"I know. Now let's get out of here before they get back up," Kate pleaded.

Dan ran in front of her and headed for the exit. The teenagers were almost to their position and had the same mind set as the employees.

Kate scanned the video game rack for new releases.

"Come on, what the hell are you doing?"

Kate sucked in her lips as she picked through the games. The two leftover employees were on their feet now and staggering closer to her.

"Kate, please."

She grabbed a handful of the games from the rack and stuffed them into her purse.

"I got them," she said.

Dan snatched her with his good hand and dragged her.

"We have to get out of here. Stay close to me," he said.

Dan ushered her through the clothing section and made a wide circle toward the exit. They avoided the teenagers and were almost out of the store when a woman dressed up as an elf lurched out from the checkout station. Where her eyes should've been were gaping holes, a pair of bloodied scissors dangling in her hand. She came at them moaning and ready to rip them apart.

Dan reared back and punched her in the face. Her elf ears flew off her head and she slammed into a cash register. Dan spotted a large candy cane on a rack. He snatched it from the aisle and approached the demented elf.

"Christmas is cancelled," he sneered, and jammed the end of the candy cane through an empty eye socket and into her brain.

The elf slumped over, motionless.

Kate stared at him.

"Come on, honey. I'll walk you back home now."

He stretched his hand out to her.

Kate intertwined her fingers with his and they ran out of the store and into the chaos of the night.

*   *   *

Cheryl was twirling her hair and watching It's a Wonderful Life, when someone knocked on the front door. She checked the time on her cell phone. Kate and Dan hadn't been gone long enough to return yet.

The knock came once more, louder this time.

She rose from the couch with a sigh. Outside on the porch, she could hear a group of people shuffling around and making deep groans.

"That's just great, a bunch of Christmas carolers." She stalked to the door.

"Go away. I don't want to hear your singing and I don't care about Christmas."

The moans continued.

The door shook in its frame as the outsiders knocked more and more.

"I said, leave me alone. I'll call the cops on you. I don't care if it is Christmas Eve or not."

The hinges rattled and the door broke free as Cheryl screamed and ran into the living room. A lumbering Santa came inside. His white beard was painted red and as he reached for her, Cheryl realized he had a hole in his lower belly which was spilling festering maggots.

Cheryl called 9-1-1 but nobody ever answered. She called the police directly and got the same response.

Two more walking corpses stumbled through the doorway. One was a man with his head split slightly open, and the other was an elderly woman missing her arm.

"This can't be happening," Cheryl sobbed. "Zombies aren't real."

Santa moaned as he grabbed a fistful of her hair and pulled. Cheryl tried to smack his hand away, but the zombie Santa's grip was much too strong. He dragged her to the couch and bit into her face.

Blackened teeth tore through her nose and part of her left cheek. Zombie Santa jerked his head and took her nose off.

Cheryl's screams were cut short as she choked on the blood and mucus now flooding into her open mouth.

The other zombies joined in. The man sunk his sharp teeth into her upper thigh, stripping her flesh and stuffing the pieces into his mouth, while the woman, in a mock attack, yanked Cheryl's arm in an attempt at ripping off the limb.

Cheryl managed one more choking cry for help. Her blood leaked onto the couch in an endless pool of red. She could feel the warmth in her body spilling out, and before everything faded to black, her arm was wrenched from its socket.

The zombies continued to feed on her long after she was dead. They tore her limbs free, ate the pulpy organs behind her rolls of flab, and sucked the marrow from her broken bones. It wasn't until they heard a door slam shut upstairs that they ceased their feast.

They left Cheryl's remains littered on the couch and they crossed the living room to the first floor landing. Fueled by endless hunger and the insistent need to kill, the trio lurched upstairs to hunt for any remaining survivors.

*   *   *

Ben heard Cheryl's screams and crawled out of his hiding place under the bed. The zombies hadn't left them alone. They'd broken down the front door and attacked his babysitter. Even though Ben hated her guts, he had to help her anyway he could.

He dug in his closet until he found his father's Army helmet. It was the only remaining relic he'd let him have, but his dad had felt bad about the divorce and wanted Ben to know he still loved him. Ben put it on his head with pride. The Army helmet nearly covered his eyes, but it took his fears away momentarily so he kept it on.

Next, he pulled his wooden baseball bat out from the closet. His mother had told him he was too young to use the bat, but Ben had promised her he'd practice with it everyday and join the Little League team when he was older. She consented and bought him the baseball bat. And now, Ben would use it to save Cheryl. Armed and ready, Ben opened his bedroom door and walked into the hallway.

He could see the light from the television in the living room but little else. Cheryl had stopped screaming and the only sound he could hear was a wet smacking noise. Ben peered down the steps and into the living room.

What he saw was pure carnage.

Cheryl was in pieces. Her arms were missing, her legs cracked open like walnuts, and the zombies were eating what was left of her head and torso.

Ben couldn't breathe. He was too late. Cheryl was dead. He ran back into his bedroom, closing and locking the door behind him.

The smacking noises ceased to be replaced by sudden groans from downstairs.

They saw me! Ben reeled.

He could hear the zombies coming up the steps, their rotting bodies dragging along the floorboards like slugs. They were coming for him and there wasn't anything he could do about it.

Ben pushed his desk in front of the door. Then he stood on his bed, baseball bat clutched in his tiny hands. The zombies made their way into the hallway and started banging against Ben's bedroom door.

Ben's grip on the bat tightened and he got ready to swing. He hoped Mr. Carpenter or Jamie came in first and not Santa. He couldn't bare hitting Santa Claus with a baseball bat, not after all those years of leaving cookies and milk out for him.

The door creaked and splintered under the zombies' combined weight, sending shards of wood sailing.

Mr. Carpenter shoved through the remains of the door and clawed the desk out of the way. Ben reared back and swung the bat with all his strength. He connected the end of the bat to Mr. Carpenter's head.

Mr. Carpenter slumped forward and didn't move again.

The baseball bat slipped from Ben's fingers. He had killed Mr. Carpenter, really killed him.

Even if he was a zombie, he was still his neighbor.

Jamie came into his room next. She wobbled into the bedroom and stepped over Mr. Carpenter without a hint of remorse. Her vacant eyes focused on Ben.

Ben leaped from his bed and his father's Army helmet fell off his head and clattered to the floor. He didn't have time to pick it up. He left it where it fell and faced Jamie. He felt like crying when he saw the ragged hole in her neck up close, but he sucked down his grief when she came at him.

Ben did the only thing he could. He ran between her legs. He moved so suddenly Jamie didn't have time to react. Ben darted under her and into the hallway. He headed for the stairs, but a strong hand hooked the back of his shirt.

"Let go of me!" Ben demanded.

He was dragged backward and spun around in time to gaze into the decayed mouth of zombie Santa Claus. Between Santa's teeth were chunks of bloody skin and plenty of room for Ben.

Ben slipped his arms out of his pajama sleeves, then tore off his top entirely.

Zombie Santa moaned and held onto the shirt in confusion.

Ben raced downstairs. He spotted the mess in the living room and whimpered. Cheryl was dead. Mr. Carpenter was dead. And Santa was trying to eat him. He had nowhere to run to and nobody to call for help.

Zombie Santa and Jamie shambled down the stairs in pursuit. They reached for him with eager hands, seeking to strip him of flesh in order to sustain their rotting bodies.

Ben saw the front door broken and sagging open and he ran toward it. If he could just get outside, he could find a policeman to help him. Ben could feel the rancid breath of the zombies on the back of his neck, and hear their hungry moans as they chased after him. He was almost outside when he slipped in a pool of blood in the doorway.

Ben tumbled onto his backside, then quickly used his legs and elbows to right himself. But it was a futile effort. Zombie Santa grabbed him by his hair and yanked him back into the living room. Santa's mouth slowly opened and it looked as though Ben's entire head could fit inside.

Ben tightened his muscles in preparation for the intense pain that was sure to come.

Then, Ben's mother and Dan intruded into the house. They took in the situation immediately. Both looked exhausted and out of breath, but resolved, and ready for action. Kate held a blood-stained fire axe, and Dan had a lead pipe, also covered with gore.

"Santa, you picked the wrong mother to fuck with tonight," Kate thundered.

She heaved the axe downward and cleaved Santa's head from his shoulders. The large body fell over, spilling hundreds of squirming maggots and black blood onto the carpet.

Kate wrapped her arms around Ben and wept.

"It's okay, Ben. You're safe now. We're here and you're safe, that's all that matters."

Ben nestled into her chest and sobbed.

Dan moved around them and smacked Jamie upside the head with his lead pipe. Her skull gave a loud crack in response and she toppled over in defeat.

Dan dropped the lead pipe and nursed the wounded hand which had been bitten earlier.

"Does it still hurt?" Kate asked him, knowing fully well by the expression on his face that it did.

"It's not so bad," Dan lied, gritting his teeth together. "But I need to get it cleaned and bandaged as soon as possible."

Kate nodded and wiped a teardrop from her eye.

"Do you think you'll ...?" she asked.

"No," Dan answered. "This isn't some late-night horror movie. I feel fine. I'm not going to turn into one of those things."

"Mommy..." Ben cried.

"Yes, dear," Kate replied. "What is it?"

"Are we still celebrating Christmas this year?"

Kate held him even closer.

"Of course, baby. We're still celebrating. Dan and I got you a bunch of presents. Would you like to see them now instead of in the morning?"

A half smile formed in one corner of Ben's mouth.

"Yes, please," he said.

Kate dug into her large purse and produced a handful of video games.

"I didn't remember which one you wanted, so I got all of the new releases."

Ben fingered the games greedily. He shuffled through them and stopped on one which had a muscle bound man carrying a gun on the cover.

"You got it! Thanks, Mom."

He put the games on the floor and hugged her.

"Merry Christmas," Ben said.

"Merry Christmas," Kate replied.

A low guttural moan escaped Dan's lips just as he lunged for them both.

YES, VIRGINIA, THERE REALLY IS A ZOMBIE SANTA CLAUS

ANTHONY GIANGREGORIO

It was well past midnight on Christmas Eve and was now officially Christmas day.

A bright red sleigh filled with presents floated across the sky, a jolly man in a red suit its sole passenger.

Chris Kringle, or Santa Claus, to the world, leaned back in his seat as the reindeer cut through the clouds, their small bells jingling on their collars.

It had been a busy night so far but the southern hemisphere was finally finished.

Below, Haiti waited for its share of Christmas joy.

Pulling on the reins, he angled the sled downward, the drop enough to make his stomach jump. He laughed, long and loud. Even after all these years, he still didn't like to fly.

Moments later he was on his first roof top, a shanty-like home with a patched roof. He was in the poor part of town, but to him it all looked the same.

Rich or poor, he had a present for every child across the world.

Turning around, he reached into his magic sack; the voluminous red bag looking like it only had a few toys in it. But when he took a toy out of the bag, another would appear almost immediately.

And this made perfect sense to Santa, as how else would he be able to carry an entire supply of presents to the world's population of children in simply one night?

The chimney was a dilapidated mess, as was the rest of the home, but he ignored it. There was a child inside and that was all that mattered to him.

Sliding down the chimney, he came up in a small living room. There was a small Christmas tree in the far corner and he waddled over to it, all the time humming a holiday tune. He didn't see the talismans to the voodoo religion, nor see the dead chicken or dried crows feet dangling from a nearby alter.

No, Santa only had eyes for the Christmas tree.

So when he set the present down under the tree, he was shocked when a shadow lunged out from the darkness and attacked him.

What was this? No one ever attacked Santa Claus; he was welcomed with open arms wherever he went.

But this dark man, with face drained of color and drawn visage, didn't seem to care who he was. Before Santa could do anything to protect himself, he felt the sharp pain of teeth on his left hand, right above the fingers.

Though he was always jolly, Santa roared with anger and punched the man square in the head. The attacker fell away and Santa kicked him once in the stomach for good measure. But the attacker was only down for a moment and was soon crawling toward Santa again.

Deciding there was no time for this and if he wasn't wanted he'd just leave, Santa fell back to the chimney and scooted up it like a worm.

On the roof, the reindeer snorted impatiently, and in seconds Santa was flying off to the next house.

His hand was bleeding profusely and he wrapped it in a bright red handkerchief.

After bandaging it, he tried to flex it and he winced in pain. The guy had gotten him good, that was for sure.

He went to the next house and the house after that, still having to do his duty as jolly old St. Nick. But as the hours passed, Santa began to feel feverish, something that had never happened before.

As Santa Claus, he was immortal, and age and sickness didn't affect him. But for some unexplainable reason, he felt ill.

So with sweat beading his forehead and his breath coming in gasps, it became harder to deliver the presents to children all over the world. But he was Santa Claus and he would continue, he had to; children everywhere were counting on him.

* * *

It happened somewhere over the Midwest of the United States.

Santa was steering the sleigh to the next city when he felt woozy, and before he knew what was happening, he passed out. The reindeer, old pros at their jobs, took the sleigh in for a landing on a nearby roof.

The roof the sleigh set down on was part of a massive, Victorian affair with ornate moldings and large picture windows. It was obvious the family living here was one of wealth.

The reindeer snuffed and snorted on the roof as Santa lay sprawled in the sleigh. This became the scene for almost ten minutes after touchdown, Santa never moving.

But then Santa's right hand began to twitch and a moment later his eyes opened.

Looking around, he had no idea where he was or how he'd arrived here. And he felt weird, sort of hollow inside. There was a strange feeling in his stomach now, similar to hunger, but that didn't make any sense as he hadn't been hungry before passing out. He had been eating all night, cookies and milk mostly, but that was part of the job.

But then he realized he didn't feel sick any more, that he wasn't sweating, and that was a bonus. There was so much to do in so little time, and to get sick tonight of all nights was unthinkable.

He flexed his hand, the one with the bite, and found it didn't hurt any longer. That was an added bonus.

Stepping out of the sleigh, he breathed in the night air, both fresh and crisp. There was a light dusting of snow across the city and he could see the blinking lights of Christmas decorations as they hung from doors and gutters of nearby homes.

Ignoring the odd feeling welling inside him, one he now felt deep in his gut, one of hunger but for what he had no idea, he reached into his magic sack and pulled out two toys. One was a train and one was a doll; then he dropped into the chimney to continue his work.

He never gave any thought to why he passed out, nor why there was no more pain in his hand, nor the odd craving in his gullet for something he couldn't put his finger on.

All that mattered was to deliver the toys to the children.

*   *   *

He dropped down the chimney and into the living room of the home. To his left was a large, eight foot Christmas tree, fill with red, yellow and blue blinking lights. A small angel was perched on top, its angelic face watching over the room.

Santa paused at a small table set up near the tree.

Milk and cookies were laid out for him like always, the cookies on an expensive China platter.

"Oooh, chocolate chip," he whispered as he reached out and took one. The hunger was growing inside him and the cookies should do the job nicely.

But instead of enjoying the first bite, he spit it out, the chewed-up mush falling to the expensive carpet. It tasted terrible. He had to wonder if this was some sort of prank, perhaps the cookies were tainted?

Deciding that was crazy, he set the half-eaten cookie down and reached for the glass of milk.

This should settle my stomach, he thought as he began to drink. But it was like he took a sip from a bucket of sewer waste. He spit out the foul tasting liquid, wiping his mouth with his sleeve. Perplexed, but not giving it too much thought, he decided this was just an anomaly. He would have a snack at the next house, but for now he had gifts to leave under the tree.

Setting the glass down, he went to the tree, admiring his reflection in the glass ornaments. As he stared at himself, he didn't like what he saw. His face was now very pale and he had dark circles under his eyes, his forehead also looking more pronounced. Gone were the rosy cheeks, to be replaced by a bluish tint.

Once again he brushed it off as the simple distorted reflection in the ornaments.

Leaning down, he set the two toys under the tree. But his left arm brushed the tree and one of the ornaments was knocked off the branch to roll across the floor.

Santa turned to retrieve it, and when he bent over to pick it up, he realized he wasn't alone.

A little girl, no more than four, was standing in the doorway leading to the rear of the house. She was in red and green pajamas and wore a pretty bow around her neck. She was holding a small brown bear, the bear too, having a bow around its neck. Her hair was done up with barrettes and she was the cutest thing he'd ever seen.

"Santa?" she asked in a small, tiny voice, her big blue eyes gazing up at a holiday legend.

Santa Claus didn't know what to do; he just stared down at her.

Normally he would have hypnotized the girl then sent her off to bed. In the morning, she would have believed she'd dreamt the whole thing, but instead of doing this, he found himself looking at her like a lion to a gazelle.

She gazed up at him with those wide orbs, so young and innocent, and Santa found his mouth watering with anticipation. She looked so sweet and tender, like Grade-A veal fresh out of the slaughter house.

Before he knew what he was doing, he leaned down and picked her up, and before the girl knew what was happening, he bit into her throat, just below her chin.

The girl tried to scream of course, frightened beyond belief, but Santa Claus ripped out her larynx and began to suck at the wound like he was a dying man just out of the desert. The small feet clad in pajamas kicked back and forth, but soon they stopped moving and only hung limp.

Santa Claus fed then, tearing off large chunkfuls of the soft, pink meat. He fed until he thought he would burst, but even then he found he was still hungry.

Dropping the carcass of the girl to the floor, he went to the back of the house where the bedrooms were located. Halfway down the hallway, there was a door with the name **Johnny** on it and he entered, another shadow amongst shadows.

Before the little boy knew what was happening, Santa Claus feasted on the little girl's brother, tearing the small form apart and feeding on the warm, juicy innards.

When he was finished he went to the parents' bedroom, killing both with teeth and fingernails. But when he began to feed, he found the taste of adult meat unappetizing and he spit it out.

No, the flesh of the children, of the innocent, was what he craved.

With his belly stuffed to the limit, he flew up the chimney and onto his sleigh. The reindeer snuffed a few items but didn't seem to pay him attention.

With a jerk of the reins, the sleigh took off to his next destination and then to every other house with children in the world.

But first he was going to the Smithfield Orphanage.

And he knew when he was finished there; Mrs. Claus was going to have to let his red suit out once more.

*   *   *

The father closed the book he was reading from and looked down into his daughter's eyes as she stared at him with trepidation from his lap.

Little Virginia Montrose blinked back a tear and touched the book her daddy had been reading from. "Is that really how it happened, Daddy? Is that why we board up all the windows and doors and block the chimney every Christmas Eve?"

The father nodded. "Yes, honey, that's exactly right. You see, Virginia, there really is a zombie Santa Claus, and every Christmas Eve he leaves the North Pole in search of the fresh meat of innocent children."

"So I have to hide and hope he doesn't find me?" she asked.

"That's correct, honey. It's so he can't get in and eat you. I wouldn't want to lose you to zombie Santa."

Virginia nodded, understanding. She knew there was once upon a time when Santa was a friend to children all over the world, and he would bring presents to them on Christmas Eve if they had been good. But now he was a flesh-eating zombie who fed on the innards of little children.

Father and daughter sat quietly for a time, both staring at the blinking Christmas tree in the corner of the living room. No pictures of Santa were to be found in the house, for he was all that was wrong with Christmas.

Finally, the father set his daughter down and stood up, crossing the room to unplug the lights of the Christmas tree. Then he turned off the lighted decorations outside and every light in the house, bathing the home in darkness.

From outside, the house looked as cold and dark as the rest of the houses on the street, nay, the entire state, or better yet, the entire country.

"Now you go to bed and tomorrow it will be all over and you'll be safe for another year," he told Virginia when the house was darkened and all the barriers were checked once, then rechecked twice.

"Okay, Daddy, I love you. Merry Christmas," Virginia said and then ran off to bed. Her father sighed as he watched her leave, wishing things could be like they once were, when Christmas was a time of joy and cheer, not fear for ones children from an undead demon in a red suit and white beard.

He walked over to the chair he'd sat in with Virginia and plopped back down, only one small night light in the corner of the room to keep the darkness at bay.

On the small coffee table next to him sat a half bottle of Jack Daniels and one small shot glass. He poured himself a shot and then took a small sip. He planned on nursing the bottle, for it would be a long night of watching over his family. His wife was already asleep, but she would be up in the morning to take over for him, just in case Santa was running behind this night and tried for one more child before the sun came up. It had happened before, some unwary parent thinking it was over when it wasn't.

After sipping the liquor, he reached around to the back of the chair and pulled out a semi-automatic rifle. Now that Virginia was in bed, he could get ready.

Flicking the selector switch to full-auto, he stared at the fireplace across the room. Though it had a sheet metal barrier across it, Santa had been known to slip past the barriers in other homes.

Curse him and his damn Christmas magic, he thought.

"Come on, Santa, I'm ready for you, you fat, dead bastard" he mumbled as he glanced at the now dark Christmas tree.

It was then that he heard, ever so softly, the ringing of sleigh bells. It was coming from outside the house, sounding like it was coming from far away, but he knew as time went by it would grow louder.

But there were many other homes to pick this night and he hoped the odds were with him that zombie Santa Claus would pass his house by.

Feeling a shiver go down his spine, he gripped the rifle more tightly.

DOWNTOWN

PETER NAGGI

"Are there any lights down here?"

"No." Nicole turned her flashlight side to side, examining the concrete walls and brickwork. "At least I don't think so."

Frank descended the last step of the staircase and entered the catacombs. None of them had guns. They were given sharpened machetes from Wales, the Samoan immigrant who owned a small landscaping business, back when the world still resembled some form of *civilized*. Wales had fled to the hotel in his Toyota Tundra bringing along all the family he had. Hundreds of dollars worth of yard equipment had to be left behind, but the more practical tools proved themselves to have multiple uses, although they were a bit messy. Isaac, the oldest son in the family, was just behind Frank. The sound of his chainsaw gently purred behind them.

"Don't turn that thing on unless we need it," Frank ordered.

"Sorry. I had a feeling," Isaac admitted. He killed the chainsaw but silence didn't follow. A German shepherd followed closely beside, panting in the stale air. "Where are we?" Isaac asked.

"I think this is the refectory." Nicole circled her flashlight from wall to wall. "This should exit into what is known colloquially as the 'Cloister Walk.' After that who knows where it goes?"

Isaac shined his light on Nicole. "So we're under the Cloister Wing."

Nicole shrugged. In the dark he could see the once-white waitress uniform now stained with red.

"All right," Frank said as he practiced swinging his machete in broad, methodical strokes. He had never handled any kind of weapon before, only the small Swiss Army knives he learned to use in Boy Scouts. Those days were long past gone, and he never thought the basic survival lessons would ever be utilized. Even though the Scouts became quite tedious as he moved up in rank, he was now thankful he'd put himself through the turmoil. "We find the opening and close it up," he said.

"Or openings," Nicole added, putted extra emphasis on the plural *S*.

Frank shook his head. "I can't believe I let Donavan talk me into coming down here." It had been even harder to talk her into lending him one of the dogs. "The science team confirmed," she had informed him, "that whatever causes the infection doesn't harm the dogs."

"So then let me bring one down with me. Otherwise I ain't gonna go."

He had expected her to say no, and although her response was quite the opposite, it still didn't surprise him. It seemed nothing could surprise him now, not after what happened yesterday. What a shock it had been for him when he first entered town and a man with blood dripping from his mouth shambled out in front of him and he slammed his foot down on the brake pedal.

Equally shocking was the fact that in the roughly three available seconds he had to react, his mind still had time to wonder why his antilock brakes did the opposite of what they were advertised to do. The front wheels fastened tightly, and suddenly his perspective of the road was not only backwards, but upside down.

A greater shock came after the car skidded to a stop, and the man he just rolled over rose back to his feet and continued his slow, irregular gait to the side of the road. The man didn't flinch. He didn't scream out in pain or bother to adjust his obviously-dislocated elbow. He just lifted himself off the asphalt and sauntered off the road and out of sight.

But nothing shocked Frank quite as much as when his girlfriend looked at him and grinned cross-eyed with the sterling-silver hairpin he bought for her birthday protruding from her neck. She had been holding it directly in front of her when the accident occurred, twirling her hair in the finger of her free hand habitually. Her seatbelt could have saved her life, but the force of the airbag exploding from the dashboard smacked into her hand and the chopstick-shaped pin flew out like a bullet straight into her throat. After rolling and skidding for another half-minute, Frank panicked and began fumbling in futility with his seatbelt. He was trying to free himself while attempting to apply pressure to Sarah's wound with his other hand. That was when her hacking and gagging stopped and her head slumped. Blood gushed from her nose, even in an upended position, almost like a low-pressure geyser.

And even though Frank clearly saw the light leave her eyes, she still stirred. It had to be a death-moan, he thought, like how people say a corpse can sometimes twitch and convulse after life has left its body. But how often do dead bodies smile? And for that matter, how often do they reach out and attack their boyfriends? By this time Frank's seatbelt was unbuckled and he was kicking his feet against the glass in a desperate bid for freedom. She clawed at his face and closed her fist around his shoulder-length hair.

And he watched her die again. After freeing his hair from her grip and pulling himself out of the wreckage, after realizing his car had come to a stop outside a Salvation Army building on Orange Street, he found more people. More shambling, struggling people pounding on the door to the building. He called for help but that sure as hell wasn't the response he received. Instead, they joined Sarah's attack; who had now also freed herself from the upside-down car. Just when he thought it was over, just when he thought the crowd would overtake him and tear the skin off his bones, a bullet went straight into Sarah's skull and out the other end, taking down both her and the attacker behind. The police showed up with their sirens on, a sound that seemed to distract the lumbering dead people long enough to receive another flurry of headshots.

But that was all in the past. Just one day earlier. Sarah's corpse was still fresh but it seemed like a lifetime ago.

"Hold it!" Nicole shouted, and Frank stopped so abruptly he nearly lost his footing. In front of him, a small group of undead lumbered out of the darkness in a slow, erratic procession. With his lips peeling back from his teeth, Frank raised his machete and dropped it into the skull of the nearest zombie.

How could it have come to this? Just over twenty-four hours ago he had woken in a cabin in the San Bernardino Mountains. His beautiful girlfriend with her muscular dancer's legs lay beside him. They kissed, despite his usual horrendous case of morning-breath. They showered, fixed breakfast, and packed up the car, then left the mountain town just as they'd found it; thoroughly and drearily normal. No throng of undead paraded the streets. No eerie moans or flesh-devouring. The drive down the mountain was uneventful. Traffic was light, but Christmas had only passed two days prior.

They were to meet a friend at the hotel and stay with him until New Years.

A car crash hadn't factored into their plans, let alone a hair pin to the throat and the dead that had somehow been given the choice to remain dead or not.

The police had saved him, but they proved to be less than amicable. Immediately after dropping the last zombie to the pavement, they turned their guns on Frank, only hesitating long enough to question him.

"Are you one of them?" an officer shouted.

"Who? Them?" Frank waved his index finger at the corpses littering the pavement, then brought both his hands on either side of his head so they could see his palms.

"You know who I mean!"

"No, I don't! I just got into town! My..." he stuttered. "My girlfriend and I were..."

Tires screeched. The officers turned. Coming to an unexpected stop was a large, red fire truck. A man sitting on top was ready with a hose. The water came out in a surge of pressure, dropping all three officers to their backsides. Another man in a yellow suit emerged from the truck and plunged an axe into both officers' skulls.

"Holy shit!" Frank ran in full reverse, then tripped over a body and smacked his tailbone on the drenched asphalt.

"Their guns!" the man with the hose shouted.

The fire fighter pulled his axe out of a cop's face and took his pistol. He stooped beside the cop's partner and now his gun was also liberated. The fire fighter's head raised and Frank could see the whites of his eyes.

"You better come with us," he said.

"How the hell can I trust you?"

"Ain't you been outside lately?" The fire fighter was power-walking toward him.

"My girlfriend's dead!" Frank said.

"C'mon!" The fire fighter took Frank by the shirt collar and looked up at the man with the hose. "If you please?" A quick stream of water sprayed from the nozzle, allowing him to wash the gore off his axe. Once it was clean, he pulled Frank away from his dead girlfriend and distributed him into the fire truck.

"What was that all about?" the driver asked as he released the brake and started on their way. Frank could see his nametag read, **Braun**.

"Guy doesn't seem to know what's going on." And now that Frank had the time to check, he noticed that the fire man in the yellow suit was named **Stanhope**, the name tag visible.

Braun looked peevishly at Frank. "Who are you?" he asked.

"Frank."

"Frank what?"

"Vernetti."

Braun held his suspicious gaze.

Stanhope took a breath to speak. "Better keep your eyes on the road," he told him. "In case there's more survivors."

But all they saw were more people shuffling in the street. Braun paid no attention to them, and apparently, they didn't pay much attention, either, because more than a few stepped right in front of the truck and were crushed under the tires. "What the hell is going on?" Frank asked.

"How could you not know?" Braun never lifted his hostility.

"I spent Christmas break at a cabin with my..." He nodded his head back in the direction of the Salvation Army building. It felt uncomfortable to talk about Sarah all of a sudden. "For a couple of weeks."

"That's about how long this has been going on," Stanhope said.

Braun brought his eyes back to the road. "Where were you headed?" he asked.

"We were supposed to meet a friend at the hotel."

Braun looked at Stanhope, who rolled his eyes. "It's fine, Chris," he told Stanhope, then turning to Frank he added, "A bunch of people are holing up inside. It's easy to defend and it still has excellent accommodations. The fire department has been searching the city for survivors."

"And the police?"

"That's a long story."

"You're the first one we've found in a couple days," Braun added. Only a few minutes passed before they came upon a rather sizeable roadblock. Stanhope waved his hand and two people in paintball masks pulled open a gate constructed from a broken freeway sign that read, **University Ave, ½ miles**.

Frank could see the streets immediately surrounding the hotel were blocked off. Few private cars were present. Instead, the curbs were crowded with a fleet of fire trucks, buses, and even a vehicle equipped with a cherry-picker. Braun pulled up to the hotel's front entrance and threw the e-brake.

"So...is this happening all over the world?" Frank asked.

Braun shot him an incredulous look.

Stanhope answered for him. "We don't know. You'll get more details inside. Meantime, we gotta get this thing back to the central station for refueling, so if you don't mind..." He gestured to the door.

Frank hopped out of the fire truck and made his way into what was once the hotel's valet drop off. An army of animatronic elves stood surrounding the compound, as well as a system of chain-link fencing and roughly a dozen people with various weapons encircling the front entrance. All the robotic elves were lifeless, but stretching across an archway above was a model of Santa Claus riding his sleigh. Every reindeer was accounted for, including Rudolph who stood at the front of the team, his big red nose held high. Every light was lit. A crudely-painted sign hung underneath saying, **All spies will be shot**.

Frank looked around at the guards. They carried everything from machine guns to axes to butcher knives and one man even had a broken pool cue sharpened to a point. A small pen had been constructed out of baby-gates, and inside was an assortment of dogs ranging from German shepherds to pit bulls.

All the guards donned some sort of protective gear: football pads, biker pads, paintball masks, and all of the gear was sloppily decorated with spray-painted raincross symbols. Only one person had actual Kevlar body armor, a woman judging by the way she walked, although it was not otherwise obvious until she removed her hockey mask to reveal a rather effeminate face. She shook her head and let a mass of short red hair into the open air.

That was Donavan. Claire Donavan. The first thing she did was cut Frank's 1970s-style mop-top, then she found him a room.

Then she sent him into the catacombs.

Frank shook his machete, splattering blood and brain matter across the walls.

"Careful with that," Nicole said, brushing off her blouse.

"What do you care? You're wearing white and it's already ruined." At his feet, the dog busied itself ripping skin from a zombie's throat.

"Dogbeef!" Isaac barked. The dog sat and looked up at him, long, stringy lengths of body mass trailing from its teeth.

"Onward?" Nicole shined her light toward the darkness.

"Yeah," Frank answered.

They moved forward but only for a short while before coming to a stop at another chamber. There were two branching pathways, one was closed by a pile of soil softener taken from the grounds keeping department and now arranged like sandbags on a battle field. A few zombies met them in the chamber, clambering over a broken fence covering the other pathway. Isaac revved up his chainsaw, but it wasn't necessary. Nicole and Frank and especially Dogbeef were more than capable of making the undead dead again. Even after a wayward stroke from a machete cut a zombie at the torso, causing its upper body to splatter on the floor only to continue inching toward them. Dogbeef pounced, taking the zombie by the neck and shaking side to side until a crack was heard and its body went limp.

"Okay," Nicole said breathlessly. "That was productive." She shined her light on the soil piled to the ceiling. "That leads to the Mission Galleria, and that..." She pointed at the broken fencing. "Was still intact when we came through here the first time."

"So I take it this is as far as you went?" Isaac said.

"Well, we lost two people bringing those soil bags down here. They weigh, like, fifty pounds each."

"And it didn't occur to you that clearing a pathway between here and the Mission Galleria would be a strategic advantage against City Hall should they ever make it inside the roadblocks?"

"Like I said, we lost two people. The mall is clear above ground. We have easy access to California Tower and all the people there. What's the big deal?"

"The only thing we have that City Hall doesn't is the element of surprise," Isaac said. "I'm just saying it would be advantageous for us to be able to move freely underground."

Frank took a look around. It was a while since he was in this town, but he knew what the Mission Galleria was; a two story antique shop with a basement and restaurant. Supposedly, the owners had used the catacombs to steal priceless artwork from the hotel and sell them in the store decades ago. Back then the hotel's founder and builder, Mr. Miller, had a rather nice art collection in storage underground. Most of it was lost after several flashfloods in the 1960s.

Frank thought about the Mission Galleria. Right now it would be decked out in Christmas trappings, just like the hotel and the rest of the Main Street Mall. Just like the hotel lobby, a long, square-shaped hall that Donavan led Frank through just one day prior. Tinsel and frilly white ropes lined the walls and about a half dozen Christmas trees stood unlit in the corners, but despite the otherwise festive decor, Donavan and whoever else was in charge of the place were mostly unable to prevent residents from adding their own flair to the surroundings. The length of the lobby featured portraits of every President who had ever stayed at the hotel and not a single one was clean of graffiti. George Bush was a particularly popular candidate for vandalism, although Taft was the only one free from a mustache drawn in Sharpie, if only because the man already had an epic butt-broom on his face (and his waist-size didn't help). Along the walls were messages and slogans scrawled in various colored ink. Sayings like, "We are reaping the seeds that we have sowed." "Somebody get the nukes." "Fuck City Hall." And the phrase, "The only good fascist is a dead fascist" was spray-painted above a photograph of the mayor. Underneath was the simple command. "Resist."

Donavan caught Frank looking at the picture and spoke: "We think whatever caused this plague originated here."

"What gave you that idea?"

"When City Hall burned down the UCR botanical gardens." She glanced at him to gauge his reaction, which was only confusion. "At the time, the professors there were researching some new drug on the streets. An inhalant that apparently causes severe brain damage. People that are on it die pretty quickly. But then the first reported cases of zombies circulated and the college was attacked. We think City Hall is somehow responsible for the outbreak. They've been hassling people, killing 'em. We started up a resistance, but unfortunately they got the entire police force on their side, which means we're outgunned by about ten to one. Riverside Community Hospital is trying to stay neutral but it's been hard because a lot of the paramedics are also fire fighters." She stopped at the foot of a spiral staircase. "The fire department is on our side, in case you haven't noticed." She started up the stairs.

"What about electricity?"

"We're still on the grid, somehow. Our theory is that it's the same grid as the hospital, so they won't shut it down as long as their officers are being treated there. Same as the water supply."

After climbing about six stories, they exited onto an outdoor landing area leading to a large a grouping of single rooms. Still more Christmas decorations covered the place, all of which were mostly animatronic carolers and short, grinning elves frozen in time.

They were causing mischief around various antiques like Civil War-era cannons and gigantic candy canes. A film of dust covered all of them. It was Frank's theory that they hadn't been switched on in weeks.

"Pick any empty room you like," Donavan said. "The war effort so far has been rough. We're losing people left and right, and more volunteers are coming up short."

"Is that you asking me to join up?"

Donavan shrugged. "If you don't mind risking your life. Or if you have any medical or botany skills you can join the science team. We got a bunch of professors from UCR working on the plague. We think City Hall was using some of the citrus plants in South Riverside as a vector." Frank quickly found a room and opened it. He turned to Donavan.

"So this it, then? My life as I know it is over? I can kiss my family goodbye and forget everything that's ever happened to me before today?"

"We all feel the same as you," Donavan told him. She looked to the reddening sky.

"It'll be night soon. Get some rest."

Frank entered the room and slammed the door. He looked at the bed situated against the back wall. It was big enough for two; Sarah would have loved it. He felt compelled to lose his composure and cry, but somehow that felt disrespectful. Sarah wouldn't want to see him in so much pain.

In fact, the idea that Sarah was still looking down on him somewhere helped him to feel more at ease.

It was said that the Music Room leading into the catacombs was haunted. Who knows what other ghosts might linger in the Cloister Walk? The hotel never let anyone in the catacombs. Frank had half-hoped to encounter Sarah's spirit on his traipse down into the depths. However, now that the walking undead were roaming the narrow passageways, he thought better of it.

"My arm is getting pretty tired," he said, after finishing off yet another zombie and flinging blood on the walls.

"Just think," Isaac joked. "Pretty soon you'll build up your strength and this'll all be second nature."

"Easy for you to say." Isaac's large Samoan frame and occupation as a landscaper afforded him the luxury of above-average muscle mass. He hadn't objected at all when Donavan wanted a team member to carry a backpack full of bricks and cement, just so long as the other volunteers would be willing to lug the water.

"I'm starting to think this tunnel might end up being about a mile long," Nicole said after a good five minutes of silence."

"Why's that?" Frank asked.

"An old rumor," she answered. "Supposedly, there's a passage to Mt. Rubidoux."

Isaac stopped and shined his light around the brick and concrete. "Maybe we should just wall it off here," he said.

"Dude." Frank shined a light right in Isaac's eyes. "Just a second ago you were saying this tunnel could be used to fight City Hall."

"Yeah, but this is all pre-code," Isaac replied. "What if there's an earthquake?"

Nicole stood cross-armed. "The hotel's been standing for over a hundred years. I'd say this tunnel is built solid." She looked down at Dogbeef, who still stood at the ready, his teeth barred in the direction of the unknown.

"Drop one brick," she ordered.

Isaac's eyebrows lowered. "Why?"

"In case we get turned around. We'll know we've been here."

"Okay," he said as he removed a broken chunk of brick from his pack and let it drop to the ground. The sound echoed off the walls and it was answered by a multitude of low-key moans.

"Shit," Frank muttered. "We don't need bricks to show where we've been, the dead bodies will do that for us."

"Goddammit!" Nicole shouted, swinging her machete and further diminishing the color white on her blouse. "How could I be so stupid!"

"It's okay!" Frank assured her as he chopped into a zombie brain. "We were gonna have to fight them, anyway!" Again and again he hurled his machete and dropped it into every zombie he could find. Dogbeef ran about, pouncing on his victims and tearing out their throats. His attacks did nothing to kill the zombies, as it had long been established that cranial damage was the only way to finish them off and the lumbering cannibals mostly ignored anything other than people. Dogbeef was free to strike at will without facing the threat of death, unlike the humans, who were now becoming overwhelmed.

"There's too many!" Nicole screeched when it became clear that piles of dead bodies meant less room to maneuver one's feet.

"Let me!" His flashlight now affixed to his coat, Isaac came running from the shadows, revving his chainsaw threateningly. Frank and Nicole took a step back and even managed to coax Dogbeef away while Isaac did his work, heaving his chainsaw toward every bare neck he could see. Just about every creature in his path lost its head and the ones that didn't, crawled along the floor only to receive machetes between their eyes.

"Damn." Isaac paused to catch his breath. "I think that's the last of them."

"For now." Nicole approached, surveying the damage. "Jesus, Isaac, you're a real hellion." She looked him in the eye. Blood dripped from his chin. "We're sure you have to die before turning into one of them?" she asked.

Another droplet of blood gathered on Isaac's chin and descended to the floor. Despite its inconsequential size, the plopping sound still managed to produce an echo in the distance.

"Dr. Singh said the virus is inside all of us, but doesn't take effect until after death has occurred," Frank explained.

"Here." Nicole removed a dinner napkin from her pocket and tossed it to Isaac. He brought it to his face and wiped. "Let's hope it's not much longer," he said handing back the cloth.

And it wasn't. Light could be seen up ahead, and in time they came upon an assortment of crates stacked against the walls. They were olden wooden crates, some splintered and broken. All of them looked like they'd been sitting there for decades. Nicole reached into one and removed an empty beer bottle, unlabeled, and chipped at the top. There were others.

Nicole grinned. "Bootleggers," she said. "This was used to smuggle alcohol during…" But before she could finish, a mangled and mutilated hand reached from behind the crates and took hold of her sleeve.

"Ah, son of a…!"

Isaac grabbed her arm and pulled her out of the fray, but the zombie's grip was vise-like. His attempt at rescue only allowed the creature a quicker exit from its hiding place, until the sleeve was torn and bloody scratches snaked along Nicole's underarm. Isaac's chainsaw revved and down it dropped, splitting the thing's head through the middle in gory spurts of red and gray. Its expression dropped, its eyes crossed, and then it crashed and splattered on the pavement.

But it wasn't alone. Ahead, a doorway could be seen, crowded by even more undead, who had been alerted by the sound of the chainsaw.

"Not this again." Frank backed up, readying his machete. Nicole was already busy hacking away at zombie heads like she was on an expedition and had to cut tree branches from her path. Isaac revved the chainsaw again, but the motor died.

"Fuck!" He pulled the cord over and over. The motor struggled and failed. A zombie was upon him, reaching toward his neck, but up leapt Dogbeef and now it was the zombie whose neck was being devoured. Frank plunged the edge of his blade into the back of the zombie's head and removed it forcefully.

"Help!"

Nicole was surrounded. Frank brought his arm across his chest and swung in swift, broad strokes. Zombies left and right were cut and dismembered, but in Frank's panic not a single one dropped to the floor. Still, he managed to clear a space big enough for Nicole to crawl to safety. She was soon replaced by Dogbeef, pouncing and tearing off pale flesh, throttling, occasionally killing. Isaac pulled Nicole to his side and took her machete. He lifted it, and screaming, charged into the crowd with the blade slicing into every skull it found.

But his fury was too enthusiastic. The adrenaline wore off before all the zombies were finished, and soon it was his turn to run, but that would be a difficult thing to do. Too many bodies had piled on the floor, and with nowhere stable to put his feet, he fell and was tackled by all the undead monsters he brought with him. Frank and Dogbeef could do little to help. It was only after Nicole successfully cranked the chainsaw motor that the multitude of attackers let up, now shuffling toward the sound of their soon-to-be deaths.

Nicole severed the last zombie's head and kicked it aside. Frank was already standing over Isaac. "I'm okay," he said.

"You're bleeding from your neck." Frank took the napkin from Nicole and began dabbing it against her wound. "But," he sighed with a smile. "It definitely missed your jugular. You're damn lucky." Then he helped Isaac to his feet.

"There's a first-aid kit in my pack," Isaac said, turning so they could find it. After the wound was properly dressed and sterilized, he was on his feet and ready to press on.

"Are you sure you're okay?" Nicole asked. "You did have a dogpile of zombies crushing your body."

"I played center on my high school football team," he replied. "I can take it."

With Dogbeef following close behind, the three of them passed through the doorway and into a larger chamber. What appeared to be beds were laid into the walls, as well as several caskets dug halfway into the earth. They were all a century old.

"This is a mausoleum," Nicole exclaimed. "We must be in Evergreen Cemetery."

"Right at the foot of the mountain." Isaac smiled.

In front of them was the exit, haphazardly torn open with the cast iron gate bent after having been trampled upon by so many zombies.

"We better radio Donavan." Isaac said and ascended the steps. Still wearing a Cheshire grin, he stepped into the daylight. The others followed.

They were in the old part of the cemetery where actual gravestones and monuments stood. It was enclosed by a strong green fence. They now stood in the shadow of Mt. Rubidoux, a white cross just barely visible on its highest peak.

"There," Frank pointed. A gate on the far end of the cemetery was open. "That must be how the zombies are getting in." He trotted to the gate as Isaac removed his radio.

"Donavan, come back. Donavan," Isaac said into the radio.

A moment passed while Frank shut the gate and secured it tightly.

"I'm here, Isaac," came the woman's reply.

"We just got out of the catacombs. You'll never guess where we are."

"Don't tell me," she barked. "We might have eavesdroppers. Just say 'yes' or 'no' if there's good news on what you were sent to do."

"Yes, but only temporarily." Isaac looked up at Frank nonchalantly approaching the mausoleum.

"Understood. Is everyone okay?"

"Yes."

"All right," she said. "Head on back. Don't radio unless it's an emergency. That is, if you get any reception."

"Right. See ya." Isaac pocketed the radio and reached out and hugged Frank. "Sweet! Let's get back to base."

"Uh, guys?" Nicole was crouching a few feet away. Frank and Isaac jogged over and found a pile of small used inhalers.

"More of those narcotics you mentioned," Nicole said, looking up at Frank. "What was it exactly that Dr. Singh told you?"

"I'm not supposed to say."

"What they don't know won't hurt them."

"All right." Frank took a breath to explain.

Donavan had told them everything. At least, Frank hoped it had been everything. "This is the science team," Donovan had said. Earlier that morning, she led him into what was once the Spanish Patio. Now it had been converted into a small science lab and makeshift greenhouse. Equipment like beakers and Bunsen Burners were situated on the dining tables, long tubes leading from propane tanks once used in outdoor heaters.

"This is Dr. Singh." Donavan referred to a skinny East Indian in a turban and beard and thick glasses encircling his eyes.

He smiled broadly. "So this is what it has come to," he said.

"What do you mean?" Frank looked at him with his eyes narrowing slightly.

"To convince someone to ramble around underground today. We don't want too many people to know." He glanced at Donavan and she added, "Spies for City Hall might find out."

"Find out what?" Frank asked.

Singh glanced at Donavan again. She nodded.

Immediately, Singh went to work picking up a wooden case containing about ten vials with various liquids of various colors. He held the glass vessels up to the morning light and said, "There has been an unusual new narcotic on the streets for about three years, now. My former colleague, Dr. Adrienne Cross, became interested in it when it took her poor son's life. At first I thought it a fool's errand, a complete digression from what we're researching, which at the time was a remedy for a disease infecting various citrus plants. But then Dr. Cross discovered that this disease is actually related to the chemical she found in the inhalers. She suspected that when the drug was exhaled, the gas had ill effects on plant life, as well. There was extreme difficulty figuring out its exact origin but we were reasonably certain it was manufactured in this city."

"Riverside has always been one of the nation's leading havens of drug labs," Donavan added.

"I remember," Frank said. "I used to live here, over off Hillside. Mom used to tell me to never buy from the ice-cream men because they were really drug dealers."

"Oh, yes, I recall that." Singh set the vials down and held up a printout of a computer rendering of a mass of small, rectangular colorful swatches arranged into the shape of what seemed to Frank to resemble a howling wolf.

"This is a chemical strain we isolated in the inhalant. It causes wild hallucinations and severe neurological damage. It also kills its victims within a matter of months."

Donavan looked from the printout to Frank. "The theory is that City Hall developed it as a means of getting rid of what they call 'the riffraff.'"

"You mean drug users and homeless people," Frank stated.

"Right," she said. "Get them off the streets, out of the hospitals, out of the prisons, and into the mortuaries. A money-saving measure, no doubt."

"How'd you figure that one out?"

Donavan hesitated and Singh supplied the answer. "Well, you notice I said 'former colleague' in reference to Dr. Cross."

"Oh, God." Frank covered his face. "I think I know where this is going."

"Yeah," Donavan said. "Cross dug a little too deep and fell in over her head. The coroner's report said she hung herself, but we think it was only made to look that way."

Frank took his hands away from his face. "Wouldn't research and development for something like that cost a lot of money, anyway?" he asked.

Singh replied, "It's simple economics. A divided by B equals C. A is profit, B is loss. If C is in the positive, it's worth doing."

Donavan included her input: "Not only that, but Riverside has one of the most corrupt local governments in the region. They've been screwing with people for years, deliberately pricing out the low-income families to make way for the former Orange County residents getting priced out of their respective cities. It was only a matter of time before the government tried to do something like this."

"Out with the poor, in with the rich," Frank muttered.

"Yes. We knew it was them when the botanical gardens were set on fire," Singh said.

Frank shook his head. "So then why didn't the zombie outbreak happen until now?"

Singh looked at him with a frown. "Flu shots."

"Flu shots?"

"Yes," Donavan sighed. "In November, one of the private hospitals handed out free flu shots for the poor and it, um..."

"It reacted," Singh finished. "The chemical in the inhalant plus the eggs in the influenza vaccine created what we think we've identified as a virus."

Frank laughed. "And since this new drug *kills*..."

Donavan nodded. "That's right. Bodies rising up from mortuaries. Babies eaten in their cribs, and everyone who died just got right back up. The inhalant went into the atmosphere and it was chaos. Plant life only acts to spread it. This thing may well have covered the Earth by now."

"Yesterday you told me they were using orange groves as a vector," Frank said.

"That's what we thought at first," Singh replied. "The intoxicant in the drug is derived from herbicides that are usually harmless to humans. The city was somehow able to transform it into a narcotic."

"With deadly results," Donavan agreed.

Frank scoffed and crossed his arms. "More like *un*deadly."

And now he was staring at the same empty inhalers Singh had showed him, explaining to his friends what had been explained to him. "It's what caused the outbreak," he finished. "More bullshit done by this city."

"Bastards," Nicole whispered.

Dogbeef barked, and seemingly in answer to Nicole's cue, a group of squad cars came barreling around the corner, driving the wrong way on a one-way street. A paddy wagon followed close behind.

"Shit!" The words shot straight through Isaac's teeth. "Don't go into the mausoleum, they can't know there are other ways into the mall."

The three of them scrambled, not quite knowing what to do. Isaac pointed to the mountain, but a loud speaker crackled and they heard an almost mechanical sounding voice.

"Throw down your weapons or we'll be forced to shoot!"

The group squirmed, but Isaac stood tall. "You're the one who's forcing us."

"Throw down your weapons!"

A shadow shuffled behind the car.

"Fuck you!" Isaac lifted his chainsaw.

"Just do it, Isaac!" Nicole screamed, dropping her machete.

"This will be your final warning!" the cop shouted. Frank saw another shadow sauntering near a house. "Throw down your..." A pair of gangrenous limbs reached out and pulled the cop down and out of sight. Other zombies entered the streets, stumbling out of the surrounding houses. It was enough to get the cops in a panic and fire wildly in all directions.

But the zombies were indiscriminate. Not only did they lunge at the police, but at Frank's group as well. They still couldn't figure out how to climb a fence, but it wouldn't do much good, anyway, on account of the fact that the tops of the metal bars were sharpened down to spikes.

Nicole scrambled to her feet in an attempt to reach the mausoleum but Isaac held her back.

"Not there!" Isaac shouted. And sure enough, the officers that kept their wits and their lives began dividing their ammo between the zombies and the survivors. Bullets were buried into the grass and pinged off stone monuments as they dove for cover. Dogbeef ran for his life, knowing full well the danger was too much for him to handle. Still, he never abandoned his masters. Isaac crawled completely prone on the ground toward the back fence.

"The mountain!" he shouted, and saw Nicole just inside his peripheral vision, running in a stooped position. She was high enough off the ground for the cops to hit her.

"Get down!" Isaac shouted at her.

Now they heard louder shots, even though they were further away. The cops had apparently retrieved their shotguns and riot gear and were now letting loose on the attacking undead multitudes. Few bullets seemed to be heading their way. Nicole reached the fence first, helping Dogbeef between the bars. Next came Frank. Nicole cupped her hands, indicating they were to be used as leverage to hop over.

"No, you go first!" Frank yelled, but Nicole's expression was not just exhausted, it was also annoyed.

"I don't need to be coddled just because I'm a woman! Now go!"

Frank took no more time to hesitate and placed his foot in her hands. She then rose to her feet heaving him over the fence, and as Frank fell down the other side, a bit of his pant leg caught an iron spike and tore not just cloth, but skin, as well.

There was no time to react to the pain. Isaac finally caught up and now it was his turn to argue.

"Jesus Christ!" Nicole screamed. "You guys don't have to be heroes, just fucking go!"

"I weigh, like, twice as much as you!" Isaac pulled the backpack off his shoulders and dropped it behind him.

"I got it! I got it!" Frank yelled, and he reached his hands through the bars to provide the extra leverage needed to heft him over the fence. He fell much more smoothly than Frank, but now Nicole was alone on the other side. She stood, taking several steps back for a running start, then charged and jumped, catching the topmost crossbar with her hands and performing the mother-of-all chin-ups, bringing her face above the fence and locking in her elbows so she now held the bar by her waste. Every muscle in her body flexed and shook with fatigue as her leg swung up. Now came the other, but it never made it. A bullet caught her in the shoulder and she screamed as she fell back down to the dirt.

"Nicole!" Isaac jumped and grabbed the crossbar. His struggle was far less elegant than Nicole's, but with some pleading and debating, he convinced Frank to boost him back over so he could help.

"Go!" Isaac shouted as his feet touched the ground. "Up the mountain! We'll catch up!"

Frank didn't argue. He pivoted and ran and soon was on a paved road next to some upper-class houses; Dogbeef all the while whimpering and scampering between him and the two left behind.

"C'mon, Dogbeef!" Frank ordered. The dog came hurrying behind. They ran up a road snaking around the mountain. Frank's calves pleaded for mercy, but he knew he couldn't stop now. Soon the paved road gave way back to dirt, and only this dirt and rocks lay before them. Somehow, Dogbeef knew what was at stake and why the summit was now the smartest option. He had a knack for finding the easiest path, so Frank followed.

"We need teams who can salvage some of the factories on the east side," Donavan had explained. *"There's some food distributors in High Grove, next to the world's biggest Dixie cup. Did you know that was in Riverside?"*

Frank scaled a rock and jumped over. Dogbeef was ahead of him, and had stopped and waited for him to catch up.

"We need more pharmaceutical supplies for the lab, so we need to send teams to some of the medical supply stores and any other hospitals, if they haven't already been raided. This is very important."

Once they were together again, Dogbeef took the lead, now pacing Frank at a much more manageable rate. There was a cramp in his side, and sweat poured over his face. Once or twice the briny substance dripped into his eyes and he squinted and wiped it away with filthy hands.

Dogbeef barked. More zombies.

"There's a mill on the other side of town that makes pet food."

"Pet food?" Frank had questioned.

"Food is food," she told him. *"And the dogs have gotta eat, too, right?"*

Frank stepped over the fresh bodies he'd produced mere seconds earlier. Dogbeef had done most of the dirty work, but the choice to make the final blow or not usually fell on Frank's shoulders, and for him there was no choice. It was kill or be killed, or be killed temporarily.

He resumed his labored hike up the mountain, now limping but thankful for the camping trip he completed two days earlier. He was still wearing hiking shoes. The thought brought him back to Sarah. She must still be on his side, wherever she was. She must be watching over him, protecting him. How else could he have made it this far?

"Some of the food we obtain," Donavan had said, *"we're gonna barter for chemicals at RCH. They need food, right? And as long as they're neutral, City Hall won't attack inside the hospital unless they want the doctors there to forget about treating their wounded."*

And they made it. All the way up top, next to the white cross overlooking the entire city. The sun was facing his back, and now he finally had time to sit and rest and take a chug of water and invite Dogbeef to do the same.

"And this is the most important detail of all." Donavan had held up her finger. There seemed to be no apparent reason why, unless she was trying to keep him from interrupting. "You can tell no one. Ever. Under any circumstances. Understood?"

"Uh, yes."

"The science team is hard at work developing a cure."

"A cure?"

"That's right. We know how this virus was fabricated. Dr. Singh assures me he should be able to figure out how to make the cure. That's why we need chemicals. It's not just for medical use."

"It's because you can save the world."

"And you can be instrumental in that," Donavan assured him. "We mass-produce a vaccine and then when the rest of the un-dead die off completely, only the fully living will be left. How's that for population control, huh?"

Standing there on the Spanish Patio at the luxurious Mission Inn hotel, Frank turned his eyes skyward. Sarah was smiling. Would she have wanted him to do this? Somehow Frank felt she would have volunteered herself.

"I just have one question," Frank finally said. "Why are you doing this? Why fight them? Why take up such a heavy burden? City Hall is pretty strong, I'll bet. You're horribly outgunned and outmanned, and then there's a city full of walking dead out there. So why go against such heavy odds?"

Donavan held her stern expression everywhere except her eyes. Her blue eyes smiled, and her red hair fluttered in a slight breeze that seemed to come from nowhere.

"Only a moron or a genius would fight them," she replied. "And I'm not a moron."

Now Frank stood above everything. Most of the downtown area was now enveloped in the shadow of the mountain. Draped across Main Street from one building's façade to the next was a large red and green banner that said, **MERRY CHRISTMAS**.

He could see the hotel way off in the distance, and City Hall not far from that, both still covered in decorations for the holiday season. Somewhere sirens blared and red fire trucks sprayed water at oncoming gunfire like the proverbial mouse flipping off the hawk.

And all around, throngs of undead could be seen shambling about the streets and giving a new half-life to the city below.

SATAN CLAUS

TOM HAMILTON

"**M**other," Seymour asked, "what are you doing out of bed?"

The old woman didn't answer. She was carrying a lit wicket inside an archaic, silver, antique candle holder, and the hot wax was dripping down onto her wrists. There was no need for this, of course, as the hallway was already ablaze with light courtesy of the best bulbs which G.E. had to offer. Plus the cold afternoon sun, which was brightened by the high piles of leftover snow outside, shone fearlessly through every available window pane.

She was wearing a long, red, flannel granny gown with green trim and printed patterns of silver bells tied together with mistletoe. Her endless white hair, which was generally piled up in a bun, hung ragged and scraggly all the way down past the backs of her knees.

"C'mon. Let's get you back into bed," he said.

After he'd pulled the blankets up to her chin, he noticed large beads of sweat dotting her gray and wrinkled forehead.

"Jesus, Mother, you're sweating...and it's freezing in here."

He turned on the electric space heater and scooted it a little closer to the bed.

"Seymour!" she barked suddenly, causing her grown son to jump. She rarely spoke anymore, as her dementia was far advanced, so the sound of her voice startled him.

"Jesus, Mother!"

"Seymour! There was a man in the backyard."

"No there wasn't, Mother. It's ten degrees outside."

"Yes there was!" she snapped. "A man came under the fence while I was tending to my garden; a wild man."

"Mother, don't tell me you went out to that garden. Why, there's a foot a snow coverin' all those plants. No wonder you've gone and gotten yourself a fever. It isn't fit for man or beast out there."

The old woman didn't say anything else, and for a moment he thought the garrulous spell had passed, so he said, "Why don't you get some sleep, Mother. I don't think anyone's going to bother you."

But instead of regressing back into her usual catatonic state, the old woman exploded. "Don't you patronize me, boy! I was fightin' in these factories when you were shittin' figgie pudding!"

"Mother?"

"Now, I *said* there was a man out there, in the backyard. A man who slithered underneath the fence amid all that red snow. A man with eyes like blue fire. And if you don't believe me, go see for yourself. He bit me!"

She pushed the blankets off and clawed back the long sleeve of her granny gown, revealing a rancid and inflamed bite mark.

"Hell's bells, Mother, how in the world did you get that?"

But the old woman was done talking. Her body straightened out on the bed as stiff as an ironing board and her mind refracted into the voiceless nostalgia of lost and darkened decades.

Seymour shook his head and went into the bathroom to open the medicine cabinet. By the time he'd fetched the bandages and Mercurochrome, he could already hear the old woman snoring softly. He thought it must have stung like hell once he applied the disinfectant, but the old woman made no reaction.

"Jesus, Mother," he said to himself more than her. "We may have to take you to see Dr. Burke tomorrow." After he'd finished bandaging her up, he turned off the light and walked out of the bedroom while scratching his head. How in the world had she received such a nasty looking bite? He checked all the doors and windows, but they were either bolt locked or screwed down tight. There was no sign anywhere that anyone had broken in, and even if someone had: Why in the world would they want to attack and bite an eighty-nine year old woman?

He plopped down on the couch and began watching a hockey game on the large color television. He didn't know what the score was or who was playing; he was just content to watch the players skate around.

Could she have really been out in the backyard? Perhaps she'd been attacked by a dog?

Concerned, he got up and began walking towards his mother's room. If she'd been out in the snow, maybe the bottom of her nightgown would still be damp. He opened the door just a tiny crack and listened carefully. But he could no longer hear the old woman's rasping breaths. He switched the light back on.

"Mother?"

No reply.

The old woman was as pale as vanilla and lying like a corpse in a casket. He tried to shake her awake, but she didn't move a wrinkle.

"Mother! Mother!"

He fumbled through the top drawer of the vanity until he came up with the old woman's ancient, gold plated, compact mirror. He held it under her nose for several seconds, but no foggy breath clouded its silvery surface.

"Oh no, *oh no*!" he said as he grabbed the phone on the night stand and began dialing. "Hello, Alice, Mother's ill. I don't think she's breathing." An inaudible squawk lisped out from the other end of the line. "No, Alice, I don't think she is. You'd better get over here. Yes, I'm calling the ambulance now. Hold on, let me check." But as he took up the old woman's wrist to feel for a pulse, the way Alice had instructed, Seymour's dead mother leapt to life and sank what was left of her halitosis inflicted teeth into his forearm. He screamed more with surprise than with terror and dropped the phone to the rug. With the damage done, the old woman's frail body dropped back onto the bed, where she writhed in convulsions and then seemed to lose consciousness. Seymour jumped back and inspected the fresh bite. Blood was oozing up into the teeth marks like swamp water filling up muddy footprints.

"Dear Lord, dear Lord," he kept repeating.

"Seymour, Seymour," the receiver called out from the carpet. After a few seconds of sucking on his wound like a mother cat, he picked it back up.

"It's okay, Alice, I thought she wasn't breathing for a minute, but now she's up. You'd better be gettin' over here pretty soon anyway. I've got to be gettin' down to the mall." After he hung up, Seymour covered the old woman with a blanket. She had quieted back down, even though her eyes were open and blazed like the torches of a lynch mob.

Once he was out in the kitchen, he let the tap water run over the wound and down into the sink. Once the blood had been rinsed from the teeth marks, the indentations were a blue color and the viscous cut still smarted even under the flow of the faucet.

He thought he heard a new noise coming from the bedroom. But when he crept back to open the door slightly, all was silent. He looked at the clock and thought that Alice should be arriving pretty soon.

Once he was in front of the mirror, he combed his white beard. It looked so authentic there was no longer a need for the frost-white fake one he had donned in previous years. There probably wasn't any need for the foam belly anymore either, but he pulled it from the closet and strapped it on anyway. A furry red jacket with white trim hung from a solitary plastic hanger.

It was the same one he put his arms and shoulder blades into every year from Thanksgiving all the way until Christmas Eve; the familiar and famous garb of Saint Nicholas.

*   *   *

"You look a little under the weather, Seymour," Stan said. "Or at least equal with it." He was referring to the blizzard which had quickly converged upon the mountain town and was now raging on outside.

"Ah, it's just my mother again."

Stan took a sip of scalding black coffee and said, "Ya know, Seymour, there ain't any shame in putting a dying person in a..."

"...nursing home, I know," Seymour finished the sentence for him. "I can't do it, Stan. Not after the way she cared for dad for all those years."

"Well, it's none of my business but..." Before Stan could finish, the eye of the walkie-talkie which was attached to his belt winked yellow and then red before spitting out a line of garbled static. After a couple of seconds, the white noise translated to words: "Stan 109, Stan 109."

Stan held the speaker up to his mouth. "You got me."

"Stan, you better get down here. I think we got a shoplifter at Spencer's."

He sighed before pressing the talk button. "Be right there." He got up from the lunch room table he'd been leaning his buttocks against. "Gotta go, big boy."

Seymour felt so weak and feverish that all he could do was nod.

"Look, don't think about any of it tonight," Stan offered as parting advice. "Just have a good time makin' the kids happy."

But as Seymour walked past the store fronts out in the mall, his limbs felt stiff and their joints aflame. Breathing was difficult, as if the oxygen was igniting a liquid fire inside his chest. He doubled over in discomfort and pawed the bite which was now hidden underneath his red and white sleeve. It throbbed with each beat of his heart, and when he pulled the cloth back to inspect it, he saw it was practically glowing with a seeping green liquid.

"Look! It's Santa!" a boy yelled in happiness.

Then the children were all around him. Usually, he enjoyed the walk through the mall. It gave him the opportunity to pass out his surplus of small, striped red and white hard candy canes to the excited kids.

"Ho, Ho, Ho," he made himself say. But what he really wanted to do was floor the first snot-nosed brat who tried to touch him. He shook his beard like a wet dog and sighed. What the hell was he thinking? He loved children, he'd always loved children. Maybe it was just that awful episode with Mother which had put his nerves on edge.

The sleigh was centered underneath a huge skylight, in an expansive circular section in the center of the huge, cross-shaped shopping mall. Above the glass roof, the ubiquitous cloudy beard of God shook out its mighty dandruff in the form of millions of snowflakes. There were eight living deer hooked to the front of the sled. They had been fastened up with reins and cordoned off in a small, chain-link pen which doubled for a petting zoo. There were some cumbersome, clumsy, artificial antlers which had somehow been fashioned to their heads to make them look like the real deal. Many children were already mulling around the small enclosure and were busy feeding the creatures some smelly, small brown pellets which could be purchased from a nearby gumball machine for twenty-five cents.

There was a very sexy teenaged girl, with legs much too long for both her years and for the elf costume she was wearing, standing over next to a display of empty but very colorful Christmas presents. Her long brown hair was so thick and shiny it still looked stunning even underneath the absurd, pointed hat. She had worked carefully with the holiday shades of green and red to create an extremely alluring look with brushed on streaks of eye shadow.

There was also a thick, tired looking, rotund, middle-aged woman who was stationed behind a big Polaroid camera, which had been mounted near a check-out desk. She wore a miserable expression and was shuffling her feet aimlessly. Seymour remembered a year when she was much more affable, but that was long before they had converted the entire mall into a non-smoking establishment.

"Jesus, Seymour," she said. "You're fifteen minutes late." She pointed to a long line of parents with their children; kids eager to tell Santa all about their Christmas wishes. "Look at these brats."

"Okay, okay, Charlene," he said. "Let's not make a federal case out of it, let's just get some of the kids through the line."

Charlene sighed as if she knew he was right and unclipped the red velvet rope which separated the first customers from Santa. As he situated himself up inside the sleigh, a crud chewing *rein*deer watched him settle into his seat without much reaction.

The sleigh was an actual mountain sled which had been donated by the local hunter and trapper's museum. The door panels had been painted a dark maroon color, and tacky, plastic, mistletoe which was sprayed gold was draped over the top half of the refurbished leather seat. The running boards were held in place by a network of wires which were hooked onto some temporary ground rods like a carnival ride.

"Hey, Sarah."

"Hey, Seymour," the ultra-attractive elf acknowledged his greeting.

The first kid of the day climbed up onto Seymour's lap and proceeded to act like a repulsive brat. "I want an Xbox and a skateboard and a GI Joe and a..." Seymour was shaking his head yes when the boy paused. "Hey? Why aren't you writing any of this down?"

"I don't have to write any of it down, my elves are recording it all."

The boy looked around as if checking for recording equipment and locked eyes with the vivacious Sarah instead. "She's got pretty big tits for an elf."

Before Seymour had to say anything else, the Polaroid's flash popped and Charlene shouted, "Next!"

Next turned out to be a sweet little girl who was dressed like a miniature Mrs. Claus in strawberry red and white. All she asked for was some sort of urinating doll and was quickly taken down. A few more like her and Seymour thought he might be able to get caught up in the fun bit, but these hopes were dashed when he took one glance at the ever lengthening queue.

But as child after child rotated past a makeshift North Pole, and request after request fell onto Seymour's rapidly deafening ears, he felt worse and ever worse. His chest felt like there were two rats inside his rib cage fighting to devour his lungs. His arms and legs were heavy and cold like scrap metal from a dissected refrigerator, and every time Charlene snapped a new instant photo, he felt as if his eyes were looking into a welder's torch with no visor.

"Are you okay, Seymour?" Sarah, the breath-taking elf inquired.

"Yes, I'm fine kiddo."

"Maybe we should close early? You don't look so good."

"Oh, no, no, sweetheart, I'm fine. These children deserve a Santa. Now call the next child up please."

She did as she was told and for a while the pace of the visits quickened. Child on lap, spiel spat, photo snapped, child down, cash garnered, next.

This rush ensued until a roll of film got eaten up by the Polaroid. Charlene busied herself with ripping it out and replacing it, a cigarette hanging from her withered lip despite the **NO SMOKING** sign which was only a few feet from her head. While Sarah had her hands full trying to fend off the verbal advances of a fourteen year old boy who had wormed his way inside the red and green velvet ropes, Seymour slumped down in his seat.

Charlene cursed as the new roll of film refused to cooperate. The lovely Sarah told the boy, who was much too old for Santa but much too young for her, to get lost. Perhaps, with all this aggravation on their plates they simply didn't realize what was going on with Seymour. Or maybe, when Seymour tilted his head back and closed his eyes, they just thought that he was taking a power nap until the camera was flash ready again. Whatever the case, they didn't notice when Seymour passed away at 4:46 Mountain time.

Even when the amorous teenaged boy gave up and strutted away; even when the camera was repaired and ready to photograph, even when the children who had been so very, very good, were cleared to tell their tale to Santa; they still didn't notice Seymour's heavy and stiffening head.

Not until a darling little girl, with a look that could challenge the style and overwhelming cuteness of Shirley Temple herself, began slapping the face of the deceased Saint Nick, did they take notice. The little girl snickered and hopped down, only to be replaced by a huge boy who was obviously much too old and oversized to subscribe to such childish fables. While Charlene and Sarah glanced at each other in confusion, the boy began running through his list.

After a few seconds he paused and said, "Santa? Are you asleep?"

"Sarah!" Charlene shouted as she snapped what was sure to be a peculiar picture, "Is he all right up there? He doesn't look so good."

"I already asked him that once," Sarah replied. "He says he wants to finish out the shift."

"Well, Jesus," Charlene said as she tilted her gray-haired head in an effort to look past the youngster on Seymour's lap. "It looks like he's passed out or something. Is he drunk for God's sake?"

Sarah walked up to the sled. "Seymour doesn't drink. Wait a minute; I think he's coming around."

Indeed, Seymour had begun to stir, and when his eyes reopened, they were as red as his jacket. Thinking that Santa had revived, the boy continued with his delayed wish list.

"Seymour? Are you all right?" Sarah tried to whisper. Seymour, his face strangely glazed and distant, didn't answer or even seem to hear her.

"... and a go-cart and a scooter and the new *Girls Gone Wild* DVD..." The big boy rambled on as a low guttural growl escaped from Seymour's slightly parted lips. His face took on the countenance of a desperately sick and hungry animal.

"Seymour?" Sarah asked.

Of all the items the boy had listed as potential gifts there was one thing he certainly didn't want for Christmas, and that was to have the first three fingers bitten off of his left hand. But that's what he got in the next instant as a Satanic new Santa, which was no longer any kin to the kind and respectful Seymour, chomped the digits off as if they were ketchup-laced French fries.

As the oversized child drew back his squirting and maimed hand, the first of what was sure to be many screams rose from the crowd. Sarah stepped away completely stunned, her gaping mouth as perfectly round as the moon, while Satan Claus continued to chew the boy's fingers. Gore ruined his beard like the blood of a slaughtered animal running from a steel trap in the snow.

For a few awe-stricken seconds, the parents and kids who had been waiting in line paused, as if there was a chance this horrific spectacle could somehow still be a sick joke or even part of the show. They faltered like this for a few heartbeats, like deflated flags in a weak breeze, before terror took hold and they dispersed in a wild zigzag of panic. People punched, kicked, and pushed past each other as vicious as carnivorous zombies.

The riot was on.

Seymour stood up, the nonplussed boy still locked in his grip. For a second he swayed drunkenly, his eyes maniacal. Then he bit a patch out of the child's scalp as if it were a juicy cantaloupe. Sarah turned and bolted down a carpeted ramp, somehow finding her way out from the fog of shock. Charlene left her post behind the camera and bravely bustled up to the sanguinary soaked Santa.

"Good God, Seymour," she said without much steam. "Stop it!"

She reached out and grabbed the gore-splattered flap of the boy's jacket. But even as she did this, the demonic Santa released the boy and switched his grip to Charlene's shoulders. When he bit into her cheek, the blood squirted out as if from a torn ketchup packet. The sound of her scream was drowned out only by the boom of gunshots. Stan was pointing his pistol straight out from where he'd been seeking cover between two, twirling display holders in front of the Sunglass Hut. The bullet struck Satan Claus in the chest; the impact knocking him back down into the sled, but it had no other effect.

"Stop, Seymour! Don't make me shoot you again!" Stan cried out.

But the zombie who used to be Seymour didn't stop. He rose and continued to bite patches out of both the boy and Charlene, the pair now rendered unconscious inside the sled. This prompted Stan to empty his gun into the red and white clad target. The final projectile, however, grazed the gray antler of one of the *rein*deer and the balsa horns exploded into dull confetti. This panicked the animals and they were so spooked that no constraints could hold them. They quickly trampled the chain-link of the petting zoo. The reins connecting them to the sleigh pulled it right out of its stanchions and away from the flimsy rods that no one had thought would be needed to help contain the docile deer.

Sparks shot from the tile floor as the sled gathered speed and mowed over what was left of the audience. A mother and several small children were trod over and clomped on by the deranged *rein*deer.

As the sleigh reached maximum velocity, a man was dragged for several yards along with Charlene's dead body. After the dragged man fell off and rolled violently into a Pepsi machine, Charlene's felled carcass could still be seen hooked onto the sleigh. One young mother, who had unfortunately fallen, had her legs scissored off by the skating blades. The detached limbs lay like reddened octopus meat, separated by several yards from her floundering body.

As the storefronts blazed past in a blur of neon commercialism, Seymour stood up and peered out over the crowd like an evil pharaoh; his eyes swirling with tiny cyclones of madness. At this juncture he let out a terrible and peevish laugh, perhaps owed to the fact that he was still an immature child of a creature inside his diseased mind. Or maybe the motion of the onrushing sleigh awakened some thrilling memory of fun, which his rotting pulp of a brain still managed to conjure. No one can say for sure. But whatever the case, the sound of that revoltingly jolly wail was disgusting and blood curdling. Hearty and horrible, it fell onto the sensitive ears of the shocked shop keepers.

The *reindeer* didn't slow down as they reached the exit. They simply veered off from the doors, which were separated by stout aluminum frames, and aimed for the much wider berth of the department store's display windows instead. They mercilessly trampled the seasonally garbed mannequins and crashed through the wide showroom-type glass pane with a sonic shatter. A large sliver of glass now protruded from Seymour's chest. But even as the wound pumped fresh blood and the shard jutted out close to where his heart must be, he didn't seem to notice.

Outside, the blizzard flew with such a robust bluster that the plows couldn't keep up. A thickening layer of powder, which was near perfect for sledding, covered the parking lot. It was already dark outside, and the headlights of approaching vehicles reflected off the menacing procession as the train continued on, careening off of cars and threatening to mow down aloof pedestrians. Then a sleigh, with eight tiny *reindeer* and one lifeless, yet blood thirsty Santa at the helm, flew down the wide thoroughfare of the mountain town's Main Street.

The quickness of the sled had pushed Seymour back down into his seat where he foamed at the mouth and snapped his teeth at anyone who was even remotely close to the carriage. At the intersection, they bustled right through the red light, causing a woman who had been driving a Honda Civic to swerve in order to avoid them. She had to cross over into another lane where a huge semi obliterated her small compact. The truck hit her so hard that the little import seemed to pop and burst like a balloon, the lady thrown out into the high drifts, now as dead as Seymour. Meanwhile, the semi slanted and plowed into a ditch, its back end askew.

A few blocks from this accident, a young family, perhaps thinking this obscenity was some type of holiday parade float, pulled up next to the sleigh. A small girl peered out from the back seat of the car and the evil Santa showed her his red and white teeth. But his mouth now looked as if he'd just chewed a ball of dentist's dye to reveal cavities. Charlene's corpse still bobbed up and down along side the carriage, reddening the fresh snowflakes. The family, then realizing they were dealing with something deplorable, quickly sped away.

Near the edge of town, they passed a speed trap and soon red and blue lights could be seen trailing the sleigh, as well as the wail of a siren.

The following conversation was heard by many curious townsfolk on the police radio band.

"What've you got, car four?"

"Uh, this is four, we're in pursuit, over."

"Request license plate number of suspect, over."

"Uhm, no plates, suspect is dressed in a Santa suit and appears to be dragging a dead body through the streets, over."

Pause.

"You have clearance to shoot out the suspect's tires, over."

"Um, vehicle doesn't have tires. Appears to be a sled pulled by some type of dogs. Over and out."

And the *rein*deers pushed on, until the traffic thinned out and the tall towers gave way to shorter three-story buildings. Then they were outside the city limits, where they rode past the unmarked county roads, all boundaries and lane lines obscured by the relentless snowfall. The drifts were so high they covered the snow fences and the barbed-wire barricades, leaving no boundaries to obstruct the path of deer and their cargo.

Soon the hills slanted. Chopped long ago by the ax of God, they dipped into steeper slopes where the angry police vehicles could no longer follow. The *rein*deer climbed all the way to the top of Mount Paydirt. Its flattened peak gazing down at Gordon's Gorge five hundred feet below; home of the Great Northern Paiute Grand Valley Indian Reservation.

Without pausing for a beat, the entire caravan ran off the cliff and began the long plunge to the sharp, man-sized boulders below. For a few seconds, they looked amazingly graceful as their forward progress held onto the neat design of the jumping *rein*deer.

It was like a classic postcard with a silhouette of Santa Claus and the outline of his eight dependable beasts. Then it all fell apart as the heavier animals were grabbed by gravity and became entangled in the reins. The sled soon turned upside down in mid-air and Seymour was thrown from his lofty perch. He fell silent and solemn, too devoid of humanity even to react in defense of his own well being.

Far down below, in a house which didn't have a Christmas tree or a wreath on the door, a young boy had seen the beauty and grace of the sleigh's brief flight. But this was before it turned into a tangle of falling creatures and twisted reins, like the strings of a fractured puppet show. He was a child with chestnut brown eyes and shoulder length black hair and he was the only one who had glimpsed the entourage before they vanished below the precipice of the rock face.

When the animals finally found the thankless terrain at rock bottom, they exploded into chunky red ribbons of brown furry gore like slabs of dead meat. At the same time, Seymour's brain burst apart on the gravel; his body shattered by an impact not even someone who was already dead could survive.

"Mama, Mama," the small Native American boy said while pointing out his bedroom window. "I just saw Santa Claus." The silhouette of his washboard-hipped mother appeared in the door-way but she didn't answer.

After a few seconds of this silence, the child turned to her and said in a confused voice, "Didn't you see him. Mama?"

But she still didn't answer, so he reached over and turned on his bed side lamp. The ceramic fixture was a depiction of a Paiute brave riding atop a spotted black and white mustang.

"Mama?" he asked again as she shuffled within range of the bulb's weak light. But those were the last words he ever spoke, for by now he could see there was something wrong with his mother's eyes.

MADE IN CHINA

MARC WIGGINS

"Come on, Dad, please? Can I get it for Christmas?" the twelve- year-old boy pleaded with big eyes.

Steve Baxter pretended not to hear while he buffed his Lexus in his garage. He wished the whine of the buffer wheel was louder so he really couldn't hear his son's nagging. The kid had been on this kick for his latest *must have* all week long and Steve was sick of hearing it. He leaned over to reach the center of the hood and continued buffing with grim determination.

The boy was relentless and tugged at the end of his dad's untucked flannel shirt. "I'll even work for it. I'll do anything you want and clean my room everyday. Come on, Dad, please?"

Steve stiffened to a stand and switched off his buffer in defeat. The shrill whine died down to an abrupt stop, without a lingering echo even though they were in an otherwise spacious two-door garage. There was too much crap in it and only had enough room for his car. His wife's Mercedes was relegated to the driveway. He looked around the garage while he considered his reply.

As he did so, he took a quick inventory of all their stuff, most of it pristine and new. Nearest to him was a thirty six inch television he bought just last spring but moved into the garage a few weeks ago because he replaced it with a flat screen. On top of it was their DVD Player which met the same fate in favor of a Blue-ray player. Just out of view was a box full of DVD's, all retired since they'd been replaced with their Blue-ray cousins. Over in the corner was a lap top he bought a few months ago, yet to be used and still in its sealed box. That was stacked on top of a heap of other boxes containing various electronics and fancy kitchen gadgets; many of them still sealed and new. At the base of the room sat his set of exercise equipment. Each machine was state of the art and gathering dust. In the center, where his wife's car should have been, were his Harley and all of his son's stuff; three bicycles, four scooters and a small off-road motorcycle yet to be broken in. Everything looked new and the timeline of each purchase was hinted at by varying degrees of fine dust layered upon many of the items.

Only his eyes noted the consumer's paradise inside his garage but his mind didn't. If it had, the credit cards in his wallet would have suddenly felt very heavy. He had other things on his mind and he absently wondered if they would need to rent more than one storage room if the house went into foreclosure.

Who's talking about 'If'? he mused. Well, that was a concern for another day, he decided. He had an anxious boy to deal with.

He looked down at his son, "Jason, I've already told you. You're already getting a big present for Christmas. That was all you could talk about last month. We got it, plus a bunch of other stuff. And I shouldn't have told you that anyways. It's supposed to be a surprise."

The boy looked up at him with desperation and hurt, "But I don't want that anymore. Please, Dad?"

Steve tried not to let that get to him. He knew his son still wanted the expensive gaming system, the one he himself had stood in a long line for several hours before a midnight sale. He told himself his boy was just being a kid. He wasn't supposed to be grateful and it was normal for children to get excited about the *latest thing*.

"Well..." he started while rubbing his chin.

The boy recognized the first chink in his father's resolve. He'd seen it many times before after successful campaigns of pleas and nagging. He had it down to a science and his eyes gleamed at his upcoming victory. The next part of their *discussion* was now a mere formality.

"Well," Steve went on with his part of the script, "what was this thing again?"

The boy sprung into euphoric animation with his hands working furiously to emphasize his words, "It's the *Stealth Leader*. It's exactly like the one *Major Fathom* has when he goes out on missions and it even has three secret compartments for your guns and gear. And the best part is that *The Renegade* comes with it. That's the Major's most powerful weapon."

Steve knew damn well what the God forsaken thing was. He'd seen the annoying commercial enough times and God knows he'd heard it from his son all week. It was basically an electric go-cart. What made it the absolute *must have*, was the cheap stickers and logos from a stupid children's show slapped on the hood and sides. But it was a very popular television show and that meant the toy would be very expensive.

"Jason, you know your birthday's in February. That's just a few months away. Why don't we make that your big present then?"

His tactic fell flat with a look of horror from the boy.

Steve bowed his head and pinched the bridge of his nose while closing his eyes to think. They were already short on this month's mortgage and that was compounded by the previous two they still owed.

Ah, screw it, he concluded, *might as well live it up while we can*. Besides, he'd already decided they were going to claim bankruptcy after the holidays and that would wipe the slate clean. They did the same thing five years ago and it wasn't really that big of a deal. Back then he was afraid his credit would be ruined but there were plenty of credit card companies that quickly welcomed him back with open arms. Besides, there was the new government bail out program that might help him keep the house. Of course, his son knew none of this.

What the hell, why not, he thought with justification. He was tired of his paycheck going to the bastards at the bank who held the deed to his home. They wouldn't be happy no matter what he did to work with them. A look of joy in his child's eye was more important than anything else.

"All right," he stated with authority. "You're already getting a lot for Christmas. This'll be extra on top of that. So, if we do this, that means I want your bedroom spotless everyday and I want you to take out the trash like you're supposed to. No more complaining or dragging your feet when we ask you to do stuff. You'll have to earn this." As a father, it was his duty to teach his son a sense of responsibility and this was the perfect way to do that.

Jason's eyes bulged as if drugged, "Yes! I promise. Every day!" But he knew the game. He would hold up his end of the bargain and within a week, his mom and dad would forget, and things would go back to normal. "Thank you Dad! I love you," he exclaimed with a hug.

Steve hugged back, savoring the important father and son moment. The boy pulled away first and left the garage. Along the way to the front door, he pulled out his cell phone to call his best friend and brag.

Steve looked on with a sense of satisfaction. He loved moments like this, valuable bonding times. A moment later, he turned and resumed his buffing. Nothing like honest to goodness manual labor to fulfill a man's soul.

Later that night, he placed an order on the internet. It wasn't from Toys 'R Us or Walmart. Rather, he decided to order the toy directly from the manufacturer so he could shave off a few hundred bucks from the retail price. He needed that savings since his credit cards were dangerously close to their limit and he only had what was left in his checking account until next payday.

Rationalizing if he was getting something for his son, he might as well get a few items for himself, his next stop was Amazon.com. He still needed to get more Blue-rays to replace his outdated DVD library.

*　*　*

"Yes, sir, right away, sir. I'm connecting you now," Chang said on the phone with cheer and a smile. He leaned over his desk to reach his phone panel and route the important call to the North Regional Manager of Ming International, the largest toy manufacturer in China.

Once done, he settled back in his chair and blew out a relaxed smile, as he bent his arms back and folded his hands behind his head. It was a very busy morning for both him and the massive toy company.

Tis the Season, as the Americans would say, he thought with a light heart. Chang didn't mind. He loved his job and he was good at it. Though his role as a receptionist might seem menial to some, he liked to think of himself as an important man. If one thought about it, he really was important and powerful. What was a receptionist after all? A receptionist was the gatekeeper to the company. Everyone had to go through him before they got to anyone or anywhere else in the multi-national organization. He knew everyone and many of their secrets. And with that, he had power.

He didn't have time to contemplate this as the phone rang again. The incoming call on the monitor was a familiar number. It was from a *mom and pop* laundry mat.

He sprung nervously to pick up the call.

"Good afternoon, this is Ming International. How can I help you?" he mechanically uttered in a serious but not quite fearful tone.

An emotionless and foreboding voice spoke into his ear.

"Yes...certainly, sir. Let me transfer you right away," he finished obediently and quickly forwarded the caller to an office within the toy factory, but an office that did not officially exist.

Yes, Chang was an important and powerful man, a keeper of secrets; and some secrets were more secret than others. He knew things not known by most. All the workers and managers in the toy manufacturing plant and even all of the executives were completely ignorant of the true goals behind Ming International. Those employees were of the *New China*, entrepreneurial and growing in affluence. However, while Chang and his secret group were all of that, too, they were also much more. They were true patriots of *The People's Republic of China* and they conducted business far more important than building plastic toys.

With the call completed, he resumed his casual recline in his chair. He had less than a moment to enjoy himself before a short, balding man in an expensive suit walked up to his receptionist desk.

"Ugh, ugh," the man curtly cleared his throat while displaying his disapproval at Chang's demeanor. This man was the Director of all Regions and thus *the most* important and powerful figure in Ming International. However, he wasn't part of the *secret group*.

"Chang," he went on condescendingly. "The inspectors will be here in less than an hour. I want you to notify me the second they enter the building. I don't need to tell you how important it is to keep them happy. We can't afford to shut everything down because of a trivial infraction."

Chang sat up and smiled a toothy grin, "Yes, sir. I'll let you know the instant they arrive."

"And I don't want them to see you slouching in your chair. You must present yourself with the utmost professionalism," the important man exclaimed.

"Certainly, sir," Chang replied with ease and cheer while motioning to straighten his shirt.

The short man grunted and turned away. Chang watched him perform his quick march towards the elevator, his destination being his office on the top floor suite.

What a pawn, Chang regarded him with a widening smile, *actually, what a toy*. It wasn't as if he disliked the man, he was merely amused.

Though that self important man was worried about the inspection, Chang wasn't. Those inspectors were all part of *the group*, and he knew that a passing grade was a forgone conclusion. The whole meeting was merely a political formality to please the Americans.

A few years back, America had discovered high levels of lead and other chemicals in the paint and composition of toys made in China. It was quite a tizzy on all the network news and cable stations. Ultimately, the general consensus was that China was taking shortcuts in expenses and quality control, and the Americans were too complacent to properly inspect until much later. It had been going on for years before detection and both countries were to blame for different reasons.

It was a big international scandal and China accepted the black eye in order to maintain their secret.

The real reason for the defective toys was a habitual screw up in supplies. Products intended for the stealth part of the business was so vaguely labeled that they were routed to and used by the public parts of the business. Toys got tainted, but for as smart as the Americans thought themselves to be, they never suspected the real reason.

To appease the Americans and ensure their continued ignorance, China promised frequent and tight inspections. So much so, that even high level people like the man who just admonished Chang were nervous and weary of those inspections. It was set up that way and they had to be honestly alarmed in order for the larger plan to appear legitimate. The real purpose of the inspections was to ensure proper delivery of chemicals and materials to the more important and darker workings of the toy business.

Another call came in, this one an internal call and technically *nonexistent*. The caller was a person who made the smiling receptionist more nervous above all others in *the group*, but for a different reason.

"Hi, Sun," Chang sweetly answered. A pleasant sensation of butterflies launched in his stomach.

"Hello, Chang," a soft and heavenly voice greeted. "Hey, our printer is out and we need a package to go out right now. Can you do me a favor and print out the label for me? You can get it off of the S drive. I'll be over to pick it up in a few minutes."

"For you, anything my dear," he cooed and then followed up in his most gentlemanly manner, "Say, lunch is in a few hours. Would you do me the honor of joining me?" He was always stunned by Sun's beauty every time he saw her. Sure, there were a lot of girls in his past, and one or two others he was seeing now. But she was different. Up until now, she had always refused his overtures but he was confident and never one to give up.

"Um, sure. I'd like that," she accepted after a moment's pause. "But hey, this is really important. Can you print it out for me? We need this shipment to go out fast."

He was stunned and elated by her decision. Always smooth and quick to recover, he only allowed the most imperceptible measure of surprise in his voice. "No problem. See you in a few minutes," he confidently concluded.

She hung up first. Even the clicking sound from her terminated call was soft and subdued. She really was demure and feminine in all ways that grabbed him. He leaned back into his chair in the usual fashion and savored his victory.

Moments later, she entered the massive lobby from a nondescript door and glided towards his desk. He allowed himself a moment to take in her wonderful vision before he leaned into his computer to print the shipping label. In doing so, a rare and unusual mistake was made. He navigated to the S drive and retrieved the label, but he was too caught up in his anticipation and daydream. The drive he accessed was from the public sector and not the secret one. He quickly retrieved the first item in the queue with a priority marking.

The home address of Steve Baxter was efficiently printed onto the label.

He pulled the sheet from the printer's cradle and held it out for her just as she approached his desk.

"Hi, Chang. Thanks," she shyly said and took hold of the paper.

He didn't let go of the sheet and he tugged it gently, pulling her willingly closer to him. With his most handsome grin, he teased, "So, where would you like to have lunch? Your choice...the finest restaurant or a picnic on the lawn?"

She giggled, herself now leaning into the desk as much as he.

She really was stunning, shy and intelligent. Though she wore the clothes of a factory worker, Chang knew she belonged in a pristine white lab coat. She was a scientist and that was all he knew.

Had he known the specific nature of her work, had he known that the antiseptic she smelled of was freshly lathered on after experimenting on a corpse, he might have thought better of his romantic notions. Instead, all he saw were those beautiful eyes.

He didn't know that she was a genius.

In fact, she was the lead researcher and that was remarkable given her young age. However, even she didn't know the true reason behind her work. Everything was compartmentalized. She only knew that she had made an important breakthrough. The most recent cadaver she had experimented on had shown great promise and now it had to be sent with the utmost urgency to another secret facility for further verifications and study.

This sweet and noble young woman honestly thought she was doing her part in furthering the betterment of mankind. With today's success, she was elated and felt anything was possible. Up until now, she always refused Chang's longstanding invitations out of shyness, uncertainty and inexperience. After all, her only dates throughout school were with textbooks.

But just now, she actually created life where there was only death. That gave her the confidence to finally accept his offer.

For her, this was a wonderful day. She reached the pinnacle of success with her God-like achievement. It was only made better with this moment, a flirtatious moment of her hanging onto her end of a sheet of paper with the handsome man tugging on his. She loved feeling desired and she finally felt she earned it.

On the matter of a lunch destination, she smiled and coyly answered, "Um, gentleman's choice." And then, with a sense of bravery and self-worth, she added, "But choose well if you want a second lunch."

"I hope to choose wisely, my dear," he played along. He looked into her eyes a moment longer before letting go of his end of the printed sheet.

She pretended to recoil back. She really wanted to lean further into him.

"We'll see..." she toyed. She never thought to look and verify the printed address.

They both continued to look into each other's eyes. Suddenly, she turned and walked away with a gait of professionalism and detachment.

Chang admired her ass and anticipated their time together while his eyes followed her cross the lobby and back through the unremarkable door.

By the time lunch came--Chang wisely chose the picnic approach with vending machine sandwiches and ice cold cans of Coke from the staff lounge--their romance began to blossom.

Just an hour before the date, the rushed package had already left the loading dock and was on its way to America.

*　　*　　*

On the morning of Christmas Eve, at the front door, a chorus of two men exclaimed, "Express Delivery!" while they placed the large package on the doorstep of Steve Baxter's house.

As promised, the item was delivered before Christmas. Here it was with a wooden thud, marking completion of their job. Another short chorus of "Thank you" marked their departure. Those guys had a lot more packages to deliver that day and the truck quickly sped off for their next destination.

Steve came out soon afterwards and he was slightly puzzled by the shape of the package. Though he didn't equate it, the shape and size of the box resembled a casket. Instead, he concluded that the product must have been in several pieces and he would have the hellish task of assembling it.

But not today, he decided with another sip of his coffee. It would be enough to drag it in and bring it next to the Christmas tree. He'd deal with the mess of putting it together tomorrow.

But, for God's sake, not now, he resolved.

He took another sip of coffee and considered the weirdly shaped box a moment longer. His son wouldn't be waking up until sometime around noon. That was enough time to get it in place and to slap some Christmas wrapping over it. Obviously, his son would know what it was, but at least the formalities would be taken care of.

He went back inside to finish his coffee, knowing he had ample time before the kid dragged himself out of bed.

* * *

The next morning, Steve and his wife, Jenna, found themselves standing in the kitchen and staring at the coffee maker with bleary eyes. The slow drip ignored them and didn't quicken from the impatient force of their glares. In fact, it seemed to taunt them.

This was the only day of the year their son was up before six a.m. This was the boy's big payday and his parents begrudgingly complied after he invaded their bedroom. However, their first order of business was to cope with the early hour, and that meant coffee.

The two tired zombies stood apart while huddled around the lazy machine. They each clutched their robes closer to their bodies to deal with the morning chill while the violent sound of rips and tearing echoed from the living room.

Jenna turned slightly to face the sound, "Jason! Don't open anymore presents! We'll be there in a minute!"

Her answer was another long rip, followed by the loud and hasty crinkling of paper being bunched up as it was peeled away from the gift. Quickly afterwards, there was another small thud and then more fresh tearing.

Jenna sighed and looked at her husband. "He's your son," she grumbled with half humor and half displeasure.

Steve broke his fixation over the coffee maker and yelled out, "Jason, you heard your mother! Stop and wait for us!" Truth be told, he wouldn't mind letting the boy go at it while he went back to his warm bed.

The sound of a final tear roared into the kitchen, followed by an excited "Okay!"

Steve grunted and took the coffee pot while it was still brewing. He poured himself a cup which didn't leave enough for his wife. He returned the pot to let the slow drip resume.

With cup in hand, he turned to leave, "Sweetheart, can you grab the camera when you come out?"

"Sure," she replied while waiting for her share of the coffee to accumulate.

Steve wandered into the living room and sat on the couch. A pile of torn wrapping paper already mounted in the center of the room. Next to that was a collection of opened and discarded presents. The boy was working his way up to *The Prize*, having started with the smallest presents first. Though he'd already opened several of them, there were still many more to race through. Jason quickly grabbed another present and looked at his father with pleading eyes.

"Whoa, tiger. Better wait until your mom comes in," Steve warned and took a sip of his coffee.

"Okay, Dad," Jason obeyed.

Both father and son looked at the Christmas tree. It was beautiful in its glory, tall and opulent. Lush green spears supported numerous crisscrossing rows of bright and blinking yellow, red and blue lights. They sparkled alongside a mix of new bulbs and ornaments. Most of the older ones were family heirlooms, or more accurately they were fixtures that managed to survive more than the last two or three holidays without being thrown out afterwards. A generous coating of artificial silver strands coated the arrangement, all carefully placed to give the illusion of icicles.

The boy continued his gaze and allowed himself to be entranced by the play of lights while he waited for his mother to join them. That calmed him while he waited for the moment when he could resume his assault on his mess of presents. Steve regarded the tree, too, but his thoughts were more about the chore of taking it down and packing everything away after the holidays were over. However industrious he would feel at that time, would determine how many of the fixtures will survive to see another holiday.

"Okay, here I come," cried Jenna's approaching voice, coffee cup in one hand and camera in the other, the camera already affixed to her eye.

She was barely out of the kitchen, and entering the living room, when Jason immediately resumed and ripped away shreds of paper from the present on his lap. The reveal elicited little response other than his tossing it aside and grabbing another colorful box from the mountain of gifts under the tree.

Jenna made her way to the couch to sit with Steve just as the quick and vicious tearing concluded and the contents were exposed. Jason smiled and tossed it on top of the growing pile. Her first picture was finally snapped and it captured a blurred image of Jason lunging for another box.

In rapid succession, each of the toys met the same hasty fate. There were too many to count. Along the way, the boy began to fabricate excitement over each assaulted gift. In his mind, these were the filler presents, a formality while he made his way to the farthest end of the tree where the largest and coolest ones loomed. As he got closer to them, he began to shower his parents with excited and obligatory "thank yous" and "wows." Some of the discoveries were actually pretty cool but he knew what he was working towards. That was the ultimate!

The lights of the Christmas tree shimmered and blinked and the ornaments glistened while he continued his attack along its base. His father grinned and slowly worked on his coffee while his mother continued to take her blurry pictures between quick sips of coffee.

Finally, the bottom of the tree was bare except for two further off to its side. Those were the big ones. Jason launched upon the smaller of the two giants and tore away the wrapping. As expected, the gaming system he once so desperately desired revealed itself in all its glory.

His requisite thanks for the system was only somewhat larger than he gave for the package of socks he unwrapped earlier.

Now there was the anticipated prize.

His obsession.

He was now upon it but, for the first time, he slowed down to enjoy and prolong the experience. He carefully tore away the first strand of paper across the length of the coffin-sized gift. He wanted to savor every second. After several slow and careful dissections of the decorative wrappings, a nondescript white cardboard box finally revealed itself. His sense of glee was still very real despite the absence of markings or pictures that should have labeled it.

He ran over to Steve and wrapped his arms around his father's neck, "Thank you, Dad!"

Steve recoiled, somewhat taken aback by the force of his son's gratitude. "Oh, sure buddy," he laughed back.

His son continued his hold for a moment and it was long enough for Steve to feel a little guilty about not assembling it already. He planned to but had never gotten the chance, then it was Christmas morning and too late.

Making the best of it, he said, "Tell you what, we'll build it together."

Jason let go and leaned back with wide and glossy eyes, "Yeah! That'll be great!"

Steve took in the vision of his son's animated face and realized this was one of those times he'd remember the rest of his life, more vividly than a photograph.

The boy stood and Steve followed, pulling himself off of the couch with a tired groan. He cupped his hand to the back of his son's head as they walked off to retrieve some needed tools from the garage. Jenna enjoyed the moment, too, taking for herself a mental snapshot of the event. Just to be sure though, she aimed her camera and took a clear picture of her departing husband and son just before they exited the room.

A few minutes later, they returned with an exacto-knife, screwdrivers and a socket wrench set. They came up to the oddly shaped package and Steve made long cuts into the cardboard encasement. Working together, they removed it as well as another layer of Styrofoam padding. Once done, they were confronted with a plain and unpainted wooden crate, tightly sealed by an overkill of nails that sealed the lid.

"What the hell..." Steve mumbled under his breath. He was growing irritated at the strangeness of the casket shaped container and the work needed to open it.

So typical, he thought. For the last number of years, he'd grown increasingly annoyed at how difficult it was to break a toy free from its container. Sure, open the box, but once done, there was a hidden base where the toy was tied down and overdone with a complicated myriad of hard twist ties that were twisted to the point of obsession. He knew all to well how some toys took up to twenty maddening minutes to unravel and break free since each strand was too thick and tough to merely cut with a knife or scissors. He could have sworn it was a silent war waged by the Chinese. A petty war designed to wear down their enemy.

He marched off back into the garage to retrieve a crowbar but he was careful not to let his son in on his growing frustration.

He returned with the crowbar and knelt down next to the package. It was sealed to the point of fusion and the first bite of his tool into it did little more than to deform the wood. With a sigh, he worked his way around. A slight grunt marked each of his digs and lifts of the bar as he tried to force his way in. It wasn't until he had made a complete trip around it that he was able to gain a satisfying screech which marked an opening. He continued with another handful of pries before he felt he could complete the task with his bare hands.

"Damn Chinese", he grumbled to himself.

Jason anxiously shuffled along with his father each step of the way around the box and he nearly ran into him when his father finally stopped, discarded the bar, and dug his fingers into the small opening.

Jason held his breath in gleeful anticipation while Steve exclaimed his most strained and prolonged grunts while fighting through the last of the lid's resistance. The object itself emitted hard and unforgiving squeaks of nails against wood before it finally gave way. Then without warning, all resistance vanished when the last nail broke free but, Steve's mighty pull continued on for a fraction of a second longer. The hood flung out of his surprised hands and landed a short distance away with an angry clatter.

All the while, Jenna had been snapping pictures. She was amused at her husband's red and sweaty face and thought it was adorable how the man worked so hard for their son.

The final image she shot was of the two peering down into the box with amazement and disgust. She brought the camera back down to her lap and asked, "What's wrong?"

"What the..." Steve muttered, not so much in reply.

"Huh?" was all the boy could gather.

"What is it? What's wrong?" Jenna asked, rising from the couch. From the looks on their faces, she wasn't sure if she wanted to walk over and find out.

"There's a dead Chinese man in here," Steve simply reported.

"What?" she asked, not understanding.

"Jeeesuuus, Christ!" Steve muttered while scratching the back of his head. He had no other words to describe the moment. He continued to look down into the box. Inside was indeed a dead Chinese man who wore nothing but a shroud to cover his midsection. His skin was ashen gray and it was obvious he was dead. His deformities were not from decay, but rather from a maze of scars on his face and body. Recent and ancient healings of cuts, bruises and lashes distorted his skin in countless places, and he was emaciated, but that wasn't from the after effects of death. This man looked like he'd suffered from starvation.

Even Steve, while looking on with his sheltered American perspective, could see this man had suffered a long time. To him, the body looked like it came from a concentration camp. Unknown to him, he wasn't that far off. In China, all test subjects at the toy factory had indeed come from labor camps.

Both Steve and Jason leaned closer into the casket for a better look, remotely hoping it was a joke and not real. No, reality didn't change and their first observation was true. It was a dead Chinese man in the box and not the toy Jason had wanted. In unison, they looked back up at Jenna with shock and bewilderment. She remained standing next to the couch. The look on their faces was enough for her and she feared to move closer.

Beneath them, the dead figure opened its eyes with a lethargic flutter. Upon seeing Steve and Jason, the dead man hissed with excitement and hunger. The sound came out more like a deformed rattle since the lungs were devoid of air.

Before anyone could react, the dead Chinese man grabbed onto Jason's arm. The boy screamed in surprise and that immediately turned into pain when the animated corpse rose to a sitting position and sunk its teeth into Jason's forearm. Blood sputtered out from the sides of the dead thing's cheeks with each rending twist of its head. When it finally pulled back with a generous mouthful of flesh, the blood from Jason's arm sprayed freely and violently back into its face. The animated corpse sat back with ease and happily chewed while still sitting in the path of the bloody shower. All the grayness in its face, neck and shoulders disappeared in a film of dark, rich red.

Jenna, still fixed to her place, screamed at the sight. Steve was in disbelief and shock, but his instincts took over and he shoved his son away and behind him. He punched the little Chinese man in the face with all of his strength. The impact of the blow was dissatisfying and too much like hitting a slab of meat. The man showed no signs of anger or pain. Aside from its lifeless recoil to the other side of the casket, all Steve achieved with his punch was to dislodge the bloody and chewed up piece of his son's arm from the mouth. The piece of flesh flew from the thing's mouth and landed with a plop at Jenna's feet.

Perhaps in mercy to her sanity, she didn't see the flying mess of meat. She unwittingly stepped on it while she took a tentative and terrified step closer towards the mayhem. Her attention was fixed on her son, who whined and squirmed in pain behind her husband. The boy clasped his hand over his deep wound while he rolled on the floor in agony.

Cries of pain from his tortured son caused Steve to turn and look back for a brief second. A sharp sense of alarm, fear and panic overtook him when he saw the rapidly expanding puddle of blood around his son. He wanted to go to Jason but the thing behind him growled. It was an inhuman and grating sound. He turned back to deal with it but was too late.

The Chinese zombie stood within the coffin with its face only inches away from Steve. Giving Steve no time to react, the bloody mouth shot forward and bit into his face. The first strike didn't earn a satisfying mouthful, only a scraping of skin and eyelid as it pulled away from Steve's brow.

Steve shrieked at the agony of teeth scraping across the bone of his forehead and the unforgiving sear of flesh being torn from him. The sensation was so intense he didn't immediately know what part of his face was gone. Though he found out very quickly when one of his eyes kept on seeing after he tried to blink in pain. Just as quickly, blood generously compensated and coated his vision. There was so much blood and pain. His hands went to cover his exposed bone instead of dealing with his attacker.

The zombie seized upon the distraction and came back at Steve. It sank its head into his neck. More by chance than plan, the deep bite pierced Steve's carotid artery.

An avalanche of blood quickly sprouted from Steve's neck.

The Chinese zombie pulled away while shaking its head to break the tougher strands of flesh still connecting the two of them. Once the last string snapped free, Steve staggered and fell back on the floor. That single bite was a lucky one for the standing cadaver. With the blood supply to Steve's brain sharply reduced, rational thoughts and any notion of defense quickly evaporated. For the moment, the zombie ceased its attack and stood contentedly and oblivious within the casket, while working its teeth on the tough strands of flesh and pieces of vocal cord.

Steve drained of blood so quickly he didn't think to use his hand to cover the outpour. He began to spasm incoherently and his pooling blood rapidly eclipsed his son's.

The hungry Chinese man swallowed the last of his bite and looked over towards the squirming activity. Jason was rolling in pain while the larger and closer victim showed himself an easier target. Without real thought, it stepped out of the coffin towards them, but somewhat deliberately, it fell over to land on top of Steve.

Now beyond reason and response, Steve didn't resist as the zombie pulled up his t-shirt and buried its face into his soft belly.

Steve could do little more than emit a low guttural moan when a quick succession of bites dug into him.

Jenna was lost in terror. Her span of vision was limited and registered the greatest degree of movement which was her son, who still rolled around in pain. He was still very much alive. That was her boy suffering!

She broke free of her panic and raced towards Jason. She leapt over the coffin and past the nearly naked attacker sprawled across her husband's midsection. The zombie was too busy to notice her.

She went over to her son and lifted him to her, cradling him within her arms. "Oh my God!" she screamed.

The sound of her voice cut through her husband's pain and fog, and it prompted his final coherent thought. His weak moans took on a measure of strength and he muttered, "Gawh, Gawh!" He only had the strength to say it twice.

She knew he meant to say, *Go! Go!*

While her mind told her to pull the half-naked attacker away from her husband, her gut told her to take her son and run. In answer to any uncertainty she might have had, she heard a soft plea from Jason.

"Mommy," Jason cried in a tired and dreamy tone. More than that, the single word was said in a scared voice that seemed less than half his age, and it was a title he hadn't used in years. Since he was four, he always knew her as *Mom*.

She lifted up her eleven year old son and rushed him into the hallway. Realizing the downpour of blood was from his arm, she decided to take him into the bathroom. Her immediate reasoning was to stop the bleeding.

Once inside, she slammed the door shut and set the lock. The small room echoed and amplified the sounds of hers and Jason's heavy breathing. She couldn't hear anything else beyond that.

In the living room, Steve drifted off into oblivion while the Chinese man ate in relative peace. Its happy grunts and moans, while it chewed and slurped its first real meal, weren't loud enough to carry through the locked bathroom door.

Jenna frantically went through the medicine cabinet. In her desperate search, she shoved away vials and tubes of useless things like aspirin, makeup and other care products. They clattered into the sink as she made her way through. She found nothing to dress her son's wound, only a useless box of band aids designed for basic everyday cuts. That landed in the sink, too.

Her only consolation was a bottle of rubbing alcohol. She grabbed it, opened it and poured it over Jason's arm. Her soothing coos did little to allay his renewed screams from the crisp assault of antiseptic. In the end, the best she could do was to use a small hand towel to dress his wound.

Agonizing moments passed before her son slowed his screams of pain. She settled in to sit on the floor with him pulled closer into her arms. She began to rock back and fourth to comfort him as much as herself. However, she could do little to calm his lingering whimpers and she added to the noise with feeble and soothing words. Blood from his arm saturated the makeshift dressing and began to drip onto the tiled floor of the bathroom.

Helpless to do anything else, she ran her blood-stained fingers through his hair and softly hummed an old nursery song with a broken and cracked voice. She was more concerned with the blood she transferred into his blond hair than to worry about the sounds of her feeble melody carrying through the door. Though only his arm was bit, there was blood everywhere, on her, on him, on the tiled floor, and on the cabinet she leaned against with him in her embrace. Still, she mostly worried about the blood in his hair.

An approaching patter of bare feet along the wood floor of the hallway caught her attention and she stopped her weak humming to listen. The steps were awkward, slapping hard upon each foot-fall, and made with a drunken rhythm. She held her breath and gently covered her son's mouth to mute his whimpers.

A sharp crash of a fist slammed against the door, followed by a sloppy thump from the weight of the body that fell into it. She could hear the fleshy squeak of a blood drenched chest rubbing against the door while the fists went on to pound with renewed vigor.

Her body jumped at each strike. However, Jason was weak and drifting into sleep. He didn't react to her repeated stiff reactions, and she wasn't sure if she should be grateful for his artificial peace or worried about his condition.

The banging settled into a slow, menacing rhythm. Though terrified and fighting back an urge to scream, Jenna chose to make no more sounds. But it was too late and the clumsy thuds against the door went on with a knowledge that she and her son were inside.

The door held but the assault continued. The attacker couldn't get in but they couldn't get out. Yet she found no comfort in their relative safety and she began to understand what eternity really felt like. Time stretched and only marked itself with each clattering toll against the door.

Then a second set of fists collided higher up against the door and the thin wood began to rattle more precariously in its frame.

A deformed shape of her husband's voice bellowed from the other side. It was an inhuman sound and only hinted at the resonance of the man she loved. It sounded angry, hungry and driven. It was not her man. She whimpered and forced herself to ignore the sounds while giving renewed attention to her son. There wasn't much for her to do other than to stroke his hair. Her lips quivered and she strained not to scream while her fingers worked their way through the dull, bloody wetness of her son's hair.

Beyond that, she tried to forget that the bathroom door wasn't very solid, and was constructed of little more than two thin sheets of painted plywood over a flimsy frame.

Despite her logical fears, she focused on the relative safety she felt and continued to caress her son's hair, though he was asleep and couldn't appreciate it. She held onto that simple act in an effort to lull her mind away from her inescapable reality.

After a time, she dozed off with that fabricated comfort. The monotonous drone of fists striking against the door continued unabated.

*   *   *

Jenna had no way to gauge time and could have been asleep for minutes or hours for all she knew. She only knew that her son hadn't moved since he fell asleep. His head still rested on her lap.

Furious clamoring at the door filled the bathroom, made more ominous with its echo bouncing against the walls of the small room. She looked over at the rattling door. She didn't know if it was her imagination, but the door was now shaking more liberally within its frame and the bang of fists upon it seemed somehow muted and less solid. She hoped it was her imagination, because she thought she heard a hint of crinkling behind each impact. Could that be the wood beginning to splinter? She didn't want to know.

She tried to stroke her son's hair but that *normal* act only gave her more reason for fear and dread. His hair was now matted and clumped with dried blood, and her fingers had nowhere to go without getting snagged. Worse was how limply his head moved to her motions.

She gently turned the boy's head to face her.

Gray skin and blue lips told her everything.

No! Please God, No! she cried within herself.

God didn't answer but Jason did. He opened his eyes and growled.

She looked into his eyes. The irises had collapsed in death and the blue in them was all but completely gone except for a slim mocking band that encircled a milky black void. The boy snarled up at her but there wasn't real rage or hate behind it. It was only instinct.

As a woman, she saw beyond this single dimension of her immediate danger. For her, this was the death of all promise, the death of her love and purpose. Accenting that, were the sounds of death and murder from her other love as he pounded on the other side of the door.

When the boy turned his head and took his first bite into her leg, she didn't resist. What was the point?

She only flinched at the pain of each bite and continued to stroke his hair with a loving hand, while she listened to the slurping and grinding noises he made. Her only consolation was her not having to see his face again. Jason's head dug itself deeper into her leg without bothering to lift up while he chewed. She sighed morosely. She never could get him to display proper manners at the dinner table.

*   *   *

Hours later, the two undead men in the hallway finally broke through the door. Both the Chinese man and former father charged inside, ready to grab and tear with their bloody and mutilated hands. Their frenzy died as quickly as they stumbled into the small bathroom.

Almost instantly, their bodies slumped with what seemed like boredom and disinterest. They showed no sense of disappointment or frustration over their hours of wasted effort on the door, only to discover two more of their kind, both bloody and gray. The female was the most disfigured of all of them since most of her left thigh and calf was little more than caked, bloody gristle upon bone.

The two invaders turned first to exit through the splintered door and out to wander the house. The two others followed. The smaller of the two, once thin as a rail, now sported a pot belly filled with the flesh of the one that hobbled along behind him.

The remainder of the Christmas festivities enjoyed that day was of the four zombies dumbly moving about the house. Numerous items throughout were either knocked over or broken while they mindlessly explored with their dead minds.

Eventually, and without plan or design, a lamp on a coffee table was knocked over. It fell into the living room window, shattering the glass. It wasn't a particularly windy day, but it was enough to filter through the broken window and disturb the curtains.

Everything in the house was still except for the curtains which fluttered with each soft gust of wind. Of course there was the Christmas tree. It had survived the zombies' previous curiosity and it stood proudly erected next to the flowing curtains with cheerful and blinking lights.

They might have overlooked the easy flow of the curtains if not for the lights of the tree both illuminating and casting moving shadows on the windy fabric. One by one, they were drawn to the quiet activity and found their way out of the house, falling out and to the lawn below the window.

None of them were capable of any thought beyond hunger as they left. If they were able, maybe they would have had a passing thought that their escape was a gift of sorts, something they might not have discovered without help from the brightly lit Christmas tree.

But then again, they ignored the cuts and gashes carved into their dead bodies by the glass shards they had to push through to leave the house.

Within the home they escaped was an accounting, a microcosm of basic exponential mathematics. It had started with one. Then two. Then four.

With the four now free, the math would go on from there.

In the end, it didn't take a billion Chinese to overtake America. It only took one.

And it didn't stop there.

CHRISTMAS HARVEST

LANCE LOOPER

The holiday season was Death's favorite time to harvest. The sweeping despair of losing a loved one during Christmas is an emotion he so loved to bear witness to. And to satisfy this craving, every year he'd pick a particularly cozy place to visit. The type of community that looked forward to its big Christmas Day parade with pick-up trucks pulling floats created by the Women's Auxiliary and Future Desk Monkeys of America, as he watched the sorrow unfold as he did God's bidding with the Devil's rage.

Eversville looked to be an ideal place from which to do this year's collecting. It was small, so each death would be felt. And it was rife with children who would carry the pain of losing a parent for all their days, until years from now when it was time for him to come for them.

But standing there in the shadows, watching the large Christmas tree aglow in the center of town, he was starting to get anxious. The streets were unexpectedly quiet even for a night so bitterly cold. He'd seen only a few people out and about and he might have taken one of them, but they were each alone. Taking someone who was alone was wholly unsatisfying because it could be hours before their absence was noticed.

No, he would wait for a group. Any minute now a family was bound to leave one of the shops. And weighed down by packages, he'd watch as one of them would mindlessly wander into the path of an oncoming bus. The family would scream and Death might even reveal himself to them in their panic. He did love to make his presence known at times like that.

The way those who saw him appear would later describe him was priceless. Sure, he was scary enough with his flowing black robes and gleaming blade, but the way his appearance was retold by those he showed himself to magnified the horror by leaps and bounds.

On the wall next to which he was standing, a mural several stories tall was painted of the man the town was named for. The inscription said he was a Civil War general who died in battle. Death recognized him. The artist was generous to minimize the general's considerable nose and wiry eyebrows and give him a graceful, noble, stare, but Death recognized him all the same. He remembered all of them. He wondered how these citizens would feel about their beloved general if they knew he really died a drunk many years after the war ended.

The snow blanketing the streets and sidewalks looked oddly undisturbed, even the footprints from the people he had seen were now mostly filled in by fresh snowfall.

And it wasn't just foot traffic that seemed light. The lights on Main Street changed from green to yellow to red with no cars around to receive the message. Finally, after almost an hour, frustration and boredom got the best of him and he drifted down into the street. The fluttering of his dark robe in the wind thundered through the silence. He considered giving up and abandoning this post altogether. After all, it was a cold night. And being Christmas Eve, everyone was probably tucked into bed dreaming of sugar plumbs.

But then he noticed a woman walking in his direction, completely blind to him, of course. Under the streetlight, he could see she was wearing a particularly tacky red and green sweater with what looked like little Santas on the sleeves. He tightened his grip on his scythe, its curved blade hovering high above his hood. It wasn't how he preferred it, her being alone and all, but he might not see anyone else tonight. Besides, tomorrow was Christmas and this square would be teeming with people. It would make quite an impression when the good folks of Eversville discovered one of their own had died on Christmas Eve and was left alone to freeze solid while they slept comfortably in their beds.

As the woman walked closer, it struck him that she wasn't wearing a coat. She must be freezing. He began moving toward her and noticed for the first time her vacant stare. He thought it odd that despite only wearing a sweater in this bitter cold, there was no urgency about her. She shuffled in slow, labored movements, as if critical thinking was required to get one foot in front of the other.

She was within a few steps of him and now he'd come to the conclusion she was likely homeless, and probably schizophrenic. It struck him how often the two go hand-in-hand. This sapped all the joy out of the chore. Still, there was a quota to make and he was already off to a slow start.

He planted the handle of the scythe in the snow and swung it around three times, the blade making a whooshing sound as it moved through the air over his head. But nothing happened. Instead of dropping dead in the snow, the woman kept walking. Death twirled the sickle again and still nothing.

This was preposterous! How was this woman resistant to Death's call? She was very close to him now and he noticed something that was much more alarming than her seeming immunity to death. She was looking at him. Before he could react, the woman lunged for him and bit into his arm. It didn't hurt of course, but it was as confusing as it was infuriating. Not only was this person impervious to his spell, but she could see him!

Frustrated, he wrested his bony arm free from her teeth and swung the scythe in a downward arc. The motion was almost instinct, and not very forceful without the use of both hands. Nevertheless, the blade severed the woman's head in a swift, short swipe.

She collapsed into the snow, her head rolling off the curb and into the street. He'd never actually used the blade in this manner and was surprised by how naturally it came to him. And the cut it delivered, clean and effortless, was a thing of beauty. In the entire course of human existence, he'd never seen anyone who was immune to death. And that this woman knew he was there was of even greater concern.

He must have been quite distracted, because when he finally looked up from the severed head, there was a crowd of people now in the square. They were dressed for the season with elf outfits trimmed with pointy hats and shoes; others were sporting colorful sport coats and ties that lit up in red and green lights. And there were at least three Santas. He felt a momentary pang of excitement; maybe there was some joy to be had tonight after all. But the hope faded when he saw their black, lifeless eyes.

And then he noticed the way they were moving. Not as much how they were moving, which was the same aimless stroll as the woman, but where they were moving. All of them, and he put the number at two-dozen or more, were meandering more or less in his direction. One of them lost his footing as he attempted to step off the sidewalk and into the street. Once on the ground, he struggled sluggishly in the deep snow to return to a standing position.

Then the formation changed. The crowd narrowed on the corners and he realized they were not just heading his direction, but they were heading directly for him. He picked one out from the crowd, a fat man in a white parka, and twirled the scythe around three times with exceptional urgency. Nothing.

The image of himself flashing through the crowd, swinging his scythe indiscriminately, came to mind. But he remembered the woman's bite and thought better of it.

He swung around as a pale hand came down on his shoulder. He'd been so focused on the crowd of people in the square that he didn't notice another group coming up from behind. There weren't as many behind him, but they were much closer, starting with the one that now had a handful of his robe. He swung the scythe and the long, curved blade caught the man above the elbow, slicing through the arm like butter and burying itself deep in his torso. Death drew the blade back, expecting the man to fall down or scream in pain, but he did neither, just staggered backwards a bit. After regaining his balance, he kept coming. He didn't even throw a passing glance to the limb falling to the snow, much less the gaping hole in his chest.

While this was happening, others grabbed Death, pulling and clawing. One even grabbed the scythe's handle. Realizing he was hopelessly outmatched, Death spun the blade and vaporized, leaving the zombies grasping and biting at the cold, thin air.

Once again on the roof of the pastry shop, Death could see almost the entire square. It was now packed with these lifeless, aimless people. The group from which he'd just escaped was still huddled in a semicircle, gazing around as they wondered where their prey had gotten off to. The order of the crowd had disintegrated, and instead of moving in one singular direction, their paths were now random.

A piercing blast exploded in the snowy air and down on the street one of the zombies fell. Even from the roof, Death could see the damage the gunshot had done. It looked male but Death couldn't be certain, the body now lying in the snow with a fist-sized hole tunneled through its head.

Voices rose in the distance. It had been so quiet for so long, it took several seconds for the sound to register. The voices were celebratory and were getting closer. On the edge of the square a group of men emerged from the darkness into the yellow and red glow of the holiday lights. There were four of them, armed like they meant to invade a small country.

Death watched as the crowd below began to loosely reorient and drift toward the men. Another shot rang out and another of the crowd staggered back, struck in the arm. But this did nothing to deter the rest of the crowd because they kept moving without a glance to their wounded comrade. The men with guns began firing into the crowd at random. One of them, a particularly fat one, was just firing his pistol into the air.

Death twirled his blade above his head and watched as the fat man crumpled to the snow a second later, steam rising from the blood pooling near his head. It took the others several moments to notice. When they did, the hollering stopped and they gathered around the body, confused and very clearly frightened.

With another wave of the blade, Death was moving toward the group. He hovered just inches over them as they belligerently tried to figure out what happened. The confusion lasted almost a full minute until one of them noticed the crowd now moving toward them. That brought the argument to a halt, but Death suspected even if they debated for the balance of time; they'd never have the common sense to figure out that a bullet coming back down travels at the same velocity as when it's fired into the air. There was a brief argument about whether to take the fat one with them, but they decided against it and were gone as quickly as they came.

In less than a minute, the horde was upon the dead fat man, dropping to their knees and pawing at him. As Death watched from above, the crowd fought over the corpse, clumsily slapping at one another. Several of them looked up at him, even raising their hands to him, but the fat man ultimately owned their attention. Others were already sinking their teeth into the still warm flesh, blood flowing down their chins. Death watched them feast on the fat man, while his robe fluttered in the wind. For the first time in an eternity he felt a chill.

He turned at the sound of whispers somewhere behind him. There were three men ducking into the drug store, their eyes trained on the undead horde feasting on the fat man. Death floated toward the entrance of the drug store where one of the men stood on watch while the others were inside. Death fluttered to the ground in front of the man, but was never seen. The man standing guard looked right past him, and to the huddled mass fighting over the fat man's bloody stumps.

After a few minutes inside, the men came out of the store, each of them carrying a cardboard box. On the way through the door, the last man slipped, spilling the contents of his box across the snowy sidewalk. Cereal boxes and cans of food slid every which way. The others scrambled to put the things back in the box and helped the man to his feet. The crowd feasting on the fat man heard the clanging of the cans and turned toward the noise. When the men noticed this, a renewed sense of urgency seemed to wash over them and they hastened their retreat into the shadows beyond the square.

Intrigued, Death followed the men into the darkness. Their tension, as well as their silence, seemed to fade the further they got from the town square. They stopped at a house along the avenue where a family congregated on the front porch. A man and a woman, as well as two teenaged girls, were huddled around a trash barrel, the contents ablaze, bits of glowing ash dancing on the cold wind as they were swept into the night.

The men from the drug store didn't seem to know these people, but they opened one of the boxes and handed the man several items from inside. After a brief bit of conversation, one of the men opened another box and looked through its contents. After a moment, he pulled a magazine from the box and handed it to one of the teenagers. She took it gratefully and began flipping through it, stopping once to show the other girl something on the page.

The men closed their boxes and continued on, but not before leaving the family with a small piece of paper. The woman read it and smiled. She handed it to the man and he also smiled and folded the slip of paper into his coat pocket. The family hugged their visitors goodbye and turned their attention back to the fire as they left. This continued for more than an hour, these men passing out the contents of their boxes to these tiny tribes they came across. And every person they saw got one of the little slips of paper. And every person reading it laughed.

When their boxes were empty, Death followed the men to a giant warehouse in the industrial district.

The first rays of sunlight took Death by surprise. It was dawn on Christmas morning and he couldn't remember the last time he'd seen the sunrise. He hadn't worked the morning shift in generations.

On the horizon, he saw a group of people walking toward the warehouse. There must have been two hundred or more, all walking in a huddled group, pushing carts and talking. They filed into the warehouse for probably half an hour. Inside it was crowded with people and each of the doors was fortified with massive chains and padlocks from the inside. In the middle of the warehouse, was a tall Christmas tree. Kids of all ages were running around the tree, decorating it and singing Christmas carols. The adults were watching them with pained, tired smiles. They were also piling gifts under the tree. Some of these were wrapped in stunning red paper with silver bows while others were stuffed into worn paper sacks with pictures of holly or bells drawn in black or colored marker.

In one corner, a man was cooking and another was serving warm cider in paper cups.

Death floated unseen above and watched them exchange presents, food and weapons, the items taking the place of electronics, sweaters, ties and coffee mugs. Whatever was going on outside, these people were managing to forget about it for now. Death watched a while longer as the men cleaned weapons and traded tips about which ammunition to use and when.

The floor of the warehouse was littered with the little slips of paper the men were handing out the previous night.

Death got close enough to read the writing:

> *The dead have risen, I've heard them say*
> *But why let it ruin Christmas Day?*
> *Dec. 25th, Eagle Wings Depository*

In the glow of the warehouse Christmas tree, Death decided to put a moratorium on the harvest. Well, sort of.

While these refugees spent Christmas day trying to forget what was happening outside, he blew through the village swinging his blade with deadly precision and staggering frequency. He reaped all day and all night, until the lifeless heads of the undead clogged the streets. He came on them suddenly and furiously, cutting down entire herds before their impaired faculties could ever grasp what was happening.

To be sure, the work wasn't as rewarding as if they'd been true-blue humans. These undead things no doubt were void of any emotion, thus robbing Death of a particularly delicious part of the experience. But if the world was now being fought over by humans and these soulless things, he knew which side he'd come down on.

He really didn't have any choice.

After all, what use would he be in a world populated only by the dead?

UPON A MIDNIGHT CLEAR

SEAN GRIGSBY

Richard Kearns handed his ticket to the usher and entered the crowded auditorium. Hundreds were already seated and waiting for the program to start. Morton City was once again hosting the annual Singing Christmas Tree at the Cerulean Opera House. The entire evening was centered on an enormous, heavily decorated evergreen in which the opera's star performers sang various holiday favorites. Every year was a battle to win the coveted spot at the top of the tree. Richard had never attended the event, nor cared to. He always had some evil-doer to apprehend, some hapless schmuck to save. But this year was different. The city had been quiet and his newest girlfriend, Eva Summers, was the star atop the green giant.

The smell of cinnamon and dusty, old curtains welcomed him as he took his seat. He had specifically asked for an outside chair near the far right exit. Bunker had agreed to take watch so he could have the night off but experience dictated there was always a chance he would have to slip away unseen. A bald man in his sixties sat next to him and was joined by a tall, wrinkled woman wearing a fur coat. They reeked of musk and cigar smoke that made his eyes water and Richard remembered why he didn't attend the theater.

The crowd's muffled banter began to die down as the lights dimmed and the chorus entered from stage right. They inched their way up the tree, following the built-in platform that spiraled around it, Eva leading the way. She winked at Richard and he smiled back with the enthusiasm of a proud parent. She wore a beautiful sparkling, green dress. Her red hair flowing above it made her look like a walking bow of holly.

The last to enter on stage was a short, portly man with a thick brown mustache; a tenor more than likely. It would fit the poorly attempted resemblance to Pavarotti. He wore a blue captain's coat with golden tassels hanging from the shoulders and a similarly colored admiral's hat that made him look like a derelict Cap'n Crunch.

He positioned himself at the base of the tree and exuded an arrogant grin as if he was carrying the entire cast on his shoulders. Richard couldn't help himself from laughing at the ridiculous man, but figured that it played some part in the show. The conductor climbed to his podium and the theater burst into applause. Taking a quick bow toward the patrons, he turned back to the stage and lifted both hands to alert the performers. The towering pine became colorfully illuminated as the choir belted out an arrangement of *Carol of the Bells*. The lights danced in sequence with the tempo, mixing blues, reds, and greens. Richard was impressed. He decided he should take more nights off, give Bunker a chance to flex his muscles. The song ended and was received with a storm of ovation.

"You soulless hack!"

Richard looked all around him to find the voice. His curiosity was answered as Cap'n Pavarotti stepped out from the glowing tannenbaum with a long barreled revolver in his grip. A single shot penetrated the conductor's forehead and sent him hurtling backwards into the orchestra pit below. The accompanying crash of instruments and all-too-common horrified screams was cue enough for Richard.

Can't get one night, he thought to himself as he rushed through the nearest exit. The doors locked behind, and he paused to turn his head, but decided to deal with it when he came back. Ushers had hurried to each door leading out, locked, and barred them with large metal poles. They each removed a handgun from their thick, red vests and took a bullying aim. The frantic mob began to scramble for the rear exit, retreating away from the crazed gunman. Before they could charge through the ushers, they were held back by a shotgun blast ripping overhead. A tall, blonde woman wearing a Viking helmet and armored one-piece appeared before the crowd.

"Please return to your seats for the remainder of the performance," her voice squeaked in a way that made her sound like Olive Oyl.

The terrified spectators froze in their tracks, several hands lifted into the air. A few girls and a lanky man sobbed quietly, trying hard to avoid any attention.

"*I said move,*" her speech now sharp.

They complied. Each of them fought and clawed to return to their seats. They had nowhere left to run.

"Thank you, Diva," said the man in the blue hat. "Ladies and gentleman, *I*...am the Showboat!"

He raised his arms as if expecting a barrage of approving claps. They came not. The lumbering blonde marched down the left aisle and stood below him in front of the stage. She steadied the double barrels at the side of her hip.

In a side hall, Richard was now dressed in black body armor, helmet, and eye mask to become Battalion, one of Morton City's many radical crime fighters. Propped up against the door leading into the auditorium, he attached his arm cannon. It was a large, black grenade launcher that clicked into place over his right arm. He lost the benefit of his dominant hand but gained the advantage of high-powered explosives.

He pulled on the door and found it was jammed shut. A brassy voice was vibrating against the metal. Battalion slid up along the wall to get a better look through the small pane of glass.

Great, he thought, *another idiot villain.*

"This production is now under my lead," the Showboat said. "You will no longer have to sit through this talentless, Mickey Mouse crap. But to ensure you remain a *captive* audience," he grinned at Diva, "how about one more Christmas song?"

The faces of the hostage audience were mixtures of confusion and horror. Was this guy serious? He rang out with the Dean Martin classic.

"*Oh, the weather outside is frightful.*"

Diva reached behind her back to pull out a small gas mask. She began singing along even as she fit it around her chipmunk face. The ushers along the walls followed her lead and covered themselves with similar masks.

"*And since we've no place to go,*" Showboat turned to the performers who had wisely remained in the tree, "*Sing,* damn it!"

They jolted to life and obeyed. And as they hit the chorus of *Let it Snow*, it did just that. Blueish white flakes began to fall from the rafters. The hapless theater-goers were covered in the cold wet snow. It was thick and icy and the audience choked and coughed but couldn't help inhaling the strange flurries. The singing dropped off. Showboat held his hand up in an "ok" toward the ushers near the ceiling. The spectators stopped moving.

"My dear audience, the sensation you are feeling is the deep paralysis induced by the Ondskalphate you are absorbing; a chemical of my own making."

The mouths of the crowd drooped and their heads hung limp. The muffled groans and assuring whispers had completely dissolved. He now had at his attention over three hundred motionless people.

Battalion could only watch. He didn't want to endanger the hostages and he still hadn't decided on a plan of action. There was an unknown number of armed ushers and he could tell the blonde had an itchy trigger finger.

The spotlights spun and joined together to shine upon Showboat as he crooned an aria from *Carmen*. Diva removed her mask and gazed up in adoration. The stilled crowd stared as well, like a gang of vegetables, while he shook out a whiny vibrato. Battalion imagined that the worst part of being paralyzed here was the inability to inspire gunfire and end the pain. As he belted a flat high *A* for what seemed like an hour, a terrible moan came from the middle row of seats.

"Who the hell is ruining my performance?"

Another groan came louder. Someone in the audience was stirring.

"Diva, darling," his face scrunched, "would you do me a favor and *blow a hole through that miserable ingrate's chest*!"

She complied and lunged up the right aisle toward the commotion. Battalion saw his opportunity and dashed for the upper mezzanine. It had been closed off for The Singing Christmas Tree to make it a more intimate setting.

What a wonderful job they did, he thought sarcastically, racing up the back staircase to take out an oblivious usher.

Diva found the convulsing man who made no attempt to quiet himself. She threw him to the aisle floor and blasted a shell into his ribcage, as instructed. The already red carpet darkened under him with the addition of fresh blood. Closing her eyes and smiling with relief, she breathed in deeply through her nose, smelling the char and smoke of gunpowder. She removed the Viking helmet, placed it on the dead man's head, and began laughing.

"Will you *please* quit playing around?" Showboat asked.

"Sure thing, Mr. S."

Before she could return to the stage, the body beneath her twitched and started pulling itself back up, growling. The Showboat and his accomplices were too bewildered to speak; to move. All of the previously frozen attendants began writhing in their seats. Their faces were lifeless, their howls deafening. The opera house shook with the bustling sound of a macabre marketplace. The dead man with the Viking helmet staggered toward the screaming blonde. Diva discharged another shot into him but it did less to stop him than the previous gory hole she had made. The mass of them surrounded her. Her cries were dwarfed by their loud and endless and aching moans. They seized her, stretching her arms and legs as if she was being drawn and quartered. She kept screaming. They chewed into her like pigs to the slop. The rest made their way toward the stage. Showboat began firing off random shots into the approaching horde he had created.

They continued to maul Diva. Her arms gave and the relentless mob ripped them from her body. Some of them attacked the freshly torn nubs, fighting for them like the last Christmas drumstick. The armor fell apart revealing her naked breasts. Bullets exploded into the attackers from every direction but they continued their assault, unaffected. Grubbing fists punched into her, flinging intestines and lungs. When they had their fill of her, they turned to the ushers along the walls of the theater.

Battalion entered the mezzanine and all of his strategies crumbled apart as he looked on the carnage below. He saw the ushers firing at the advancing creatures. He looked toward the stage. Showboat had run out of bullets and was swinging his revolver at the group surrounding him. A pair of twin little girls pounced and bit into each side of his neck.

The opera singers were bustling one by one down the tree but the things were on them quicker than they could escape. Eva still stood at the top, screaming her head off. Battalion's eyes darted around for a way to her and saw that a naked, armless shell of a woman had stumbled onto the stage. It was the gun-happy blonde, or what was left of her. She looked up the expanse of the Christmas tree and attempted to climb it. Her legs slipped off of the branches and she fell backwards. The others scrambled over her and started up the tree. Eva saw no way out and threw herself off, landing on the stage with a loud *smack*.

"No!" he screamed.

Battalion leapt for a curtain and swung toward the stage, the crowd grabbing at his legs as he swooped above them. Landing next to her, he tried for a pulse but couldn't get a good position. His hands were trembling too much. More of them, including the mangled ushers, climbed onto the stage and enveloped the crime fighter as he held Eva's lifeless body. Their arms grabbed at the air, eyes fixed on wounded prey, slime and blood oozing from their mouths.

Battalion cocked his arm cannon toward a few standing in front of the brick wall at the back of the stage. The armless blonde was among them. He blasted a bomb in their direction, covered his head, and spread out on top of Eva. The grenade went off instantly, sending a blanket of fire over them. The entire building shook and threw the crazed patrons to the ground. Stone and guts rained onto the stage, bringing a terrible stench and a crimson cloud of gore.

He threw Eva over his shoulder, escaping through the hole that had been blown open, out onto the busy street outside. The black Mustang was parked two blocks down and he loped after it, pushing multiple pedestrians out of his path. His only concern was Eva and he didn't know if she was still breathing.

The legion of infected cannibals followed through the opening and began attacking citizens wandering the sidewalk. A man in a business suit was pummeled to the ground. Rotting fingers sank into his eye sockets and blunt teeth ripped the flesh from his chest. A horribly disfigured Showboat tackled a young couple walking their poodle. The dog skipped away, yipping and dragging a severed hand at the end of its leash.

A corner Santa Claus rang a bell for generous donations. The large flock each dropped whatever heart or leg they were devouring and glared at the man in the red suit. The golden bell rang out into the cold night air along with his jovial "Ho, Ho, Ho's". He was clueless of what lumbered slowly behind him. Turning around, he dropped his bell and cried out as the entire swarm focused their attention on him. He pumped his legs backwards and tumbled over the collection stand, sending coins scuttling into the street as they charged onto him.

Battalion made it to the car and laid his girlfriend inside. Jumping into the driver's seat, he removed his cannon, threw it to the floor below Eva, started the engine and stepped on the gas pedal. He pressed a small, green button on the dash and a dial tone sounded. It rang twice before a gruff voice answered.

"What you want, B?"

"I'm in deep shit, Scorch."

"You need me to suit up?"

"You might want to," Battalion was out of breath, "but I need somewhere to regroup."

"Come by the store then," he hung up.

Battalion made a sharp left and glanced at Eva. Her eyes were still closed and she swayed violently with the motion of the vehicle. He looked back at the road and noticed several dark figures a few hundred yards ahead. He secured the locks and squinted to make out who it was outside of the nearing bank building. As he passed, he saw a woman in tight fitting, pink leather swinging a large whip in each hand. Stumbling toward her were three bloody cadavers. He slammed the brakes and looked into the rear view mirror. She hooked one body around the leg and sent it flying into the air. It landed hard on its head with a loud *squish* against the asphalt. Battalion popped the Mustang in reverse, rolling over the first body and slamming the others into the bricks behind it.

"You all right, Lash?" he called through the passenger window.

"Thank God it's you. I don't know what the hell is going on," Lash said.

"Hell is exactly what's going on. I'm headed to Scorch's. I can shed some light on this and then we can figure out what to do from..."

One of the dead men climbed up from under the car. There was nothing below his chest except mangled intestines hanging from a bloody gash. He clawed into the window on two arms and pulled Eva out and onto the ground. Battalion screamed in helplessness while the woman in leather stabbed a dagger into the creep's back. Battalion fell out of the car, crawled toward them, and wrestled the thing off of Eva. He hammered several punches into the zombie's head until there was nothing left but gobs of bone and puss. He grabbed Eva and inspected her for bites. A huge chunk of meat was missing from her left shoulder and she was bleeding intensely. Battalion began crying. He held her tight and sobbed into her green dress.

Lash put her hand against him. He looked back at her.

"Lash, I..."

"I better drive," she said.

He stood, still bawling, and turned to the car. Lash went around to the driver's side and sat down. A gurgling wail sounded from behind and Battalion twisted around. Eva sat up and bared her teeth in a menacing scowl. Battalion reached to the side for his glaive. She clambered toward him. He slashed a three-bladed weapon against her throat and sent the head rolling down the sidewalk.

The body dropped to the concrete and his did the same, head in his hands, weeping. Lash ran back around, dragged him into the vehicle, and sped off. He blacked out as the streetlamps passed with increasing speed overhead.

He woke to the sound of a loud, steady knocking. His eyes were closed and the exhaustion was still wearing off. *Bump...bump*, it came again. There was no tempo to it, the radio was off. His eyes opened and he saw Lash still driving, turning the wheel in jerky motions. He sat up and quickly flinched back in his seat as a body collided with the windshield.

"Damn it," she said.

Lash swerved left, dodging an abandoned Neon. The neighborhood was dark except for the occasional twinkling streetlight. There were zombies flooding the street, debris and wreckage all around. How long had he been out? The car accelerated and smashed into an obese woman, spraying her entrails onto the hood.

"These things are everywhere," Lash said, pressing a button to spray cleaner onto the glass.

She could feel his disapproving glare. "It's not like everything you have isn't armored."

This didn't help.

"I'll pay for a paint job, that is if there's anyone left to do it," she said.

He didn't respond, didn't feel like talking. The mindless drones kept trailing along the pavement. The same people he protected from muggers and plots of world domination were now the very things he was fighting against. A kid with a torn out throat limped with a boom box on his shoulder. Dead shoppers still lugged around their shiny papered boxes. A blood-soaked mother pushed along a stroller missing its front right wheel.

He looked away.

They pulled up to J.B.'s Hardware Store and saw the windows were busted and boarded up from inside.

"Think he made it?" Battalion asked climbing out of the car.

"One way to find out," she replied, hurrying up to the smoke-stained door.

Lash knocked while Battalion watched her back, cannon loaded. The nearest zombies were a couple hundred feet away. It was enough space to buy them an entrance but it had to be quick. There was no sound on the other side of the barricaded door. Lash knocked again, harder and faster this time.

The things were getting closer.

"Call him from your car."

"No time," he said.

He whipped out his three-pronged glaive and jammed it into the crack near the doorknob. The groans grew louder and closer. He jiggled at it but the door wouldn't budge.

"*Hurry...*" she whispered.

Lifting an armored boot, he kicked it open and rushed in with Lash on his tail. He lifted his head and swore aloud as a cloud of hot flames rushed toward them. Lash pushed him to the ground and dove out of the way. The burning orange flames flew over them, filling the room with smoke, making it hard to breathe. The inferno subsided and they got to their feet.

"You better 'nounce yourself before you get burnt!" a voice said.

Scorch stood with his palm raised toward them, a smoking hole where the blaze had burst forth. He had crazed charcoal hair and wore red lens goggles that hid his eyes. There was a bulky gas tank strapped to his back, connected to multiple tubes encircling his arms and attached to each gloved hand.

"Well, don't just stand there, get the damned door shut before we all get chomped!"

Battalion closed the door. Scorch brought in a pile of two-by-four's, nails, and a hammer and they began securing the wood against the entrance.

"Seems your shit leaked into my backyard," Scorch grinned.

"When did they get here?" Battalion asked.

"'Bout twenty minutes ago. I kept hearin' this awful racket like a bunch of retards were selling candy bars. I came from around back and saw a bunch of 'em breaking through the windows. Fire kept 'em away but didn't hurt 'em at all."

"What the hell are they?" Lash asked.

"Some wannabe villain at the opera house doused the audience with a chemical he concocted. They didn't move for a while but when they did..." Battalion started.

"Zombies is what they are! Cold blooded, eat-your-ass zombies?" Scorch interrupted, removing his goggles.

"It seems that way. There must be an antidote," Battalion said.

"There's no antidote for being dead," Lash said.

Battalion knew she was right. The chemical didn't just *turn* them, it *killed* them. The only solution would be to destroy them all before it spread further.

Scorch led them deeper into the store. It was much larger than the exterior suggested. He had cleared everything out and set up his arsenal of flammable weaponry. It was more like a large warehouse with only a few relics of the hardware store it had once been. A pile of Christmas trees lay at the base of the far left wall. Chainsaws and power tools were strewn out elsewhere.

They followed him to the back where the glow of a small television lit up the room in a blue haze.

"I've been watchin' for reports. This shit's spread over the city at a bullet's pace. Started at the Cerulean, you said?"

"Yeah, I found Lash fighting off a group of them on 29th," Battalion said.

"Thought it was a bank robbery," she added. "They got Eva."

"Aw, hell, B. I'm sorry," Scorch said and reached into a desk and pulled out a small piece of glass. "Where's Bunker?"

Bunker. He had completely forgotten. Battalion stepped away and dialed his cell. It rang a few times and went to voicemail.

"Bunker, it's me. Lash and I are at Scorch's. I need you to call me ASAP."

He made sure the volume was loud enough to hear and placed the phone back into his belt. Scorch had one fiery finger lit under a small glass bulb and he held it to his mouth. He blew the smoke out above him and wheezed a round of coughs.

"You're still doin' that crap?" Battalion asked.

"Only when I'm stressed."

"You're always stressed," Lash said.

"Yeah, well, it's a tough city."

"Meth-head crime fighter..." Battalion shook his head.

"Can we get passed this petty shit? We have bigger problems and we need to move," Lash said.

The television ended the conversation as a female reporter's voice broke in through the speakers.

"*Kevin, you can see behind me that the city is in ruins as hundreds of angry rioters have taken to the streets.*"

"Rioters? Give me a break!" Battalion said.

"*We still have no clue as to what caused the outbreak of violence. We do know that Mayor Brimley has been killed as well as several Morton City police officers attempting to put an end...*"

The reporter screamed, sending a burst of feedback into the microphone. Several of the dead charged her and the cameraman, sending the picture to a sideways view. Her body dropped to the ground and blood poured down her face as unseen attackers rummaged into her body. The screen went to color bars and a loud high-pitched tone filled the airwaves.

"Dumbasses," Scorch whispered.

The three of them sat there for a moment. They needed a plan. They needed heavier artillery. A loud pounding came from the front of the store. They each looked to one another. Scorch jumped up from his desk and ran to a large cabinet against the wall. He pulled out a .12-gauge and handed it to Battalion.

"Think you can use this for a bit? I don't want you blowin' up my stronghold with that cannon of yours."

"Not yet anyway," he grabbed the shotgun and began loading shells into the magazine.

Lash went out into the store and found two hefty containers. She rustled through a heap of junk and brought out a large bag of razors and a box of nails. Dumping the contents into one of the containers, she grabbed two jugs of fast drying glue and poured them into the other. She unhooked both whips from her holster and dipped them into the sticky liquid, then shook them around in the mixed pieces of shrapnel.

More pounding from the front. They could see a thousand fists scraping at the wood through the small slits between the planks.

Scorch reattached his goggles. "It's show time!"

They all stood ready. The beating against the door and windows became more intense, angrier. They could hear the horrible moaning and screaming of the dead army. Something was pelted against the barrier, making a loud crash like a metal dumpster. The fluorescent lights above flickered and buzzed.

"They're screwin' with the lights!"

A board broke through, revealing the rotting face of a man wearing a Santa suit, complete with white beard. Battalion fired and the man's snarling face exploded into bits of flying goop. An arm busted through the wood near Lash. She jumped back and flogged it with one of her jagged whips. It hooked into the skin, tearing deep into the tissue. She jerked it with a snap, sawing off the arm, and it flew to the ground.

Battalion discharged another shot through the hole, but another zombie soon filled the void. Scorch launched a small rocket from his arm that whizzed past Battalion's helmet and into the corpse on the other side. The creature was flung back into the others and a burst of hot yellow ruptured from its core. This motivated Battalion to hit the floor and a spray of guts and bloody hair rained down on top of him. He spit out a glob of crimson slime and turned to face Scorch.

"And I couldn't use my cannon?"

"I've got better aim," Scorch shrugged.

Lash shrieked and both of their heads jerked toward the noise. An arm wrapped in nails and razors was pulling her by her whip, dragging her closer to the open gap. Another hand grabbed at the leather, trying to get a hold of her neck. Battalion chucked his glaive. It made a hollow hum as it twirled through the air, slicing into both arms of the zombie before lodging itself into the wall. Lash fell backward and panted for oxygen.

The lights shut off.

The sound of snapping wood and moaning creatures continued while Battalion held out his arms to find Lash. He could feel swipes of air and flying splinters against his face, but he kept moving.

"Need a light?" Scorch held up five blazing fingers for a torch. He moved ahead, lighting the way, but they couldn't see Lash. They listened closely, and could hear her breathing under the racket of the intruding horde, but the store was thick with darkness. Small beams from the streetlamps started entering with every crack of the two-by-fours. Battalion turned and pumped a quick shot into a dark figure climbing through a small opening. It dropped out of sight and they hurried forward. Scorch stopped and pointed at the corner in front of them. There was a crumpled, pinkish-red shadow that he couldn't make out. Battalion brushed by Scorch and bent down to pick Lash up off of the floor but she wouldn't turn to him. He finally gave an impatient pull and the hideous thing turned and jumped onto him. The fluffy white ball of its hat bobbed in his face as he strained to keep its crooked teeth away. He pushed his left hand against its shoulder and his right against its throat.

Scorch ran over, kicking into its side with no avail. In the orange glow, Battalion saw that he was pinned beneath another undead Santa Claus. The putrid wash of its breath brushed against his face. Slobber oozed down in slow, drooling beads. It snatched Scorch's leg and threw him into the pile of Christmas trees.

Battalion fought, but the rotund body was crushing him. He couldn't breathe; beginning to wear out. He looked beyond the fat man's red shoulder and his eyes widened.

The speeding blades of a chainsaw sung above Lash's messy, brown hair. Her arms dropped and metal met meat. Blood splattered everywhere and Chris Kringle shrieked in agony. The blade ripped down the shoulder, the chest, and into its enormous, jiggling belly. The metal *tinked* against the hard bones and sloshed through plush organs. Lash turned off the gas and uprooted the saw from its gory crevice. The two pieces of Santa fell along the sides of Battalion's indignant face. Lash giggled with a hand over her mouth, trying hard to be serious but failing miserably.

"Did you forget the situation we're in?" he gasped.

"Sorry," she helped heave the over-sized elf off of him. "You just looked so pissed!"

Gunfire blared in from outside, sending her sprawling onto him. Hundreds of bullets flew in, ricocheting off of rusty pipes and sheet metal. Lash clung tightly against him, her breasts buried into his chin. He wished it could have been under better circumstances. A thousand pinholes of light penetrated the wooden barriers like some backwoods planetarium. It was a symphony of rattling lead, thumping meat, and splattering liquid. The shooting stopped. Scorch remained buried in the conifers, puffs of white smoke blowing up from their branches. Everything went quiet. The moans of zombie citizens only echoed in the mind. The street seemed empty except for the blinding of headlights, and few dropping cartridges that jangled against the pavement.

"There are *people* in here, ya know!" Scorch yelled from under the Christmas trees.

Lash rose and crouched toward a hole to see out. Battalion retrieved his arm cannon from behind an overturned table. Scorch stayed put.

Rotting bodies, ripped apart by the spray of iron slugs, some still twitching and clawing along the ground, were strewn in front of the hardware store, leading into the street below a large, black jeep. It was empty. The bright lights on top of the front roll bar forced Lash to squint, lifting a hand to shade her view. The engine sputtered with a soft rumble. Steam rose steadily into the freezing night from a machine gun turret resting between the twin head-lights.

It started snowing.

A dark figure jumped up in front of the hole. Lash screamed and jerked back into Battalion, sending them both to the floor. It was becoming a pattern.

"Are you guys okay?" a voice called from outside. He wore a black mask over eyes that were too weary to belong to such a fresh face. He'd seen a lot of Hell in a short time. The falling snow stuck to his brown hair and lashes that blinked with concern.

"We're making it," Lash said, standing up.

"Bunker, you asshole!" Scorch sat up against the green pines, lighting his pipe again.

"What?" Bunker asked.

"Don't mind him," Battalion assured, "he's just got the tweaks." Scorch huffed at this and took a long drag.

"You did great," Lash said, "I don't know how else we would have gotten out of here."

"Yeah, well I think we have a bigger problem than you think."

"What do you mean?" Battalion asked.

"Haven't you seen the news?"

"Well, before the power went out, as you can see," Scorch jeered, "we saw a news crew get chomped after the reporter said all the cops and the mayor got killed."

"Then I guess they failed to mention that before Mayor Brimley was dismembered by a dozen of those things. He closed off the entire city."

"He doesn't have the resources for that," Battalion said.

"Made a call to the Governor after all of this broke, declared martial law, called in the National Guard and closed off all the bridges leading out."

"Son of a bitch," Lash said.

"What about the harbor?" Battalion asked.

"That's the next place I checked. Every yacht, canoe, or Jet Ski is gone. Hell, they even confiscated the damn paddle boats."

"We could swim," Scorch said, walking closer to the opening in the wood.

"Current would be too strong. We'd drown. Plus, there would be soldiers waiting on the bank for anybody who survived the swim," Battalion said.

"Well, I've got good news and I've got shitty news," Bunker said.

"What's the good news?" All three of them demanded.

"I was scaling some buildings in the business district earlier tonight on my watch and I remember seeing a helicopter on the Saffron building."

"That's *wonderful*," Scorch was indignant. "Who's gonna fly the damned thing?"

"Bunker can drive anything," Battalion said.

"Okay, so what's the bad news?" Lash asked.

"After I got your message, I hauled it over here as soon as I could. But when I got to the..."

Suddenly, a bloody hand came through Bunker's neck like his throat had exploded. His head bobbed in a lifeless jiggle, spurting a fountain of blood. The three crime fighters backed away from the hole in the wall, watching an undead homeless man struggle to free his arm from their young comrade's throat.

Scorch ran to the Christmas trees and lifted one out in front of him. The zombie was busting through the wood without effort. Its growl was a deafening, otherworldly roar, spouting from a drooling and dirty, hair-covered mouth. They were getting stronger; faster, too.

Scorch ignited the tree as the zombie charged into the store toward him. He lunged forward, impaling the dead man through the chest and forcing the zombie out onto the street. The body caught fire in an instant.

Fighting to free himself from its burning clutches, Scorch pounded a fist into its skull. It thrashed around, biting at him, as the flames engulfed them both. Scorch finally managed to roll off and get to his feet. He shot an inferno from both palms, ensuring the homeless man did not get back up. All that was left was a smoking block of red and black.

"We need to burn Bunker," Scorch said.

"No, we can't. He's one of us..."

"Scorch is right," Lash said. "He'll change like the rest of them."

Scorch stepped over to his crumpled body and released a stream of flame. Bunker didn't move, didn't make a sound. Just burned.

"That's why you never have a sidekick."

"You piece of shit!" Battalion punched him in the jaw and tackled him to the ground. He continued laying hits into Scorch's face, one after the other. Every ounce of fear, of frustration and rage, came out with each blow. Lash cracked her whip against his back. His scream pierced the snowy air around them. He fell off of Scorch, crying.

"We're probably the only three people uninfected in this city and I suggest we use our time more productively. Don't you?" Lash asked.

"I'm no expert but I've had a chopper lesson or two. It'll have to work," Lash said.

Of course they all agreed. Lash hopped into the jeep and gave each of them a hurried look. Battalion jogged toward the awaiting vehicle and sat beside Lash. Scorch stood up from the sidewalk with a heavy glare at Battalion. Whatever disagreement they still had would be dealt with later.

Lash leaned close to Battalion and whispered, "The tank's on empty. I don't know if we'll have enough fuel to get all the way to the Saffron building. We may need to walk the last half."

"So why are you only telling me?" he asked.

"You may have a tendency to be depressed every now and then but *he's* on the complete opposite side of the spectrum."

"Best not to tell him then," Battalion said, glancing at Scorch.

"Are we goin' or what?" Scorch asked. He limped toward the jeep, wiping his mouth. Single drops of crimson fell to the white snow, staining it like bloody breadcrumbs. They leaked in a slow drip, running down from his right arm. The other two didn't notice this, or the bite from where the flow was coming.

Scorch had taken the spot behind the machine gun. The others didn't feel too comfortable about this but made no argument. Lash wanted to drive and Battalion liked sitting back and having the frosty air blow in his face; anything to keep him awake. They were coming up on 41st when Lash broke the silence.

"What do you think he was going to tell us about before he..." Battalion asked.

"Looks like we're gonna find out. Don't it?" Scorch said.

The engine coughed and choked. The gas fumes in the tank had finally run their course.

"What the hell!"

"Calm down, Scorch. We ran out of gas," Battalion said.

"What are we gonna do now?"

"Get out and walk," Lash said.

They left the jeep in the street and headed for the corner of 41st and Langdon Ave. Morning light was breaking through the skyscrapers as Lash paced out in front, then turned back with a confused look on her face. There was a strange rushing sound, like river rapids but lower in pitch. The men didn't know what to make of it either. Battalion had heard a similar sound only once before, during the Morton City marathon. They caught up to her and rounded the corner together.

41st street was packed with zombies.

There had to be hundreds, thousands, every last resident of Morton City, now turned into flesh-hungry cannibals. It was a Mecca of the decaying multitude, wrestling over each other and making their way straight toward the debilitated crime fighters.

Scorch began wailing.

"*Shut up*," Lash whispered.

He didn't listen.

The first wave of zombies stumbling in front of the undead army noticed them first. It wasn't long before the entire mass drew their focus onto the three heroes. The dead hollered and moaned in unison, a terrible sound that shook the heroes from deep inside their marrow. Battalion grabbed Scorch with his free hand and pushed Lash to the left. They rushed into a building across the street as the mob stormed after them.

"There's no time to bar the doors!" Battalion yelled, leading them into the stairwell.

"We can still make it to the Saffron building but we'll have to go on the rooftops."

They marched up the stairs as the sound of the crazed dead echoed up the steps from the first floor. Battalion pushed harder. At the top of the next flight, there stood a decrepit janitor, chewing a bloody hunk of meat. Lash shot forward and jammed her dagger deep into his eye. The janitor fell down the stairs, Battalion and Scorch tripping over the body to reach the top landing.

Stepping out onto the roof, they leaped over a gap onto the adjacent building. Scorch fell hard against the gravel, and Battalion bent over to help him up. Behind them, the dead burst from the rusty door leading onto the roof. A few of them attempted to scale the expanse but were too sluggish and fell to the deep alley below. The three heroes sighed for a moment, realizing they may have bought some time with the crevice now separating them from the dead.

Two of the things bolted toward them and flew across with startling speed. The heroes dashed for the other end of the rooftop. Scorch was howling behind them, and he backed against a tall A/C unit. The Saffron building, along with the helicopter, was waiting just over the next ledge. It seemed so far away, too far to jump. The two zombies were getting closer.

"*Duck*!" Battalion screamed and the other two complied. He made a quick click on his cannon and shot a grenade in between the approaching zombies. It exploded upon impact, sending the bodies over each side of the building in a hail of fire. This further enraged the multiplying group gathering on the neighboring rooftop. They staggered back, preparing to launch themselves over the divide.

"What are we going to do?" Scorch asked.

Battalion made another click with his arm cannon and reached into his belt. He removed what looked like two small, metal arrowheads connected to a thin silver cable. "This won't hold for long. We're going to need your whips, Lash."

She handed one to him.

"What about me?" Scorch asked.

"You're going to hold onto me," Battalion said.

A loud thud came from the far side of the building. Scorch's whining became more frantic. Another thud. Battalion set the two arrows into his cannon and blasted one into the radiator. He then took aim at the far building, catapulted it into the roof, and slung the cannon across his back. Lash jumped with her whip onto the cable and soared across the skyline before landing into a body roll near the helicopter.

"*I can't...I can't...*" Scorch cried.

"You gonna stay here?" Battalion yelled as he pointed to oncoming zombies.

Scorch wrapped his arms around Battalion and they flew down the cable with Battalion using Lash's second whip for a handhold. They were going too slow. The residue of remaining glue on the whip and added weight was slowing them down. Lash had started up the helicopter, its blades gradually picking up speed. Scorch began to twitch. His eyes rolled back into his skull and he began jerking around.

"Quit moving! You're going to kill us both!" Battalion yelled.

Scorch went for his neck, his teeth bared. Battalion wriggled on the line like a dangling worm. He caught both ends of the whip with one hand and held back Scorch's gnashing teeth with the other.

Lash could only watch helplessly.

The two men began to pick up speed. Battalion could see Scorch's face was bulging with thick, red veins. He drooled like a rabid dog, searching for a place to bite. The cable began to make a metallic whine and Scorch's hands slipped. He clawed at Battalion's torso, trying to regain his grip. The hollow pain of each jabbing finger resonated through his skin. Scorch slid down to Battalion's left ankle, squeezing hard with both hands as his body swung in the air like a broken pendulum. The fingernails on each of Scorch's hands dug into Battalion's leg. He kicked at him but he wasn't letting go. The zip line was loosening. He could feel it with the weight pulling him down. The ground had to be more than a five hundred feet below. It was dizzying. Battalion looked up and kept his gaze forward.

The edge of the Saffron building was approaching fast. The creature was still taking bites at him when Battalion swung backwards as hard as he could. Scorch lost the grip of his right hand, but still clung to him with the left. They flew forward like a giant slingshot. Scorch's back slammed into a sharp edge of the structure while Battalion sailed over the edge and onto the roof. The gas tank strapped to Scorch's shoulders ruptured, spilling a profuse amount of fluid as he plunged toward the distant cement below. The contraption exploded in mid-air, showering a cloudy, gray mix of snow and ash onto the ground and the zombies below.

Battalion laid there for a moment, catching his breath, and let the wash of the helicopter's rotors flow over him. Lash was waiting in the cockpit, looking understanding yet impatient. He picked himself up and checked his ankle.

No bites.

Walking to the helicopter, he sat down in the passenger's seat and looked out through the windshield. A mass of zombies crowded the roof of the distant building, thrashing and groaning as usual. Lash prepared to take off.

The aircraft lifted smoothly at a slow climb. They passed over the vast row of buildings and across the river. The holiday decorations were still hanging on homes and streetlamps, plastic reindeer and sleighs on rooftops.

The two heroes took one last glance at the city below, their city at one time. Both of them knew they wouldn't be coming back. Morton City, the city they had protected, was forever closed off; the city of ravenous dead, where it was now Christmas all year round.

THE END OF CHRISTMAS

ANTHONY GIANGREGORIO

Thomas Jurgensen wandered the cold lonely street, wrapped in nothing but rags. The snow on the ground was two feet deep and he could feel the ice crystals inside his worn boots.

All around him were the signs of a dead neighborhood, the same as every other one he'd passed through in the twelve months since the dead began to walk and swarmed across the world like locusts.

Stopping in the middle of the street, he stared at the house to his right. It was a standard two-story house with a two car garage and a large picture window in front. In that window, Christmas decorations still hung, the scotch tape holding the cardboard cutouts of Santa and his reindeer firm.

After a full year of hanging in the window, the sun beating on the facades, the colors were now washed out and only the dark lines of the shapes could be seen.

On the front lawn, buried under two feet of snow, three unlit plastic reindeer frolicked. Their white skeletal frames were once lit up, but now they truly looked like skeletons.

Hanging askew on the roof, a life-size sleigh clung to its moorings. Exposed to the winds and weather, it wouldn't be long before the sleigh was forced off the roof to crash to the ground below.

Thomas shook his head in sadness, wondering how it could have come to this.

It wasn't a long story how the dead came to walk, it was quite simple actually.

A cure to the common cold, it was heralded as. Finally, no more runny noses and chests full of phlegm. But the cure hadn't been tested as well as it should be, the drug companies in a rush to get it on the market. To make up for the loss of cough syrup and allergy medicines, the price of the cure was incredible, but nine out of ten people were happy to pay it.

So when the first fatality was admitted into a local hospital, no one gave the woman much thought. At least until the patient died and returned as a living corpse, sinking her teeth into the nurse administering over her.

From there it was a domino effect, and in the blink of an eye, a year later, Thomas was standing on a holiday festive street in the middle of Nowhere, USA, shivering in the cold. The wind blowing in from the north felt like it would freeze him to the bone, and he turned and headed for the ranch house.

All around him were the frozen corpses of zombies, each as stiff as the day it had frozen months ago. But Thomas knew when spring came they would thaw out and be free to roam once more.

There was a time when he would have tried to destroy them, to chop off their heads and break their legs as they lay helpless in the snow. But months ago he had finally given up. There were just too damn many to destroy.

So now he used the winter time to stock up on whatever he could find, and when spring arrived, he would hole up somewhere until winter returned.

The front door of the house was locked, so he went around to the back. This door was locked too and it was a heavy wooden fabrication. But there were more ways to enter the house and he found it by using a basement window. After kicking out the glass with the heel of his worn boot, he scurried in like a worm sliding into its hole.

The basement was dark and dingy, but was slightly warmer than outside.

That made Thomas nervous. Anywhere the temperature wasn't below freezing, a zombie could be lying in wait.

He remembered the last time he found a zombie in a house.

It was three weeks ago to the day. He had climbed in through an open window to find the bedroom door leading to the rest of the house empty. Upon opening the door, he found himself standing face to face with a dead man in a Santa Claus suit. With the door closed. The rest of the house had managed to stay above freezing.

But Santa wasn't as jolly as days past. This Santa had a massive hole in his throat, a missing arm and intestines hanging like dangling rope from his abdomen.

As the dead Santa raised its one remaining hand, Thomas heard the tinkle of jungle bells, the three red bells sewed to the sleeve of the red suit. As the zombie moaned, the bells jangled, and Thomas slammed the door in the festive ghoul's face.

As the holiday zombie pounded on the bedroom door, Thomas had climbed out of the house to find another hiding place.

So now here he was again, inside a house searching for anything useful. Empty cardboard boxes sat on his left, the words **XMAS** written on them in black marker. He chuckled slightly at the sight. Of course they were empty. All the decorations were set up around the home. It was like this in every house he went to. When the outbreak began, it had been three days to Christmas, and though the world died, at least it left a festive corpse.

The basement was relatively empty, though he found an old claw hammer on a dented and rusted metal shelf. The hammer was better than nothing, so he tossed away the cracked bat he'd been using, knowing the bat's days were numbered. Swinging the hammer once or twice to get a feel for it, he turned and began climbing the steps to the first floor.

The door was locked, but his new acquisition saw him through. With the door lock now splintered and lying on the top step, he pushed the door in and waited for signs of trouble. He was confident that any zombies would have been attracted to the noise he made breaking the lock. He waited for a full minute, and when still nothing arrived to attack him, he stepped inside the kitchen.

It was a kitchen like any other he'd seen over the past year. A snowman cookie jar sat on its side on the counter, even the crumbs now gone. Christmas potholders hung from the cabinets and small statues, five inches in height, sat on the edge of the stove, while salt and pepper shakers of elves lay on their side in the middle of the kitchen table.

That was the only sense of normalcy in the kitchen, however, as the rest was a maelstrom of tossed aside empty boxes and brown, dirty dishes. When he reached the kitchen sink, he turned up his nose as the sight greeting him. A large, dried turd, human by the size and shape, lay in the bottom of the sink, and Thomas had to wonder what kind of human would feel the need to climb up onto the counter to defecate like that. But he'd seen worse in his travels and he moved on.

As Thomas searched the cupboards, they were as bare as the preverbal old woman in a shoe. When he was through searching, not finding so much as a crumb, thanks to the looters before him, he went into the living room.

He had his fingers crossed about what he might find there, and sure enough, he was correct.

In the center of the large living room, stood a brown Christmas tree, all the needles now on the floor. Ornaments still hung from it, but as the once fresh tree was now long dead, the branches looking unappealing and ugly in their bareness.

The tree was like the world now. A few pretty baubles on its surface, but underneath, it was dead and rotting.

But that wasn't what Thomas was looking for. It was what was below the tree that had him coming to the living room in the first place.

Below the dried and brown tree, a fire hazard in the waiting, sat the presents of this home's family, every one still wrapped with care a year ago.

For some reason, looters didn't think to check the presents, only going to the obvious places, such as the kitchen, pantry and medicine cabinets in the bathrooms.

But Thomas had figured out long ago that there were hidden treasures to be found sitting under desiccated Christmas trees. Setting the hammer down, he dropped to his knees and bean ripping open the presents.

To: Timmy, Love, Mom and Dad, the first one had written on the wrapping paper, and when Thomas opened it, he saw it was a video game. He tossed it aside and went for the next one.

To: Sally, Love, Mom and Dad, the next card said and this one had a pink ribbon on the corner.

Thomas ripped the ribbon off and tore into the present, to an outsider looking like a kid on Christmas morning. All he got for his trouble was a new cell phone.

Beyond worthless, he thought, as he tossed the box aside.

But this had happened before which was why looters didn't bother.

Thomas picked up the next one. *To: Daddy, From: Timmy*, was on a homemade card. There was a drawing there, too. Timmy had used crayons to draw Santa and his reindeer as they flew across a happy town. Thomas ripped the card off and threw it behind him, then he ripped open the present like a hungry dog and cried out in relief to see what was inside.

It was a summer sausage gift set, complete with two blocks of cheese, mustard, and crackers. The perfect present to give a man who needs nothing but you have to give him something.

Ravenous beyond imagining, Thomas tore into the package and feasted on the sausage. Though it was processed meat that he would have shunned a year earlier, now it tasted like the finest New York sirloin. He ate half the sausage and then a quarter of the cheese, devouring half the crackers with it. Then, his stomach feeling better, he continued opening presents.

He went through four more, one was a new IPod for the little girl, the other was an action figure from some Japanese cartoon for the boy. The second to last was a sweater for the mother, cashmere if he was right. Not worried about fashion sense, he set it aside to take with him. Warm was warm and there was no one to impress anymore. And besides, the dead didn't judge you, they only wanted to eat you.

The last present was addressed to the father, and when Thomas opened it up, he gasped in happiness to see a brand new Browning Hi-power, complete with a box of ammunition. This was the find of a lifetime. And to think, it had been sitting here for all this time, ignored by others!

After loading the gun, he felt so much better, knowing he wouldn't have to get close to an attacker to defend himself.

Going to the front door, he stepped outside and grabbed some snow from the front porch, eating it. It melted in his mouth and he sighed, washing the salty taste of the sausage and crackers from his palate. At least with the snow he had all the water he could ever want, but he still needed food. At least now, for a day or so, he had both.

When he had his fill, he closed the door and went back into the living room. This time he noticed the rest of the holiday decorations spread out across the room.

Near the front window were two animatronic statues of Santa and Mrs. Claus. Both were covered in a layer of dust and hadn't been on in more than a year. Off to the right was a fireplace, the family stockings hanging in front like a classic Christmas card. Two large ones had Mom and Dad on them, while the other two had the names Timmy and Sally.

Made sense to Thomas, especially after ripping open the presents and reading the cards.

On the walls were holiday cardboard cutouts similar to the faded ones on the front window. Rudolph, Santa, and Frosty all smiled down onto the living room, where once a happy family had laughed, loved and played together.

That had Thomas wondering where the family might be. Had they evacuated like so many families had in the beginning? He felt for them if they did. The rescue stations had quickly become concentration camps, where death and sickness ruled with an iron fist.

Luckily Thomas had been alone when it all started. He was already a widower and he and his wife had never had kids. All his family was either dead or estranged when the world crumbled. Which was why it had been easy for him to adapt, as he had no one to worry about but himself.

With a full stomach and the inside of the house much warmer than outside, he felt his exhaustion sneaking up on him, and he decided it was time to get some rest. He did a few things before he slept, however. The first was to use the bathroom, not caring about his waste being left behind in the empty bowl. The second was to use one of the kitchen chairs to block the basement door from opening. If he thought to enter the house that way, so could another. He hadn't seen many other people in this part of the town, but one could never be too careful. At least if one wanted to stay alive, that is.

When the house was as secure as it could be, he went back to the living room and dropped down on the dusty couch. There was a dust-covered throw blanket on the back cushion and he pulled it down onto him.

Then, snug and comfortable, he drifted off into sleep, into a world where Christmas didn't equal death, and if you saw Santa Claus on the street, he wasn't going to try and rip your throat out.

*　　*　　*

Thomas came awake with a startled groan. He'd heard something, the question was: What was it?

Always on the run, he had learned to sleep lightly, and no matter how tired he was, he always managed to do this.

So he knew something had woken him from his troubled rest.

He sat up and could barely see, darkness having descended almost completely. Checking his wristwatch, he saw he had been asleep for almost four hours.

His bladder required attention and he silently padded to the bathroom, took care of business, and then proceeded to go back to the living room.

That was when he heard the noise again. It was a scratching sound, like a dog wanting out and its claws brushing the door.

It was coming from the second floor. He hadn't checked the second floor, not feeling the need. The gun was in his waistband, but he went back to retrieve the hammer, then, as well armed as one could be in this day and age, he began to climb the stairs leading to the second floor.

Halfway up, he paused to study the family photos hanging on the wall. There was a small fixed window that allowed light in and the wan illumination was enough for Thomas to see the smiling faces in the pictures. A man, woman and two children, a boy and a girl, looked out at him, with cheerful eyes and wide smiles. This must be the family that lived here, the two children named Timmy and Sally.

They looked so happy and Thomas couldn't help but feel his heartstrings tugged just a little.

But then the scratching could be heard again and he was brought back to the here and now. He reached the top landing, and he walked down the small hallway, peering into each room as he went. There was the parents' bedroom, the dust thick with disuse, the floor void of fresh footprints; the bathroom was empty and the first child's bedroom was empty also.

That left the last room at the end of the hall.

The door was closed and the name **TIMMY** was on a small sign tacked to the middle of the door.

Thomas stepped closer and placed his ear to the door.

There it was again, that scratching noise.

While there was absolutely no reason for him to open the door, he felt his curiosity get the better of him. It didn't hurt that he now had a gun and if there was any true danger he could shoot the problem and then leave.

For once he felt in control and he was damned if he would run away.

He wanted to know what was in the room, and had been inside for a year or so.

So with treacle-like slowness, he reached out to the doorknob with his free hand.

Turning it careful, he pushed the door open and took a step back, lest a hidden ghoul attack him.

But there was no attack, nothing happened. But the scratching began to grow louder.

When he was sure it was safe, he raised the gun and stepped into the room.

Immediately he was blasted by the rank odor of stale death and the reason for this aroma was apparent the instant he entered the room.

There were two zombie children, a boy and girl, only the clothing allowing Thomas to know this for sure. Both were tied by the necks like dogs, their small bodies far too weak to ever hope to break their leashes.

Below them, on the floor, were the remains of two adult bodies. There was no meat left and the skeletons pieces that were till intact looked chewed on, like someone had been gnawing on them for some time.

The heads were tossed to the side, the skulls empty, as if a small hand had plunged into the neck cavity of each to scoop out the juicy brains within.

Thomas took the room in at a glance. There were pieces of rotted, dried meat off to the side, and a few of the pieces looked as if they may have been human.

It wasn't too hard for Thomas to piece together what must have happened.

Somehow, the two children had been infected and had turned into the walking dead. The parents hadn't the heart to destroy their offspring and so had penned them up, tying them up like wild animals. Then the kids had been fed a diet of raw meat and human when possible. But something had gone wrong, perhaps the kids getting the drop on their parents. And then the parents had become a meal for their children.

The two little zombies snarled and hissed at him, their drawn visages basically nothing more than human skulls wrapped in dried skin. The small zombies hadn't eaten for a very long time and were ravenous for human flesh.

They were an odd sight, the two wearing festive holiday clothing, though now it was covered in brown and crusting blood from meals long past. The boy wore a yellow sweater with Santa Claus on the front, while the girl wore a blue sweatshirt with a snowman with a black top hat.

Frosty, had to be, Thomas figured.

Thomas stared at the kids and then at the gun in his hand. In the end, he decided he didn't need to waste two bullets on them. They were trapped and small and he had the hammer.

Shoving the gun in into his waistband, he raised the hammer and stepped closer to the boy. He was less than a foot away, but the leash was short and the boy couldn't reach him. He raised the hammer high and then brought it down hard; the skull cracking like it was made of plaster. The boy dropped to the floor, gray brains seeping out the hole in his head.

Thomas barely felt anything as he turned to face the girl. She hissed and snapped; her hands out in front of her. The leash was taut as she stretched to reach him.

He laughed, feeling powerful, knowing it was petty, but still relishing his power. After a year of being on the run by these *things*, it was nice to be in the driver's seat for a change.

Almost casually, he raised the hammer again, his attention barely on the task at hand. He was already thinking about eating the rest of the summer sausage with mustard.

His carelessness was his undoing, as he had learned a long time ago any zombie was a danger, no matter how helpless it might seem.

As he raised the hammer and looked away for the briefest of seconds, the leash holding the zombie girl snapped, and she came at him with mouth open wide.

He brought the hammer down, but only glanced her head, the blow breaking her clavicle instead of her skull. But the little girl could have cared less. Before Thomas could stop her or jump away, she sank her brown teeth into his right leg, just above his knee joint.

He screamed in pain and anger and raised the hammer again, this time his attention fully on the killing. The hammer cracked her skull like a melon and the point of the hammer sank halfway into the small skull, the girl twitching on the end of the hammer like she was being electrocuted.

Her teeth clamped down in her death throes and tore a two inch size chunk of flesh from his leg. Howling in pain, he kicked the corpse away from him and dropped the hammer.

The girl was very dead now, the small body dropping onto the two skeletons of her parents.

Moaning in pain, Thomas left the bedroom, slamming the door behind him. He wasn't cursing himself as he wasn't thinking that far ahead. Instead, he rushed to the bathroom and ripped open the vanity.

He found what he needed, but it was in short supply after looters had taken what they wanted, but he ripped open his pant leg and cleaned the wound. Then he bandaged it.

With nothing left to do, he went downstairs and sat on the couch, his leg throbbing with each beat of his heart.

He still didn't want to admit it, but he knew what that little zombie girl had given him for Christmas.

A death sentence.

Though he was hurting and upset, eventually he fell back to sleep, though now his dreams were plagues with even more zombies, and by the end he found he was one of them.

When he woke up his leg was numb, and when he checked under the bandage, he saw the wound had festered. It had already started and there would be no stopping it.

He finished off the sausage and cheese, sucking every last ounce of mustard from the packet. He wasn't worried about eating it all. He didn't need to save it anymore and at least this way he would die with a relatively full stomach.

Then he sat and waited, only getting up to use the bathroom and eat some snow.

By the second day, he didn't bother to do that, and the last time he needed to pee, he'd said the hell with it and had simply leaned over the edge of the couch and urinated on the floor. Hell, it wasn't his house and in another day he wouldn't be alive to care.

That night he was holding on to life by his willpower alone. He knew if he passed out that would be it.

And he knew for a fact he didn't want to become one of *them*.

He picked up the Browning and held it in his grip. He remembered just a day or so ago when he'd found it how lucky he'd felt.

In fact, he had been so happy it had been just like Christmas to him, what with finding the gun and the summer sausage. He wasn't sure, but he was pretty sure December 25th was close, the anniversary of the outbreak the same week. So it was Christmas again, albeit a rather lonely one for him.

As he placed the gun to his temple and closed his eyes, he mumbled one last sentence.

"Some Merry Christmas."

He held the gun there for almost ten minutes, not having the courage to go through with it. But then he felt a sharp pain in his chest, one that filled him with agony.

That pain gave him the courage to do what had to be done.

He squeezed the trigger.

RED CHRISTMAS

KEVIN COCKLE

"They got Mrs. McWhirter," Josh whispered, peering out through the circular attic window of his two-story Victorian. Snow covered the grounds, and weighed down the boughs of nearby pines and elms. It would have been an idyllic setting, a perfect white Christmas, if not for the sight of Mrs. McWhirter's intestines being pulled from her belly as she screamed into the frigid afternoon air. Great pumping gouts of blood splashed snow in nightmare Rorschach patterns all around her.

A wolf about to bite a housecat, Josh thought on reflex. *A bird smashing into the windshield of a moving car or a butterfly.*

"Jesus," Josh breathed, unable to look away. His breath fogged on the pane of glass as he leaned in close to it. "She must have run out of food. Why the hell else..."

"Come away from the window," Celia said, her voice sharp with tone. *The* tone.

"They can't see me," Josh said defensively. "They never see me. Or if they do, they don't care."

Mrs. McWhirter was twitching as greedy gray hands helped themselves to her vitals. Steam rose from the gaping cavity that had been her midsection. Josh tried not to think of what it must smell like, with her bowel exposed like that. Eventually, he moved away and sat upon the old guest-bed with a creaking protest from the decades-old springs.

Celia sat in the far corner, knees drawn up to her chest, arms hugging knees, shoulders shrouded in an old gray blanket. Dark circles rounded her hazel eyes, and her hair--normally so perfectly nonchalant--drooped limp across her shoulders. Dark roots were beginning to show as time whittled away on her dye job.

She'd hate that, Josh reflected.

"What's the date?" he asked, just trying to fill the room with conversation.

"I think it's the twenty-fifth," Celia muttered.

"Damn," Josh said wearily. "Merry Christmas."

*   *   *

Merry Christmas, Josh thought, three weeks previously, when he'd finally sat down to deal with the divorce papers. It was only December 7th, a day that would live in infamy for sure, but the holidays were in the air. He'd put the lights up a week before, on the house, and upon the trees in the front yard; strings of small electric blue pin-point bulbs that his daughter Kelsey absolutely loved. He'd started buying presents in July as he always did, because he hated the last second rush at the malls. He'd mailed out cards to friends and family in the last week of November as he did every year, to beat the frenzy at the post office. Celia called the behavior *anal*, but Josh thought of it as *proactive*.

Must be what they mean by irreconcilable differences, Josh thought as he stared at the signature line on the fifth page of the document.

She was taking the house.

She had secured Kelsey; Josh had supervised visitation.

They both earned well in professional careers, but Celia made more. Nevertheless, she was taking 200k to be held *in trust* for Kelsey.

Note to self, Josh had thought. *Never marry a lawyer.*

A year and a half of constant, protracted, and bitter warfare, and Josh had been decisively, irrevocably beaten. While he'd raged, and tried to bully the early arbitrators, Celia had been laying her traps, conducting reconnaissance, sowing the ground ahead with mines. His behavior in arbitration had been exquisitely baited by Celia's outrageous opening positions. She had never meant to deal in good faith in those sessions. What she had meant to do, was to provoke him, and get his reactions on the record. Right off the bat, she'd held the strategic initiative, and had used it to slowly choke off all his options.

While he'd focused on the legalities and the asset-picture, she'd been working their friends. Once again, he'd been distracted, tricked into looking at Celia's right hand while her left hand did the magic. Friends they'd known for eight years, people they'd golfed with, done dope with, taken trips to Cabo with, some of them had signed Celia's affidavit.

"Excessive drinking and lack of self-control..."

"Inappropriate touching..."

"Frightening Kelsey with his bouts of temper..."

"Moody, and unpredictable..."

"Erratic behavior...unstable..."

Masterful. And overkill. Her PI had already caught him on film with one of his young female associate-architects. That alone would have been enough to win. But Celia didn't just win. Once he was down, she still went for his throat. She'd gone for his throat the way those things had tucked into Mrs. McWhirter. The same greedy hands; the same cold-blooded determination.

He'd lost almost seventy five pounds off a portly two hundred and twenty five pound, five foot eight frame, in fighting that war. Celia hadn't changed a bit. That gym-built, marathon-tight, fat-free chassis of hers had performed magnificently well through all the difficulty. It was almost as though she had consumed him, literally, physically diminishing him, as though killing him had been the objective all along. He hadn't had one non-pharmaceutically assisted night's sleep since the war had begun. Not one. Every night, his mind would go over and over the details, gnawing on minutiae as he lay sweating in the darkness. At one point, the sleeping-pills and wine had put him--humiliatingly so--into the emergency ward. Another entry on another affidavit. Another defeat.

"Get your shit together," Layne, his partner at C-tech Architecture and Design had said at last, driving the final nail into the coffin of Joshua's war effort. "Settle this. Settle this, or I'm suing you for your half of the business. Your choice, J." Some choice. But that was it. Once the divorce had begun to threaten the company, Layne had made an executive decision. "I'm not on anybody's side," he'd always say. But his threat more or less handed victory to Celia on a silver platter.

Broken physically, emotionally, and financially, Josh had accepted unconditional surrender. The divorce papers were more than a domestic legality; they were an armistice. Josh signed out of exhaustion; bombed into submission. He would have couriered the papers in the morning, but Celia had shown up that night. It had been December 7. She retrieved them in person because he was *taking too long.*

That was how they came to be in the house together when the televised emergency broadcast started telling everyone to stay in their homes.

*   *   *

"You should eat," Josh said, his voice little louder than a whisper. Empty cans littered his side of the attic, along with plastic picnic knives and forks. They still had a few items left: canned pumpkin pie filling; smoked mussels; canned tomatoes; canned creamed corn.

"I can't," Celia said, miserable. She shuddered in her gray woolen blanket, her cheeks looking hollow. Outside, the sun was going down, and the creatures began to moan as though afraid of the dark. There was always noise as they milled about; a door being banged at; a window being broken.

"You don't look well," Josh said, trying to suppress a certain grim delight.

Am I really that petty? he wondered. Then he marveled at what it had actually taken to break his formidable ex-wife.

"Happy?" she asked, flicking him a rheumy-eyed glare.

"Oh, Jesus. Here we go."

"I cannot believe I'm in here, with you."

"Maybe if you weren't so goddamned impatient."

"Why the hell didn't you just sign the papers and turn them around?"

"I'm sorry if I have a life, and your business isn't my top priority."

"Two seconds. Sign. Return."

"You don't even like this house. You never liked being out in the country. Why would you go after this place?"

"Oh, Please."

"Seriously, Ceel, I'm curious. Why the house? I'd have mortgaged to buy you off; why take the property?"

Celia just glared at him, trembling.

"Because I love it," Josh answered his own question.

"Hurts, doesn't it?"

"I can't believe you," he said.

"And I can't believe you, you fucking cliché."

"Because I banged an associate? Please, like you didn't blow your way to partner."

"You'd like to think that wouldn't you?" she said.

Josh double-clutched, feeling his temper rise. His *unstable, erratic* temper. She had him there, he did wish she'd slept her way to the top. But he knew she hadn't. She'd made partner by billing more hours than any other associate at the firm; year in, year out. He'd grown to hate the fact that she only seemed to need four or five hours of sleep; a ninety-hour work week was nothing for her. After a while, her physical drive had come to seem like a kind of subtle insult.

One of many, many such insults.

"Maybe I would," he managed at last. "At least it would mean you were human. But sex would be the last thing you'd offer, wouldn't it?"

Score. Josh watched as the barb bit home, saw it the way a bomber pilot could see flashes far below his plane; bombs striking the target in the darkness. Genuine hurt flared bright in her exhausted eyes, and the corners of her thin lips twitched.

"What are we doing?" she asked at last. He knew what she meant; he'd been thinking the same thing.

"I know," he said, half chuckling. He could see his breath in the air. "Zombies have taken over the neighborhood and we're still at each other's throats."

"Christ, I hope she's okay," Celia said.

Josh could see her eyes brimming again, and knew she was thinking of Kelsey.

"Come here," he said. "Get warm."

* * *

"I have to," Josh said, pulling on his coat. "We're out of water."

"I'm..." Celia cut herself off. Even now, she couldn't say it. Josh let it go.

"I know," he said. "I'll be out and back fast. Promise. Do me a favor?"

"What?"

"Eat something."

She looked over at the tins with sallow eyes. The sight of the cans seemed to be making her physically ill. He assumed she must have eaten something since they'd holed up. You couldn't go this long on attitude alone.

"Whatever," Josh mumbled when she didn't move.

He lowered the small attic staircase to the second floor landing. He hadn't heard any of the things inside the house, but he took no chances, arming himself with a Ping five iron. Taking a moment to listen, he stepped quietly down onto the second floor, feeling his heart slapping in his chest.

Relax, he told himself. *Breathe.*

The house had a main staircase, but it also had a narrower and direct servant's staircase leading from the upstairs into the kitchen. It had been one of the main selling features for Josh; just the quaintness of it, the datedness of it. He took the servant's stairs because two of the creatures wouldn't be able to come at him at once, if any were in the kitchen. And, once he was in the kitchen, he could leave directly through the back door, which would be much quicker than going through the front door.

Once in the kitchen, he looked out the window, which had a good view of the long backyard, and the trees along the fence line.

Empty.

He proceeded to the back door and opened it, immediately detecting the footprints of shuffling feet from visitors who had come and gone in the night. Curling around the north side of the house, Josh reached his front yard and looked past Celia's black SUV in the driveway into the empty street beyond. Something was moving in the McWhirter's front yard. Josh knew what it was.

Scanning up and down the street, Josh made his way to the McWhirter's lawn, stopping a few feet away from Mrs. McWhirter. Her arms were moving up and down in a hideous parody of someone making snow angels, her lifeless eyes staring up into the overcast, mercury-colored sky. Like water, her eyes reflected the color of the sky, giving her a robotic, doll-like aspect. Her dentures were half in/half out of her mouth, as she slowly worked her jaw open and shut.

Her legs weren't moving, and peering into the gaping body-hole, Josh thought he knew why. Bits of spine shone white in the morning sun. The zombies had hollowed her out and damaged the backbone. She could flap and gape, but apparently, getting up and shambling about was out of the question.

"Jesus, Helen," Josh whispered.

At the sound of his voice, her mouth made a hideous smacking noise; her head craning up out of the snow. She hissed, her eyes shining like brand new nickels, and her teeth dropped out onto her chest. Josh had no idea if the things communicated, but he didn't want her drawing attention to herself or him. A swing of the Ping took her in the forehead with a wet crunch, the toe of the club penetrating skull. As per the TV reports, Helen McWhirter stopped moving. Josh worked the club free with a grunt and fought down his rising bile.

Stay focused, he chided himself.

That first night, December 7th, Josh and Celia had watched the television in silence. After they'd had an explosive, shrieking argument over the papers of course, and him being drunk when she'd arrived, and her taking Kelsey to her folks' place in Toronto, and on, and on, and on. He actually couldn't remember that fight all that clearly. Maybe he'd had more to drink than he thought. He remembered shouting, and hurting inside, because it was all finally over, but he really couldn't recall the details of the back-and-forth. All he remembered was that at some point, the TV in the background had made its presence felt, and at the repeated phrase of *walking dead*, they'd shut up and listened.

For weeks, reports out of New York and the other big cities had been mind-blowing, but for the most part, the rioting and violence had seemed to be under control. But the truth was that things had been tipping *out* of control for some time. It now seemed that *rioting* wasn't altogether an accurate description of the unrest that had been experienced in the cities of the nation. Up until now, images had been carefully controlled and spun, but now it was all coming clean. Cameras brazenly recorded walking corpses taking bullets in the chest; falling down; struggling back up. The National

Guard had been forced to draw back and regroup, *temporarily* leaving people to their own devices.

"Stay in your homes, stay calm. Plans are in place to restore order just as soon as possible," was the familiar restrain.

"That's mostly for New York," Josh had said. "We're fine out here. It's the cities they need to secure."

But that night, they'd heard gunfire from the Winston's down the road, and they'd seen figures like the ones on TV staggering uncertainly in the middle of the street. Cars had peeled out, not everyone was staying put, but Josh had physically stopped Celia from going outside.

"Think, Ceel," he'd said. "The interstates will be a nightmare. You don't want to be caught out there."

And just like that, the die was cast. They'd go to the attic and wait it out.

That had been just about three weeks ago, in a house with a few decent bottles of wine and a jar of olives in the fridge. Josh rarely ate at home.

In two days, the power and utilities went out.

In four days, cell phones no longer obtained good signals.

Josh had left his laptop at the office, so internet was out of the question.

Within a week, they were rationing tiny morsels of foraged food, and sipping bottles of water. On one trip outside to raid nearby kitchens, Josh had almost been killed by Ben Tinsley, who had holed up with a skeet-shooting gun.

And on Christmas day, they had both been alive to see Mrs. McWhirter get disemboweled on her front lawn.

Get a grip on yourself, Josh scolded himself when he realized he'd been staring at the dent in Mrs. McWhirter's forehead. There would be plenty of time for reminiscing once he was back in his attic.

Stepping to the McWhirters' front door, Josh could see that it was still ajar. Pushing it open with the bloody club-head, Josh stepped inside.

Doesn't make sense, he thought. *If she'd gone out to forage, why leave the door open?*

Maybe she hadn't gone out to forage.

Josh stepped through the door, momentarily paralyzed by the choice of leaving it open or closed, finally settling on leaving it open. The things were slow. The only way they could catch him was if he got trapped somewhere. He'd take his chances with the open door.

Through the living room and then into the kitchen.

The door to the pantry was closed but the door to the basement was open.

Hefting the club in both hands, Josh made his way to the basement steps, peering down into the darkness. Almost immediately, he heard a heavy footfall on the bottom stair and could see a pant leg in the gloom. Another step, and then a throaty groan. It was definitely one of those things, lurching its way up the steps.

Another few steps, and Josh knew why Mrs. McWhirter had left the safety of her house in such a hurry.

Mr. McWhirter tottered into view, yellow smoker's teeth bared; dull eyes focused with animal intensity.

Poor bastard must have gotten himself bitten on a forage, Josh thought. *Got bit, and came home anyway.*

Dumb prick.

Josh cracked Jason McWhirter a good stroke in the forehead, hoping the creature would fall back down the stairs. He did fall, but not backward; the creature stumbled forward into the kitchen, bellying-in with his legs behind him on the stairway. Biting back a scream, Josh struck again and again to the back of the skull, crunching his way into whatever remained of Mr. McWhirter's brain until the thing stopped moving.

The five-iron was holding up well. The shaft was a little bent, but all in all, the Ping had been worth the money.

There was a sound behind Josh, and then hands fell upon his heavy green parka. A low moan of revulsion escaped his lips as he spun in the thing's grasp, slipped on Mr. McWhirter's brains, and staggered back into the counter. A woman, frozen nearly blue in a t-shirt and panties staggered forward, her mouth open to reveal jagged, broken teeth. Josh sidestepped to his right, pushing the thing in its left shoulder and sending it reeling down the basement steps. The thumping and thudding sounded like someone had thrown a bunch of shoes down the stairs.

That was the last of Josh's nerve. In something close to blind panic, he rushed into the living room, where he nearly charged headlong into a man staggering around with his entrails hanging down to his knees. Josh cried out, stepping around the creature and hurtling out the front door. More zombies were coming; they'd seen him. If he'd been calmer, he might have tried to lead them away before going home, but he wasn't thinking clearly.

All he could think to do was get home.

Get home, and get into the attic.

Wait for help.

He charged through the faded Rorschach pattern of Mrs. McWhirter's blood spatter, and catapulted across the street. He made it to his front door, entered, and slammed the door shut behind him. Looking out his front window, he could see creatures shambling towards him, and his skin crawled. They'd seen him, and they were coming for him.

He locked the door and hurried up into the attic.

He pulled the stairway up behind him, then sat huddled on the guest-bed as an awful pounding began to sound out from his front door.

Celia sat huddled on her side of the room, baleful eyes staring accusations at him.

Like all this was his fault.

*   *   *

They bickered through the night.

Celia was exhausted, groggy from hunger and thirst, but somehow never so spent that she couldn't mount her attacks.

"This isn't about me not signing those papers," Josh finally said, exasperated after two hours of rehashing the past eight years of their life.

Downstairs, zombies had gotten into his beloved house; he could hear them stumbling about in the kitchen.

"What, Celia: what? For Christ's sake! You won."

That stopped her.

In the dim gloom, Josh imagined he could see her eyes reflecting the moonlight. He could hear her seething in the darkness.

"What?" he repeated.

She didn't answer.

* * *

Josh lost track of time.

They had no water left; little food. Celia wouldn't eat: she looked like a concentration camp survivor; sunken eyes; bony cheeks.

Hours would pass in silence, then one or the other of them would start.

The fighting would proceed in mumbles and whispers, each trying to score points in a game that had long ago ceased to have any meaning. The same cratered battleground, the same tired battles.

Zombies roamed through the house, sometimes even on the second floor, directly below the attic entrance. When that happened, Josh and Celia lowered their voices, but if they had the chance to sting, they stung; undead be damned.

Maybe we can live on hatred? he reflected dreamily, after striping Celia for the umpteenth time for being frigid after Kelsey had been born.

Maybe that will see us through.

* * *

It was broad daylight when Josh first heard the helicopter.

"Shut up," he said, cutting Celia off in mid-insult. She sat huddled in her blanket, glaring at him from its musty depths. "Do you hear that? It's a helicopter. More than one."

She sat in silence, her drained face stretched in a weird expression of triumph.

In an hour, they heard the first gunshots, high powered rifles. M16s.

"Come here, baby," Josh croaked. Celia was crying dry-eyed, just releasing tension. "They're coming. Come here."

Celia joined him on the bed, sitting with their backs against the wall.

"It's gonna be all right," Josh said, putting his left arm around her. She was shivering. She felt so frail, so thin.

"*Celia*," Josh sang in a thin warble, singing the song he'd sung all the time in the early days. "*You're breakin' my heart...*"

He sang to her and held her close as he heard his front door being kicked in, and shots ringing out loud from the living room, then the kitchen.

After a while, he heard the voices of men on the second floor; heard radio static. More helicopters flew overhead, and ground support was driving slowly through the streets. Someone was speaking on a loudspeaker in slow, measured tones.

The attic stair was lowered from below, the steps cautiously ascended by booted feet.

"Jesus!" a helmeted soldier cried out, firing wildly into the wall.

"Don't shoot!" Josh croaked. Celia lay silent in his arms, staring at the soldier who was little more than a kid. "Don't shoot," Josh repeated.

"Christ...it talked!" the soldier said. He stepped all the way into the attic, rifle trained on Josh's face. An officer stepped into view, eyes narrowed.

"Son of a..." the officer said.

"He's human," the kid said.

They stared at Josh and the skeletal remains of his ex-wife. Josh's face and hands were covered in her blood, making him look, at first glance, like one of the creatures. There wasn't much left of Celia after three weeks. Her marathon-lean meat having kept Josh alive, barely, until rescue. There were no cans or plastic cutlery evident, there never had been. There were a few water bottles lying scattered throughout the room.

"We're saved," Josh said, giving the corpse at his side an encouraging hug. "Ceel? We made it." Josh paused, cocking his head as though listening. "Don't start," Josh mumbled, his voice cracking. "Don't start with me, Celia. Not again."

PEACE ON EARTH

KELLY M. HUDSON

On Easter day of this year, the dead rose and walked. They didn't just walk, however, they walked and they ate...people.

They devoured human flesh, intestines, internal organs, eyeballs...pretty much whatever they could get their fingers or teeth on. Society collapsed. It happened quickly and in ways that nobody saw coming. And by the fall, the dead outnumbered the living.

I thought about that sometimes, about how fast things had changed. Just a year ago I was a dentist, a partner in a small firm hoping to open my own office and have a practice entirely to myself. I'd built up a good reputation and had a solid core of patients, so it was just the matter of a little more money and I was there.

Easter changed everything. The funny thing is, as fast as the world fell apart, those first few days, everything moved slowly. A few scattered reports were on the news here and there, but the deaths and mutilations were chalked up to maniacs, or cults; nobody took it seriously, at least, not the coming enormity of it.

I was in the office that Monday morning and my partner, John Deeds, was already working on a patient. I liked John, he was a good guy, but I had an itch to get out and run my own ship. He knew it and realized I would be going soon. He tried not to let it bother him, but there were some days he could be snippy.

He wasn't that Monday. He was in one of those helpful moods, where he'd run across some abnormal case and call me in to show me how to handle the situation. I was always grateful, and on that fateful morning, he wanted me to observe work he was doing on an impacted wisdom tooth.

"Get in here, Frank," he said.

The nurse, Carol Saunders, a pretty young lady fresh out of college and our dental technician, came out of the room and ushered me in. She was a sweet girl, with blonde hair, a nice body, and a smile that could make a man go out and do silly things all to get that gleam turned his way. I liked Carol, and being single, I let it show. Carol had a boyfriend, though, so I left her alone for the most part. That didn't stop her from flirting with me, though. She always used to tease me about not wearing a tie to work, saying that it would make me look more professional. I told her I hated ties. She'd laugh and swear that one day, she'd buy me one and then I'd be forced to wear it because if I didn't, I'd break her heart. I'd just laugh and shake my head.

John was seated next to his patient, laughing gas nozzle firmly attached to the nose of the big man. The patient looked like he weighed close to three-hundred pounds and it was all fat. He had a pudgy, squished face that reminded me of a hamster for some reason. Anyway, the guy was out, having been given the combo of laughing gas and anesthetic, and he didn't care what I thought about him at all.

"Check this out," John said. He had the guy's mouth open and his fingers inside, along with a small, hooked instrument we used to clean teeth. "This is the most God-awful impaction I've ever seen."

John was in his forties, heavy-set, with graying hair and smart, sensible glasses, a sharp nose and chin, and deep brown eyes. He was married, with two kids about to graduate high school and head off to college. John was who I wanted to be in about ten or fifteen years.

I leaned forward and looked into the patient's mouth. The guy on the chair suddenly farted and a terrible smell filled the room. I gagged and covered my nose but John, he just laughed.

"I think he's having a reaction to the gas," he said. "He's farted like that three times already. This guy's a stinker."

I looked at the patient's chest and it didn't move. I stared for a second, not believing it.

"Is he okay, John?" I asked.

John looked down at the man and studied him for a moment, confused.

"God," he said. He used his free hand to check for a pulse, pushing back the layers of fat on the man's neck. "I can't find it," he said.

I leaned forward to help when the smell of the man slapped my nose like a drunk beating his wife. I staggered back, my stomach retching, and as I fought the urge the vomit, the man's eyes fluttered open.

They were vacant, the emptiest eyes I'd ever seen.

The man bit down, chomping on John's fingers. John screamed and tore his hand free, leaving behind three of his fingers and the dental hook he'd been using. The man chewed on the fingers, blood bubbling between his lips and dribbling down his chin. He gnawed on the digits and then swallowed them. The dental hook worked around in his mouth until it turned sideways and then tore through the man's left cheek; the pointed hook end stuck out and gleamed in the office light, a thick glob of blood at the end of it.

The man sat up and opened his mouth. A piece of John's rubber glove that had been covering his fingers was stuck between the man's teeth. It flapped and flopped around as the fat man slid off the chair and stumbled towards me, his mouth opening and shutting.

John fell into the corner of the office, knocking over the tray of instruments. They clattered to the floor as blood squirted high into the air from the stumps where his fingers had been. He screamed and slipped, holding his wounded hand and bellowing with pain.

Carol ran back into the room, colliding with me and knocking me into the fat man. She screamed, her cries joining John's, as I stumbled forward and ran into the patient, our chests butting. The fat man's mouth opened and the most horrible stench came from between his teeth as that piece of rubber hung there, flapping, his maw foaming with blood and saliva.

I punched the man in the stomach with my fist, nearly breaking my wrist. He may have been fat, but he was solid, and the blow did nothing. He leaned his head back and rolled his eyes like a shark and lunged forward, his teeth clacking together. If I hadn't slipped in the blood from John's hand, I would have been bitten and that would have been the end of the story for me. As it was, I slid and next thing I knew, I was on my side on the floor and the fat man was leaning over me, his thick, grubby fingers digging into my arm.

Carol saved me, God bless her. She dipped down, grabbed a scalpel from the spilt instruments, and jammed the blade deep into the fat man's right eye. She let go and jumped back with a gasp as the man turned from me and looked over to her, his ruined eye dripping with clear fluid and blood, mixing together like yolk in a frying egg. The fluid and blood mixture streamed down his cheek as he stumbled forward, reaching for Carol.

It was my turn to be the hero. I wrapped my ankles around the man's legs and tripped him. He pitched forward and his head slammed face-first into the wall, ramming the scalpel further into his skull. It must have pierced his brain because this time, when the man hit the floor, he stayed dead.

Carol stood at the doorway, shaking violently. I got to my feet, out of breath and completely out of my mind. John's sobbing distracted me, and I gazed at him, sitting there and holding his ruined hand up in the light. The blood glistened from the finger stumps as it kept pouring out, seeming to drown him. John's eyes were bloodshot and dazed; he'd lost a lot of blood. I stepped over to help him when he fainted, his body falling back and his head hitting the wall behind him. He slid down, leaving a long, wet trail of blood where his skull had cracked.

I would have tried to save him if not for the screams from the parking lot. Carol and I ran to see what was going on outside and the sight greeting us was one I'll never forget.

The dead were in full invasion mode at that point, with panicked people spilling into the streets heading straight into a slaughter. There were dozens of them out there in the corner of the lot where our little building stood, dozens of humans and triple that amount of the walking dead. They swarmed the living, tearing and grinding and rending. There was blood, so much blood, filling the streets.

I stood, numb and unmoving, and stared as the blood flowed into the gutters, emptying into the storm drains like it was a monsoon downpour. Intestines, body parts, eyes, toes, fingers, arms, legs...they were all strewn about, savagely torn from fleeing people, as the dead walked, eating and killing, perfect engines of destruction.

That was the first day, for me and Carol. There would be many more like that for us in the time to come. We escaped the office and fled, heading to the countryside, hoping that somehow we would find safety in the open spaces. We met other survivors, and some of us banded together, hoping for safety in numbers. But it was all a joke, because the dead soon outnumbered all of us and there was no place out of harm's way anymore. Days were spent running and nights full of restless sleep and guard duty.

We survived, though. We made it where others didn't. And in the process, Carol and I fell in love. We clung tight to each other, and months later, when the winds turned cold and the leaves fell from the trees, when summer turned to fall and then fall turned to winter, we stayed together.

Carol was very thorough, keeping track of the time with a small, pocket daybook. She informed us each day what the date was and when we closed in on any holidays. Most of us didn't care much, but it was important to her, so I encouraged her to continue. She'd always smile at me, her face still pretty, despite the anxiety, despite the constant grind and lack of rest. She was the most beautiful woman I'd ever known.

Did I mention an *us*? That's because we were part of a small group, seven in all, including Carol and me. We kept each other as protected as possible and were always on the move, never settling in one place for too long, always fearful that the dead were tracking us or would stumble on us if we ever stopped being mobile.

The group consisted of five others, three men and two women. There was Curt, a former attorney turned guerilla fighter. Curt was one mean bastard. He'd had some training in the National Guard when he was in college, so he was our weapon's man. Nobody could shoot like Curt, and nobody was as ice cold about killing as he was. One time, when a woman in our group got bitten, Curt calmly strode over to her and, despite her protestations and mine, leveled his gun and erased her head. I hated Curt. I hated him because he was so virile, so strong and so right. He was tall and lean, with a gaunt, chiseled face. He'd started with a crew cut, but like all of us, there wasn't much time for personal grooming. He had long brown hair now, pulled back in a ponytail.

The other two men were brothers, Dan and Paul. They were nice enough guys, if a bit quiet. They'd operated a service station back in the old days, doing car repairs and doing some illegal chop-shopping on the side. They were very forthright with their story because they had nothing to fear anymore; at least, not from any sort of law. Dan and Paul were average-sized guys, both in their early thirties, with dark hair and eyes and a slouch in their shoulders. They'd started out with a paunch, but time and scarcity of food had turned their fat into sustenance and now they were trim and lean, just like the rest of us.

The women were related, too. Bobbye and Amber, they were cousins. Bobbye was ugly; I wanted to be nice about it, but there was no other way to put it. She had the kind of face a bulldog wouldn't lick even if the face was covered in ketchup. She was tall and skinny, with long blonde hair and really bad breath. But Bobbye was strong, like a bull, and was great in a fight; nobody was better with a hatchet than she was. Amber was pretty, but she was close to retarded, I think. She did whatever Bobbye said, except when she slipped off in the night and had sex with one of the brothers. I heard them sometimes, grunting and squealing, trying to be quiet but not really succeeding. They took turns; the brothers did, on the occasions when things were safe enough for them. Amber had brown hair, long and curly, and really big breasts, the kind that turned a corner before she did. But like I said, she was lost without Bobbye and was luckier than us to survive so long. I never heard Curt take a turn with Amber, and although that should have made me somewhat happy that he wasn't taking advantage of her like the others were, it maybe bothered me even more. Curt didn't seem human any more. In any case, and I'm sorry to say this, but I was happy none of them tried for Carol. I would have killed them if they did.

That was our little family, and we managed to make it to December before the weather got so cold we were forced to look for some decent shelter. We were out in the sticks, where there weren't many houses or barns even, and those that we found were either so gutted by other survivors they were useless. Many were burnt down. This forced us to get closer to the cities, and this was dangerous. Most of the walking dead were gathered in the towns, clumped together like blood clots. We avoided urban areas as much as possible.

But like I said, we were pushed into having very little choice.

We entered a small town with a main street and some shops and stores. Curt had reconnoitered and come back to tell us the town was mostly deserted and, except for a few stragglers, wandering up and down the empty streets, it should be easy pickings. We discussed it as a group, finally deciding to go on in and see what supplies we could find, and if it was possible to hole up there for the coming winter.

Carol nudged my arm as we walked; a bright smile on her face. She held her small daybook out for me to see. She thumped a date on the calendar with her finger as her eyes danced with delight.

"You see what tomorrow is?" she asked. I looked and nodded, feeling a lump form in the back of my throat. "It's Christmas. As of midnight tonight, it's Christmas!" I thought she was going to jump up and down with excitement.

"You know what this means?" she asked. I shook my head. "When we get to town, you need to leave me alone for a few minutes. I want to shop for a present for you."

"It may not be safe," I said.

She slugged my arm and giggled. "Okay, Mr. Grinch," she said.

"Seriously."

She stopped and stared at me, those happy eyes clouding over. She crossed her arms in front of her chest.

"I need this," she said. Tears welled in her eyes. "Please. For one day, let it be like it used to be."

I studied her for a moment. Like I said before, she was the most beautiful thing I'd ever seen, and I couldn't bear to see her hurting like that.

"Okay," I said.

She threw her arms around my neck and hugged me tight. She kissed my face and neck. Curt turned and glared at us.

"That's enough," he said, his harsh bark cutting through our joy. "Let's get moving."

I stared at Curt and he offered me one of his funny little smiles, the kind that said he would kill me in my sleep without blinking an eye if I wasn't careful. I stuck out my tongue to relieve the tension and he turned and walked away.

"Don't let him get to you," Carol said. She held up her wrist and showed me her digital watch. "I set the alarm. At midnight, we celebrate!"

I didn't really know what to say; she kept up hope, regardless of the situation. The rest of us, I guess we'd pretty much given up at that point, resigning ourselves to a life on the run, always hiding like scared little field mice, afraid that at any moment the evil hawk was going to swoop down and snatch us up.

We worked our way into the town. There were a few roaming dead, stumbling around. We stayed away from the zombies we saw, four in all, who drifted around, lazy, seeming to have no purpose, until they saw us. We were in front of an abandoned department store when one of them moaned and Curt turned, brandishing his knife.

"Go on in," he said. "I'll take care of this." He jogged over to the zombies, his knife glittering in the pale afternoon sunlight. Good old Curt, he was always dependable for a kill.

All of us carried some type of knife or hatchet and we also had handguns, but we tried not to use the pistols because for some reason the noise attracted the dead. Each of us grabbed our guns anyway because you could never be too sure. When I stepped towards the entrance, Carol stuck her hand out to stop me.

"You stay out here," she said. When I opened my mouth to protest, she put her hand to my lips. "I don't want to hear it. I'm going in and I'm picking out your present and I don't want you to look."

I nodded. Carol could take care of herself if there were other zombies inside, and if there were a lot of them, she could just call out and I'd be there in an instant. I gave her a quick kiss and watched as she followed the others inside, then I turned and stared off at Curt.

I have to give him credit. He was really good at what he did. He moved quickly, scampering across the road and driving his knife under the chin of one zombie, a construction worker, and up through his jaw, shoving it deep so that the brain was destroyed. He jerked the knife out, spun, and swung the blade in an arc, burying it in the next closest zombie's head, right through his left ear. This one was some kind of Scout Master or an overgrown Boy Scout, I wasn't sure which. He fell forward, the bloody medals pinned to his chest clanking on the street. Curt turned to greet his next assailant, this zombie was a teenager wearing a white t-shirt, torn jeans, a ball cap, and had a pair of earphones attached to his ears, the plug end dangling at his side. He had no face; it must have been raked off when he was killed, or shortly thereafter, and over time the raw, exposed nerves and veins dried and he looked like some kind of prune-headed monster from a surreal horror film. Bits of garbage and dust had stuck to his open wound so that his face was a collage of withered gunk and pieces of paper and even a torn soda can that had stuck to where his right cheek had been. Curt, as always, wasted no time. He ran around the zombie and jammed his knife into the back of its head. The teenager went down with a moan and didn't move again. That left one more. This one was maybe the ugliest thing I'd ever seen. He'd been a cop, or a security guard, I couldn't really tell which, his uniform caked in dried blood, staining the blue material even darker. He had a badge, once bright and shiny but now just a dull glimmer over his right breast. He was missing the flesh on his right arm from the elbow down. All that stuck out was a long bone, sheared off at the wrist, that had flecks of dead skin and, like the teenager, bits of dirt and dust clinging to it. The left side of his neck was gone, like an apple bitten halfway through, and that side of his face was smeared. The skin ran down like a violated watercolor painting. The cop moaned and reached out with his one good arm and I watched Curt smile and step back. He plunged his knife into the cop's mouth, smashing out teeth and then twisting the blade and pushing it up. I heard it chunk through the roof of the cop's mouth and then the cop pitched forward.

Curt stepped out of the way and turned to give me a wink.

"Easy-peasy," he said.

I shot him a salute and then froze when I saw what was coming around the corner over his shoulder. There were at least a hundred zombies shambling as fast as they could manage, all of them headed straight towards us.

"Shit," I said.

Curt spun and stood for a moment, transfixed. We hadn't seen such a large mass of the walking dead since we'd first gotten out of the cities, and the sight was still staggering.

I screamed into the department store for the others and they came running, all but Carol.

"We have to get out of here," I said. I looked around and when I didn't see Carol, panic surged into the back of my throat like a hot wad of steaming vomit. Then she poked her head out, her eyes wide with shock.

"Let's go," I said. I started to move off to my right, to head down the street and out of town, when Curt called out to me.

"Hold it," he said. He backed up slowly towards our group. The dead were more than a hundred strong and they were growing closer by the second.

"If we run away, they'll just follow," Curt said. "We should lead them into the department store and leave the back way. If we bar the doors, they'll think we're still inside. Then we can get away clean."

It was a great idea and I hated that he came up with it. Anybody else but Curt and I would have been thrilled. We went back into the department store, Carol falling to my side. She had a plastic bag in her left hand that had the words **Thank You** printed in red on it. When I looked at the bag, she shook her head.

"Not 'til Christmas," she said.

We shoved the sliding glass doors shut behind us and headed to the back of the store. Dan led the way. "I saw a door back here," he said. "It was for employees only, but I bet it leads to the loading dock."

The dead slammed into the glass doors, the weight of their numbers straining the already rusted and weak entrance. It wouldn't be more than a few minutes before they were inside and swarming. I glanced over my shoulder. It looked like a parade out there, all these zombies, swaying and marching in time, walking straight into the glass and bouncing off and then going forward again. Soon they were thick against the entrance, the zombies in front pressing against the doors, their bones cracking as the glass fractured.

We hustled through the door that Dan led us to and it emptied into a stock room. Big boxes were sprawled across the floor and to our left was a small kitchenette. There was a table, some chairs, a microwave and a refrigerator with its door hanging open. Brown, dried blood was smeared across the top of the dinette table and splashed against the wall. Dan darted between the boxes, leading us through a maze until we reached a back wall.

There was no door.

The room didn't lead anywhere. We scrabbled along all the walls, searching in vain for some type of exit or entrance but there was none. Inside the department store, we heard the glass doors shatter and the moans of the dead echoed off the walls.

"We'll find another way," Curt said.

We crept to the door and then out into the department store again. The dead were staggering into the building, the destroyed front doors vomiting forth a wave of zombies like a womb squirting out children. They were still far enough away that we were safe for the moment, but if we didn't find a way out soon, we were doomed.

Curt found another door and we all crouched down, hiding behind a row of empty shelves.

"Stay here," he said. "I'll go check."

We stayed. The groans of the dead were growing closer by the second. I looked at Carol and she smiled at me, still cheery despite our situation. I never understood where her optimism came from, but I'd be a liar if I said it never comforted me. Carol was probably the only reason I'd made it this long without putting a bullet in my head.

The zombies scuffled straight towards us, even though we were hidden. A lot of people used to speculate how they tracked us; some said it was sense of smell, others said it was supernatural, that they were demons sent from Hell. I think they can sense our body heat. How else can you explain zombies that feast on the living until that person dies, still chomping away until the meat goes cold and the person turns? As soon as that happens, the dead stop eating their victim and instead welcome another of their own into the world. Sight and body heat, that's how they follow us.

Curt stuck his head out of the doorway, a big smile on his face. He nodded and we crept through the entrance. We came out into a large dock area with big garage doors at the opposite end. All of the doors were shut except one, which was edged open at the bottom by two feet.

Paul, following Dan, shut the door behind us as we ran for the back of the room and scuttled under the opening and out into the fresh air.

Behind us, the moans of the dead rang, filling our ears and drowning out any other sound. There was never any real escape from them, just a delay of the inevitable.

We made a circle around town and then went back to our small camp, dejected. We'd hoped to find some food and whatever else popped up to aid us in our efforts, but instead, we'd barely gotten out with our lives. We should have been thankful for that, but none of us were, really. We were bone-weary from the constant struggle.

Curt walked the perimeter a few times, just to make sure the zombies didn't follow us, and after a time he seemed satisfied. We gathered around a small campfire we built to keep warm and baked our last two cans of beans. Nobody said a word. We ate in silence, all of us wondering where our next meal was going to come from.

Day passed to evening. The temperature dropped and still, no one talked. Carol snuggled next to me, a slight smile on her face despite everything. I held her tight, tears filling my eyes.

"Tomorrow is Christmas," she said. "We'll have a Christmas miracle. You wait and see."

I stroked her hair until she fell asleep against me. When she finally nodded out, I looked out over the campfire at Curt who sat silently, staring at us, his face blank. Paul, Bobbye and Amber had already fallen asleep and Dan was out on watch duty. I was next up on the roster and then it was Curt, who preferred the deepest, darkest hours of the night to do his patrolling.

He kept staring at me and I was about to yell at him when I realized he was asleep. He did that sometimes, slept with his eyes open. It was creepy. He only did it when things were really stressful around us. It had been a long time since I'd seen him do it. I shrugged and let it go, lying back on the ground, pulling Carol close to me. I closed my eyes and drifted off.

I dreamed of Christmas, of Santa and his elves and bustling shopping malls. I dreamed of times gone past, of goodwill to all men, of streets teeming with people all out shopping and full of merriment. In my dream, I stumbled down a crowded city sidewalk, stopping in front of a little blonde-haired girl who held an empty teacup in one hand and an alarm clock in the other. She looked at me and smiled, her clear blue eyes sparkling in the holiday lights. Then her alarm clanged in her other hand and she stopped smiling, her face melting into a grave frown.

"Wake up," she said. I opened my eyes to find Carol leaning over me, her watch alarm beeping.

"Wake up," she said; her eyes shining like the girl in my dream. She pointed to her watch. "It's ten minutes until Christmas!"

None of the others moved; they were all still asleep. Even Curt had closed his eyes by that point and lay on his side by a fire that had all but gone out.

Almost twelve? Where was Dan? He was supposed to wake me over an hour ago to take his place. I looked around, the blackness of the night thick and impenetrable.

"What is it?" Carol asked. Her voice was a hush.

I held my finger up to my lips. Off to our right, something swished across the grass, heading towards us. I pulled my flashlight out of my backpack and pointed it in the direction of the noise. The beam splashed on a scene from a nightmare.

A zombie, a woman in a wedding dress stained forever brown with crusty blood, stumbled towards us, the hem of her dress stirring the grass. Her face was caved in on one side like she'd been hit with a hammer, and her nose hung on by a small flap of skin, skipping and bouncing across her face with each step.

Behind her were countless zombies, headed for us, all less than twenty yards away.

Carol screamed. I jumped up, grabbing my pistol and pointing it at the surging mass. The others came awake, too, getting up and getting armed, but it was too late for us. I heard Curt cuss behind me, and when I whirled to look, I saw we were surrounded. The dead had followed us back from town and now here we were, pinned in and doomed. To my right, my flashlight beam found Dan walking towards us, very much dead now.

Where his throat had been was a wet, crimson patch of meat. Chunks were missing from the cheeks on his face and his shirt had been torn off, revealing a glistening, raw torso, stripped clean of flesh from the bottom of his neck to his waistline. He looked like he was wearing a fresh, red tattoo where his skin had been. Dan moaned, louder and more vigorous than the others and staggered towards Paul.

Curt was the first to open fire. I heard his gun go off and it spurred me on. I sighted the zombie in the wedding dress and blew her head off, her dried and desiccated brains splashing on a crossing guard behind her. I shot him next, then the armless priest behind him. I kept firing until my gun was empty, then I dropped down to search through my backpack, finding spare bullets, and quickly reloading. Next to me, Carol had her gun up and blasted nine zombies before she was out, too. We worked it as a team, like we always did, one firing while the other reloaded. I looked up at her face, grim in the flickering, dying firelight, as she sent one after another of the walking dead to their eternal rest. She was a good shot, probably better than me, and despite her holiday cheer, she was serious as a church mouse. I loved her more in that moment than any before.

I stood and sighted a small boy who wore a bicycle helmet, knee and elbow pads. I blew a whole through his ruined right eye, the bullet blasting out the back of his skull to then strike a skinny, naked woman behind him in her shoulder. She spun with the impact but kept coming, like they always did, relentless and without emotion.

All around, I heard the roar of gunfire as our little group made its last stand. We knew it was hopeless; we were surrounded and there was no way out. There were so many of them, too many of them, and we could feel their dark bodies pressing forward through the black night, shambling to murder and feed.

Carol screamed and I spun and stared as a legless male zombie crawled across the ground and buried his teeth into Carol's left ankle, biting down and tearing out a huge chunk of gleaming red flesh. Blood squirted from the wound at the same instant my lips formed into a shriek, and I pointed my gun and punched a hole through the side of his head. I was too late, though, because Carol fell in a heap and more zombies collapsed on her, their fingers and teeth clawing and biting at her warm, supple flesh.

Behind me, I heard Bobbye scream and I turned in time to see a fireman zombie grab her by the top of her head and rip a chunk of her hair out, scalping her. Bobbye put the muzzle of her gun in his face and pulled the trigger, turning his head into a bright spray of blood and gristle, just as another zombie crept up behind her and buried its teeth into her neck. It chomped on a thick wad of flesh and blood burst from the hole, spurting and spraying the advancing dead like a water sprinkler. Bobbye dropped to her knees, eye-level with a little girl zombie in a bright pink dress. The little girl leaned forward and bit her nose, tearing it from her face and chewing like a rabid animal until she swallowed the snout whole. After that, Bobbye disappeared under an avalanche of bodies.

Next to her, Amber wasn't doing well, either. She'd run out of bullets and was using the butt of the pistol to hammer a plumber's head in. His skull collapsed with a crunch, like that of a bottle smashed under a car tire, and he fell to his knees and then to the side, forever dead. She swung again and caught a zombie in a business suit in his jaw, clipping the left side of his head and dislocating the lower jawbone. She hit it again and the lower jaw broke off and flipped through the air like a thrown horseshoe, landing on the soft grass two feet away. A zombie in a maid's dress stepped on the fleshy jowl, crushing it beneath her heel. Meanwhile, a zombie had grabbed Amber's arm and yanked it until she pitched forward, falling flat on her face. Four zombies bent down and ripped the flesh from her back, their fingers digging in, tearing off her shirt and her skin with it, acting almost as if in concert. More zombies followed, gouging her back, legs, and buttocks, scratching out hunks of flesh and bone, shredding her skin and tendons until there was nothing left but a squirming, screaming mass of pulsing blood.

Paul ran out of bullets and turned to run away, but in vain. He tripped over Curt who was busy knifing the zombie closest to him. Paul fell on the fire, snuffing out what was left of the flames and dousing the area in complete and utter blackness. I heard Paul scream and the dead moan and I knew he was gone, that his fight was over. And all around me, I could feel them, even if I couldn't see them, the writhing mass of the living dead, all pressing forward and surrounding me, ready to at last make a feast of my body.

The clouds above parted and the moon, brilliant and full, blazed in the night sky, sending down shafts of pale light that illuminated the entire area. I could see Paul, still struggling on the ground as zombie after zombie pulled pieces of his intestines out, stringing them along and sticking them into their rotting, foul mouths. Two baseball player zombies grabbed his right arm and wrenched it from its socket, tearing the appendage free and falling back with their prize. Blood spewed from the stump where his arm had been. Another zombie, this one dressed like a coal miner, dove down between Paul's legs, ripping at his pants. The miner bit down on the inside of Paul's thigh, gnawing a wad of skin and blue jeans free. Another zombie moved in, this one a redneck, with blood-blackened overalls and bare feet. He jammed his hand into Paul's crotch, grabbed his testicles, and ripped them out through the fly in his pants. Long streams of blood, nerve filaments, and ropes of spermatic cord followed, plopping wet on the ground. The redneck kept pulling until the external abdominal ring came out, and then he gathered his bounty in the palms of his hands, dipped his face in, and dug in. He raised his head once, his gray flesh painted with blood, little giblets of testicle meat hanging from between his teeth. Paul's screams filled the night air, mercifully cut off forever when another zombie, this one a woman in a housewife's robe, curlers still fastened tightly in blood-matted hair, tore his throat out and shoved it into her mouth.

Curt was still fighting, busy killing zombie after zombie, stabbing and shooting, holding his own for the moment. But that moment was going to pass. There were too many of them for us to handle and there was nowhere to go to get away.

I looked down at Carol who was kicking at the zombies trying to grab and eat her and then at the mindless mass of undead just two feet away from me, shuffling forward, an unstoppable tide of living death.

Carol's watch alarm went off again.

It was the secondary alarm, the one she'd set to tell her it was midnight and officially, Christmas. When it rang, a strange thing happened.

All the zombies stopped.

I staggered back, dozens of zombies just one step away from me, all ready to tear me apart, now standing still, arms at their sides, like an off switch had been thrown. I tripped over Carol and fell, cracking my head on the ground.

Blackness swirled in my vision until it blanketed me. Then I passed out.

When I woke up, it was morning. The sun was out but weak and pale, and a chilly wind blew from the north. I sat up, dizzy, unsure of what had happened the night before and wondering if I'd died and this was what it felt like to be a zombie.

I hoped not, because my head throbbed and my back ached.

"Frank," Carol said. Her voice was weak and hoarse. I rolled over and she was lying next to me, pallid as the gray morning skies. She'd bled quite a bit throughout the night and it was a minor miracle she was still alive. She smiled up at me, her eyes glassy and distant.

"Oh, baby," I said. I bent over her and swept her torso up into my arms and squeezed her tight to my chest. She was so cold. Her entire body shook, a slight tremor running through her and into me. I knew she didn't have long to live.

"I love you," she said. She leaned up and kissed my cheek and that was it. The last breath left her body and she went rigid and then limp in my arms. I ducked my head and pushed her face against mine and wept like I never had before.

In the distance, I heard a siren, its wail growing closer and closer, louder and louder, and I wondered where the ambulance was and why there was even one operating when I realized the wail was coming from me. It rumbled in my chest and burst forth, a spiral of sound, fury and anguish.

I wept for what seemed like hours, and all around me, the living dead stood in place, not moving one inch.

After a time, exhaustion overtook me and I was on the verge of passing out when a strong hand clamped my shoulder. I spun; ready to face my end, only to see Curt's grim face staring back at me. He was covered in blood, with black circles ringing his eyes, and cuts, gouges, and bruises dotting his chest and arms. His shirt was gone, ripped off at some point, and in his other hand he held fast to the knife I'd seen him use the day before.

"I must have passed out," he said. He sounded as weary as any man I'd ever heard.

"She's dead," I said. "Carol's dead."

Curt nodded. "She's going to turn, you know."

"Shut up! Shut the hell up, you bastard!"

"You know I'm right," Curt said.

I did know, but I didn't care. She was gone; the only reason I had to keep on going was dead and I wanted to join her.

Curt looked around and spat a wad of phlegm onto the ground next to Bobbye, long since dead and now revived. She was sitting up and staring at me with the one eye she had left. Grass and dirt was tangled into the wounds she'd died from.

"They just stopped," Curt said. "I don't know why. We were in the middle of it, both of us about to die, and then they stopped. I spent a good couple of hours cutting down as many as I could, but brother, I tell you, I got tired at some point and passed out; that's all I remember. Then you started crying and it woke me up."

I said nothing. I looked out over our small camp. Paul and Amber were sitting up, too, but what remained of them made no move to attack. Like the others, they stayed still; they just sat and rocked slightly with the breeze. I stared down at Carol, her dead eyes looking back up at me. I bent my head and kissed her lips.

A hiss came from her throat and then a soft moan. I leaned back and watched as Carol pulled away from me and sat up on her own, dead as dead can be. She'd turned, and fast, too.

"Oh, God," Curt said. He jumped back and brandished his knife. I held my hand up.

"Hold it," I said.

I studied her face and gazed deep into her eyes. She was dead, of that there was no doubt, but she didn't attack me. She sat and stared back, unmoving.

"What the hell is going on around here?" Curt asked.

Carol reached over to her right. Her fingers roamed over the plastic **Thank You** bag she'd carried with her from the department store. My Christmas gift. She lifted the bag and faced me with her arm extended, holding the bag out for me to take.

"Good Lord," Curt gasped.

I took the bag, tears streaming down my face. "For me?" I said. "You shouldn't have."

"You're losing it," Curt said.

I ignored him and opened the bag. Inside was a neck tie, black with pink horizontal stripes. I took the tie out of the bag and held it up, a grin creasing my harried face. I showed it to Carol and kept right on smiling and acting like nothing in the world had happened.

"Thank you," I said. I leaned forward and kissed her cold lips, expecting her teeth to bare and for her to bite my face off. She didn't do anything. She sat and watched me as I pulled away and stuffed the neck tie into my front pocket.

I turned to face Curt. "She made good on her promise," I said. Tears filled my eyes and then spilled over, running down my cheeks. I took the tie and put it around my neck and tied it, just like I would have if I was wearing it with a dress shirt for work. I turned back to Carol and puffed my chest out.

"How does it look, honey?" I asked.

She just looked at me.

Curt got up. He hocked another wad of phlegm and spat it on the ground.

"We got to get going," he said, ignoring my madness.

I stared at Carol a few more minutes.

"Christmas," I said.

"What?" Curt asked. He was going through the remains of the weaponry we had that had been tossed aside or dropped, gathering it up to pool it together.

"Peace on earth, goodwill to all men," I said. It all made perfect sense to me now.

"You really have lost it," Curt said.

I turned to him.

"No, think about it. Back in what, World War One, was it? The troops stopped fighting on Christmas day. Sworn, bitter enemies stopped their battles and shared gifts with each other. Then the next day, they went back at it like nothing had ever happened."

"So?" Curt said. He wasn't getting it.

I smiled. "Today is Christmas," I said. "Peace on Earth, goodwill to all men."

Curt studied me for a moment and then turned his gaze onto the zombie horde surrounding us. He thought on what I'd said and eventually, he nodded.

"So you're saying that these zombies, these dead people, they knew it was Christmas and stopped attacking us?"

I nodded.

Curt shook his head slowly. "I don't know."

"Think about it," I said, getting to my feet.

"I suppose you could be right."

"I bet at midnight, they go back to how they were," I told him.

"If so, then we need to get out of here."

I looked back at Carol. She'd given me a wonderful gift and here it was, Christmas day, and I had nothing to give her, even if she was dead. Then an idea occurred to me and I smiled.

I snapped my fingers and Curt gave me a funny look as I held my right hand out.

"Gun," I said.

He handed a pistol over to me. I checked to make sure it was loaded and then turned to face Carol, still sitting on the ground. I pressed the muzzle of the gun to her forehead. I was going to give her the best present ever.

"Merry Christmas, baby," I said.

I pulled the trigger. The gun bucked and sprayed the ground behind her with the back of her skull and brains. Carol slumped over to the side, a slight grin on her face. I gave her the gift of freedom, the gift of true death.

"Let's go," I said to Curt.

We marched away from that awful place, only the two of us left alive of our group of seven. We walked for miles and miles before stopping by a road to rest for a few minutes. We passed several zombies on our way and each of them stood or sat wherever they were, paying us no mind.

Sure enough, at midnight, the dead walked again, searching the countryside for warm human flesh.

Curt and I kept pressing forward, doing our best to survive, thoughts of that strange night never far from our minds.

A ZOMBIE CHRISTMAS

PAUL C. SNIDER

Christopher Barbour put on his black boots, long red sweat pants, a red and white overcoat stuffed with one of the pillows that was in his room, and wrapped around his black belt. Then he looked in the mirror. He just had to do three ultimate touches to make the transformation complete: the red Santa hat, white gloves, and the fake beard.

He wasn't looking forward to the next part; his wife Tisha had pushed and prodded him to play Santa for their two kids, Jackie and Jamie, both girls. He argued at first but knew deep down the fight was lost before it even began. His argument was that the kids were too old for Santa, Jackie was fifteen and Jamie was seventeen.

They even agreed on something which was rare these days; he would make an attempt to try and climb down their own chimney! They both made sure before he tried that there was no fire going of course; but still he was nervous as hell.

Christopher then snuck around the back patio, ran around to the two-door garage and lifted it open. He grabbed the silver ladder that was hung up on the right wall and carried it to the right side of the house with ease.

He steadied the ladder first, which was difficult due to the snow and ice covering the ground. Once he managed to steady it, he began his climb to the roof with a heavy sigh and one slow step at a time.

Now at the top of the roof, he looked down the chimney and yelled heartily, "Ho, Ho, Ho, Merry Christmas!" Then jingled some bells around his waist for good measure. The sound of the bells echoed through the chimney and he thought, how eerie.

He swung both legs over the chimney's opening and started his descent, desperately pushing both hands against the cold, dark bricks.

When he looked up, he could see the full moon as bright as it could be in the clear night sky.

Thank God there was no storm tonight; it had been snowing for the past couple of days.

Just after the thought, he had an itch under his nose like never before.

"Damn this beard," he said to himself as he took his right hand and rubbed against the itch.

By the time he realized what he had done, he was already at the bottom of the chimney, choking on the left over ashes they had forgotten to clean.

"Fuck that hurt!" He covered his mouth quickly hoping he caught the curse word before the kids could hear.

"I mean, um, yeah, Ho, Ho, Ho, Merry Christmas!"

I'm glad I don't have a red sack full of toys, too, he thought to himself as he staggered to his feet. That's when he noticed no one was in the room. The lights were all turned off; the only thing penetrating the front window was the moonlight from outside.

"Where the hell is everyone?"

The sofa was there, the TV set, the Christmas tree; everything was in order except for his family.

I don't have all night for this shit, he thought to himself. *I have to go to work tomorrow morning!*

"Okay, you guys, this isn't funny! Where the hell did you go? Now's not the time for hide-and-seek," he called out.

First thing he decided to do was recheck the driveway and verify the family car was still there. They had a new, bright-red Cavalier. They had saved up for what seemed like forever just for the down payment on it.

He threw down his Santa hat when he noticed the vehicle was nowhere in sight.

"Seriously, why the fuck do I even bother?" As he yelled those words, his neighbor, Mark Vinson, was standing to the right of him, and the man gave Christopher a *you-must-be-crazy* stare. Christopher flipped him off before going back inside; making sure the old man saw the gesture first.

I never liked him anyway, he thought, slamming the door and leaving the Santa hat behind in the snow.

Christopher turned on the lights with one flick of the switch and the living room lit up. Deciding he was going to get something to eat, he walked to the kitchen. What he saw next at first was hilarious to him. His wife *was* still home, but she was stumbling all over the place like she was drunk, her arms bent upward at an odd angle as she moved slowly from one side of the kitchen to the other. Every time she hit part of the kitchen, a low moan escaped her lips.

Damn, this would be great for TV, he thought as he considered grabbing the camcorder.

But before he could step away from spying on his wife, he was attacked by his other neighbor, Amanda Waldack, from behind.

Her hands and arms looked leathery and flakey, and most of all blue with frost bite all the way to her shoulders. He noticed this at a glance as she attempted to claw and bite him.

She was an attractive, blonde-hair woman. She had just gotten married last year and was around twenty years old. She had deep blue eyes and was wearing a pink-shirt that said *boys suck on it*, and blue jeans.

No wonder her arms were that way; look at what she's wearing at this time of year! Christopher thought as he tripped her to the ground and ran downstairs to the basement for his gun cabinet.

When he opened it, he grabbed the first gun he saw, a .12-gauge shotgun he'd used as a police officer before he quit after a short term to become an electrician.

Amanda and his wife had already reached the door to the basement by the time he got the shells loaded, and they looked absolutely ravenous.

As the first shot went off, he winced at the report.

The blast struck Amanda in the right side of her neck and blood squirted onto the white plastered wall. Still they both kept coming, and Amanda didn't even flinch! He aimed for her right leg then, not wanting to kill her, and fired again.

She went down all right, but was still going, crawling down the stairs and reaching out to him. The blood from her leg was smearing over the stairs. His wife tripped over her body and he heard a loud crack from her head as she landed on the cement floor face first.

"Fuck! Tisha why'd you do that?" he gasped in shock, forgetting about Amanda's second attack as he checked to see if she was okay. He lifted her head to the right and checked for a pulse.

"Damn it, she's dead! I've killed my own wife!"

He dropped the shotgun to the floor, and as he did, it went off again and caught Amanda square in the head, her body tumbling the rest of the way down the stairs to land on top of his wife.

Tears then flowed from his eyes and dripped from his white beard onto the dead bodies below him.

I'm going to rot in jail for the rest of my life! he thought. *My poor wife, and Amanda—Jamie will never forgive me for this. Amanda was her best friend.*

Christopher went back up stairs and dialed 9-1-1 to turn himself in. He was surprised to hear a busy signal and thought that he'd never heard that before as he hung up the phone.

Feeling guilt and sorrow over his dead wife, he paced the living room for the next five minutes, until he heard more god awful moans coming from the backyard. He decided to see what was going on, but first he went downstairs and grabbed the shotgun and loaded some more shells.

He was horrified by the sight when he got back up and reached the back door.

Standing out his back patio door, he noticed the steel fence separating the property line was completely trampled, and smack in the middle of his backyard were about thirty zombies!

Were they there the entire time I was climbing on the roof? he pondered. He blasted four of them, and he saw in the middle of the pack...a snowman.

He wasn't shocked just yet as it was winter and snowmen were a common sight. That is until he squinted, then focused, and saw what the arms and eyes were made of.

Real human parts!

The torsos were still being eaten and intestines were being dragged across the lawn by a really tall female zombie. The severed heads were just being kicked around by the other ones, and Christopher thought it looked like they were playing soccer.

He couldn't help but chuckle a little and realized he was probably cracking up.

That's what my two girls must have seen and I bet they took off for help or a shelter, he thought.

He fired a couple more shots, missing two zombies by inches. Then they all stopped moving and turned around to stare at him. That's all they did, at first. Just stared at him as if in awe.

Christopher stared back to see what they would do, he even teased and taunted them, laughing the entire time at the absurdity of it all. With his red Santa suit on, he was quite the sight, the crimson color of the material a sharp contrast to the white of the snow-covered backyard.

That appeared to be the last straw for the zombies, because that was when they started stumbling towards him!

Okay, now that was a stupid idea, he thought and ran back inside, locking the door behind him.

He ran out the front door and coincidentally a cab was parked in front of the house across the street. A dark-haired black woman was looking at her watch and turned the ignition back on.

"Wait! For God's sake, please wait!" he called while panting. As he ran towards the cab, he grabbed the Santa hat still lying in the snow. It was still cold out and he put it on tight.

He opened the passenger's door and climbed in while still holding the shotgun.

"Fine, I was going to head home for bed, but I guess you'll be my last fare. I've waited for at least ten minutes, who lives here must not be going out anymore. I wish people would at least have the courtesy and call in and cancel their ride instead of leaving me out here like this!" She glanced in her rearview mirror and saw him in his suit. "Nice Santa suit."

"Yeah, tell me about it," Christopher said.

"Where're you heading, stranger? Hey, what's with the shot-gun?"

"First of all, my name's Christopher. You can call me Chris. The gun's not for you, so relax.

Now just start heading downtown. I need to find my kids and I have a feeling where they might be."

"Nice to meet you, Chris, mine name's Carmen. Just don't do anything hasty with that shotgun. Also, Merry Christmas."

"Yeah, I guess, Merry Christmas to you, too."

"What do you mean *I guess* Merry Christmas?" she asked while pulling out onto the road. Before she drove ten feet, two zombies struck the cab and started clawing at it, moaning the entire time.

"That's what I mean. That's also the reason for this," he replied, raising the shotgun.

"Holy shit. Where the hell did they come from? What's wrong with them?"

"Who knows, I just want to get out of here, get my kids and go from there."

"You have a wife?" she asked.

"Had a wife."

"I'm sorry."

"No problem. How about you? Do you have any family?" Carmen steered around the zombies and stepped on the gas, the cab shooting forward. She'd seen crazy people before and it didn't bother her that much. She had no idea the two attackers were zombies.

"Nope just moved here on my own," she said. "I'm going to the University to be a doctor, this job is only temporary, I hope. My family lives in Baltimore, Maryland."

"Why come to Toronto?"

"Change of scene, and people is all."

"I see. You like it so far?"

"Yeah I think I do."

"Well, that's good."

"Yeah, it is," she added.

"So what was with the two nutjobs who attacked my cab?" she asked.

"Don't ask," Chris said, and when he didn't elaborate, she let it go.

As they reached downtown Toronto, they noticed more and more zombies coming out of the buildings and walking the streets. Carmen asked him again and this time he filled her in on what had happened. She didn't believe him but then her eyes weren't lying to her either.

"Do you think this is a good idea?" she asked.

"I told you I have to find my kids."

"I have a cell, do they?"

"Shit, why didn't I think of that before!"

"Stress does a lot of crazy things to people," she added.

When he tried the cell phone to dial Jackie's number, there was no service, not one bar of signal. He tried one more time after removing the battery and plugging it back in. The cell rang and a glimmer of hope showed on his face.

"Anything?"

"Nope, just a fast busy signal. Then it went out again!"

"Technology sure bites the big one sometimes, don't it?" Carmen said.

"Damn right it does!"

As if on cue, the engine began to sputter and the cab came to a complete halt in the middle of the road.

"What's wrong, why'd we stop?" Chris asked nervously.

Carmen was trying to start the cab but it refused. The engine light was blinking and a loud, grinding sound carried from under the hood each time she turned the key.

"I don't know, damn piece of junk. They said they fixed it!"

Zombies were now moaning all around them, and more were slowly walking towards the vehicle.

"Forget it, we need to go or we're gonna be trapped!" Chris yelled and threw open his door. "Come on!"

They both rushed out of the car and started dashing down Main Street. The zombies were slow walkers so it was very easy to out run them.

"What are we doing now?" Carmen asked, panting.

"I have no fucking clue! Just keep moving, even jogging should be okay with these slow clumsy idiots!"

"Good idea!" she replied. "Do you have any other guns on you other than that shotgun? I have a feeling it's not going to give us any advantages at this point."

"Nope, but it's better than nothing."

She only nodded.

"The worse case scenario is I use it as a club against them when I run out of shells!" he said.

"Right. Got it," she said.

Chris immediately grabbed Carmen by her arm and started dragging her with him towards a bank on the corner.

He shoved her through the bank's glass doors and she landed forward on her hands and knees. As she looked up, she was relieved there were no zombies. The lobby was decorated in standard holiday fashion. A large Christmas tree was set up in the far left corner, decorated from top to bottom with lights and tinsel. On every wall were wreaths, and plastic statues of snowmen and penguins lined the velvet rope used for directing bank customers to the tellers.

There were three tellers behind the counter and each stared at Chris in his disheveled Santa suit and Carmen like they were two homeless people who had wandered in to get out of the cold.

"How did you know?" she asked.

"I didn't, I just guessed!"

"You did what?"

"I told you I guessed!" Chris said. He had made sure to hide the shotgun, not wanting to get shot by a nervous security guard.

They walked up to the counter.

"Hi, how may I help you?" a short haired brunette behind the counter said in the most polite tone Chris had ever heard.

"We're just resting, don't you know what's going on outside?"

"No, I've been in here all day." She looked to her right and asked one of her co-workers; a short girl with long blonde hair and bright blue eyes.

"Do you know what's going on outside, Laura?"

"Nope, same reason why you don't! Why, is there something happening?"

She looked to her left to the other co-worker peering over her PC and with a small pause of silence asked, "Do you know?"

"Hell, no, stop asking me stupid questions all the time, jeez!" the woman snapped.

"Nope. We know nothing," the first teller replied, making her answer as serious and confident as she could, as if trying not to be embarrassed.

"Okay. Well let me be the one to give you the bad news." Chris said and looked for her name-tag, which was upside down on her right breast. Turning his head almost upside down to read it, he replied, "Rachel, if that's what it says, or whoever you are, there are zombies outside!"

She blinked at him like he was crazy.

"That's right, I'm telling you that there are zombies out there! Bloodsucking, brain-eating, intestines ripping..."

Both tellers, except for the one he didn't know the name of, busted out in laughter.

"My name's Ashley... thank you very much," the last teller said. "Now please leave. If you two don't have any bank account concerns you have no business in this bank." She finished by crossing her arms and glaring at him. "Don't make me call the bank manager."

"Thanks for that demonstration of a crazy man. You could really make it as an actor," Laura replied chuckling as she looked at Chris.

"I'm not acting," Chris said. "And no I don't have any fucking bank account questions. Look, I'm trying to find my kids. They're out there somewhere and probably scared shitless!"

"Have you had your break yet?" Laura asked Rachel out of nowhere, still laughing a little herself. With Chris in the Santa suit, it was hard to take him very seriously.

Chris had had enough. "Fine, we'll just let the zombies in here and you can see for yourselves." He started walking towards the front doors where he noticed one of the zombies was attempting to walk through the rotating doors, but failing miserably.

No wonder the tellers are safe in here, he thought. *Those zombies are definitely stupid.*

"Wait! He's telling the truth," Carmen said and slammed her right hand down on the counter as if to confirm her response.

"Okay, fine. If there are zombies outside, then there are zombies outside. What do we do now?" Rachel responded.

"Why not tell the boss. Maybe we can leave early?" Laura responded while chuckling.

"I don't think Mr. Sarvis would mind us leaving due to a zombie invasion Laura," Rachel said.

"Mr. Sarvis!" Laura called out.

"What do you want, Laura," a man's voice replied.

Chris and Carmen stood back at the loud response that came from the closed office door behind the tellers. On the door in neat script was **Paul Sarvis, Executive Manager**.

"Can we close the bank early?" Laura asked.

"For what possible reason?"

"There's a zombie invasion taking place outside," Laura informed him.

"A zombie what?"

"Invasion..."

"I think you mean an apocalypse," he chuckled. He checked his watch and saw it was close to quitting time anyway. "Are there any customers out there?"

"Are you two customers?" Laura asked.

"Nope." Chris and Carmen said in unison.

"No, sir! The lobby's empty!"

Then you can leave early if you want to, Laura," Mr. Sarvis said. "But Rachel and Ashley must stay until closing time, six p.m. sharp!"

Both women glared at Laura in pure hatred as she got her purse from under her desk, turned off her PC after saving her files, and walked around the counter as she waved goodnight.

"Do you mind if we hitch a ride?" Chris asked Laura.

Laura looked Chris and Carmen up and down for the tenth time since meeting them and finally, she shrugged.

"Sure, I guess I could give you a ride. After all, it is the Christmas season. But I won't go out of my way; you need to pick someplace that's on my way."

"Fine, that's fine," Chris said and Carmen nodded too.

"Okay, stay here," Laura said. "I have to get my car from the garage across the street. I'll beep when I pull up front. Don't keep me waiting,"

"We won't," Carmen replied.

They both sighed in relief as she walked out the rotating doors and then Chris chuckled as the zombie moaned due to the revolving door trapping him inside it. The zombie who looked like a bank teller wore black pants, black overcoat, blue tie and white buttoned t-shirt. He had on a name-tag with the name **Stan Ryland** on it.

"Is that Stan?" Rachel called from behind the counter. "He works here."

"I don't know, I guess so." Chris replied, "That's what his name-tag says."

"He looks stuck in the revolving door. Could you help him, please?" Rachel asked.

"I don't think that's a good idea," Chris warned.

"Why?"

"Because I think he's a zombie."

Stan started to claw at the glass door, moaning loudly, but still unable to move the rotating door.

Suddenly, a scream was heard through the glass doors, coming from just across the street.

"Told her there were zombies out there," Chris said with a frown, shaking his head at the stupidity of the woman. "I'll bet there goes our ride."

At that moment, Stan managed to work his way inside the lobby, and he started to stumble towards Ashley and Rachel.

"See, he's dead!" Chris said.

"But he's walking just fine," Ashley stated.

"He's not walking, he's stumbling," Chris said.

"Whatever," Rachel added, checking the clock on the wall to see how much longer until the bank closed.

Chris pulled out his shotgun from under his red suit and shot Stan once in the back, but he kept moving.

"Now if he was alive, he would have fallen to the ground dead. But he's a zombie. Have I made my point?"

He then shot Stan in the head and this time he went down for good, his brains and pieces of skull splattering across the polished tiles of the lobby.

"I'm tired of this crap. Where's Wendy's from here? I think my kids went there as that's where they work."

"Actually it's just two blocks down," Ashley said, her face frozen in horror as she stared at Stan's corpse. She was shaking in fear, expecting Chris to shoot her too. Mr. Sarvis came out of his office at the sound of the shotgun, but once he saw what happened, he dashed back into his office, slamming the door like a good coward would.

"You're shitting me..." Chris said. "It's only a few blocks away?"

"Yup, right on the corner of Dalton St."

"I knew I was close but didn't think I was that close! Jesus. I'm getting out of here." He gestured with the shotgun to the corpse of Stan. "Sorry about the mess."

"Think nothing of it," Rachel replied as she swallowed the lump in her throat.

With a wave goodbye, Chris pushed his way through the rotating door, keeping the shotgun with him, he was out of ammunition now but figured he would take Carmen's advice and use it as a club. Carmen followed behind him, not knowing what else to do.

Laura's body parts were scattered across the street and her head tumbled down the sidewalk as the zombies walked over her. A dozen zombies had pieces of Laura in their mouths, chewing happily. One, zombie dressed up like Santa Claus, glanced at Chris and did a double take, as if he was looking in a mirror. Then he went back to eating, content for the moment.

More screams could be heard as the city began to break down, the zombie invasion in full swing.

Using the shotgun like a club, Chris fought his way down the street with Carmen close behind him. Twenty minutes later, breathing hard and covered in gore, he crashed through Wendy's front door with his right elbow pushing the door open. Slipping on the blood-covered white tiles, he struggled to keep his balance which he managed to do by holding on to the bar on the door.

Then a wave of dread washed over him as his two children, Jackie and Jamie started to stumble towards him, arms stretched out and clawing at the air. They had immerged from the women's washroom, he noticed as the door swung closed. They also had red drool dripping from their mouths.

Behind the counter to the restaurant, the counter barricaded high with boxes and chairs, he saw two cashiers. Both were heavily built men. Chris watched them raise their guns from behind them and aim them in Chris' direction. Both were pistols and were aimed at his kids and himself.

"No, don't shoot! They're not zombies...they can't be!"

He noticed someone sitting in the booth beside him, and saw it was an old man with a beard, and a Santa suit just like his. The man was dead as a doornail. He saw the pistol jutting out of the dead Santa's pocket and quickly grabbed it, dropping his shotgun as he pulled the body in front of him just as the two cashiers fired their weapons.

He counted four or five shots fired at him. Possibly there were more, but it was hard to tell as the gunshots echoed throughout the restaurant. He used the dead fake Santa as a human shield against the oncoming blasts.

He didn't see the zombie behind him as he returned fire, not realizing only clicking sounds emerged from the gun. He screamed out in agony when he felt the zombie's teeth sink into his exposed neck. Blood shot out, staining his Santa suit a darker crimson.

Then, as he tried to stand up, a bullet from one of the cashier's pistols went through his forehead and he dropped to the ground face first. His two kids fell over shortly after two more shots were fired.

The first cashier glanced over to his buddy and said, "He dead?"

"Yep. We killed Santa Claus again."

"Does that mean... we just killed Christmas?"

"Sure does, buddy, Christmas is most definitely dead."

They started polishing their guns and loading them up again, on the counter, as the song, *Have Yourself A Merry Little Christmas*, played through the restaurant speakers, the Christmas lights glowed and changed amongst their many colors.

ZOMBIES OF THE CARIBBEAN

VAL MULLER

Standing in line to see Santa Claus, Ali huffed. "It's too hot," she complained. "It's not Christmas without snow. And the *real* Santa doesn't wear shorts."

Her parents, Marion and Ted, sweltered in the Yacht Haven Grande shopping plaza. Marion, ready with her camera, sighed. "Imagine not wanting to spend Christmas in the Caribbean."

"I don't have to imagine it," Ted muttered.

Maybe you're just too far from Tiffany, Marion thought, but she didn't say it. She hummed along with the Christmas songs playing through the plaza's outdoor speakers. "Come on, where's your Christmas spirit?"

"It must have melted," Ted groaned. "And if Ali complains to my mother, that's all I need. She's already pissed we won't be there for Christmas."

"It was *your* idea not to see your parents this Christmas."

"How could we spend Christmas there with you acting the way you do?"

"What way is that?"

Like a bitch, Ted wanted to say, but he kept quiet. "They'd know something was up."

"Well, maybe they should."

"Geez, forgive and forget already!"

"I'll forgive when you act like you're sorry."

Ted crossed his arms. The plaza was too crowded for an argument. Besides, he'd still been seeing Tiffany in secret even after Marion found out.

From the nearby cruise ship harbored nearby, a group of tourists screamed strangely and ran off the boat and into Yacht Haven shopping plaza. On the ship's main deck, high above the plaza, someone shouted and dove into the water below. A police officer hurried by the Santa display toward the splash, muttering into his radio.

"Cruise ships," Ted mused. "I'll bet they've been drunk since they first boarded."

"Wouldn't that be right up your alley?" Marion smirked.

"Actually, it would be."

The group had stopped screaming and was now weaving clumsily in and out of the crowd.

"Lousy drunks," Marion mumbled.

The couple turned to Ali, who was next in line. Marion squatted to get a shot of Ali and Santa with the lighted palm tree in the background.

"Santa doesn't look too good," Marion whispered as she steadied her camera.

"It's the heat," Ted said. The man wore a heavy white beard and a long-sleeved red and white fur coat over red Bermuda shorts.

"And who do we have here?" Santa asked Ali.

"Mo-om, do I have to?" Ali asked.

"Come on, honey, don't you want Santa to bring you any gifts?"

Ali crossed her arms, quite precocious for a five-year-old. "This isn't Santa. Santa lives at the North Pole. Everyone knows that."

"It's Santa's helper," Ted offered. "Now go sit on his lap."

Ali shuffled to the man. "He smells!"

"Ali!" both parents scolded.

Santa seemed not to notice. "Ho, ho, ho," he said. He stopped and stared, unsure what to do next.

"Have you been good this year?" whispered one of his elves.

"Have you been good this year?" Santa repeated brainlessly.

Behind Santa were three elves, all female, dressed a little too scantily in little green furry skirts and matching bikini tops.

"Some elves!" Ted said. "Make sure you get a snapshot of them!"

Marion eyed them. *How could I have married such an asshole?* she wondered. "They're not that sexy. Look at the one in back. Looks like she's about to keel over. Probably hung over…"

"Have a merry Chri…" Santa started saying, but then stopped. His right hand rested heavily on Ali's lap so that she couldn't get up.

"Okay, already, I get it," Ali said. "Have a Merry Christmas, be good and all that." Ali moved to get up, but Santa's arm remained heavy on her lap.

"Let me up already," she said.

Santa looked at her with unfocused eyes and mouth agape. Two elves exchanged nervous glances.

"Mom!" Ali called. "He won't let me up."

Santa turned to her. "Something's wrong. I feel so... so..."

"Ali," Ted said. "Come here. We're leaving."

"I'm *trying* to come there!" She pulled, but Santa's hands wouldn't budge. The sickly-looking elf used the distraction to slump to the floor, shutting her eyes. The other two tried to pry Santa's hands off of Ali. As if someone cut the cord of a marionette puppet, Santa's head dropped, making a dull *clunk* as it landed on Ali's skull.

"Ouch!" she screamed.

"Santa's fainted!" a tourist shouted.

"He's got the same thing as that woman on our ship," another tourist said, pointing to the cruise ship harbored nearby.

"Get him off!" Ali screamed.

One of the elves ran to the security booth while Ted tried to pry the man's arm off his daughter.

"Hurry, Ted!" Marion called.

"I'm trying, but he's..."

"He's what?"

"Like rigor mortis! His arms are locked stiff."

"Get me out!" Ali yelled.

"Ted, get Ali out right now!"

The elf that stayed let out an ear-piercing scream. Ted couldn't help but turn to her and notice the way her body shifted under her uniform as she scrambled out of the way.

"Ted, focus!" Marion called. "I can't believe you!"

Ted turned back to his daughter. Without warning, Santa's head had popped up. In a moment of lucidity, he looked Ali directly in the eye, then brought his head quickly to her shoulder and bit down hard.

Ali screamed hysterically.

"Get him off!" Marion yelled. The elf joined Ted and pushed Santa away.

Santa's eyes rolled back completely, and he sank his teeth into his co-worker. "Duke, you bastard!" the elf screamed, "You bit me, too!" She sucked a few drops of blood from her forearm.

In the line to see Santa, parents leaned awkwardly to shield the sight from their screaming kids. Shop employees ushered them into the air-conditioned stores, but most tourists just stood frozen in awe. A Jeep drove wildly onto the pavilion sidewalk driven by the elf.

"I told security," she screamed. "Angie, get in!"

The second elf ran to the vehicle, still nursing her forearm. "What about Amie?"

The two elves looked for their co-worker, who was still slumped over, comatose.

"Leave her! She's drunk or something. Just get in!"

Tires squealed as the Jeep sped away. Seconds later, a security guard arrived on foot. He spoke into his radio. "Call 9-1-1," he said. "A girl's been...attacked by Santa Claus." He turned to Marion and Ted. "Everything'll be okay." It was clear from his accent he was a transplant from the States. His shirt was freshly-pressed and bore the nametag **Jones**.

"Look, Jones," Ted said, "I want that asshole handcuffed." He pointed to Santa, who remained seated in the chair, his head hanging limply and a few droplets of blood dripping down his beard. He appeared to be chewing.

Jones nodded and handcuffed Santa to the light post just behind him. "Stay back," he told the crowd.

In the long line of children that wrapped around the shopping center, hundreds of eyes stared in amazement or fear, disgust or horror.

"Did you see how Santa bit a chunk out of that girl?" a wide-eyed boy asked.

"Yeah, Jason!" shrieked his younger brother. "She's so lucky! They should call him Santa Claws!" He flexed his fingers menacingly to illustrate the pun.

Nearby, a four-year-old was crying. "Momma, why did Santa *do* that?"

"That wasn't really Santa," insisted the child's father. "It was an imposter. I'm calling management!" He stormed out of the plaza, wife and child in tow.

Meanwhile, Santa had slid out of his seat and sat slumped on the ground against the light post. His arm hung by the handcuff uncomfortably over his head.

The wide-eyed Jason approached, followed by his younger brother Timmy.

"Maybe we should wait for Mom and Dad," Timmy whimpered.

"They're gonna be shopping forever. Come on!" Jason stepped closer.

Santa raised two bloodshot eyes to the boys. One white eyebrow had fallen off his face, and the other had slid to an unnatural and menacing angle. The man's blood-stained beard was also half-detached.

"See, Timmy?" said Jason. "He isn't really Santa."

Timmy nodded. "But look how yellow his eyes are. And his skin is blue!"

Santa's eyes rolled back in his head, and his skull fell forward against his chest.

"Is he...d...dead?" asked Timmy.

"Nah," Jason insisted. He picked up a fallen palm frond and poked Santa with it.

Santa sat still at first, but as Jason continued to poke him, he sat erect, snapping at the boy with heavy teeth. Only the handcuff kept Jason safe.

"No, boys!" cried another security guard, this one a native. "You must leave dis man alone. Where are your parents?"

"Shopping." Timmy pointed to the stores.

"Go find dem," the security guard said. "Don't touch not'ing. Just go to your parents. Now!"

The boys scattered.

"What took you so long, Louis?" Jones shouted. He had been applying a temporary bandage to Ali's wound. Louis quickly ushered the crowd out of the way. They hurried into the safety of air-conditioned stores, but their wide eyes stared from inside the display windows. Louis turned back to the Santa.

"Jones, come here. Don't touch dat girl. Come right here."

Jones packed up his first aid kit and joined Louis on the other side of the cuffed Santa.

"Did you call 9-1-1?" Jones asked.

"9-1-1? Are you crazy?"

"That girl is injured. And who knows what's wrong with this guy!" He lightly tapped Santa's leather sandal with his foot. The man moaned and snapped half-heartedly at Jones.

"I do," said Louis. "I know just what's wrong with dis man. You continentals have never seen it, but I know."

"What's wrong with him? Why didn't you call 9-1-1?"

"Ever heard of a zombie?" Louis asked in a hushed voice.

"A zombie!" Jones nearly shouted.

"Shhh! Not so loud."

"A zombie?" Jones whispered. "Are you kidding me?"

"No. And do you have any *idea* what could happen if we brought it to de hospital?"

"Maybe they could help him?"

"Help him! Only one person I know on dis island could help him. And with the price and pain of de cure, better not to help at all."

"Is an ambulance coming?" Ted asked, approaching the security officers.

Louis turned to Jones. "Don't mention zombies."

"No ambulance," Jones told Ted.

"No? Then what are we waiting around for?" Ted complained.

Jones looked uncomfortably at Louis.

"Dis is not an emergency," Louis said. "Take her to de clinic. Follow dis road about three miles down. There's a clinic on de left. You'll see it."

"Some vacation this is, Marion," Ted said.

"Can we save our fighting till later?" she asked.

As Ted and Marion trudged toward their car, carrying Ali like a sack of potatoes, Louis whispered to Jones. "Do you have any idea what would happen if we brought dem to de hospital? Do you know how many bodies dey could infect?"

"Infect? How?"

"You continentals can't understand. It's been so long since a zombie attack. You all t'ink dey only exist in de movies. But now you see; dey *are* real!"

Jones shook his head. "Whatever." He reached toward Santa who was slumped again.

"No!" Louis shouted.

"What?"

"You must be more careful. He bites," Louis warned.

"Yeah, I know. He's a real asshole. I don't know what kind of drugs you'd have to be on to bite a little girl like that. And at Christmas time, too." With that, Jones uncuffed Santa's hands. "Come on, buddy. We'll get you some help."

Jones was pulling dead weight. It took a good four minutes just to get Santa to his feet. All this while, Louis watched from a distance.

"A little help?" Jones asked, drenched in sweat.

"I don't mess wit' zombies," Louis insisted.

When Jones finally got the man to his feet, he led him to the security van. Santa shuffled behind Jones without any resistance, his body threatening to collapse at any time. His arms swung stiffly as if to keep balance.

"Louis, you gotta stop your zombie talk. You've got this guy acting like one. Must've heard you."

Jones finally got Santa to lean against the van. Its dark blue paint absorbed the sun and awoke Santa from his trance.

"Meeeer!" he growled, raising his head. His yellow, bloodshot eyes had trouble focusing. His skin was pale, blue, and dry.

"This guy sure is sick." Jones opened the door and reached to guide the man inside when Santa's head suddenly jerked forwards. It slammed into the car door, but Santa seemed unfazed. With a guttural grunt, the man lunged forward and bit a chunk of flesh from Jones' thumb.

"No!" Jones screamed. Santa's head swung back, and his jaw moved up and down, chewing loudly on Jones' bitten flesh. Louis was screaming and approaching and reaching into his belt. In one continuous motion, Louis pushed Santa onto the ground and pulled Jones away. Louis grabbed Jones' bleeding hand and slammed it onto the hot metal hood.

"Ow!" Jones tried to pull his arm away, but Louis held tight.

"Stay very still," Louis said. He raised his arm into the sky. Jones could see it held a shiny object that glistened in the sun. A knife. Louis screamed as he brought it down with all his strength.

It cut cleanly through both flesh and bone, leaving a straight gash on the otherwise pristine hood.

When Jones looked down, he could hardly believe that was his thumb right there, rolling down the hood and onto the blacktop below. The blood pouring onto the hood was already sizzling in the heat.

"What the hell, Louis!?" he yelled.

"It was de thumb or de soul," Louis said. He pulled off his undershirt and wrapped the white cloth tightly against Jones' wound. The cloth turned red almost immediately. "You will t'ank me when you see. Now hold dat tight. I'll drive." He pushed Jones into the passenger seat.

"What about Santa over there?" Jones asked weakly.

But it was too late. Louis had already put the car in reverse and backed the front tires over the man. Switching gears into drive, Louis maneuvered the van over the body with a *thud-thud*. Jones told himself he wouldn't look in the rearview mirror to see Santa's crushed skull bleeding brains onto the pavement; but he looked anyway.

*   *   *

The clinic was a dilapidated one-story building nearly hidden from the road by unkempt palm trees.

"State of the art," Ted said sarcastically as he parked along the gravel shoulder. "Place looks deserted."

Marion was too focused on Ali. "A little help!" She tried to exit the car while cradling Ali, who slept awkwardly in her arms. "She has a fever."

"Oh, Marion!" Ted came around to the passenger side and grabbed his daughter. "Maybe a little hot," he admitted.

Marion opened the clinic door for him, but before she could follow, someone caught her eye.

It was a strange old woman, her white hair thin and wispy in a loose bun. Her skin was dark and wrinkly, her eyes shut tight in two puffy slits. She wore a colorful dress that looked as old as she. As Ted ventured inside with Ali, the woman's nose sniffed and sniffed, and the expression on her face changed to alarm.

When the old woman's eyes popped open, Marion jumped. They were large and watery, one hazel and the other brown.

"I seen dem comin' on de ferry from St. John. Dey do so every now 'n den. She's a child, so it'll work more slowly on her, but it'll work none de less. You take care dat she don't bite you now, chil'."

"Bite me?"

"You know, chil', what bit her. Deep down, you know."

The door opened, and Ali shuffled out. "Mommy, will you wait with me?"

"All right, honey," Marion said, but her eyes remained locked on the old woman. "I'll be right there, Ali. Wait inside with Daddy."

Ali lingered at the door.

"You know, don't you?" the old woman asked again.

"I don't know what you're saying. That man was on drugs."

"Ain't no drugs powerful enough to do dat. Dat man was a zombie!"

Marion turned to the door, but it was too late, Ali had already heard, her eyes bulging at the idea. In the clinic, the nurse stitched Ali's shoulder and gave her some topical cream and a fever reducer.

"What a bullshit Christmas," Ted whispered to Marion on the way out. "I should have never given in to this stupid idea of yours."

"Then go fly home to your parents, Ted. Or to Tiffany for all I care."

As she got into the car, Marion saw the old woman again.

"Wait a minute," Marion told Ted, and returned to the woman.

"Dem zombies got only one cure besides killin' em, and it's so painful and cost so much money dat it's only worth it for de chil'." The woman pointed a withered finger towards Ali. "She got her whole life in front o' her. By de time she grow up, she won't even remember nothin' about it. But for him," she said, pointing to Ted, "de cure wouldn't be worth de pain or de money. Especially for you, sweetie." She smiled at Marion. "He ain't worth none of it."

"I..."

"Don't say nothin', chil'. I know how it is. Your motherly love don' let you believe, but when you see how she gets, you come lookin' for me. Come to Water Island. By de time you need me, de ferry won't even be runnin' no more. You swim out to Water

Island. Bring money and courage. I'm de only one who still knows de cure. De only one who still knows de ol' ways. Mama Claudette, dat's me. Bring all de money you can. Don't bring your man. He's bad luck."

"Marion, let's go!" Ted screamed from inside the car.

"Coming," Marion said, glancing at Ted. When she turned back to the old woman, she was already gone.

*   *   *

After a short nap, Ali's fever broke. Marion put extra cream on the wound as it looked likely to fester.

Ted had spent hours at the airport trying to find a flight back home. "They're all overbooked," he said. "We couldn't even get on standby until the 27th. Everyone started freaking out and buying up seats home."

Marion fussed over Ali.

"Let's get out of this damned hotel room," Ted said. "How 'bout going into the ocean. Salt water'll do her some good."

"Ali?" Marion asked. "Do you feel like going into the ocean?"

"I dunno. Do zombies like the ocean?"

"Zombies? Honey, why does that matter?" Marion put a hand on her daughter's shoulder and stared her in the eye.

"You heard what that woman said. I got bit by a zombie, and I'm gonna be one, too. So I might as well get used to it."

"This is bullshit," Ted muttered. He dug through a drawer, retrieved his swim trunks, and slammed the bathroom door behind him.

"Mommy, is Daddy gonna love me when I turn into a zombie?"

"Honey," Marion said, "Daddy's going to love you no matter what. And you're not turning into a zombie. That woman didn't know what she was talking about."

"She sounded like she did," Ali said.

"No, honey, she..."

Ted opened the door and stormed past them, carrying a towel. "You coming or not? We're working against sunset here."

*   *   *

At the beach, Ali sat in the sand with her bucket and shovel. Ted had already jumped into the ocean, complained about the tepid temperature and lack of waves, returned to the beach chair, and ordered a pina colada from the scantily-clad server roaming the beach with a pink Santa hat.

Marion sat watching her daughter with concern. "You think she's all right, Ted?"

Ted huffed. "Didn't we come here not to worry? Every Christmas you're a bundle of stress. The whole reason I agreed to this God-forsaken trip was so you could actually relax for once. Now you can't even do that."

"That's not the only reason we came," Marion muttered, wishing he'd just get drunk and happy already. "Besides, how can I relax after that awful Santa?"

"Hopefully that asshole got hit by a bus," Ted said. He tilted his drink back, emptied it, and waved to the server for a refill.

Marion turned to Ali. "What are you doing, honey?

Ali, intent on digging in the sand, seemed not to hear.

"Are you building a sand castle?" Marion asked patiently.

Again, Ali didn't answer.

"Damn it, Ali, when your mother asks you a question, you answer her!" Ted snapped.

Ali seemed unfazed by her father's anger. She dug a few more shovelfuls of sand before looking up at her parents with a strange, solemn expression.

"I'm digging a grave," she said.

Ted chuckled.

"A grave, honey?" Marion asked. "Why?"

"It's where zombies sleep."

"But you aren't a zombie, Ali."

"Not yet. But soon."

Marion looked at Ted, but he was too busy making googily eyes at the server, who had arrived with another drink.

"This is just what I need, baby," he was saying.

The server smiled but looked awkwardly at Marion. "Anything for you, ma'am?" she asked.

"No." Marion pulled off her t-shirt and trudged toward the shore. "Watch your daughter, Ted," she said over her shoulder with disgust.

"Wives," Ted said to the server, throwing up his arms. He took a sip of his drink, then reached into his pocket. "Let's say you start working on a refill for me." He put a roll of cash in her bikini top. She giggled and bounced toward the bar.

Halfway through his drink, he turned to Ali. "Ali, you don't *really* think you're a zombie, do you?"

By now, Ali had dug a significant hole, longer than her height, and she was deepening it. She worked intently for over a minute before answering her father.

"Would you still love me when I'm a zombie?" She peeked over her sand-grave just in time to see the server coming back with another frosty drink.

"I'll watch you play sand castle in a minute, honey. Daddy's got to pay for his drink."

Ali turned back to her work. She stretched out in the hole, like a cadaver, and covered her legs and torso with sand.

Ted lost himself in conversation with the server.

After a few minutes the server's smile faded. "Where did your daughter go?"

Ted turned to Ali's grave, but it was nearly filled in, and she was gone.

"Damn it!" He looked out to sea, where Marion was floating on her back, staring straight at the sky. "I'll never hear the end of it if Ali's gone when Marion gets back." He got up quickly, spilling the colada. "Shit!" he said too loudly, and tossed the cup out onto the beach. "The damn kid thinks she's a zombie. She was digging a grave, and..."

"A zombie? I'd be careful who I repeated that to," the server said.

"What?"

The server frowned. "About being a zombie. I'm not originally from around here, but I know plenty of people who would murder anyone suspected of being one."

"Murder a little girl? Never."

"I'm serious. The locals here, they... just keep it to yourself, okay?" She walked slowly back to the bar, her face a little paler than when she arrived.

Ali was still nowhere in sight. "Damn it!" Ted cried, kicking his chair across the sand.

"Quiet, Daddy. You'll scare away the kids."

"What the?" Ted saw a small opening in the sand, through which he could see Ali's mouth and one eye. "What're you doing?"

"Trapping victims," Ali chanted. "Children are the easiest."

Ted shook his head. The alcohol was starting to work its magic, but not quickly enough. "Honey, are you going to stay like that, under the sand, while Daddy gets a drink to replace the one you made him spill?"

"Yes."

"Good girl." Ted trudged to the bar.

Minutes later, Marion was coming out of the ocean and Ted was at the bar when they both heard the same high-pitched shriek. They ran towards the area where Ali had been digging.

"Excuse me!" screamed a woman in a red cover-up. She was consoling a teary-eyed child. "Is that your daughter?" She pointed to a squirming mound of sand.

"Yes," Marion sighed.

"Well, she scared the wits out of my son, popping out of the sand like that. And then she tried to *bite* him!"

"She *did* bite me, Mommy!" the boy held up his pinky.

"You all need to be quiet!" Ali insisted from the sand. "Else I'm never gonna catch another victim. I almost got him, but his stupid mother got in the way. Not sure if I bit him hard enough. Didn't get any meat."

"She thinks she's a zombie," Ted explained.

"What horrible people!" the teary-eyed mother cried, ushering her son away. "Degenerates!" she called over her shoulder.

"Ted, did you see her burying herself?"

Ted nodded.

"You asshole! You figured since she was all tucked away under the sand, you might as well hit the bar?"

"I'm not the one who wanted to spend the goddamn holidays in this Hell-hole."

"Hell-hole? This is a tropical paradise."

"Doesn't seem like paradise to me," Ted grunted.

"Would you just get your daughter out of the sand?"

"Can't get a moment's peace," he groaned.

"Why don't you go back to Tiffany? Maybe she'll give you some peace."

"Babe, that was six months ago. When are you gonna drop it?"

"Just help me get Ali," Marion said. She was on her knees and digging at the sand, but Ali buried herself faster than Marion could excavate.

"Leave me alone, I'm a zombie," Ali's muffled voice protested through the sand.

"Give me some room," Ted said, pulling Marion out of the way. He dropped to his knees and stuck his arms into the loosened sand, trying to catch Ali between them. As he did so, sand exploded all around him as Ali sat straight up. Her skull bashed into his.

"What the…" he said.

She looked horrid, with the damp sand clinging to her hair and skin in uneven clumps. She barely looked human.

"Ali!" Marion cried.

"I *said*, leave me alone! I'm hungry!" She lunged forward and sunk her teeth into the flesh of Ted's bicep.

"You little bitch!" he cried, pushing her away.

"That's your daughter!" Marion screamed. She ran to the sand-covered girl, gave Ted a nasty look, and ushered Ali towards the ocean. "Let's try to clean you up," she said as gently as possible.

"What about me?" Ted called. "Do you give a rat's ass about me?" He paused, but neither responded. "I'm bleeding," he offered, holding up his arm. A few scarlet drops soaked into the sand. "Fuck it," he said. He yelled inaudibly, throwing his half-empty drink cup toward the ocean. "Fuck it all!"

*   *   *

Hours later, Ted sat at a beach bar miles from the hotel. He'd meant only to walk to the resort next door, but each time he tried to stop, he felt nauseous and couldn't fathom the thought of more alcohol.

When the nausea finally subsided, he parked himself at a stool at The Tiki Bar, a hole-in-the-wall on the beach that looked likely to blow away in the next hurricane. Tonight, it was adorned with LED candy cane lights.

"What can I get you?" the bartender asked. He looked barely old enough to drink.

"You sure look like you need one," said a bar patron in a proud Texas accent. He wore a black felt cowboy hat and a gaudy bolo tie secured with a bright snowman clasp.

"Just want an end to the bullshit."

"My name's Jimmie. What can I get you?" the bartender asked again.

"What's your special?" Ted asked.

"The zombie," Jimmie said. Ted's expression remained blank. "It's sweet, full of rum..."

Slowly, Ted spoke. "The zombie, huh? Where'd you come up with a bullshit drink like that?"

The Texan laughed. "It's in honor of that girl."

"What girl?"

"You jus' get here, partner? Some little girl was visiting Santa at Yacht Haven. Well, Santa stroked out and bit her. All hell broke loose, and Santa got run over."

"They say he was a zombie," Jimmie added, sliding a cold zombie drink to Ted. "And now everyone's looking for that girl."

"Why?"

"She was bitten by a zombie. Or so they say," Jimmie said.

Ted pounded his fist. "You believe that shit? How long have you lived here?"

"Long enough to know that there's stuff out there best left alone." Jimmie shook his head.

"A young lady was jus' here," the Texan said with a blush, "and telling us of a similar thing that happened on her cruise ship. Why, she refused to get back on board. Now she's stuck here 'cuz the airline's all booked up. I offered her my room, but she refused."

The Texan shared a laugh with the bartender.

Ted slammed his fist on the counter. His movements seemed labored. He wondered why; he wasn't even that drunk yet.

"Ain't you on vacation?" the Texan asked. "You look like an anemic. You need to get some sun. And take a sip o' that zombie. You need to jes' relax. What's got you, partner?"

Ted looked at the man with disdain. He hadn't noticed the horrid red-nosed reindeer on his belt clip before. "None of your business," he said slowly.

The Texan put his hands up to show he wasn't a threat. "Look, buddy. All I'm saying is to enjoy your vacation, all right? Get some sun, and some sleep. It's the holidays, remember. Peace, love and goodwill."

Ted nodded and sipped his drink. Though it tasted sweet and tangy at first, it made him feel nauseous as it went down. "So what'll they do with this girl when they find her?" Ted asked no one in particular.

Jimmie chuckled. "Around here, she'd probably just disappear."

"Disappear?"

"You know, have an accident or something. Disappear."

"Ain't not'ing more sorry den de child zombie," said a bar patron who had been sitting in a shadowy corner.

Ted looked at the stranger. "What are you saying? You mean they're going to kill the little girl?"

The stranger leaned forward into the red glow of the candy cane lights. His muscular, ebony skin glowed in the lights. "It's de bes' way."

"The best way?"

"To stop de spread. It's why dey killed Santa."

"Stop the spread?"

"If she was bitten, she'll turn. She'll bite others, and pretty soon, we all be zombies."

The Texan shook his head. "I don't know 'bout no zombies, but I don't see how anyone could kill a little girl."

"It's not a girl no more," the stranger explained.

Jimmie shook his head. "I'll tell ya, I'd love to see a zombie in person."

"No you wouldn't," the stranger insisted. "Dey need to kill her."

"Damn it!" Ted slammed his drink onto the counter. "This tastes like shit!"

"I don't think it's so bad," said the Texan.

"Well, fuck you, buddy!"

"Hey now, that ain't called for," he said, straightening his hat. "That ain't the Christmas spirit at all."

"Watch it, buddy," Jimmie warned Ted.

"No. I mean it. Fuck you and you and you." Ted pointed a finger at each. "And fuck Christmas, and this dumb drink, and your stupid hat, these dumb lights, and..."

Before Ted could finish, the Texan got up and threw a punch right into Ted's jaw. Ted felt the crack before he saw the Texan; his perception and movement seemed encumbered as if his body were suspended in gelatin.

"Out! Both of you!" Jimmie said.

Ted's face throbbed from the blow, but somehow it didn't hurt as he thought it would. He struggled to focus his eyes. The Texan stared him down, feet squared and fist poised for another blow. Ted's body reacted without his consent. He felt himself lunge forward quickly, forcefully. He took the Texan by surprise and knocked him to the floor. His teeth gnashed at the air with an unbearable sense of frustration. The satisfaction finally came as his teeth bit through the flap of skin above the Texan's collar. His victim's body froze with shock as Ted pulled off a chunk of skin.

Jimmie shuddered. "You sick bastard!"

"You wanted to see de zombie," the stranger said without moving. "Dere you go. Dis man's been bitten."

"He doesn't look like a zombie."

"Not yet. But it's in dere. He'll turn before long. He already can't stand de drink."

Jimmie jumped the counter and struggled to pull Ted off the Texan, who backed away in terror. Ted smiled at the bartender. The world had finally stopped spinning, and Ted widened his smile, revealing a row of red teeth fresh with the Texan's blood.

The stranger moved quickly to pull Jimmie out of harm's way. "Who bit you? Who bit you?" the stranger was asking Ted over and over.

Without answering, Ted tried to run, but the world again felt enclosed in gelatin. He settled on a shuffle-walk through the sand and headed in the direction of his hotel.

"We got to get dat bastard!" the stranger screamed. "Dere's only one real way to get rid of zombies! Kill dem!"

Shaken, Jimmie put his hands in the air to show he'd have no part of it.

"Don't just stand dere," the stranger said. "Get a knife. A knife!"

Jimmie fumbled and grabbed the first thing he saw, a plastic disposable knife for guests who ordered bar food.

"Dat ain't a knife!" the stranger cried. He jumped over the bar and searched under the counter until he found what he was looking for; a large chef's knife, its handle sticky with coconut juice. "Dis is a knife!"

He jumped back over the counter and knelt to the ground, where the Texan huddled against a bar stool. His wound dripped blood, and his eyes looked straight through the stranger. Already, the color was draining from his sunburned skin.

The stranger removed the Texan's hat. "You would t'ank me if you could. It's better dis way." The Texan looked blankly at the stranger, who raised the chef's knife behind his back. In a swift, stealth motion, he ran the knife around the Texan's throat. Blood poured out, absorbing into the sandy wood beneath the stool. The Texan tried to speak, but it came out only as a bloody gurgle.

"Urg!" Jimmie held his stomach.

"I had to do it," the stranger said. "He was already becoming a zombie."

He ran the knife the whole way around the neck and sawed firmly at the man's vertebrae to loosen the head. "Jus' to be sure," he said. Jimmie watched, frozen in horror and unable to remove his eyes from the gore.

Moments later, the stranger's brown shirt was visibly soaked in the dark red blood. "Burn him if you can," the stranger said, motioning to the lifeless pile of parts. "Keep de fire going. I'm gonna get one more."

The stranger ran down the beach. "Come back here!" he cried. He squinted against the darkness, trying to make out Ted's form. It was difficult to see, with palm trees, beach chairs, and other obstacles in silhouette against the sky. With outdoor Christmas lights reflecting in the water and on the horizon, it would have otherwise been a picturesque night.

Meanwhile, Ted had hobbled down the beach. He felt invigorated after chewing on the Texan's flesh, but now that exhilaration was wearing thin. The world moved again gelatinously, and Ted thought only about finding someone else to bite. Shuffling along through the sand, his foot caught in a hole, and he tripped and fell. Sand showered on him from above, and a figure towered over him, groaning.

"You zombie asshole," Ted said, gaining a bit of his former self.

The zombie was covered in sand, much as Ali had been earlier that day.

"You smell like rotten seaweed!" Ted shouted.

The zombie lunged forward, jaw snapping at Ted. But then the zombie stopped, sniffing at his would-be victim. With a sighing groan, the zombie turned away.

"Bite me, you asshole!" Ted shouted. "What, am I not good enough for you? You zombie freak! Just bite me!"

The zombie ignored him and trudged, much more slowly than Ted, toward another beach bar a quarter mile away.

"I don't think so, asshole!" Ted shouted. "I'm not one of you. Bite me! Bite me!" He picked up a lounge chair and ran after the zombie. Ted overtook him easily and slammed him across the back with the chair. The zombie stumbled a bit but continued his slow shuffle.

"I'm not done with you," Ted said, throwing the chair to the side. He ripped an umbrella out of its stand and held it like a baseball bat, swinging it at the zombie. Again, the zombie stumbled but didn't stop. "That's bullshit," Ted said. He swung the zombie around and slugged him across the face.

"Murrrrr," the zombie groaned. He fell to the ground then rose awkwardly.

Ted thrust the umbrella like a spear into the zombie's heart. It made a sinuous crunch as metal splintered against bone in the chest cavity. This time, the zombie's groan mixed with a gurgle and struggled to get up.

"Not dead, eh? How does it go? It's not a stake through the heart. That's vampires. Damn it. How do you kill a zombie?"

"T'rough de brains," a voice said behind Ted. It was the stranger from the bar, and he had the bartender's chef knife held out in front of him.

"Ah," Ted said. He used all his might to pull the umbrella out of the zombie's chest, then raised it high again and smashed it into the zombie's head with a harsh *crack*. The zombie twitched for just a moment before brainy sludge poured into the sand.

Ted turned his attention to the man with the knife. "What the hell do you want?"

"Dat will be you within' de week. You feel it already. De desire to bite. De nausea. De world spinnin' round. De only t'ing to stop de spinnin' is biting."

Ted eyed the man skeptically, especially the hand that held the knife. "So you're gonna kill me?"

"I'm protectin' my home. I don' want it to be de way it was years an' years ago. We had to move de whole family to Water Island jus' to stay safe from dem zombies."

"Water Island?"

"De ferry stop' runnin' on account o' de zombies. We had to swim. Zombies don't swim. We surrounded de place with guns. Small island. Easy to protect. But no grocery stores. No gas stations. We near starve to death! I don' want my kids to see dat terror."

Ted tried to think, but he felt only the urge to bite. How it would feel to sink his teeth into this man's flesh! But this man was motivated, and fast. Ted was slowing down, his consciousness drifting like a boat in the current; sometimes near, and sometimes floating out to sea.

The stranger didn't have time to strike. Just behind him, another zombie popped out of the sand. This one looked like it had been buried much longer than the first. It wore ragged clothes, its hair disheveled and covered in sand, its gender impossible to determine.

"What is dis? Night of de Living Dead?" The stranger swung his knife at the grotesque creature. It moaned but maintained its slow shuffle. The stranger swung again, this time cutting into the flesh of its arm. Though the gash was deep, it barely bled. "Dis a bad zombie, an ol' zombie," the stranger said to no one in particular. "It bite you, an' you turn fast!"

He slashed and slashed, ducking adroitly to avoid injury. Within minutes, the stranger was drenched in sweat. It soaked through his already blood-saturated shirt and ran down his legs in pale red streaks. But the zombie looked worse. Pieces of flesh hung from its body. It was missing an ear. But still it hobbled towards the stranger.

The stranger ran down the beach, easily outrunning his attacker. He remembered something that might help. Just up toward the line of resorts was a gift shop, and he remembered its large display of conch shells in the front window. As he ran towards the shop, another zombie emerged from the sand just in front of him. He pushed it over and continued on, smashing through the gift shop door with a rock found nearby.

From the large glass display, he chose the largest two conch shells. He put one on each fist, the spiky points facing outwards. "Dese will get dem zombies," he assured himself, hoping he wasn't cut too badly. On the beach, he ran circles around the first zombie he saw. When it was thoroughly dizzy, he smacked the back of its skull with a conch-covered fist. It moaned and turned around to meet its attacker. And the stranger was ready with the other fist. The zombie's skull looked like a cherry bomb had gone off inside it: open at the top, brains and dark blood gushing out, a single eyeball hanging by a torn optic nerve.

When the other zombies had been killed, Jimmie trudged to the stranger; speechless.

"You start a bonfire," the stranger said. "We need to burn dese bodies. De one from de bar, too. Den get cleaned up."

On normal nights, a bonfire at the beach would have attracted tourists from all around. Tonight, however, rumors of the zombies spread quickly, for the fire burned solemnly with just two lone attendants.

"What happened to that asshole from the bar? The one who bit the Texan?" Jimmie asked later, as the fire died.

"Dat bastard," the stranger said. "He got away."

*   *   *

The hotel room was quiet with Ali sleeping and Marion reading. When Marion heard Ted shuffle into the room, she didn't bother turning around.

"Try not to wake Ali," she said curtly. "And for Christ's sake, if you're gonna puke get it in the toilet."

Ted groaned.

"And I hope you're not too hung over. We have that timeshare presentation in the morning."

"Huh?"

"Oh, don't' tell me you forgot. Our first day here, that cute little thing in the pink bikini came up to you on the beach and got you to sign up for the presentation tomorrow morning. She promised a free dinner cruise for attending."

Ted groaned again.

"You signed up for it, not me. If you don't want to go, then don't. Not my idea of a perfect Christmas Eve morning."

Ted headed for the bathroom and closed the door.

"Ali's doing okay," Marion said. "She's just really tired. Thanks for asking," she added.

From the bathroom, Ted pounded the door twice. Marion shook her head and crawled into the pull-out couch bed with Ali, leaving the empty queen bed entirely for Ted.

*   *   *

After his Santa ordeal, Jones recovered in the hospital, losing consciousness soon after arriving. Louis waited with him.

"What happened?" Jones asked as he awoke.

"You remember not'ing?"

Jones looked at his hand. "What happened to my thumb?"

Louis summarized the day's gory events.

"Hmmm," Jones groaned, trying to picture it.

"Now do you remember what I told you about de Santa?"

"These painkillers are really strong," Jones told Louis. "I can't remember what you told me five minutes ago."

"Dat's okay," Louis said. "Dey'll wear off when you're ready." He looked concerned. "In de meantime, here. Keep it hidden away from de doctors." He handed Jones a green U. S. Virgin Islands hooded sweatshirt.

"You think I'll get cold?" Jones asked.

"Look inside!"

Concealed within the sweatshirt was a machete.

"I didn't want to risk sneaking a gun into de hospital. But when you get out, I have plenty."

"What do I need a gun for?"

"Do you remember not'ing about de zombies? Do you remember Santa bit dat little girl?"

"What Santa?" Jones asked as the nurse entered.

"My, you're looking even paler than before," she said. "Best get back to sleep." She turned up his morphine drip, and Jones passed happily into slumber. "Best not to come back 'til tomorrow," she told Louis.

Louis nodded. He was clenching the machete under the sweatshirt, and when the nurse left, he tucked it into Jones' night table. "I sure hope I got to your thumb fast enough," he sighed. He patted Jones on the chest, then left.

* * *

Ted's cell phone rang at seven in the morning, waking only Marion. She'd had a rough night, checking on Ali and being awoken by Ted's snoring, which was much louder than usual. Who else would be calling at seven in the morning on Christmas Eve except Ted's parents! If she ignored it, they'd just keep calling back. Best to get the conversation over with.

"Where's Ted? Where's Ali?" an older female voice cackled as soon as Marion answered.

"Merry Christmas Eve to you, too," Marion said. "They're here. They're both sleeping."

"Sleeping at this hour? How late were they up? When we go on vacation, we never..."

Marion sighed. "Let me get Ted." She took the phone to the queen bed. The bed was still made, and Ted slept on top of the bedspread, fully dressed down to his bloody sandals. "He's in the bathroom," Marion lied into the receiver. "Let us call you back."

She hung up without waiting for a response.

"Ted!" she shouted. He didn't move. "Ted!"

He groaned, opening one eye.

"Did you get into a fight last night?"

"No," he groaned and rolled over.

"Don't give me that shit. It's Christmas Eve. You came in drunk and now I find you covered in blood."

"Leave me alone," he moaned.

"Your parents just called. They're waiting for you to call them back. And you're scheduled to do that time share presentation at nine. That's two hours from now."

Ted groaned again.

"Mommy, I would stay away from Daddy," Ali said. She sat up groggily on the bed, looking very pale.

"Honey, how are you feeling?" Marion asked.

"Daddy's going to become a full zombie before I do, and I think he's gonna bite you."

"Ali, honey," Marion said, trying to sound normal. "Let's forget about this zombie talk for now. Grammy and Grampy called, and they want you to call them back. How 'bout you not mention anything about zombies? I don't think they'd understand."

Ali nodded.

"Ted? You going to talk to your parents?"

Ted groaned.

Marion dialed the number and handed the phone to Ali. Meanwhile, she turned on the television in the other room. She knew how the conversation would go, how Marion herself would be blamed for Ali sounding tired, for Ted being hung over, for anything else the in-laws didn't like.

The television clicked on to a news station. "...creating rumors about zombies on this Christmas Eve." The screen cut to an interview of a sunburned teenager chewing gum. "And the Santa just *bit* the girl! Just like that!" The girl chomped into the air to demonstrate. "The security guards ran over the Santa in their van, and then someone came to take the body away. There was an elf, one of Santa's helpers, and she looked real sick."

The screen cut to another tourist, this one a middle-aged man. "I'm not saying I believe in zombies or anything, but something weird is happening. Last night I was on the balcony trying to enjoy a glass of Christmas cheer, when I see these bodies popping out of the sand. It must be some kind of game, or maybe a cult. They started attacking each other, or maybe they were attacking tourists. I even think someone may have been killed. I went inside and locked the balcony door. Later there was a huge bonfire. You can guess what they were burning."

Back in the studio, the news anchor continued speaking: "Rumors haven't stopped the holiday preparations in Charlotte Amalie, where Santa will be delivering gifts in a buggy pulled by zombies..." The anchor blushed. "I'm sorry. Zombies on the mind! Santa will be delivering gifts in a buggy pulled by *donkeys...*"

Marion switched off the news and listened to Ali's side of the phone call.

"So that's what we did the first couple days," Ali said. "It was lots of fun. But then we went to see Santa, and everything got messed up." She paused a moment. "Well, first thing is I got bitten by a zombie. So it won't be long till I become one myself. Grammy, are you still gonna love me when I'm a zombie?"

Ali got off the bed and approached Marion. "She wants to talk to you," Ali said.

"Hello, Patrice," Marion sighed into the phone.

Patrice, half screaming into the phone, told Marion about a news story she'd seen about a zombie scare in the Caribbean involving a girl and a shopping store Santa. "They say that groups of people are still looking for that girl. They think she's a danger to everyone. They'll probably try to kill her! Are you trying to get my grandbaby killed?!"

Marion rolled her eyes. "Why would I do that to my own daughter?"

"Where's Ted?" Patrice insisted.

"He's still in the bathroom," Marion lied. In fact, Ted was comatose on the bed, a foul smell emanating from him. "Ted booked some standby tickets for the twenty-seventh, so it's possible we'll be home then."

"Look," Patrice said, "if there's only two seats on standby, send back Ted and Ali."

Marion frowned. "And if there's only one, I'll send your Ted back to you," Marion said, and hung up.

On the bed, Ted stirred. "I should make you attend that time share presentation," she told him. "It'll serve you right; always flirting with whatever eye candy you happen to see."

Ted bolted upright. "Maybe I *will* go," he said. He was feeling nauseously hungry, and as much as he wanted to, he knew he shouldn't bite his wife. He thought about those annoying time share presenters, how satisfying it would be to crunch into their arm or neck. "Yeah, I will go," he said.

He moved slowly into the bathroom, followed by lots of noise.

"Need help in there?" Marion asked.

"Maybe turn on the shower for me," he said.

When Marion entered, he had already stripped down. His skin was paler than she'd ever seen it. Patches of hair were gone all over his body. He tripped twice just trying to get into the stall. He smelled like road kill.

"Ted, maybe you should just..." For now, all the anger had melted from her voice.

He turned to her, eyes rolled back, and growled. She backed off and closed the door behind her.

* * *

At the time share presentation, a few other hapless couples sat, some in Santa hats and others in beachwear. In the hallway was a local children's choir. They sang holiday songs to the background of steel pan drums. Ted sat holding a cold bottle of water against his head. Ali stared at a fish tank, which contained a baby nurse shark.

"Ted and Marion?" a cheerful saleswoman said. "I'm Pepper Slates, number one in sales for four years now! Pepper Slates, Happiness Makes!" She sat them down at a table and brought them coffee and pastry and started questioning them about their vacation habits. It seemed she'd never stop. "A timeshare can really benefit a family like yours, which will continue to grow over the years. I'm sure your daughter will love traveling the world."

"Zombies don't travel," Ali whispered, still fixated on the shark.

Ted groaned. He wanted breakfast, but not what was on the table.

Oblivious, Pepper went through brochures, numbers, and financial figures. "So," she said when finished. "What do you think? You'd be stupid *not* to buy!"

She stared at the family. Marion sat looking exhausted with her half-eaten pastry. Ali stared into the aquarium looking as pale as ever. Ted stared at the saleswoman with something in his eye that Marion didn't recognize; for once, it wasn't lust.

"The shark is part of the cure," Ali whispered to Marion.

Ignoring her, Ted bent down to look more closely at one of the numbers Pepper had written. "Look at this here," he said. It was very hard for him to make such fine movements; the world was once again trapped in Jell-o.

Pepper confidently leaned in. "I can tell you're smart as an engineer," she said. Ted smiled and head-butted her, chomping a thick piece of flesh from her neck.

She screamed, of course, and the other hapless families sitting through similar presentations jumped from their tables, spilling coffee and pastry all over.

Marion bolted upright, grabbing Ali. Ted trudged after them, happily chewing on the woman's flesh.

"Stay the hell away from me!" Marion screamed. She ran to the rental car, but it was futile. She had given the keys to Ted before the presentation, as she didn't have any pockets.

He held them up, flashing a bloody smile. "I won't bite you," he promised. He reached into his mouth and pulled out a piece of half-chewed flesh. "Here, honey," he said to Ali. She eagerly grabbed the meat and shoved it into her mouth.

Marion grabbed the keys. "Get in the back seat, both of you," she said. She pulled out, tires squealing. She didn't care much about Ted, but she didn't want anything to happen to her daughter. Once she hit open road, she let out an ear-piercing, cathartic scream.

"What was that for, Mommy?" Ali asked.

"I just don't know what to do. I don't know how I can help you!"

"I know how to stop us," Ali said.

But before Marion could respond, Ted's cell phone rang. "Yes!" Marion screamed, hoping it wasn't the in-laws again. Luckily, it was the airline.

A polite and businesslike voice told Marion that due to 'recent events,' a seat had opened up this very afternoon. "We normally wouldn't try to split up a family," the operator said. "But your husband told us how urgently he needed to get back to be with his sick mother. We've got just the one opening today."

"Oh, yes, she's very sick," Marion said, rolling her eyes at Ted. "I promise you Ted will be on that flight."

Marion sped away not to the resort but to the clinic where they had taken Ali.

"Where's the old woman who usually sits outside here?" she asked inside the clinic.

"You mean Mama Claudette. She lives on Water Island," a nurse said. "Can *I* help you?"

"My husband broke his jaw in a fight," she said. "He's in pain, but he's taking a flight home this afternoon. In fact, I've got to get him straight to the airport. Would you be able to wire it shut; temporarily, just until he can get back into the States? I'll pay you whatever it takes."

The nurse turned around to a doctor who sat at a table playing solitaire. "Not my way of spending Christmas Eve morning," she said. "But it can be done. Bring him in, honey. It's your lucky morning. We don't close for another hour or so."

Marion ran to the car. "Ali, honey, go inside and wait for me. The doctor is gonna help Daddy."

Ali obeyed without a will of her own.

Meanwhile, Marion pulled the half-comatose Ted from the back seat and leaned him against the car. "Stand right there," she said, opening the trunk. Then she found what she was looking for; the tire iron.

Even with such a lousy spouse--a cheater, a drunk, a selfish mama's boy--Marion had to summon the anger to do the deed. She thought about the in-laws, how they held Ted on a pedestal. How they blamed everything bad Ali and Ted encountered on her, and gave Ted credit for all the good. She thought about Tiffany and the hotel receipts and the credit card statements for jewelry and flowers and candy she herself had never seen. It was enough. She swung hard and steady. It did the trick.

Ted groaned in pain as the iron made contact with his jaw. Even he felt the snap.

"You fucking bitch!" he tried to scream. Blood gushed from his jaw, disguising the morbid breakfast he'd eaten.

"Come on, honey, we've got to get you help!" she screamed, loud enough for the nurse inside to hear. "He's delirious!" she yelled over Ted's screams. "Doesn't remember what happened."

With the nurse's help, they got Ted on the table. He was screaming and clawing and clamping his teeth.

"It'll never work this way," the doctor said. "This will help, but you'll have to get him on the plane." The doctor gave him a sedative so she could wire the jaw. "Now this is only temporary," the doctor warned when she was finished. "He's got to get it fixed permanently back in the States. And you should get him looked at more thoroughly. He doesn't look so good."

Ted looked terrible, a metal brace holding his jaw shut and half his head wrapped in gauze. When he opened his lips to speak, his teeth stayed clamped together like a skeleton's. Marion only hoped it was good enough to get him home.

*　*　*

At the airport, Marion pushed her stolid daughter in a rented stroller. Marion had spit-cleaned the blood from her daughter's face, but she still looked sickly. Not to mention Ted, whom she was dragging by the wrist.

"I'm Ted's wife," she told the attendant, holding out Ted's passport. "Ted Parker. You called us from standby. Do you still have a seat for him?"

The attendant looked skeptically at the family; the sick daughter, too big for the stroller, the sweat-drenched Marion, and grotesque Ted barely able to stand. Blood still oozed from his jaw, and his eyes rolled back in semi-consciousness.

"He's drunk," Marion explained.

"We do see our share of passengers drunk on Caribbean rum... but why's he look like that?" the attendant asked.

"He got in a fight," Marion said. "He's so upset. About his sick mother, you see. That's why he needed a standby ticket. He wasn't thinking, and he picked a fight at the bar."

"It's probably true," said another attendant. "He was here yesterday. I've never seen a man so upset."

"I see," said the first attendant.

"I've written a note." Marion presented them with something scrawled on hotel stationary. "It explains about the fight, the painkillers. He can't speak with his jaw like that. I've written his parents' contact info," Marion explained. "They'll be there to pick him up. Since it's a direct flight, he won't have to worry about transferring. Once you get him into a seat, he'll just sleep the whole time." She borrowed a stapler and attached the note to Ted's shirt like a kindergartener.

The attendant chomped on her gum. "All right," she told Marion. "I'll have someone escort him. I'll tell you what, though," she said, looking at his wired jaw, his limp posture. "I'd give just about all my Christmas presents to see the way they handle him down in security."

Marion watched as an attendant arrived with a wheelchair and sped Ted off to security. "Mommy," Ali said as they watched him fade into the crowd. "Daddy's gonna want to bite Grammy and Grampy."

"I know," Marion said. Despite it all, she couldn't help but say it with just a little smile.

*   *   *

Despite everything that had happened, Marion wanted to make it a special--somewhat normal--Christmas for her daughter. She couldn't deny the truth in the zombie rumor, but she couldn't believe that her daughter was one of them. Upon leaving the airport, she saw a sign for the Water Island Ferry, but she drove onwards towards town.

"Ali, honey," she said. "How would you like to see Santa?"

"Is he a zombie, too?

"No," Marion said.

Ali shrugged. "Okay, I guess. It'll be a while before I'm hungry again."

Marion shivered. Part of her hoped that maybe the power of suggestion had taken over her daughter's imagination. Maybe some big crowds would be just the stimulation she needed to drop the zombie act. But if not, there was always Mama Claudette.

In Charlotte Amalie, there was a strange feeling among the crowds. Children clung close to parents. Although small bands and choirs performed Christmas carols and the sun shone brightly, the mood was somber.

"Let's go in here," Marion suggested, ducking into a brightly-decorated store on the corner of Main Street and an alley. A huge artificial Christmas tree sparkled with red and white lights and golden ornaments. On the floor, someone had sprinkled artificial snow, and a life-sized felt snowman stood just next to the checkout counter.

"Good day to ya," the shopkeeper said. She was a middle-aged woman with a scarf around her hair.

"Good day," Marion replied. "And a Merry Christmas."

"Oh, de same to you, dear. I hope you be keepin' safe."

"Safe?"

The shopkeeper looked skeptically at Ali. "You know, from dem zombies." The shopkeeper eyed Ali's pale skin, the dark circles under her eyes.

Marion ushered her daughter behind the large Christmas tree.

"Hey," Marion said, trying to distract her daughter. "Doesn't it feel like Christmas in here?"

Ali nodded. Marion led her around the store to kill time in the air conditioning before Santa arrived. Normally, she would be shopping for gifts for friends and family, but right now she was just trying to stay calm; for Ali's sake.

"Can I help you find somet'ing'?" the shopkeeper asked.

Marion tried to smile. "Just looking."

The shopkeeper watched her skeptically.

"Mommy," Ali whispered. She motioned with her finger. "There's a zombie inside that snowman."

"What? Ali! You need to control your imagination. Really!"

"Well, there is. You should be careful."

Marion reached into a refrigerator case for a bottled water.

"Mommy, don't pay for it."

"Why?"

"The register is too close to the zombie."

"Honey, Mommy's got to pay for it," Marion explained.

"Then give me the money, and I'll pay for it. The zombie won't bite me. I'm already turning. He's hiding in there because he wants to bite you. I know what he's thinking."

"That's nonsense," Marion said. She took out a five-dollar bill.

Ali screamed and plunged to the floor.

"She wanted to pay," Marion explained in embarrassment.

"Well, it's Christmas Eve for goodness sake," the shopkeeper said. "Let de chil' pay if she want it dat bad."

Marion nodded and handed Ali the drink and the money. "Go wait outside," Ali insisted.

Marion stepped closer toward the door but watched her daughter closely. Ali politely paid for the drink. Waiting for her change, she turned to the snowman.

"You're a bad, bad zombie!" she screamed. Then she kicked the snowman, her foot denting it.

The snowman trembled, rose, moved a few inches, then toppled over groaning.

"Chil', how did you know dat zombie was in dere?" The shopkeeper showed unexpected physical prowess as she jumped from behind the counter, shotgun in hand.

"Ali, come away!" Marion called. She ushered Ali out the door but couldn't help peeking inside. The shopkeeper kicked the snowman shell away to reveal a male zombie writhing on the floor. His skin was a bluish-green, and tufts of thinning hair stuck straight up on his skull. He wore a green U.S. Virgin Islands sweatshirt over what looked like a hospital gown. He looked strangely familiar.

"Murrrr," the zombie groaned. Then with a loud report, the shotgun fired, and the zombie's head exploded like cherry bombs packed inside a watermelon. Blood and brains splattered on the cash register and pooled in the hooded sweatshirt before the torso collapsed to the ground. Red flecks dirtied the pristine white artificial snow. And on the Christmas tree, clotted pieces of blood, brains and flesh hung from the branches and glittered in the lights.

Marion couldn't help but catch a Christmas Carol playing ironically on the speakers outside. *How lovely are your branches…* "Ehck, let's go," she said, running out just as a crowd of onlookers rushed in.

"Dat was a bad zombie!" the shopkeeper screamed to the crowd. "And dat little girl knew about it. I t'ink she a zombie, too!"

"Get her!" someone yelled.

"Maybe it's the girl who got bit by Santa!" cried another.

"It is!" shouted a child.

"Somebody kill her!"

"Down here," Marion whispered, pulling Ali into the alley. The shops here were less frequented as they were on Main Street. "Let's try on some sundresses!" Marion pulled Ali into a clothing shop. She smiled awkwardly at the cashier, grabbed a handful of dresses off the rack, and ran into the fitting room.

It wasn't until she looked in the mirror that she saw just how blood spattered she was. She heard the cashier speaking into the phone. "Bloody," she said, and "like the girl on the news."

"Ali, listen to me," Marion said. "Let's get you into one of these sundresses. And me, too. We can't wear our bloody clothes anymore. Then, when I count to three, we're going to run out the door and toward the car. If we can't get to the car, try to make it to the ocean."

"The ocean, Mommy?"

"We've got to swim out to Water Island, or take the ferry if we can."

"Why?"

"There's someone who can help you there."

"The old woman from the clinic?"

"Yes."

Ali nodded. "Mommy," she said.

"Yes?"

"They're not going to want you to go."

"Who isn't?"

"The zombies," she said matter-of-factly.

Marion peeled off her blood-stained clothes and Ali's as well, choosing a dress for each. Hers didn't have pockets, so she stuffed her wallet, cell phone, and keys down through the top. She felt them secure and snug between her breasts.

"Ready?" Marion asked.

Ali nodded.

On the count of three, they ran for the door. No one tried to stop them. The cashier huddled in the corner. At the door, Marion saw why. There were three female zombies dressed as scantily-clad elves headed straight for the cashier, who was now screaming. Marion ignored her and ran into the alley, her daughter dragging behind.

"There they are!" someone cried from Main Street. A crowd followed into the alley with bats, sticks, and even guns. Bullets whizzed by, each missing narrowly. Marion pulled Ali into an adjacent shop. They could cut through here to the next alley over and hopefully avoid the crowd. It was a cigar store, and no one seemed to have heard the ruckus outside. Christmas music was playing loudly, and a few men crowded around an expensive-looking display at the counter without turning towards Marion.

She passed through the store to the next alley over. In the alley, however, shuffled three more zombies. Each looked worse than the next, with hair falling out, skin pasty and blue, and eyes unfocused and yellow.

"Zombies, Mommy!" Ali squealed.

She grabbed Ali and dashed back into the store. "Zombies!" she screamed to the men at the counter. Marion looked more closely this time. The men were only slightly pale, and their hair was in fairly good shape, but their mouths were covered in blood. When Marion looked at the display, she saw the bloody hand of the clerk, who now slumped half over the counter and half behind it. They weren't men at all, they were zombies, and they were feeding.

Meanwhile, the crowd had followed Marion into the cigar store.

"There they are!" someone shouted.

"Shoot 'em!"

"They're zombies over there!" Marion screamed, pointing to the three men at the counter and ducking with Ali just in time to avoid a bullet to the head. From behind a display of lighters, Marion watched as a gunshot hit the shoulder of one of the zombies. Unfazed, he kept feeding. The second shot didn't miss. Zombie brains exploded on the display case, turning the clear glass a dirty red. Bits of brains oozed down the glass.

"Uh-oh, Mommy," Ali said.

"Uh-oh, what?" Marion asked.

"All this blood is making me…"

"It's making me sick, too, honey. I'm trying to find a way out."

"No, Mommy, it's making me hungry."

"What?"

"I'm turning, Mommy."

"No, honey, I…"

"I might try to bite you."

"Shit!" Marion grabbed her daughter and ran out the back entrance, barreling through the three emerging zombies. "That way," she told them, pointing to the crowd. They grunted and continued on.

"They may not come after you if you're with me. Zombies don't like to eat other zombies. But I'm awfully hungry, Mommy. I think I may just bite your arm…"

Marion clasped her daughter's jaws together just as they chomped towards her.

"Shit," she said again. She ran down the alley toward Waterfront Highway. There was a convenience store, and she ran inside. "Duct tape?" she shouted.

A startled clerk pointed to a shelf in the back. Still carrying her daughter, Marion grabbed the tape, ripped it open with her teeth, and began winding it tightly around her daughter's mouth. Ali protested inaudibly, but Marion continued. When Ali's mouth was securely fastened, Marion rushed out the door.

"You gonna pay for that?" the clerk asked.

"No, sorry," Marion said, throwing the used roll at him.

"Hey!" He chased her onto Waterfront Highway, but stopped when she disappeared into the crowd. Santa Claus, pulled in an old-fashioned donkey cart, moved down the street, and children and parents alike were smiling and cheering.

Marion ducked behind a large family. "Be quiet, Ali," she whispered. Ali closed her teary eyes and nodded. "Stay there."

Marion worked her way to a police officer a few yards away. "How can I get to the ferry to Water Island?" she asked.

"You can't today. Not anymore. The ferry's all closed down. It's all this talk of zombies. Silly as it may sound. You want to get to Water Island today; you're going to have to swim." He laughed. "Merry Christmas!"

Before Marion could say anything else, the holiday cheers turned to screams.

The zombies from the cigar store and the scantily-clad elves, now joined with other decrepit fiends, all shuffled slowly into the crowd. They emerged from inside holiday displays, trash cans, anything large enough to conceal them.

The officer unholstered his gun, aiming at the anomalies. The crowd parted, but the streets were packed, and people jammed together like cattle. In such conditions, their speed gave them no advantage; they were defenseless against the zombies. Here and there, a tourist went down, covered in a mass of hungry zombies. From behind, a crowd emerged with guns and sticks, but there were so many people it was difficult to tell who was a zombie and who wasn't. The blood from human victims only served to escalate the zombies' lust.

Marion rushed to her daughter, who stood alone watching events unfold.

"The donkeys," Ali mumbled through her taped mouth. Marion turned in time to see a group of zombies pull the flesh off of two of Santa's donkeys. Meanwhile, Santa used the opportunity to jump off his sled and run across Waterfront Highway 30 into the water. Clearly, he knew that zombies can't swim.

"Ali, can you swim?" Marion asked. Ali had been swimming since infancy when Marion took her to Mommy and Me swim time. Now she could swim freestyle as well as any seven-year-old.

Ali shook her head. "Mmm-mmmm mmmm mmmm!" she mumbled through the duct tape. Marion didn't need a translator, she knew what Ali said. *Zombies can't swim.*

"We're too far from Water Island," Marion said. "The ferry's not working. We can better reach it from further west. Maybe from Frenchtown. I'll have to carry you. We need a car," she resolved.

The crowd was a mess from Main Street to Waterfront Highway. Worse, the roads had been closed for the Christmas celebration, and the only two vehicles visible were Santa's carriage--now hitched to half-eaten donkeys--and a police officer's SUV.

"I hope you were right about the zombies," Marion said.

She took Ali in her arms and ran toward a group of zombies busy devouring an obese tourist. Two of them turned to look at her. They sniffed the air briefly but turned right back toward their kill.

"Great!" Marion shouted. She ran toward the crowd surrounding the officer's vehicle. A dozen panicking tourists were trying to get into the SUV. The officer stood on the hood of his car, kicking at zombies and tourists alike. He had his gun aimed down at the crowd, but he wasn't shooting. "Get away. This is my car!" he screamed. "I'm gonna start shooting, zombie or person. Get away from me!"

"Get his gun!" someone yelled.

Three or four tourists in tropical shirts and Santa hats climbed on the SUV's roof and jumped the officer from behind. They took his gun and kicked him down into the crowd. Someone screamed, and the crowd instantly parted; one of the *tourists* turned out to be a zombie. He bit fervently at the fallen officer. People tripped over each other trying to get away.

Meanwhile, the man with the officer's gun got into the driver's seat. His accomplices were still on the hood of the SUV, but he wasted no time. He waited about two seconds before flooring the gas pedal. His friends flipped off the roof and into the air. One landed right on his neck, becoming zombie food.

The SUV swerved right and left, trying to find a route through the crowds. Some tourists tried to jump inside. Some clutched to the roof. Others fell under the tires.

"We've got to get that car," Marion said. "Ali, are you still feeling hungry?"

Ali nodded, her eyes looking a little jaundiced.

"Okay. Be ready." Marion put her daughter down, and used her car key to rip some of the duct tape, being careful to leave a bit on Ali's mouth, just for safety.

Marion left Ali on the side of Waterfront Highway and ran to the alley in the opposite direction as everyone else. She emerged moments later with a fully-decorated artificial Christmas tree. She swung it from side to side, then motioned to the SUV.

"This way!" she called like a deranged traffic cop. The SUV maneuvered around the crowds, running over a body here and there to follow the path Marion cleared. Marion worked her way through, sweeping the crowds with the tree. As she swung, ornaments fell and smashed on the road. When she reached Ali, she grabbed her under one arm, dropped the tree, and dashed toward the SUV. As she ran, she pulled off the duct tape. "Don't bite me," she pleaded to Ali.

The driver was still recovering from running over so many people.

"All right, I get it," he told Marion. "You scratch my back, yadda yadda. Get in."

Marion pulled open the door and shoved Ali inside. Immediately, Ali lunged for the man's arm.

"What the hell!" the man screamed. The SUV slowed and swerved. Marion tried for the wheel. Her daughter was chewing happily on the man's arm. "Lady, you gotta be nuts!" he said.

Marion grabbed the gun from his shocked hand and slammed the butt down on his head. "Go ahead, dear," she told Ali as she climbed over the corpse and floored the gas. "Feast away."

*   *   *

Crossing to Water Island proved more difficult than Marion thought. The zombies had already inundated Frenchtown, and Marion had to use all her ammo on them just to gain access to the ocean. Ali seemed better after feasting on the driver, but she still couldn't swim. Marion took an inflatable raft that had been drying on someone's front porch and strapped Ali to it with a stolen fishing net.

The water sent Ali into a panic, and Marion had to struggle just to keep her afloat. Worse, the current worked against her, and it took hours to reach Water Island. When she finally got close to the shore, she was met with the barrel of a shotgun.

"Don' trespass on de island," an angry local insisted.

"No!" Marion held up her hands. "I need to see Mama Claudette."

"Wait right dere," the local said. He called loudly to his son, who was patrolling the beach with a machete. "Go fin' Mama Claudette. Tell her she got a visitor."

Marion stood where the water was shoulder deep. Ali floated on the raft in front of her, her eyes closed. She had finally stopped struggling, and Marion hoped it wasn't too late.

After an eternity, the old, withered woman hobbled to the shore. "What took you so long? You finally bring your daughter to me?" Mama Claudette yelled.

"Yes!"

"You bring your courage? De cure is so bad dat it might kill her."

Marion thought for just a moment. "She'd be dead anyway," Marion admitted. "I believe in you."

"You bring de money?"

Marion paused. She reached inside her dress top. Luckily, her wallet was still wedged there. "You can have everything I've got. And I'll owe you the rest."

"Where's your man?" Mama Claudette asked.

"Bitten," Marion said. "Gone back to his folks."

"Dat man have life insurance?"

Marion nodded.

"Den you sho' can pay me de res' afterward. Bring her to shore." Mama Claudette motioned to the man with the gun. Reluctantly, he lowered his weapon.

"Dis will take a long while," Mama Claudette told Marion, holding her arm. "You don' want to watch. Trus' me. You would never forget what you see. It don't do no good for her to see you upset, anyhow." She turned to the man with the gun. "Watch her, honey. Try to make her comfortable."

"Yes, Mama," the man with the gun said.

"Baby, come help me with dis chil'," Mama Claudette said to the boy.

"Yes, Mama," he said.

"You're lucky," the man with the gun told Marion after Ali had been taken beyond the tree line. "She don' do dis for just anybody."

Marion nodded. She couldn't help but look towards the main island, where people were shouting and jumping into the ocean.

"She done it to me, years ago," the man said, relaxing. "I had nightmares for years, but den, one day I jus' forget. It will be de same wit' your daughter. Even Mama was a zombie once. Her own Mama cure' her, and she ain't never forget. Lucky your daughter so young."

He smiled at Marion, and she smiled back. Even after all that had happened, she was lucky, wasn't she? That reminded her of something she needed to do.

"Do you have a phone I could use? I need to make a very important call."

The man gave her a cell phone from his pocket. "Keep it short. Save de battery."

Marion nodded and dialed. The other end was picked up on the second ring "Patrice," she said a few moments later. "Great news about Ted. Grab a pencil 'cause you're gonna want to write down his flight number. He'll need you to pick him up from the airport tonight."

As she waited for Mama Claudette to work her magic on Ali, she pictured in her mind the feeling of holiday joy that would unite Ted with his mother. She could just imagine the look on Patrice's face when she saw her son staggering to her at the airport, knowing that he'd be home for the holidays after all.

Marion smiled as she thought what would happen next.

Maybe this wouldn't be such a bad Christmas after all.

FRIGHT OF THE REINDEER

JACK BURTON

Christmas Eve 8:30 p.m.

"R...R...Rod," Tim stammered, approaching his co-worker. Tim was a shy twenty-year-old, severely lacking in the social skills department. He had a hard time confronting people under the best of circumstances, and having to deal with Rod Tearny put his stomach in knots. At six-one and covered in tattoos, Tim felt it was a miracle the ex-con could secure any job let alone working for Teddy's Christmas Trees and Santa Land.

Rod finished locking up the company chainsaw in the cabinet underneath the register before staring at Tim with icy eyes. His shift ended at ten and he wasn't in the mood to stay a minute later. As far as he was concerned, if someone didn't have a tree by now, they weren't getting one this year. Even Santa and the elves had changed out of costume and left hours ago. So what could Tim possibly want?

"What now?"

"You...you..." Tim struggled.

"Jesus Christ! Spit it out, man!" Rod was cold, tired and desperately wanted to get back to his apartment to start on a fresh bottle of Cutty Sark.

Tim had anticipated the harsh reception, hence his nervousness. Rod Tearny was the only person in the small town of Farley who didn't cut Tim an ounce of slack, regardless of his disabilities. In truth, Rod's anti-social behavior stemmed more from his struggle to readjust to life in the outside world again than to anything else. He'd only been a free man for five weeks, and had spent the majority of his time working nonstop for Teddy, in an attempt to make enough money to get back on his feet. Unfortunately, Tim was unaware of Rod's hardships and assumed the man just hated people in general.

"You gotta see the reindeer," Tim spat out. "They look real sick and smell bad, too."

Rod clenched his teeth, "Tim, they're animals. They aren't supposed to smell like roses." He cursed Teddy for scheduling the two of them to close up tonight. It was always *something* when you were working with Tim. But of course, they were the only two without families to rush home to and were the perfect candidates to close up shop on Christmas Eve.

"Yeah, but I think they're dead. Probably that stuff you gave 'em," Tim kept his gaze focused on the ground, but he could feel Rod's anger boiling over without even looking at his face.

"Listen," he said, grabbing Tim by his thin arm. "Those shots were supposed to...oh, the hell with it." *What's the point of trying to explain it to an idiot*, he thought. "Let's just get to the damn stables and see what the hell you're blathering about."

Rod released his grip and walked through the rows of unsold Douglas Firs. As he turned on his heels, causing Tim to nearly run into him head on, Rod exclaimed, "And don't say shit about the fucking shots I gave 'em, you hear me!" Rod used the same voice that got him through two years behind bars and Tim shrunk back in fear.

He couldn't believe Tim was accusing him of poisoning the caribou, or reindeer, or whatever the hell they were. The only reason he'd used the tranquilizers in the first place was because Dasher and Vixen, the charming names Teddy had christened them with, had been wired since they arrived at Santa Land. Their tempers had further rocketed in the past two days and the last thing Rod wanted to see was some poor kid getting their teeth knocked out because Vixen didn't feel like getting his picture taken.

And this is what I get for caring, Rod thought to himself. *Should have just let it happen and watch Teddy get sued.*

But that's not what would have happened. After all, Rod had been put in charge of the animals. Rod would be holding the reins if something happened and he'd be the one everyone blamed. It didn't matter that Teddy was a cheap bastard who bought the two wild beasts from a shady foreigner two towns over. No one would take into account that Teddy had refused to spend the money required to go through a reputable company that would have at least provided a trainer and legal tranquilizers. The issue would be him, a recently released jailbird for two counts of drug possession. And after his PO got involved, which he surely would, Rod would fail his drug tests and that would be the end of it. So he had asked a favor of his old dealer and eagerly accepted two vials of a yellowish liquid the man claimed was a tranquilizer. But the stuff did the trick, the reindeer were tame, kids were happy, and Rod wasn't in the spotlight. Until now. Until Tim, the only one who knew about the illegal tranquillizers fingered Rod for poisoning the animals.

Stupid, he thought, stepping over the train tracks that circled Santa's miniature village.

They passed under the candy cane arch leading to Santa's workshop. Six hours earlier, the shop had been teaming with kids, until Santa made his announcement that he'd be leaving to start on his yearly journey. Now the lights were off and the fake village resembled a ghost town in the dim moonlight.

The pair was about eighty feet from the small wooden stable when the smell hit them. Rod stopped and looked at Tim. For once they were on the same wavelength; even animals shouldn't have smelled that bad. Something was seriously wrong.

They quickened their pace and with each step, the rancid stench intensified. When they finally reached the small stable doors, the smell bordered on unbearable. There was no sound within the wooden shelter and Rod knew that was a bad sign. He lifted the wooden brace and swung the door open.

"Oh, God," Rod said, staring down at the two reindeer who had once been Dasher and Vixen. Now they were just two lifeless heaps on the cold straw bedding.

"Are...are they dead?" Tim asked.

Rod didn't answer; he just kept staring at the two carcasses. The fur of both animals was wet and stringy, marked by open sores that were already festering despite the cold weather. Dasher's tongue, purple and spotted, hung out of his mouth and green bile formed a sticky puddle around his muzzle.

I've done it now, Rod thought. How was he going to cover this up now that Tim had seen it? "Okay, lay your hands on him and see if you can feel breathing or a heartbeat."

"Smells bad," Tim replied.

"Tim! Just get down there and do it."

Tim pulled his shirt over his nose and reluctantly knelt down in front of Dasher. Careful not to touch any open wounds, Tim placed his hands on the enormous flank of the reindeer and waited.

"Anything?" Rod asked.

Tim shook his head sadly, tears welling up in his eyes. He was a simple man and didn't want to see anything dead, man or beast.

What the hell was in that shot? Whatever it was, Rod knew it was more than just a tranquilizer.

Tim was turning away from the deceased carcass when it happened. Dasher let out a grunt and suddenly sprung to life, jerking his head up. Tim froze and that was his mistake. Dasher took Tim's tiny leg in his mouth and crushed down like a vise. Tim's piercing scream rang out through the stable as Dasher's powerful jaws applied enough pressure to snap the bone.

Rod could only watch Tim fall helplessly to the ground, shrieking in pain, as Dasher released his death grip on the young man and slowly tried to stand up.

"Help me! It burns!" Tim wailed, in response to his shattered tibia.

Rod grabbed Tim and slung him over his shoulder. He carried him out of the stable and back towards Santa's workshop. The cold air hit them hard and was a welcome relief from the tepid, death-infected stew brewing inside the stable. Rod paused briefly, taking in the fresh air, trying to figure out the best course of action. Aside from the tiny village and tree nursery, there were two small modular homes on either side of the parking lot. The factory-built quarters served as the home-base of Teddy's business and held a few small offices, a lounge, and rooms for employees to change in. The one on the left housed Ted's office and Rod knew the first aid kit was there.

"It's coming," Tim moaned as he watched Dasher.

Rod turned to see Dasher attempting to gallop towards them, but swaying like a violent drunk under the effect of whatever drug Rod had pumped into him. Rod headed for the building on the left, jogging as best he could with Tim crying on his shoulder, the deranged reindeer not far behind.

Reaching the steps, he dug his hand furiously into his pockets, trying to retrieve the key. The sound of the impending hooves pounding hard on the cold ground intensified both men's fear.

"Oh, God," Tim closed his eyes, unable to stare at the charging beast.

"Got it," Rod said, mounting the three steps and stabbing the key hole. Safely inside the modular building, Rod locked the door before setting Tim down on the employee couch. Before either of them could speak, the room shook from a powerful blow to the door. It was Dasher, and he tried twice more to penetrate the building before staggering off.

They waited. Tim on the couch, Rod crouched over him, both praying the deranged animal had given up.

After what seemed like an eternity, Tim spoke. "I need a doctor. I think I got rabies."

Rod was already up and retrieving the first aid kit. "Listen, I'm gonna wash it out real good, so the bite doesn't get worse while we're waiting for a doctor." Rod didn't bother telling him that whatever Dasher had was a lot worse than rabies and probably incubated a hell of a lot faster.

Rod put on gloves from the first aid kit and ignored Tim's cries of anguish as he cut back the fabric of his jeans to expose the masticated flesh. Rod was horrified to find the leg before him was beyond any normal animal bite that could be dressed. In just the five minutes it took to get to safety, the injury had produced thick, green pus around the edges, and red lines were radiating outward from the initial bite like a spider web of infection.

Rod did the best he could with hydrogen peroxide and water, but Tim's screams became too much.

I've gotta bite the bullet, and get this kid to a hospital. Shit's outta control! Rod knew there was nothing more he could do. "Just hang in there buddy. I'm gonna call an ambulance." *God, I'm sorry.*

Tim's head rolled back and forth as if in a fevered dream and he could only mumble an unintelligible response.

The make-shift lounge didn't offer much. A couch, water cooler, card tables and chairs, but no phone. Rod rushed to Ted's office, annoyed that the only telephone was going to be inside, which he assumed would be locked. Trying the door, his fears were confirmed and Rod's key wasn't authorized to open Ted's office.

"Shit," he kicked the door. *Once again the cheap bastard screws me*, he thought. *It's a business for Christ's sake. He should at least have two phone lines.*

"Kick it down," Tim said, blood and vomit dripping from his lips.

"Kick it down? It's a solid oak door!" Rod said, turning to face Tim.

Tim fell silent. His glazed eyes rolled back inside his skull whose pale skin now shared the same purple and red veins of infection as his leg. Whatever infection Dasher was carrying was flying through Tim's body like a tornado.

This isn't possible, Rod ran his fingers through his hair.

Rod placed his hand on Tim's chest, searching for a sign of life. He pressed harder and thanked God when he finally felt the faintest of thumps pressing upward from somewhere deep inside Tim's infected chest cavity.

"Don't worry, man. I'll get you to a hospital." Rod hoped that somewhere inside Tim's fevered brain he could hear him and that the words gave him hope.

Rod opened the door, knowing if he didn't act fast, Tim would die. His breath formed in front of his face as he looked back and forth, checking for any signs of Dasher, or Vixen, assuming he too had been able to regain some form of life.

The coast was clear and Rod ran fast. His first stop was the nursery where he retrieved the chainsaw, knowing that he had no other means of protection against the mad beasts should they return. With chainsaw in hand, Rod jumped into his Z28 and skidded to a stop in front of the steps. He left the engine running and passenger door open wide so he could quickly get Tim in.

It took barely a minute for Rod to lift Tim's sickly body and position him in the front seat. He revved the engine and sped out of the dirt parking lot, sending chunks of dirt and gravel flying in the wake of the tires.

Within two minutes they were almost to Farley's Good Samaritan hospital which was just on the outskirts of the town center.

He roared into the hospital's parking lot, blaring the horn and shouting for help. The car skidded to a stop in front of the emergency room's sliding glass doors, and was met by two nurses who came out to see what was wrong. To Rod's relief, they didn't waste time with a bunch of questions. Once they saw Tim's condition, a crew loaded him onto a gurney instantly. The only information Rod provided was that he was attacked by an animal.

Rod properly parked the car, then headed into the hospital. He didn't know if Tim was right about the shots, but either way Rod felt terrible about what happened.

Inside the waiting room, the admitting nurse asked Rod questions for five minutes straight, none of which he could answer. He knew nothing about Tim's home life, allergies, blood type, or even where he lived. The only information he could provide was what happened.

"A reindeer?" the nurse asked, skeptical.

"Yes!" He didn't care if no one believed him. That was the truth. "The stable was left open so they might be anywhere by now. We need to call animal control or something."

"I'll let the doctors know." She walked back through the triage door and behind the reception desk. Through the sliding glass window Rod could see her inputting information into the computer, but she made no attempts to call anyone.

Christmas Eve 10:00 p.m.

Not more than six miles from Good Samaritan, Dasher was reaching the town center. The streets had emptied in the past hour and the majority of shops were now closed for the day. A few families still strolled leisurely past the store fronts, admiring the beautiful lights and numerous nativity scenes on their way to church, whose parking lot was already filling with cars in anticipation of midnight mass.

"I can barely hear you," Jessica Helms, spoke into her cell phone. Jessica released her grip on her daughter momentarily, using the free hand to plug her other ear. "Yeah, but it must be bad reception."

"Look, Mommy, a reindeer," Sarah said, free of her mother's grasp.

With both ears engaged, Jessica didn't hear her daughter's statement, nor did she see the infected animal lumbering up to her daughter. "Why don't you just meet us at church," she pressured her husband over the phone.

"You're probably looking for Santa," Sarah said. "Here have a cracker." She held up her gloved palm containing the last of her animal crackers.

"Honey, stay by me," Jessica said, without looking at her daughter. "Honey?" She turned in time to see Dasher bend down and take hold of Sarah's hand.

The eight-year-old's expression transformed from happiness to pure shock and pain as Dasher's teeth sunk deep into her wrist.

"Nooo!" Jessica yelled, dropping the cell phone. "Help!" she cried out, grabbing hold of Sarah's shoulders as the child's screams mixed with her mother's.

With a simple twist of Dasher's head, a sickening crack sounded out over the howling child. Sarah's frail bones were no match against the strong jaws and her hand popped off, releasing a geyser of blood high into the air. Jessica and Sarah fell to the ground and Dasher sauntered away, munching on the bloody treat.

The streets quickly filled with bystanders, calling 9-1-1 and offering assistance. No one attempted to approach the reindeer until the paramedics and police arrived.

Good Samaritan Hospital 10:15
Rod was the lone occupant of the ER waiting room. The triage nurse had disappeared to the back, and her absence robbed the sterile hospital of its last sounds of life. There was no typing on the keyboard or shuffling of files, and in the deafening silence, it dawned on Rod that he hadn't seen or heard anyone in the last fifteen minutes.

Rod wasn't sure if it was just his nerves reacting to the desolation, but the waiting room felt like it was getting hotter. He took off his jacket, stood up and made his way to the reception window. He stuck his head through, but couldn't see anyone or hear anything beyond the door that led to the ER.

I hope Tim's okay. But Rod knew that regardless of what was happening behind that door, there was nothing he could do except wait.

The heat in the hospital became too much, so Rod slipped back into his thick leather jacket and walked outside, hoping the fresh air would help him pass the time. He headed towards the rear entrance of the hospital, where only the paramedics and their patients were allowed to enter. He expected to see at least one doctor or nurse taking a smoke break, but the area was deserted. The landing pad was without a helicopter and the docking bay was void of emergency vehicles.

Some Christmas this turned out to be.

His head spun quickly towards the whine of approaching sirens. Within seconds, the ambulance was squealing haphazardly into the parking lot. With lights flashing, the giant vehicle veered left then over compensated to the right while the driver struggled to straighten out. Whoever was driving showed no signs of braking and appeared to be accelerating as he plowed through the parking lot.

He's not gonna stop! Rod backed away from the rear entrance.

The ambulance clipped a parked car and spun out of control before crashing into the side of the hospital, just missing the entrance. The driver's door swung open and a blood drenched EMT stumbled to the pavement.

"We need help here!" Rod shouted, hoping someone would hear him. *Where is everyone? How could they not have heard the crash?*

The wounded man struggled to his feet and took three more steps before collapsing. Rod rushed to him, but realized instantly that he was again powerless to help. The man held one hand to his bloody neck, and reached out for Rod with the other. But Rod was too scared to take the man's trembling hand.

"I'll get the doctors," Rod said, running for the doors. Behind him, the man tried to speak but was unable to form coherent words.

Rod nearly flattened himself against the doors when they didn't open automatically. He pounded and kicked the glass but the hallway in front of him remained empty. "We got an accident out here!"

There was probably a swipe card or code needed to authorize the emergency entrance to open and Rod knew the EMT was in no shape to give it to him. He was just about to give up and head for the front entrance when a shadow appeared in the hallway.

"Hey!" Rod called, smashing his boots repeatedly into the glass door.

The shadow lengthened slowly in the hallway until a doctor finally appeared.

What the hell is he waiting for!

Rod continued shouting, but the doctor inside didn't respond. Rod looked back at the EMT, now motionless on the ground, wondering how much time the man had left. Rod returned to the glass door and was shocked to see the hallway was now filled with at least eight individuals, all wearing scrubs of one type or another, but still no one came forward.

Has the world gone crazy!

Finally the hospital staff started for the door, and the closer they drew, the more apparent it was to Rod that something was wrong. What he had mistaken as colorful patterned scrubs, were actually splotches of blood. Closer still, and Rod could distinguish the same dead, cold eyes and infected tissue that plagued Tim just after being bit by Dasher.

Rod's brain told him to run, but for some reason he couldn't. His legs only allowed him to inch away from the mass of... of what?

Zombies? Did he actually just think that word? Unfortunately, his vocabulary wasn't vast enough to find a different word for the people staggering towards the door.

What else could they be?

The first of the zombie doctors collided with the glass door and fell backwards. A second and third member of the infected staff hit the doors with a similar result. Rod continued backing away as the whole legion of the dead began pushing against the door with decaying hands.

There was no longer a shred of doubt in Rod's mind, these things were definitely dead. They couldn't even remember how to open the doors, and their attempts simply smeared strips of flesh and bloody handprints across the glass.

Shock was the only word to describe what Rod was experiencing. He moved at a snail's pace and his head continuously snapped back and forth, half watching his forward progress, half making sure nothing snuck up on him. Rod passed the EMT, dead for now, and felt he had a good chance of making it to his car before the zombies figured out how to breach the doors.

A shuffling noise made his body freeze. Out of the corner of his eye, he saw two forms emerging from the back of the ambulance. A woman led the way, ragged chunks of flesh dripping from her mouth. A child, missing her right hand, followed closely, her feet scraping slowly across the pavement. Behind the mother and daughter was a second EMT, who was lying inside on the ambulance floor. His stomach was torn open, organs strewn wildly around him.

They ate him! Rod concluded. And based on their unyielding advance towards him, they weren't full yet.

This time there was no barrier between him and the living dead and Rod had no trouble turning his back. Not only did he turn, he ran full force back to his car. The first thing he saw upon entering was the chainsaw. Rod looked up at the hungry zombies, still thirty feet away, and an idea hit him. There was a possibility, although slim, that he could end this and keep the infection limited to the hospital.

It was unlikely the doctors and staff could escape the hospital just by hitting the glass. Their actions suggested that all reasoning and logic had deteriorated within their infected bodies. The only drive that appeared to remain was a thirst for fresh blood and anyone unlucky enough to escape an attack with only a bite or scratch, would face the fate of joining their ungodly quest.

But then again, he might be completely wrong about everything.

It didn't matter, he had to try.

If I leave, they may just go back into the hospital. After all, they've got three floors of sick patients to feed on. It was a horrible thought, but at the same time it made sense and it meant the zombies would be kept busy until help arrived. However, the plan hinged on him killing the two zombies outside the hospital, and murder was something Rod had never considered in his life.

You're not killing anyone, remember? They're zombies! Just take them out and get help without worrying that they'd be roaming the town searching for their next meal.

Rod exited his car, chainsaw in hand. He cranked the Aosika brand chainsaw to life and prepared to strike. The spinning blade did nothing to deter the advancing zombies. The model provided an eighteen inch bar length, and combined with his out stretched arms, Rod felt confident he could attack without risking a bite.

The mother lurched forward, Rod side-stepped and buried the blade into her arm. The woman's body shook as the powerful chainsaw ripped through her appendage. The limb detached, falling to the ground, followed by black blood and shards of bone. Rod pulled the saw back, thinking it was over, but the woman continued, and the handless child was still right behind her.

God help me, Rod prayed, then swung the saw into her neck. The dead flesh offered little resistance against the steel blade and her head toppled to the pavement. The headless woman sunk to her knees, then crumpled to the ground.

The child stepped over her mother's decapitated head. Rod took a deep breath and reminded himself that the girl was already dead. The thunderous chainsaw entered the top of her tiny skull and traveled straight down to her chest. The two halves of her putrefied head separated with a sickening squish, and she joined her mother on the street.

Rod clicked off the chainsaw and turned away from the gory massacre. He dropped the chainsaw in the car then ran to the pay phone just outside the hospital's front entrance. Dialing 9-1-1, he contemplated what he would say. *Help, I'm being attacked by flesh eating zombies!* Probably not the best idea.

"9-1-1, what's your emergency?"

"We need help at Good Samaritan hospital. Bring lots of guns." Rod let the receiver drop while the confused operator continued questioning the empty ear piece.

He got back into his car and headed for the center of town. With luck, he could find a bar that was still open, kick back a few drinks, and wait for the cavalry to arrive. Once the Farley cops saw what they were up against, they'd be forced to call the county or state for help. Maybe even bring in the National Guard, but either way Rod assumed things would be okay.

He took his time driving to the heart of town, but his confidence fell as he turned onto Main Street and found it deserted. Except for a lone squad car parked diagonally across the road, the street was eerily empty. Rod drastically reduced his speed, scanning the streets to see what brought the cop out. In case something was going on, Rod decided against passing the vehicle, and instead pulled up along the curb and stopped.

Just over the swirling emergency lights of the Crown vic, Rod thought he may have seen someone. Someone, or something, standing on the other side of the car. He grabbed the chainsaw and stepped out of the Camaro.

"Hello?"

A soft smacking sound carried over the car. Rod took another few steps and something came into view over the Crown vic's roof. He couldn't tell what was poking up over the car, but whatever it was, no one was answering. Rod edged up to the trunk, left hand on the cord of the chainsaw, ready to rev it if need be.

"Officer? Anyone there?"

He walked around the Crown vic and found Dasher's head down in the stomach of his newest quarry. This time his victim was a Farley police officer. His 9mm lay just inches from his hand, which was about the only part of the officer not caked in blood.

The chainsaw chugged to life and Dasher raised his head up from the human feast, entrails spilling from his muzzle. Dasher's eyes, if they could even be called that, were now just black sunken holes in a decaying skull. It was hard to tell if the bloody puss and hanging flesh was his own or just from previous meals.

The decision to decapitate this creature was much easier than it had been with the little girl and Rod felt no apprehension as the eighteen inch Aosika blade drove into Dasher's head near the left antler. Dasher pitched forward and Rod leapt back, forced to withdraw the chainsaw before he finished the deed. The minor wound he inflicted was isolated just below the antler. Dasher took another step towards Rod. His antler, now only supported by a few strands of rotted fur, gave loose and fell to the ground, taking with it the skin and fur attached to its base. As the left antler fell, the skin peeled back, exposing the skull on Dasher's left side. Rod found that the hideous creature now resembled an animal version of Two-face from the Batman comics.

Focus man, you can do this! He struck again, this time coming from Dasher's wounded side. The chainsaw severed vertebrae, thus preventing the risk of further attack. It took a lot more strength to cut through the thick beast but eventually he fell, just as the other zombies before him.

Rod tilted his head back and blew out a sigh, then looked down at what remained of the officer. It was unlikely that the deputy would be returning as a zombie, he'd been eaten straight through to the pavement. But, just to be on the safe side, Rod lobbed off what was left of the cop's head. He doubted he would ever have to answer for his action, not after the state found what was waiting for them at the hospital.

"Fuck it," he said, rising up from the officer's headless, mangled body.

Two faces peered out at him from the front window of Chasers bar across the street. He headed for the front door of the bar and pushed it open. The two waitresses who had been watching his every move pulled back from the window and stared dumbfounded at Rod in his soiled clothes. A family of four was huddled in a corner booth, the parents talking fast, trying to distract the young children from what had transpired outside. In the back, a woman in motorcycle boots and a denim jacket shot pool by herself.

To keep things festive in the bar, a small Christmas tree with half the lights burnt out flickered in the far corner.

Rod walked up to a table, leaving a trail of bloody footprints on the floor. He set the chainsaw down on the table, globs of gore dripping from the steel to the wooden surface. The waitress cautiously approached him but stopped at least five feet away and continued to stare.

"Can you please call the police and bring me a beer," Rod stated, as if unaffected by the grisly bloodbath he just participated in.

"We did, that's why officer Mabi was out there," she said.

He turned and looked directly at the young woman whose age he placed at about twenty-two. "Well, didn't you think to call them again after you saw the first cop get eaten by Santa's helper out there?"

"Of course we did!" the second waitress said as she walked up to assist. "The operator told us all units were out on calls and she'd get help as soon as it was available. We've been scared to death. Everybody ran in and has been holing up in here," she pointed to the family in the corner.

"Well, looks like I showed up just in time then. How about that beer while we wait?" Rod said again.

"Yeah, sure," she laughed, as if the situation was making her delirious.

"Dark if you have it, please."

"Dark lager coming right up," she smiled and disappeared behind the counter.

"Well, I'll be damned. If it ain't Rod Tearny," a voice spoke from the pool table.

Rod turned, finding that the woman who addressed him was Chasey Schmidt. He could barely believe his eyes. He hadn't seen her in years. He used to ride with her and a guy named Jake, but those friendships had dissolved years ago.

Rod never once missed Jake, the guy turned out to be a jerk and Rod still partly blamed Jake's involvement in the job that landed him in jail. Chasey, however, had often been on his mind. He always regretted letting her run off with Jake and wondered how different things might have been had she stayed. Then again, Chasey wasn't the type of woman one could keep. She was truly a wild child.

Chasey laid the pool cue down and dragged a chair up to his table. She flipped it around, laying her arms on the head rest and leaned her chest against the back.

"Didn't think I'd be seeing you again," she smiled. It was a beautiful smile, but devilish at the same time.

"Likewise," Rod said, not wanting to show that he was excited about seeing her.

Chasey was hot shit, and she knew it. She loved playing hard to get and always made sure a guy knew how lucky he was if she decided to grace him with her presence. Deep down, Rod knew there was a sweetheart under the fast-riding, denim-clad beauty, but Chasey rarely let that side out. Rod had glimpsed it just once before. The thing was, you had to be careful with girls like Chasey. If you got too mushy too quick, she'd split on you. Rod had made that mistake once before.

"Shit, man, from the looks of it, you've had one hell of a night!"

"That's one way of putting it," Rod said with a laugh. *Hell of a night* didn't even come close to covering it. The waitress put the beer down on the table in front of him and departed. Rod pulled back his jacket sleeve, reading his watch, then looked up. "And I'm guessing it's only gonna get worse."

"Really? I find that hard to believe," Chasey said. "What I saw out that window earlier was damn near the craziest shit I've ever witnessed."

"Didn't Jake show you some crazy sights? Isn't that why you took off with him and left this place behind? Where is old Jake by the way?"

She shook her head, "Jake's somewhere out west now. And turns out he wasn't *that* exciting. Anyways, I was sure you left this dump a long time ago."

"I like this dump," Rod said. "Didn't realize how much I liked it till they put me away for a while." He drained the last of his mug. "What brought you back?"

"Rode in a few hours ago. Just before that deer went apeshit. Thought I'd surprise my folks tomorrow for Christmas. Hey, what do you say we do a shot? For old time's sake."

He nodded and Chasey ordered two whiskeys. Rod welcomed the burn of the harsh liquid, the way it warmed his insides and calmed his head, especially after what he'd gone through. Chasey threw back her shot like it was water and slammed the glass on the table.

"Now, the past is the past. So why don't we pick up where we left off? Tell me about this crazy night of yours?" she smiled. "Besides what I've just seen."

"You wouldn't believe me if I told you," he said.

"Try me."

"Okay. That reindeer out there used to work at Santa Land where I was employed to cut trees and walk the fucker around so the kids could see him. It got sick with…something." Rod decided it was best not to mention his possible involvement in the illness. "It went crazy and bit this guy I worked with. Two more whiskeys, please!" he called out, taking a break from the story. "This guy turned just as sickly as Dasher, that's the reindeer. Anyway, one thing led to another. I get him to the hospital and he turns into a mindless, flesh-eating zombie."

The waitress set the shots down, clearly disgusted by the conversation, and departed quickly. Rod sucked down the second shot.

"Whoa, wait a minute. Did you say zombie?" Chasey asked.

"Yep," Rod answered, very matter-of-factly.

"Yeah, sure. Well then, here's to zombies," she laughed, and raised her shot glass.

"Okay, fine, you like excitement and danger. So how 'bout I show them to you and you can decide what they should be called?" Rod grinned, already feeling the effects of the alcohol.

"You're bluffing."

"Nope. I bet you that everyone fled here after Dasher came into town and bit off some kid's hand. Possibly took a chunk out of the mother, too."

The color started to drain from Chasey's face, but she remained skeptical.

"That's right. I saw them at the hospital, only they weren't *them* anymore. They were infected, just like my co-worker. And now it's spreading through the hospital. Why do you think no one has come here to help that officer out there? Cause every cop in town is at the hospital."

As crazy as his explanation sounded, Chasey knew that something major *had* to be happening. There was no way the sheriff would allow a fellow officer to get devoured without sending some kind of assistance. Rod fished a twenty out of his wallet and held it up in his blood-soaked fingers. "Sorry to bother you again, but we're gonna need one more round."

The waitress reluctantly did as she was asked, cautiously taking the twenty by a corner that wasn't touching Rod's filthy fingers.

"Highly doubt you got this kind of excitement with old Jake." Rod took his third shot then stole the one from in front of Chasey.

"Hey! I thought that was mine?"

"Sorry, babe, but I need it more than you. I'm planning on heading back to the hospital and seeing if I can fight these fuckers off until more help arrives," Rod said.

"For argument's sake, let's say all this is true. You're gonna put your neck on the line for a bunch of pigs and townsfolk who don't give a shit about you? Doesn't sound like the Rod Tearny I know." Chasey folded her arms, having made her point.

"Yeah, and an estranged daughter coming back to give her folks a surprise visit on Christmas morning doesn't sound like the cold-hearted, selfish bitch that I used to know. Guess anyone can change on Christmas, huh."

Chasey's lips began to curl up in a smile. He had a good point and she was unable to come up with a witty comment.

"Maybe you'd like to join me? For old time's sake?" Rod felt confident he had her, but it could have been the alcohol. "Whether I'm right or wrong, it's gonna be an adventure you won't soon forget."

"Hot damn!" she smacked the table. "I must be outta my fucking mind but I'll go! I'll go zombie hunting with you!"

"You don't believe me, but I'm glad you're coming anyway," Rod smiled.

"It's not that I don't believe you. I know something's up in this back water town. I just don't know what, but I'm itching to find out."

Rod headed for the door. "You packing?" he asked. Carrying a firearm was a right the state had taken away from him, but Rod knew they were going to need more than the chainsaw.

"Got a lovely Winchester defender in my saddle bag and a shit load of shells. Stole it from Jake," she winked, following Rod. "My bike's just around the corner. Also took a Sig 225. Real nice looking. I was gonna pawn it after Christmas, figured I could get a decent price."

"Great, get them. You know how to drive a stick shift?" he asked.

"Oh, yeah. You taught me on that old Camaro of yours, remember?"

Rod tossed her the car keys. "Of course I remember. I just wanted to see if you did. And that old Camaro is a classic muscle car, by the way."

They walked out, barely detecting the significant drop in temperature. Adrenaline and alcohol kept the pair warm as they retrieved the guns and ammunition.

Midnight

Chasey down shifted as the Good Samaritan Hospital came into view. In the foreground were six police squad cars. Probably all the force Farley had to offer. Pulling up to the vehicles, they found each car abandoned. Past the deserted cars sat the hospital.

Above the main doors of the hospital was a large wreath, the ring decorated with colored lights. Snow dusted it where ever a flat surface allowed, and Rod thought the hospital didn't look very terrifying at the moment. But he knew sometimes things were calmest just before the storm.

"Is that smoke?" Chasey asked, pointing up at the second story.

"I think so," Rod said, but couldn't be sure.

They watched the windows, looking for a tell tale sign of danger inside the building. Within a minute there was no need for further debate. Glass started to shatter from the heat and smoke poured out from the ruptured panes of the second story.

"We're not equipped to fight fires," Chasey said.

Rod didn't have a chance to answer; a figure emerged from the front entrance of the hospital. Rod knew the person running was too fast to be one of the zombies, but he kept his finger on the Sig's trigger just in case. Chasey looked to him, as if asking what she should do.

"Hold tight," he said.

The figure was coming straight for them and as it approached, it took the shape of a female officer. She nearly threw herself against a squad car and fumbled to retrieve the keys. In her fear and haste, she didn't notice the civilian vehicle not more than five feet from her.

"Need help?" Rod called out the window.

"Whoa!" she yelled, not expecting to see anyone. "No," she said, composing herself. "We got a criminal on the loose and he set a fire in the hospital," she lied. "Best thing you folks can do is head home, lock yourself inside, and don't answer the door for anyone."

"Save it," Rod cut in. "I'm the one who called 9-1-1. We're here to help."

Seeing that the farce was up, she let her anger and frustration come out.

"It was like an ambush. Would have been nice if you told us what we were up against! Whatever those things are inside that building, they killed everyone! I can't radio the rest of the county from the car. I gotta get back to the station to call for help. We'll probably need all units from Dubuque County or maybe even the fucking National Guard. But if those things get out of the hospital, this town is dead!"

"The fire's gonna drive them out," Rod said, knowing that eventually they'd find the front entrance.

"I know, that's why I gotta move fast. I suggest you do the same." The cop got into her car and started the engine.

"You got a cell phone?" he asked Chasey.

"Yeah."

"Give me the phone number," he said.

She gave him the number, Rod got out and rubbed the piece of paper on the cop's window, who was already about to leave. She rolled down the window and grabbed the number.

"We'll stick around and try to hold 'em off till you get help here. Call us when backup's on the way."

"I'll call, but I'm telling you it's no use," she said.

"Just call," Rod pleaded. The woman nodded and sped away, lights flashing and siren wailing.

"I can't believe it," Chasey said, as Rod got back in the car.

"Believe it, baby," he cocked the shotgun. "She's right about one thing. We can't stop all of them. I'm guessing that half the hospital has been completely eaten alive like Officer Mabi. But the other half probably turned to zombies just like that poor mother and her daughter."

Chasey just stared wide-eyed at Rod as he continued with his assessment of the situation. A situation that felt more like a bad nightmare than reality.

"The cops screwed up by getting in close quarters with them," Rod said. "Not enough room to maneuver. Every zombie I killed was relatively easy, but I did it out in the open with plenty of room to move around. And that's the key to staying unbitten. Once they leave the hospital, we can take 'em out from the safety of the car." He looked at Chasey, "Here's the question. Do you really want to do this? These fuckers could kill a lot of innocent people before help gets here. We might be able to reduce that number if we stay and fight, but there's always the risk of getting killed ourselves. Or worse."

"I came for adventure," she replied, finally finding her voice. "Let's do this!"

She backed up then swung around the remaining squad cars. As she did, the sliding glass doors swung open and the first wave of zombies began to file out.

"Oh my God," she breathed, stopping the car. "What should we do?"

"What we came here to do. I want you to drive slow, get as close to them as you can and I'll take care of the rest."

Keeping an easy twenty mph, Chasey approached the slow-moving zombies. Most were dressed in hospital gowns, or scrubs, and a few roamed naked, suggesting that the gowns had been torn in a struggle. While there was space in between the hordes that were now pouring out, they all seemed to be heading south, as if some instinct was guiding them. Perhaps the smell of warm flesh.

"Here we go," Rod leaned out the window, chainsaw in hand. He pulled the cord and the saw barked to life. His position out the window put him at head level with most of the oncoming zombies.

"Be careful," Chasey screamed, over the howl of the blade.

The razor-sharp teeth of the Aosika blade sliced right through a man in his sixties. His head rolled under the tires, causing the Camaro to buck slightly. Rod kept his balance and readied for a second attack. This time the target was a young woman. Her gown was missing, exposing a bloated and bitten stomach and a half decayed left breast, the other one missing. Rod brought the blade up under her jaw and sliced through her head. The naked women collapsed with enough force to push the rest of her decomposed organs out through the gash in her abdomen.

Chasey turned in a circle, coming up on a pack of five zombies, one of which appeared to be a doctor. Rod took a deep breath and swung as hard as he could. The chainsaw contacted the doctor, but he hadn't suffered as much decay as the previous victims and the chainsaw didn't slice as easily through his neck.

"Slow down!" Rod yelled, fearful he would be dragged out of the car window.

Chasey slowed, but that allowed the other zombies to inch closer to Rod. The doctor flopped to the ground after his head was finally severed, but the other zombies reached out for Rod's arm. "Shit!" he screamed, dropping the chainsaw to the road and falling back into the car.

"Did they get you?" Chasey asked, concerned.

"No, thank God. The chainsaw only works when they're alone or in pairs. I'm not fast enough for large groups."

Chasey circled the car back behind the line of cop cars and paused, the engine idling. The zombies continued to flow from the open doors of the building and almost reached the road block of squad cars. They would have no trouble walking past the vehicles and straight into town.

"Now what?" she asked.

Rod handed her the shotgun, "How good are you with this thing?"

"Good," she took the firearm. "I've been practicing. Plus, we have a shitload of shells."

Rod loaded up all three magazines for the Sig, replaced one into the bottom of the handle, and cocked the gun. He placed the two remaining magazines into his jacket. They got out of the car and leaned against the hood. The zombies maintained their slow but steady course for the police roadblock, as if they all agreed on where they were heading.

"Do you think they know what they're doing and where they're going?" Chasey asked.

"I think they're looking for food. It seems to be the only thing they need," he replied.

"And that food is...?"

"Exactly, it's us."

Rod gestured over his shoulder with his head. "Gotta be at least three hundred people in that church for midnight mass. I bet these fuckers can smell 'em." Rod looked at the impending army of the dead. "Just a few more feet and start firing."

"What chance do we have if the cops failed?" She was skeptical of his plan.

"I told you, close quarters. Plus, cops are trained to go for body shots. Go for the head, it's the only way. Got it?"

"Yeah."

"Now!" Rod yelled.

They opened fire, taking down the first line of zombies. The remaining dead continued past their fallen comrades, unfazed by the gunfire. Chasey emptied shell after shell into the crowd, taking down twice as many zombies as Rod with the powerful shotgun. Rod's fire didn't cover as much area as the shotgun and he had to choose his targets carefully.

Rod focused on a young man, his beard saturated with blood and puss, fired, and caught the man in the shoulder. The dead man staggered backwards, regained his balance, and continued forward. Rod fired again and this time the bullet entered the man's right eye socket, blowing chunks of brain matter out the exit wound. Rod turned and fired at a woman who seemed to already be burned by the fires inside. He missed her. He frantically loaded the last magazine into the gun and tried again. With his remaining nine bullets, he was able to stop five more zombies.

"Back in the car!" he yelled, tugging at Chasey's arm. She fired one last round, missing her mark, then hopped back in the car. She threw it in reverse and rolled back another twenty feet.

"What now? We only got about twenty so far."

"Give me the shotgun," he said, picking up the box of ammunition she'd brought along. Rod wasn't ready to give up yet. "Same plan as before. Let's cut back and forth just in front of them, and I'll take out as many as I can before we run out of ammo."

Chasey nodded and maneuvered the Camaro. Rod resumed his position out the window and loaded the chamber. His first three shots missed their mark, but when he quickly adjusted to the change of firing while moving, his aim improved.

He destroyed at least forty more zombies before the ammo box ran dry. The impending zombies had only gained another ten feet, which meant that Rod and Chasey's efforts, however minimal they may have seemed, *were* making a difference.

Chasey retreated fifteen feet, then spun the car around, facing the masses. "We're out of ammo, no chainsaw, and outnumbered. Now what?"

Rod just stared out the windshield at the walking dead that continued their drunken march towards the town. Behind them, the hospital blazed in the back ground, sending smoke and flames high into the night sky.

Chasey's phone started to ring.

"Answer it," Rod said.

"Hello," she paused. "Yeah, we're still here. No. Thank God." She hung up the phone and looked at Rod. "It was that chick cop. She said the Guard is fifteen miles away and to get the hell out."

"Well, what are you waiting for?"

Chasey shifted and floored the gas pedal, leaving the zombies behind. She turned on 5th St., so they could escape through side streets.

They traveled in silence for fifteen minutes while the car approached Farley town limits. They passed the turn off for Teddy's Trees and Santa Land, but Rod didn't question where she was going. Chasey took the exit for Waddell, the next town over, and pulled into a motel parking lot. She turned off the engine and looked at Rod.

"We did it," Rod said. "Where are we?"

"I have no clue," she burst out laughing and Rod joined her. "I just had to get outta town after that," she said between fits of giggles. "But you're right, we did it."

"Probably a wise choice," Rod agreed. "After things are under control, they'll have to set up some kind of quarantine and make sure that the infection is definitely contained. But I'm sure your parents will be okay," he added.

"I'm sure they are. Thanks to us. I'll see them another time," Chasey brushed hair out of her eyes. "You think the Guard can finish off the rest?"

"Sure, they're better equipped to handle this kind of shit. Well, better than a biker babe and an ex-con like me, anyway" Rod said.

Chasey leaned over and kissed him once, then got out of the car. "I'm gonna get a room. I suggest you do the same." Implying that after everything they went through, Rod was still going to be sleeping by himself tonight.

"Chasey," Rod called from the window and she stopped. "We make a damn good team, don't you think?"

"We sure do," she smiled. "Really gave 'em hell too."

"No, shit," Rod agreed.

"No, shit," she whispered.

"Will I see you around?" he asked, careful not to let too much anticipation creep into his voice. He'd wanted her badly every night since she left.

"Definitely. And you better get your rest, because I expect to see you in my room at nine o' clock sharp!" She tried to hide a smirk and turned away.

"Yes ma'am." *I got her after all!*

She took a few steps then turned back, "Merry Christmas."

"Merry Christmas, babe," he called back.

*   *   *

Christmas Day 10:00 a.m.

Thirty miles west of Farley, on a long stretch of highway, Vixen, formerly from Teddy's Christmas Trees and Santa Land, was trotting across the road. A station wagon, containing the Miller family, barreled down the same highway on their way to share Christmas morning with relatives.

In the rear of the vehicle, colorful presents were piled high, each more garishly wrapped than the last.

"Look, Mommy," the little girl said, from the back seat. "It's a reindeer."

"That's nice, honey," her mother responded, without glancing out the window. "I bet he's looking for Santa."

ZOMBIE SANTA IS COMING TO TOWN

DAVID BERNSTEIN

It was December 24th, Christmas Eve, seven p.m. on the east coast. A man in Vermont died of a sudden heart attack, only to rise within minutes and attack the paramedics that arrived. A nineteen year old girl was at a party doing drugs. She overdosed, went into cardiac arrest and died. Two minutes later she awoke biting off her boyfriend's lips as he attempted CPR. The epidemic wasn't limited to just the east coast. From all corners of the globe, reports were coming into to hospitals, fire departments, and police precincts about the dead returning to life. News stations were only beginning to pick up on what was happening, reporting nothing, until an actual event could be confirmed. It was only the beginning.

Martin Hickey sped along the snow-covered country road. Flakes were coming down as if a giant pillow had burst in the sky, covering the land in a blanket of white. The temperature was below freezing. The road to Sayville was dark, the moon's glow blocked by cloud cover, street lamps non-existent.

Martin cruised along in his 1989 station wagon, the heat barely blowing from the vents. He was a large man, three hundred pounds of overweight goodness and dressed as Santa Claus. In the back seat were his three little helpers, all dressed as elves and each wearing a different colored outfit.

With no other cars on the road, the station wagon laid the trail, cutting through the unmarked snow. It had rained earlier in the day before the temperature dropped, the puddles becoming patches of ice.

Martin was late for the Christmas party, an engagement he was hired to attend. There would be children at the party taking pictures with him and the elves. He was already ten minutes late, but almost to the house. He hit the accelerator, disregarding all caution. He'd lived in the region his whole life and had never had an accident during the winter. The elves, Bobby, Darren, and Cindy, had asked him to slow down, but he ignored them. He was, after all, their boss.

Coming into a sharp turn, the tires hit a patch of ice. He lost control, the car skidding sideways. He tried turning out of it, but the car proceeded as if no one was driving. It slammed into a bank along the road, flipped over sideways and proceeded to tumble down a hill, stopping upside down in a small rivulet.

The creek had begun to freeze over, but the car smashed what ice had formed, as the interior began to fill with water. Martin tried undoing his seat belt, but couldn't get the damn thing to release. He turned his head around and called out to his helpers, but received no answer. Panic began to set in as icy water breached his bald head; the Santa hat growing cold and heavy with water, held on by a string under his chin. His beard had flopped over his face, impeding his vision. The water kept rising and it was only a matter of time before death found him.

Maggie Steward looked at her watch as she waited by the front door. The Santa was late. She'd dock him a portion of his pay and if he didn't arrive soon, then she'd call the company that sent him.

She turned, looking at the living room with the Santa-less display. Empty boxes wrapped to look like presents, white cottony fabric along the floor, a giant candy-cane, and a Christmas tree decorated with colorful lights and beautiful ornaments, decorated the area. The children would wait in line before sitting on Santa's lap and tell him their wishes while grinning parents looked on, snapping pictures. Maggie stomped her foot and grunted in anger.

That Santa had better show up soon.

Back at the station wagon, one of the elves awoke in the back seat. It was Darren, shivering, his blue elfin outfit soaked with freezing water. He could barely see; the ravine the car was in shrouded in gloom.

He called out. "Guys?" But only the sound of the creek flowing through the car answered, the trickle adding to his need to urinate. He saw a silhouette next to him. It was Cindy. He felt for her head, then found her neck. She had no pulse. Darren pulled his hand back. He looked around the dark car. Bobby lay on the floor, face down in a pool of icy water. He pulled his elfin brother up, checked for signs of life, but found none. Bobby was as dead as Cindy.

Martin moved in the front seat, startling him.

"Martin!" Darren yelled, happy the fat bastard was alive. He saw the big man's seat belt was still on. "Can you talk?" Darren scrambled from the wreck, crawling out of one the broken windows, managing to nick his hand on the glass.

Outside the air was bitter. Darren's water soaked suit was a death trap in these elements. He'd have to hope his change of clothes was still dry and put them on as soon as he freed Martin.

He ran around to Martin's window, which was also smashed out. It looked like the man's head was under water, but he reached in anyway to check on him. He felt no pulse, but thought maybe if he could just pull his head from the water he could somehow save him. He tried lifting it out, but it was no use. Suddenly, he felt a sharp pain in his fingers, not too bad because the icy water had numbed them. Pulling his hand out, he saw that his fingers were missing, blood leaking from the stumps to dot the white snow red.

On the way to the kitchen, Maggie grabbed a bottle of Zinfandel. She sat down at the table, the rest of the party in the living room or downstairs in the playroom. She poured herself a glass, filling it, and began sipping away. She glanced up when her best friend Kate walked in.

"What are you doing in here all by yourself?" she asked, wearing corny reindeer antlers on her head.

"I'm not alone," Maggie said. "You're here." She took a swig of the wine this time. Kate grabbed a glass from the cupboard and poured herself a cupful.

"What's the matter?" Kate asked.

"The damn Santa hasn't shown up yet and he's not answering his cell phone."

"Have you looked outside?"

"I know it's snowing, but he could've at least called. The kids..."

"Stop with the kids," Kate interrupted. "They're downstairs playing Twister, having a ball." She nudged Maggie with her hand. "I think you care more about Santa than the kids do," she said with a chuckle.

"I just want everything to go smoothly. It's Christmas Eve and it's my first party since moving into our new house."

"Your parties have always been fun. Everyone loves them. Why do you think they keep coming back?"

Maggie took a sip and smiled. "I guess you're right. Screw Santa. If he doesn't show, I'll make Ted dress up and play the part."

"I'd love to see that," Kate said, laughing.

"Thanks," Maggie said. "I needed someone to set me straight."

Darren was shivering uncontrollably. He managed to tie a tourniquet around his wrist, minimizing the blood loss of his missing fingers. With the cold water from the stream numbing his hand when he checked on Martin, the pain had yet to hit him, the hand still numb.

It was ten minutes since he'd dialed 911 on his cell phone which, incredibly, had stayed dry in his pocket.

Climbing the hill to the road was tough, especially for a little person, but he'd managed, dragging his duffel bag with him. His entire body was numb from the cold and through the bitter wind and snow he'd stripped off his clothes and changed into dry ones.

Finally, after sometime, he saw the red and blue flashing lights of the ambulance as it approached. Jumping up and down and waving his arms, he got their attention. The ambulance pulled over, rushed him inside and began warming him and tending to his wound.

"The others are down in the ravine," he told the paramedics. "I'm pretty sure they're dead."

"We'll check it out," one of the paramedics said. He had wavy blonde hair and glasses. His name was Jim. The other paramedic's name was Frank, a forty year old with twenty years of experience.

"You said there are three other people in the car?" Jim asked.

"Yes."

"And your boss, the guy in the Santa suit, just bit you?" Frank asked.

"Yeah."

"Probably in shock, didn't know what he was doing," Jim said. He looked to his partner. "We better head down there, if he's still alive, it won't be for much longer in this weather."

The paramedics radioed for additional support, but were told it would be at least an hour, as the town seemed to be having one problem after another. They left Darren in the back of the ambulance.

The paramedics climbed down the hill, both carrying supplies. Using flashlights, they found the overturned station wagon, lit flares, and tossed them around the wreck.

Frank peered in the back, while Jim tended to Martin.

"Got two bodies back here," Fred said. "Both deceased and frozen."

"This guy's a goner too," Jim said. "I'm gonna cut the harness, see if together we can pull this guy free. Make it easier for the meat wagon." Jim began cutting the seatbelt. It snapped apart when he was three quarters of the way through, the fat man falling to the car's roof in a splash.

"Lucky you weren't under him," Frank laughed. "Or I'd be calling for an extra baggie."

"Holy shit!" Jim yelled. "This guy's moving! He's still alive." Frank, his upper body still in the car, echoed his partner's sentiments as the two people in the back began moving.

"Damn," it looks like we both need to practice our first-aid. These guys are waking up. I swear they were dead." Frank grabbed Cindy and pulled her from the car before going back in and grabbing Bobby.

Jim was busy trying to maneuver Martin, but the big guy was too heavy. "A little help here."

Frank came over to help.

"We better get something nice this year," Frank said. "We saved Santa."

They got the body so the big man's head was sticking out of the window. His face was paler than chalk with a hint of blue from being frozen.

"I don't know how the hell these people are still alive," Frank said.

Martin was raising his arms and moaning. "The guy must be confused, out of it, but he's got a massive amount of will power," Jim said.

They continued to drag Martin out, while shoving his hands away as he tried to grab at them. They had his body almost all the way clear of the car when Frank yelped in pain. He spun around to see the little female clawing at his leg. She'd bit him and was devouring a piece of his flesh. She came at him again, mouth open, and he shoved her to the ground, falling with her after losing his footing on the snow and ice.

"What the hell? She just bit me!" Jim cried out in surprise.

Jim let go of Martin, wanting to take a breather. He turned to see the little elfin female shoved to the ground after Frank yelped. She was getting back up and so was the other elfin-dressed male. Jim went to rise when he was pulled forward onto Martin. He tried pushing himself off, but the big man was strong. A sharp pain erupted on Jim's chest. Santa Claus was chewing through his jacket and had nipped his skin.

"Frank, help!" Jim screamed.

Frank turned to see his partner lying on top of the fat man in the Santa suit. "What the hell are you doing, Jim?" Frank yelled as he ran over and started pulling Jim off, but the two elves grabbed onto Frank's arms and began biting him. Frank let go of Jim, who was pulled back down, and began punching and kicking the elves.

Jim landed with his neck near Martin's mouth, immediately smelling the nasty odor of his breath before the painful bite from his teeth. Jim cried out, feeling a chunk of flesh leave his neck and the warm flow of blood pour out of him. His strength was quickly diminishing as Martin continued to feed, the fat man's strength never fading.

Frank continued to fight the elves, their faces void of emotion, no matter how many times he hit them. They kept rising and attacking and he was beginning to tire. He turned to Jim and gasped when he saw the huge pool of blood around his and Martin's body. Santa Claus was holding Jim down, a slurping sound coming from in between them. He ran over and shoved Jim off of the Santa. Upon seeing the fat man's face, covered in blood, a huge piece of flesh sticking out of the mouth, he wanted to vomit.

Jim lay still on the snow, blood continuing to pump out of what was left of his neck. The elves were coming after him again. Not knowing what else to do, he took off running for the ambulance.

He arrived at the rig, huffing and puffing. He opened the driver's door, plopped onto the seat, and used the walkie. "Base come in, this is Frank over on Pine Ridge Road, over."

"Ten-four, Frank, it'll be a little longer on the back-up, over," the female voice said.

"Screw the back-up!" he yelled. "Get the cops down here, now!" He heard a moaning from behind. Turning his head, he saw the tiny mouth close over his cheek, ripping the rosy flesh from his face. The now very undead Darren had his cheek in his mouth and began to chew as his fingers, stumps included, tore at Frank's eyes, rupturing the left one. It popped like a grape, the juices runny. Frank screamed in horror and pain, dropping the walkie. Darren's skin had paled like Martin's and he had a vacant look in his eyes, as if no emotion existed there. Frank shoved him away, grabbed for the door lever, opened it, and fell out onto the snow-covered road.

He got to his feet and started to run, bumping into zombie Santa. Walking just behind him were the two little zombie elves. Zombie Santa wrapped Frank in a bear hug, pinning his arms to his sides, and bit off his ear. The other two undead members of Santa's toyshop began biting Frank's legs, ripping pieces of his pants and skin off.

Frank tried screaming, but Martin had his Adam's apple in his mouth, chewing it like it was a juicy wad of tobacco. Frank slumped as the life drained out of him. He lay on the road as the Christmas zombies, joined by the elf in the ambulance, huddled over his body, tearing his intestines out and eating them.

Back at the party, Maggie was sipping her third glass of wine and enjoying herself. The guests were all eating and merry, no one asking where Santa was until her husband came up to her.

"Where's the Santa guy?" Ted asked.

"No idea and I really don't care," Maggie said. "The party's a success and we didn't pay the guy yet so he can shove it."

"I think you better slow down there, honey," Ted said, attempting to grab her glass.

"No, no, no. This is a party and I'm finally enjoying myself. You should do the same."

"Maybe the guy went off the road or something. It's nasty out there," Ted suggested.

"So go take a quick, but careful, drive, and see if you find him."

"All right, I will," Ted said. He left the room and grabbed his coat and car keys. Pete, his friend from work, stopped him. "Where're you going?" he asked, holding a bottle of beer in his hand and a cocktail weenie in the other.

"Just for a short drive up the road. The Santa Maggie hired hasn't shown up and he isn't answering his phone."

"I'll get my coat and keep you company," Pete said and dashed off to the bedroom containing the coats, found his, and joined Ted outside.

Ted started his Jeep after scraping off the snow from the windows, then pulled out of the driveway. He informed the guests prior to arriving not to park in the driveway, leaving the space for Santa.

They drove the Jeep slowly, keeping an eye out for any cars parked alongside the road. The snow was thick and coming down so fast that hoping to find any tracks was hopeless. Pete brought a fresh beer, popped it open, and started drinking.

"I normally don't open containers in vehicles, but I figure we aren't going to run into the law out here."

"I normally don't allow people to drink in here at all, especially alcohol, but you're right, so enjoy, my friend," Ted said. He hit the brakes upon seeing figures walking up ahead. "Look." He pointed. "Does that look like a Santa with three elves walking in the middle of the road to you?"

"Sure does, and if you weren't with me I'd think I was tripping," Pete said, letting out a long belch.

Ted drove a forward little, but stopped. The people in the road weren't moving to the side. They looked strange, too, as if they were sleepwalking. "Wait here, I'm going to get out."

Ted got out of the Jeep, closed the door, and approached Santa and his elves. "Hey, guys. Car trouble?"

None of them answered. Instead they picked up speed and began moaning. "Guys?" Ted asked, feeling a little scared. Upon further examination, he saw Santa's face and beard, both covered in blood. Behind him the three elves were glistening with crimson, their green suits saturated with blood, too.

"Were you guys in an accident?" Ted asked hesitantly.

The zombie Santa drew close, within a foot, before Ted began back-pedaling. He turned to run upon seeing the fat man's face, but was grabbed by the jacket collar. He was being pulled into Santa's grasp, the little elves enveloping his legs. Pain erupted in three areas, including his crotch. Ted looked down to see the elves biting him, tearing away at his slacks, taking chunks of flesh with them. A rotten, horrid odor struck his nostrils and Santa's beard tickled his cheek before pain seized his ear. Santa Claus gnawed at it, tearing it off. Ted was screaming now, struggling to break free. The large Santa squeezed his fingers into Ted's skin through his jacket and began tearing his flesh as he took another bite from Ted's scalp.

Pete was busy trying to find some rock and roll on the radio. All the stations had either Christmas music or gospel. The front window had fogged up, making it impossible to see out, and he finally gave up his search.

"There's nothin' good on," he muttered as he turned off the radio.

Finishing his beer, he pushed the window button. The cold night air struck his face, the sensation refreshing. He stuck his arm out the window to toss the can when a bloody hand grabbed his wrist.

"Holy shit!" he yelled and tried to jerk his hand back into the Jeep. It was a giant, gore-covered Santa, his beard wet with red. The jolly old North Pole resident opened his mouth and began eating Pete's thumb.

The beer can fell to the ground as Pete began screaming to be let go, but the zombie's grip was too strong. Pete, not wearing his seatbelt, was yanked halfway out the window. Zombie Santa bent over and began gnawing at Pete's face, biting the flesh over his right eye and taking the eyebrow with it.

As blood ran into his eyes, blocking his vision, Pete continued to scream.

Maggie went to the kitchen and tried for the third time to get Ted on his cell phone. Kate, Pete's wife, was standing next to her.

"He's not picking up," Maggie said, clearly frustrated.

"Maybe he left his cell home," Kate suggested. She whipped out her cell phone and dialed Pete's number. After a few seconds, she said, "Went to voicemail." She had a concerned look on her face. "You think something happened?"

"Nah, they're probably just ignoring their phones. Come on, it's time for the snow angel contest."

"What snow angel contest?"

"The one I just made up. I've a bag full of prizes and it's getting late. And I told all the parents to make sure their kids brought their snowsuits."

Maggie left the kitchen, Kate following. She announced to all the children that there'd be a snow-angel making contest in ten minutes. The kids cheered and ran to get dressed.

Ten minutes later, the front lawn was littered with children, their parents watching from afar. Flashes of light exploded as pictures were taken. A few snowballs were thrown, but most kids had spread out and were busy waving their arms and legs on the ground.

"Hey, look over there," one mother said.

Maggie turned and looked in the direction the woman was pointing.

A group of people were walking down the snow-covered road. They looked haggard and drunk. One was wearing a Santa costume. The others looked like little elves. Then it hit her. "Hey, that's my Santa," she said, the alcohol buzz impairing her a bit. "Guess they had car trouble."

Kate grabbed Maggie's arm. "Where're our husbands? They should've run into them while they were driving."

"Let's go ask," Maggie said.

Maggie and Kate began walking toward the group of Christmas characters when off in the distance, they saw more people coming. "That must be them," Maggie said. "Shit, they must've gotten stuck and had to walk back."

The two women continued on, drawing nearer to the first group.

"Hey, guys," Kate said. "Are you all right?"

"They look awful," Maggie said. "Was there an accident? Are you guys hurt?" When they didn't answer, Maggie asked again, but still received no reply.

Kate rushed forward. "I think they're in shock. There's blood all over them." She halted as the Santa zombie reached for her, his face coming into the light.

Maggie saw the gaunt face, the hollow eyes. Working in a hospital, she thought they resembled the cadavers she'd worked on in nursing school.

The two women rushed to the people's aid, putting an arm around the Santa, who in turn took a chunk of meat from Kate's clavicle. She screamed as blood gushed from the hole in her jacket.

Maggie pulled away, but one of the elves had her leg and began biting her thigh. Both women were screaming, attracting the attention of the party-goers.

Everyone in the front yard watched in horror as the two women were torn to pieces. Shouts of "call the police" rang out. The children were ushered inside as they screamed and cried for their parents. Some of the men from the party came to the aid of Maggie and Kate.

Two more zombies approached the melee, but from a distance, no one knew they were part of the walking dead yet. They just looked like two people out for a walk in the snow.

One of the men, who had come to help the women, waved the two zombies over. "Hey, you two, come over here and help." The men saw the medical jumpsuits of the two zombies and were glad to see they were paramedics. They were glad they were joining the fray until they noticed their ripped out throats, missing stomachs, and pieces of intestine dragging along the ice-covered road. When they were close enough, the paramedic zombies began attacking.

The men punched and kicked the undead, but to no avail as they just kept coming. Many had gotten bitten and after realizing they weren't normal people, took off, running back to the house. Maggie, Kate, and a man from the party, now lay on the ground as the zombies closed around them, ripping them apart and eating their fill.

Inside the house, most of the people received messages that all phone lines were busy upon calling for help. One person managed to get through, but she heard a recording. After listening to it herself, and hardly believing it, she yelled for everyone to be quiet.

She put the phone on speaker setting so everyone could hear.

"This is the Sayville Police Department. No one is available. The police are out dealing with the epidemic. Please stay in your homes and wait for help. Do not approach anyone looking sick. If you are bitten by anyone, seek medical attention immediately. Everything will be under control once the police sort this out."

Outside, zombie Santa and his three elves roamed the street, looking for flesh, joined by other members of the undead. Their flock grew, and like Christmas carolers, they walked from house to house, moaning their song for all to hear. People ran and screamed, were eaten and slaughtered.

You better cry, you better not pout, because Zombie Santa Claus had come to town.

ABOUT THE WRITERS

Scott M. Baker was born and raised in Everett, Massachusetts, and now lives in northern Virginia with his wife and six house rabbits. His short stories include, "Rednecks Shouldn't Play with Dead Things," which appeared in the autumn 2008 edition of the e-zine Necrotic Tissue, and "Cruise of the Living Dead," which appeared in Living Dead Press' Dead Worlds: Volume 3 anthology. Scott recently contracted with Shadowfire Press to publish The Vampire Hunters, a novel, as an e-book.
Please visit the author's website at scott-m-baker.com.

David Bernstein, a.k.a. Macabrezombie, can usually be found writing some type of horror and when he isn't writing, he is either reading or watching it. He's been published in a number of horror magazines and anthologies, many of them zombie oriented. He lives in the NYC and may be reached at dbern77@hotmail.com or dbern77@gmail.com

Jack Burton resides in the Arizonan deserts. When he's not busy preparing for the zombie apocalypse he spends his time teaching, listening to heavy metal and indulging in all things horror related. Some of his stories can be found in the upcoming horror anthologies due out between 2009 and 2010: The Middle of Nowhere(Pill Hill Press), Creature Features (House of Horror), Dead Worlds 4 (Living Dead Press), Bonded by Blood II (SNM Horror), and Elements of Horror.

Kevin Cockle is a published boxing journalist, a frequent contributor to On Spec magazine, and has had honorable mentions in a number of the "Year's Best Fantasy and Horror" anthologies. Kevin's upcoming work will be featured in a variety of anthologies, incorporating zombies, vampires, and unclassifiable weirdness in between.

Anthony Giangregorio is the author and editor of more than 25 novels, almost all of them about zombies. His work has appeared in Dead Science by Coscomentertainment, Dead Worlds: Undead Stories Volumes 1, 2 , 3, & 4, and an upcoming anthology (Zombology) by Library of the Living Dead Press and their werewolf anthology titled Wolves of War. He also has stories in End of Days: An Apocalyptic Anthology Volumes 1 & 2, and 2 anthologies with Pill Hill Press.
Check out his website at www.undeadpress.com

Sean Grigsby is a new face to horror and has done everything from stand-up comedy to broadcast radio. He lives with his wife in central Arkansas.

Tom Hamilton is an Irish Traveler. He has recently had short stories accepted by Withersin, Existere, Necrography and Tales Askew. You can read some of his earlier zombie stories in Living Dead Press' Dead Worlds series. Along with his wife Mary Theresa and their three small daughters, Tiffany, Hope and Catalina, he lives in Loves Park, IL USA.

Kelly M. Hudson grew up in Kentucky, lives in California, has been lucky enough to get published in most of the fine Living Dead Press publications, and has been in a few others, too! If you'd like to know more, www.kellymhudson.com will provide links.

Lance Looper spends his Christmases in Austin, Texas and when he's not writing scary stories he spends his time working as a copywriter in the technology industry. He can be contacted at lancelooper@yahoo.com

Keith Adam Luethke obtained a B.A in English from the University of Tennessee and is currently going after his M.A in Writing Concentration. His new novel Dead House, which was picked for publication by Living Dead Press, will be released later this year. His other works can be found on Amazon and he's currently working on an action packed novel about zombies entitled: Shelter from the Dead: Marauders.

Rick Moore, originally from Leicestershire, England, moved to the US ten years ago and now lives in Phoenix, AZ. Rick's fiction has appeared in numerous zines and anthologies, including Dead Worlds Volume 2 & Book of the Dead by Living Dead Press, The Undead: Flesh Feast, History Is Dead, The Beast Within, Cthulhu Unbound, Harvest Hill, Dark Animus, the 2009 Stoker nominated Horror Library 3 and Bound For Evil.
Visit him online at http://www.myspace.com/zombieinfection

Val Muller is a high school English teacher in Virginia who enjoys writing middle-grade fiction. Despite this wholesome exterior, the long, cold winters of her childhood in Connecticut permanently imprinted themselves upon her in her lasting love of the horror genre.

Peter Naggi is a writer hearkening from Southern California. "Downtown" is his second published work, the other being "Damned" which can be found in Dead Worlds Vol. 4, also available from Living Dead Press.

Rob Rosen, author of the novels "Sparkle" and "Divas Las Vegas", has had short stories featured in more than seventy anthologies, most notably: Short Attention Span Mysteries; Modern Witches, Wizards, and Magic; Southern Comfort; Hell's Hangmen: Horror in the Old West; By the Chimney With Care; Strange Stories of Sand and Sea; Damned in Dixie: Southern Horror; Twisted Fayrie Tales; Ruins Metropolis; Don't Turn the Lights On; Speculative Realms; Bloody October; and Middle of Nowhere: Horror in Rural America. Please visit him at his website, www.therobrosen.com, or email him at robrosen@therobrosen.com

Paul C. Snider currently resides in Napanee, Ontario, Canada with his wife Crystal. Is an aspiring writer of horror fiction, and enjoys Horror, science fiction, action and comedy movies. This is his second short story published, the first one is available online. You can visit the online web site at http://www.paulcsnider.com or e-mail at paulcsnider@gmail.com

Marc Wiggins has been an avid lover of post-apocalyptic fiction ever since he saw his first zombie movie in seventh grade. He has always loved the written word and favors zombie novels over movies. Marc lives with his loving wife and kids in Southern California. This is his fourth story published, the others being in Dead Worlds: Volume 1 and 2 and End of Days: An Apocalyptic Anthology.

BOOK OF THE DEAD 2: NOT DEAD YET
A ZOMBIE ANTHOLOGY
Edited by Anthony Giangregorio

Out of the ashes of death and decay, comes the second volume filled with the walking dead.

In this tomb, there are only slow, shambling monstrosities that were once human.

No one knows why the dead walk; only that they do, and that they are hungry for human flesh.

But these aren't your neighbors, your co-workers, or your family.
Now they are the living dead, and they will tear your throat out at a moment's notice.

So be warned as you delve into the pages of this book; the dead will find you, no matter where you hide.

ANOTHER EXCITING CHAPTER IN THE DEADWATER SERIES!
BOOK 6
DEAD UNION
by Anthony Giangregorio

BRAVE NEW WORLD

More than a year has passed since the world died not with a bang, but with a moan.

Where sprawling cities once stood, now only the dead inhabit the hollow walls of a shattered civilization; a mockery of lives once led.

But there are still survivors in this barren world, all slowly struggling to take back what was stripped from their birthright; the promise of a world free of the undead.

Fortified towns have shunned the outside world, becoming massive fortresses in their own right. These refugees of a world torn asunder are once again trying to carve out a new piece of the earth, or hold onto what little they already possess.

HOSTAGES

Henry Watson and his warrior survivalists are conscripted by a mad colonel, one of the last military leaders still functioning in the decimated United States. The colonel has settled in Fort Knox, and from there plans to rule the world with his slave army of lost souls and the last remaining soldiers of a defunct army.

But first he must take back America and mold it in his own image; and he will crush all who oppose him, including the new recruits of Henry and crew.

The battle lines are drawn with the fate of America at stake, and this time, the outcome may be unsure.

In a world where the dead walk, even the grave isn't safe.

DEADFREEZE
by Anthony Giangregorio

THIS IS WHAT HELL WOULD BE LIKE IF IT FROZE OVER!
When an experimental serum for hypothermia goes horribly wrong, a small research station in the middle of Antarctica becomes overrun with an army of the frozen dead.

Now a small group of survivors must battle the arctic weather and a horde of frozen zombies as they make their way across the frozen plains of Antarctica to a neighboring research station.

What they don't realize is that they are being hunted by an entity whose sole reason for existing is vengeance; and it will find them wherever they run.

DEAD WORLDS: Undead Stories
A Zombie Anthology Volume 1
Edited by Anthony Giangregorio

Welcome to the world of the dead, where the laws of nature have been twisted, reality changed.

The Dead Walk!

Filled with established and promising new authors for the next generation of corpses, this anthology will leave you gasping for air as you go from one terror-filled story to another.

Like the decomposing meat of a freshly rotting carcass, this book will leave you breathless.

Don't say we didn't warn you.

VISIONS OF THE DEAD
A ZOMBIE STORY

by Anthony & Joseph Giangregorio

Jake Roberts felt like he was the luckiest man alive.

He had a great family, a beautiful girlfriend, who was soon to be his wife, and a job, that might not have been the best, but it paid the bills.

At least until the dead began to walk.

Now Jake is fighting to survive in a dead world while searching for his lost love, Melissa, knowing she's out there somewhere.

But the past isn't dead, and as he struggles for an uncertain future, the past threatens to consume him.

With the present a constant battle between the living and the dead, Jake finds himself slipping in and out of the past, the visions of how it all happened haunting him.

But Jake knows Melissa is out there somewhere and he'll find her or die trying. In a world of the living dead, you can never escape your past.

DEAD MOURNING: A ZOMBIE HORROR STORY
by Anthony Giangregorio

Carl Jenkins was having a run of bad luck. Fresh out of jail, his probation tenuous, he'd lost every job he'd taken since being released. So now was his last chance, only one more job to prevent him from going back to prison. Assigned to work in a funeral home, he accidentally loses a shipment of embalming fluid. With nothing to lose, he substitutes it with a batch of chemicals from a nearby factory.

The results don't go as planned, though. While his screw-up goes unnoticed, his machinations revive the cadavers in the funeral home, unleashing an evil on the world that it has not seen before. Not wanting to become a snack for the rampaging dead, he flees the city, joining up with other survivors. An old, dilapidated zoo becomes their haven, while the dead wait outside the walls, hungry and patient.

But Carl is optimistic, after all, he's still alive, right? Perhaps his luck has changed and help will arrive to save them all?

Unfortunately, unknown to him and the other survivors, a serial killer has fallen into their group, trapped inside the zoo with them.

With the undead army clamoring outside the walls and a murderer within, it'll be a miracle if any of them live to see the next sunrise.

On second thought, maybe Carl would've been better off if he'd just gone back to jail.

ROAD KILL: A ZOMBIE TALE
by Anthony Giangregorio
ORDER UP!

In the summer of 2008, a rogue comet entered earth's orbit for 72 hours. During this time, a strange amber glow suffused the sky.

But something else happened; something in the comet's tail had an adverse affect on dead tissue and the result was the reanimation of every dead animal carcass on the planet.

A handful of survivors hole up in a diner in the backwoods of New Hampshire while the undead creatures of the night hunt for human prey.

There's a new blue plate special at DJ's Diner and Truck Stop, and it's you!

DEAD WORLDS: Undead Stories
A Zombie Anthology Volume 2
Edited by Anthony Giangregorio

Welcome to a world where the dead walk and want nothing more than to feast on the living. The stories contained in this, the second volume of the Dead Worlds series, are filled with action, gore, and buckets and buckets of blood; plus a heaping side of entrails for those with a little extra hunger.

The stories contained within this volume are scribed by both the desiccated cadavers of seasoned veterans to the genre as well as fresh-faced corpses, each printed here for the first time; and all of them ready to dig in and please the most discerning reader.

So slap on a bib and prepare to get bloody, because you're about to read the best zombie stories this side of Hell!

THE DARK

by Anthony Giangregorio
DARKNESS FALLS

The darkness came without warning.

First New York, then the rest of United States, and then the world became enveloped in a perpetual night without end.

With no sunlight, eventually the planet will wither and die, bringing on a new Ice Age. But that isn't problem for the human race, for humanity will be dead long before that happens.

There is something in the dark, creatures only seen in nightmares, and they are on the prowl. Evolution has changed and man is no longer the dominant species. When we are children, we're told not to fear the dark, that what we believe to exist in the shadows is false.

Unfortunately, that is no longer true.

SOULEATER

by Anthony Giangregorio

Twenty years ago, Jason Lawson witnessed the brutal death of his father by something only seen in nightmares, something so horrible he'd blocked it from his mind.

Now twenty years later the creature is back, this time for his son.

Jason won't let that happen.

He'll travel to the demon's world, struggling every second to rescue his son from its clutches.

But what he doesn't know is that the portal will only be open for a finite time and if he doesn't return with his son before it closes, then he'll be trapped in the demon's dimension forever.

SEE HOW IT ALL BEGAN IN THE NEW DOUBLE-SIZED 460 PAGE SPECIAL EDITION!

DEADWATER: EXPANDED EDITION

by Anthony Giangregorio

Through a series of tragic mishaps, a small town's water supply is contaminated with a deadly bacterium that transforms the town's population into flesh eating ghouls.

Without warning, Henry Watson finds himself thrown into a living hell where the living dead walk and want nothing more than to feed on the living.

Now Henry's trying to escape the undead town before he becomes the next victim.

With the military on one side, shooting civilians on sight, and a horde of bloodthirsty zombies on the other, Henry must try to battle his way to freedom.

With a small group of survivors, including a beautiful secretary and a wise-cracking janitor to aid him, the ragtag group will do their best to stay alive and escape the city codenamed: **Deadwater.**

DEAD END: A ZOMBIE NOVEL
by Anthony Giangregorio
THE DEAD WALK!

Newspapers everywhere proclaim the dead have returned to feast on the living!

A small group of survivors hole up in a cellar, afraid to brave the masses of animated corpses, but when food runs out, they have no choice but to venture out into a world gone mad.

What they will discover, however, is that the fall of civilization has brought out the worst in their fellow man.

Cannibals, psychotic preachers and rapists are just some of the atrocities they must face.

In a world turned upside down, it is life that has hit a Dead End.

DEAD RAGE

by Anthony Giangregorio

An unknown virus spreads across the globe, turning ordinary people into bloodthirsty, ravenous killers.

Only a small percentage of the population is immune and soon become prey to the infected.

Amongst the infected comes a man, stricken by the virus, yet still retaining his grasp on reality. His need to destroy the *normals* becomes an obsession and he raises an army of killers to seek out and kill all who aren't *changed* like himself.

A few survivors gather together on the outskirts of Chicago and find themselves running for their lives as the specter of death looms over all.

The Dead Rage virus will find you, no matter where you hide.

FAMILY OF THE DEAD
A Zombie Anthology
by Anthony, Joseph and Domenic Giangregorio

Clawing their way out of the wet, dark earth, these tales of terror will fill you with the deep seated fear we all have of death and what comes next.

But if that wasn't bad enough to chill your soul, these undead tales are penned by an entire family of corpses. The zombie master himself, Anthony Giangregorio, leads his two young ghouls, his sons Domenic and Joseph Giangregorio, on a journey of terror inducing stories that will keep you up long into the night.

As you read these works of the undead, don't be alarmed by that bump outside the window.

After all, it's probably just a stray tree branch...or is it?

The Lazarus Culture

by Pasquale J. Morrone

Secret Service Agent Christopher Kearns had no idea what he was up against. Assigned on a temporary basis to the Center for Disease Control, he only knew that somehow it was connected to the lives of those the agency protected...namely, the President of the United States. If there were possible terrorist activities in the making, he could only guess it was at a red alert basis.

When Kearns meets and befriends Doctor Marlene Peterson of the Breezy Point Medical Center in Maryland, he soon finds that science fiction can indeed become a reality. In a solitary room walked a man with no vital signs: dead. The explanation he received came from Doctor Lee Fret, a man assigned to the case from the CDC. Something was attached to the brain stem. Something alive that was quickly spreading rapidly through Maryland and other states.

Kearns and his ragtag army of agents and medical personnel soon find themselves in a world of meaningless slaughter and mayhem. The armies of the walking dead were far more than mere zombies. Some began to change into whatever it was they ate. The government had found a way to reanimate the dead by implanting a parasite found on the tongue of the Red Snapper to the human brain.

It looked good on paper, but it was a project straight from Hell.

The dead now walked, but it wasn't a mystery.

It was The Lazarus Culture.

END OF DAYS: AN APOCALYPTIC ANTHOLOGY VOLUMES 1 AND 2

Our world is a fragile place.

Meteors, famine, floods, nuclear war, solar flares, and hundreds of other calamities can plunge our small blue planet into turmoil in an instant.

What would you do if tomorrow the sun went super nova or the world was swallowed by water, submerging the world into the cold darkness of the ocean?

This anthology explores some of those scenarios and plunges you into total annihilation.

But remember, it's only a book, and tomorrow will come as it always does.

Or will it?

DEADFALL

by Anthony Giangregorio

It's Halloween in the small suburban town of Wakefield, Mass.

While parents take their children trick or treating and others throw costume parties, a swarm of meteorites enter the earth's atmosphere and crash to earth.

Inside are small parasitic worms, no larger than maggots.

The worms quickly infect the corpses at a local cemetery and so begins the rise of the undead.

The walking dead soon get the upper hand, with no one believing the truth.

That the dead now walk.

Will a small group of survivors live through the zombie apocalypse?

Or will they, too, succumb to the Deadfall.

DARK PLACES
By Anthony Giangregorio

A cave-in inside the Boston subway unleashes something that should have stayed buried forever.

Three boys sneak out to a haunted junkyard after dark and find more than they gambled on.

In a world where everyone over twelve has died from a mysterious illness, one young boy tries to carry on.

A mysterious man in black tries his hand at a game of chance at a local carnival, to interesting results.

God, Allah, and Buddha play a friendly game of poker with the fate of the Earth resting in the balance.

Ever have one of those days where everything that can go wrong, does? Well, so did Byron, and no one should have a day like this!

Thad had an imaginary friend named Charlie when he was a child. Charlie would make him do bad things. Now Thad is all grown up and guess who's coming for a visit?

These and other short stories, all filled with frozen moments of dread and wonder, will keep you captivated long into the night.

Just be sure to watch out when you turn off the light!

BOOK OF THE DEAD
A ZOMBIE ANTHOLOGY
VOLUME 1
ISBN 978-1-935458-25-8
Edited by Anthony Giangregorio

This is the most faithful, truest zombie anthology ever written, and we invite you along for the ride. Every single story in this book is filled with slack-jawed, eyes glazed, slow moving, shambling zombies set in a world where the dead have risen and only want to eat the flesh of the living. In these pages, the rules are sacrosanct. There is no deviation from what a zombie should be or how they came about.

The Dead Walk.

There is no reason, though rumors and suppositions fill the radio and television stations. But the only thing that is fact is that the walking dead are here and they will not go away. So prepare yourself for the ultimate homage to the master of zombie legend. And remember... Aim for the head!

DEAD TALES: SHORT STORIES TO DIE FOR
by Anthony Giangregorio

In a world much like our own, terrorists unleash a deadly dis-ease that turns people into flesh-eating ghouls.

A camping trip goes horribly wrong when forces of evil seek to dominate mankind.

After losing his life, a man returns reincarnated again and again; his soul inhabiting the bodies of animals.

In the Colorado Mountains, a woman runs for her life, stalked by a sadistic killer.

In a world where the Patriot Act has come to fruition, a man struggles to survive, despite eroding liberties.

Not able to accept his wife's death, a widower will cross into the dream realm to find her again, despite the dark forces that hold her in thrall. These and other short stories will captivate and thrill you. These are short stories to die for.

REVOLUTION OF THE DEAD
by Anthony Giangregorio
THE DEAD SHALL RISE AGAIN!

Five years ago, a deadly plague wiped out 97% of the world's population, America suffering tragically. Bodies were everywhere, far too many to bury or burn. But then, through a miracle of medical science, a way is found to reanimate the dead.

With the manpower of the United States depleted, and the remaining survivors not wanting to give up their internet and fast food restaurants, the undead are conscripted as slave labor.

Now they cut the grass, pick up the trash, and walk the dogs of the surviving humans.

But whether alive or dead, no race wants to be controlled, and sooner or later the dead will fight back, wanting the freedom they enjoyed in life.

The revolution has begun!

And when it's over, the dead will rule the land, and the remaining humans will become the slaves...or worse.

KINGDOM OF THE DEAD
by Anthony Giangregorio
THE DEAD HAVE RISEN!

In the dead city of Pittsburgh, two small enclaves struggle to survive, eking out an existence of hand to mouth.

But instead of working together, both groups battle for the last remaining fuel and supplies of a city filled with the living dead.

Six months after the initial outbreak, a lone helicopter arrives bearing two more survivors and a newborn baby. One enclave welcomes them, while the other schemes to steal their helicopter and escape the decaying city.

With no police, fire, or social services existing, the two will battle for dominance in the steel city of the walking dead. But when the dust settles, the question is: will the remaining humans be the winners, or the losers?

When the dead walk, the line between Heaven and Hell is so twisted and bent there is no line at all.

RISE OF THE DEAD
by Anthony Giangregorio
DEATH IS ONLY THE BEGINNING!

In less than forty-eight hours, more than half the globe was infected.

In another forty-eight, the rest would be enveloped.

The reason?

A science experiment gone horribly wrong which enabled the dead to walk, their flesh rotting on their bones even as they seek human prey.

Jeremy was an ordinary nineteen year old slacker. He partied too much and had done poorly in high school. After a night of drinking and drugs, he awoke to find the world a very different place from the one he'd left the night before.

The dead were walking and feeding on the living, and as Jeremy stepped out into a world gone mad, the dead spotting him alone and unarmed in the middle of the street, he had to wonder if he would live long enough to see his twentieth birthday.